A.J. SCUDIERE

NIGHTSHADE
FORENSIC FBI FILES ✦ BOOK 2

FRACTURE
FIVE

NightShade Forensic FBI Files: Fracture Five

Copyright © 2016 by AJ Scudiere

FIRST EDITION

FOREWORD

There's so much in a book that's not on the page. During the course of writing *Fracture Five*, I started a master's degree program at the University of Tennessee in Forensics. As you read, you'll see the contribution of that new knowledge. You'll find it in book #3 *The Atlas Defect,* as well. Huge thanks go out to all the professors in the program, particularly to Dr. Murray Marks who has faithfully gotten this massive undertaking underway. (Keep an eye on that name . . .) Thanks also go out to my friend Katherine Coble. Deeply knowledgeable about religions in general and a writer herself, she was incredibly helpful with this text. She pointed me in the direction of Saint Issa— the history of which made this story richer.

As always, much love to my support system at home: Eli, Daddy, Guy, Jarett & January. As well as the puppies, Mayhem and Travesty, and our kitty, Delilah. Snuggles are excellent for writers.

Thank you all!!

This one is for my lifelong friend, Heather Widener Debord.
I've been a writer since I was taught to compose a paragraph. I wrote an 80-page novella in third grade—and Heather motivated me to do it. She was a writer, too, and she always encouraged me to write and to write more. We wrote our stories longhand, me on whatever I could find, but Heather always wrote on yellow legal pads, with Bic erasable blue pens. I can see her small, round writing in my mind to this day.
What's even better is that a portion of the book you now hold in your hands was written with Heather across the table from me. Now we write on laptops and tablets. Her with a fortune taped to the top of her screen, me with my squishy keyboard; sometimes we're in a coffee shop. It's a much more grownup endeavor these days.
Heather—you are such a large part of the reason there are any AJ books out today.
Thank you.

PRAISE FOR A.J. SCUDIERE

"There are really just 2 types of readers—those who are fans of AJ Scudiere, and those who will be."
  -Bill Salina, Reviewer, Amazon

For *The Shadow Constant*:

"The Shadow Constant by A.J. Scudiere was one of those novels I got wrapped up in quickly and had a hard time putting down."
  -Thomas Duff, Reviewer, Amazon

For *Phoenix*:

"It's not a book you read and forget; this is a book you read and think about, again and again . . . everything that has happened in this book could be true. That's why it sticks in your mind and keeps coming back for rethought."
  -Jo Ann Hakola, The Book Faerie

"For we are the granddaughters of the witches you could not burn."

--author unknown

"We stopped checking for monsters under the bed when we realized they are inside us."

--author unknown

1

Cooper Rollins figured he knew how to say goodbye.

His son didn't. Christopher had sticky fingers and a wandering attention. He squirmed a lot.

"You're holding him too tight." His wife's voice was sharp as she stood over them. Alyssa Rollins knew better than to pull Christopher away from him, but she didn't have any patience either. "Cooper!"

Lately it seemed her voice only grated. Was the change in him or in her? He couldn't be sure. Cooper didn't trust his own senses anymore.

Still, he abruptly scooped the toddler up tight and whispered in his ear. "Daddy loves you, more than anything." Then just as abruptly, he let his boy go.

"Come on, Chris." Alyssa reached out with baby wipes and cleaned the sticky fingers. She didn't offer any to the man who was still legally her husband.

Didn't matter. Cooper could wash his own hands.

She didn't say goodbye to him either.

Also didn't matter. She hadn't said goodbye to him since she'd said it in the grand sense six months earlier.

For a moment, he watched the two of them walk off together—his son's tiny stride not quite keeping up with Alyssa's. She was patient with him. She'd turned to sandpaper where her husband was concerned, but she was always soft with their boy. He'd give her that.

Cooper had no legitimate complaints against her parenting. He just wanted to be a part of it—and not an every-other-Sunday, if-he-was-feeling-up-to-it kind of part. Unfortunately, it seemed he wasn't good for much more.

He'd slept through their initial meeting time, so she was right to be pissy. He just wished she wouldn't be so sharp.

Cooper turned away, unable to watch any more. Unable to wonder—as he always did—if this goodbye would be the last one. He'd been to too many last goodbyes. He'd missed too many of them, too.

Inside his skull itched. On the right side. Above his ear.

He was used to things rattling around in there—thoughts bouncing randomly, voices that wouldn't shut up, friends saying goodbye over and over—but the itching was bad.

Someone was going to die.

He felt his stomach turn and for a moment he wished that someone else could be him so he wouldn't have to have this feeling again.

His skin grew cold, his breathing shallow, and he started to sweat.

Noises came rushing back from his memory, putting him somewhere else. He couldn't tell if it was real. Not the noises, not the words, not even the gut-deep certainty that someone was almost done.

Had he said goodbye?

Would it be Christopher? Or Alyssa?

Cooper felt the curb under his ass, though he didn't remember sitting down. A cigarette butt taunted him from the dirt in the gutter. A hand came down on his shoulder and a voice, louder than the others, asked, "Are you all right, man?"

The sound that exploded from his throat was primal and out of his control. The hand shouldn't have been there. They shouldn't touch him. He curled away and didn't pay attention as the Samaritan muttered and walked off.

A popping noise made Cooper look around, but he saw nothing other than beautiful, sane people walking down the street. They gave him a wide berth. The sun was out. A shadow from the puff of a palm tree brushed the ground next to him. He scooted away, his breath still coming in short gasps.

It was too late.

The popping noises, the wet color.

He could see it, the awfulness of the vision creeping around the edges of reality, though he knew both worlds were real.

It was already over for someone. He just couldn't remember who.

Eleri Eames looked out the window at the Pacific below her. The flight pattern took them out over the water, then swung back before landing at LAX. She felt as though she'd just been plucked from the opposite ocean and plopped into this plane.

It was almost literally true. Her beach vacation had been ended early. Thoughts of returning to the office and waiting for another case to come along had been banished as quickly as she'd hung up the phone.

She blinked, the world she was in now so different from her days with the profilers. Then, she'd worked at the FBI home office, each night she'd returned to her own apartment, left alone with her dreams. Now she was being thrown from one end of the country to another, a field agent under odd circumstances at best.

Next to her, Donovan Heath flipped through a newspaper, his long face set off by dark eyes turned downward to the print. His jet black hair fell over his brows, slightly longer than the usual nearly-military style favored by so many agents. He looked like the nerd he was, not FBI.

Then again, he looked completely human, too—which was also a bit deceptive.

He flipped another page and Eleri pulled her shoulders to the side to get out of his way. First class. Wider seats. A magazine would have fit comfortably, but the man found a print newspaper. Where did he get that thing? Couldn't he e-read like everyone else?

Biting back a sigh, Eleri reminded herself there wasn't much that Donovan did like everyone else. And besides, who was she to complain about a little oddity?

Okay. A *lot* of oddity.

She turned her gaze out the window again. Public access plane. No reading classified files. She was left turning the case over in her brain.

Two bombs.

Two people, practically vaporized in their own space—one at home, one at a rented office only he used.

Connected by not much more than their method of death.

And the hint of terrorism.

She wondered if Donovan had ever seen anything like it in his ME days, and she wanted to ask, but did not want to start a discussion of bombs on a plane. Besides, would a medical examiner even get the body when there wasn't one? Likely anything similar in the past would have gone straight to forensics, or maybe odontology for a dental identification. If any teeth could be found.

She wanted to ask him not to take up so much space, but she couldn't. He'd switched seats with her after she'd suffered a panic attack upon first sitting down. The sudden fear of flying wasn't her own, but the result of the seat's occupant from the previous flight. Three hours of near hyperventilation had permeated the upholstery and leached out into Eleri's conscious. Donovan absorbed no such feelings from the seat and traded places without comment.

Eleri quickly shifted right, closer to the window, to avoid the edge of the wide newspaper as Donovan flipped the page again.

Disturbingly, her stomach lurched as the plane began its descent into L.A. Not because of the dip in altitude and not even because she was headed to see bodies that were merely a collection of remaining bits of tissue in sealed plastic bags. Her stomach rolled because she was excited.

She'd survived her first assignment and been given a second. She'd survived her partner despite great oddity, and he'd survived her. Eleri almost smiled.

Leaning toward him this time she asked, "Does the change in altitude hurt your ears?"

His expression stayed flat, his body going still. He only softly replied, "No."

He didn't like to talk about it, but she did. He was remarkable. While she wouldn't put him under glass, or cage him, or even call him a freak, she was going to study him. "Hmmm."

His ears were so sensitive. Then again maybe not so much when in human form. Not that she could say such things on this plane.

People around her were putting their things away, pulling out their earbuds, and starting to look around as they approached the runway. Eleri didn't have much to gather—her bag at her feet, her firearm checked in her luggage. There had not been a Sky Marshal on this flight, but she hadn't wanted the gun, could think of no situation where it would be better than what she had. Or rather, what Donovan had. She almost laughed.

As she studied him and he ignored her doing it, he slowly folded the paper with nerd-like precision and tucked it under his arm. Then he leaned back and stared straight ahead for a moment before saying, "What?"

"Nothing." She shook her head and looked out the window as the ground came up.

Fifteen minutes later, she stepped off the ramp and into the chaos that was LAX airport. Even inside, the air felt different. People pushed past them as they made their way to baggage claim. Despite not having to fight the crowd at the carousel—due to the badges and checked guns—getting their things was still a bitch. They still had to hit the lower level and weave their way to the office.

No one paid them any attention. What a change from the small Texas towns they'd been in for their last case. There, they'd stuck out like sore thumbs, just because no one knew them and their family histories for about three generations back. Here, people bumped into her and didn't say 'excuse me.' They didn't seem to care that she carried herself like a cop. She stopped for a moment and someone bumped into her back.

Shit.

Donovan had moved on ahead, almost to the floor-to-ceiling window that was the baggage check. If he hadn't been so tall, she might have lost him in the effort to reclaim their bags, get a rental car, and find the local Bureau branch.

The logistics were a struggle.

Though she'd driven in L.A. before, it was always a struggle. Even the traffic patterns she remembered from before seemed to have changed. Wilshire was more crowded, 3rd Street less so. By the time they got to the office she was ready for a nap, though she didn't think that was very agent-y of her.

It seemed the two of them didn't rate any special treatment. It meant she still had her carry-on slung over her shoulder as she pocketed the envelope and the address to a small house then followed Agent Vasquez down the hall to a conference room.

Marina Vasquez was the only one who sat down with them and after a moment, Eleri became convinced she was the only one who was going to. On top of that, Vasquez was irritable. "I've been on this thing since the first death, six months ago."

Ahh. Finally, something Eleri understood. "You finally caught something and you have to hand it over to us."

Vasquez didn't answer, just pushed the slim file across the table, her eyes showing a rough combination of anger and acceptance. Eleri fought the urge to apologize.

"I found Rollins." The words were flat, just a self-acknowledgment that she'd uncovered the one break there was.

"No one found him yet, I thought." Donovan spoke before Eleri could, but she felt her own frown forming. Had something happened while they were in the air?

No, Agent Marina Vasquez backpedaled on her choice of words. "I mean, I found the connection; apparently I'm not qualified to find the man."

Eleri couldn't tell the woman that it may have less to do with Vasquez and her qualifications than the fact that the case had been handed over to the NightShade Division.

Not her fault, Eleri reminded herself and watched as Vasquez visibly swallowed her bitterness and became a professional. "Here's what we know, and what you need to know."

Flipping open the file, she began spreading out pictures by feel. "You've seen this one, but these are worth looking at and knowing. He'll be hard to find."

Her fingers deftly sorted through shots from various angles, some with sun-bleached hair that was nearly blond, some with beards and without.

"His eyes." Eleri reached out a finger and touched a photo.

"He's not above using contacts, but you're right. His eyes are a bit unique." Vasquez tipped her head, nearly black hair sliding off her shoulder in thick curls.

Her brain churning, her gaze checking each picture for what she could pull from it, Eleri wondered if his eyes would look as bright all the time or if that was an effect of something else. But Vasquez was already onto the next topic.

This then was the issue with the new job. Someone else

started things and handed them over. Often reluctantly—most people didn't like having their project taken away. But the low-toned, female voice pulled her back.

"Here's his military history. I suggest you memorize it. It's quite varied and has likely played into why no one can find him." This time she looked directly at each of them, her eyes conveying the seriousness of the case and her attachment to it. They weren't supposed to get attached, but if anyone understood, it was Eleri.

"How did you find the connection?" Donovan broke in again.

This time Vasquez looked at him. "Too much reading. First victim was just a retired man. Turned out he was retired military. Second was a psychologist in his own office. Cooper Rollins is the only name that showed up twice. It's tenuous at best, but the fact that no one can find him to question him is concerning."

"He knows you're trying to question him?"

Vasquez answered to Donovan again as Eleri watched like a spectator at tennis. "He must. I told people to tell him we'd like to meet with him."

This time Eleri added her own two cents. "Military history like his, highly decorated, why wouldn't he come in?"

"Exactly." Vasquez's face held that same disturbed look.

"Is he dead?"

This time the woman shrugged, once again disturbing the curls that wanted to stay on her shoulders. "Could be. But there's no body. I've checked every death record, every morgue, every John Doe and every body that was ID'd but could have still been him. Nothing."

As Eleri stood gathering the file, she assessed the other woman. Vasquez was young, at least occasionally irritable, and so far very good. "When did you graduate the Academy?"

DONOVAN ROLLED his shoulders and felt the city pressing in. Eleri may have been happy to leave the beach house behind; she seemed to be dreaming of her sister more often there than when they were out.

He, on the other hand, had loved the place with unadulterated joy. It was big, airy, beautiful, and stocked. Maids changed the sheets and brought food. Eleri cooked sometimes. There was sand on the beach and no one much around in the off season.

Now, in the city, his skin felt like it wanted to stretch and pull. Just the thought of being surrounded by all these people made him itch. He'd been offered a Medical Examiner's position here once. He was good at what he did. Though the pay had been crap, that hadn't been the deciding factor. No, he'd turned down even the idea as soon as he heard "Los Angeles."

The rental house assigned to them was small, and he wondered how rich-girl Eleri handled coming from such a privileged background to this. For him, it was a step up from the trailers and one-bedroom apartments of his youth, but a step down from his own home in South Carolina. A far cry from a large backyard and a gate that opened onto a National Forest.

His sensitive nose felt the pollutants moving up through his sinuses and down into his lungs. His ears picked up on traffic and the horns that people here seemed to apply as liberally as they should have applied sunscreen.

Setting his bag in one of the two small bedrooms, this one at the back of the house, he wandered out to see where Eleri had gone.

With the small square footage of the place, he could easily hear her in the front bedroom. A drawer rolled along a runner, and a slight whisper of fabric told him she was actually putting her things in the drawers. They would be here a while.

Given the last case in Texas, then FoxHaven, and now this, they'd been in each other's pockets for over a month. And he didn't know when he'd get home again, get alone again. His chest pressed in, and he guessed the sooner he got the case solved the sooner he could run in his forest and breathe clean air filtered by trees. What he wouldn't give for a single dead body laid out on his table from a suspicious death.

But it wasn't his table now. The job had gone to someone else. Now he had a soldier to find and two dead bodies that weren't bodies anymore.

Eleri called out, seeming to know he was standing in the hallway. Maybe she wasn't quite human herself; he had been pretty quiet. "What do you think of Vasquez?"

He paused. There was something more, something Eleri wanted, but he didn't know what. So he just listed his impressions and hoped that helped. "She seems competent, but she was unhappy about having to hand the case over to us. She seems young. She's well put together, well spoken, pretty . . . Why?"

"Alyssa Rollins is Alyssa Gutierrez Rollins—Hispanic and young. You and I don't have an initial visual connection to her. . ."

Click. Eleri's gears were now obvious. "But Vasquez does." Even the name "Marina Vasquez" might appeal to Alyssa Gutierrez Rollins. As long as she didn't figure out she was being psychologied up to. "You want Vasquez to run the interview? I got the impression she'd never been out of the box."

"I don't think she has either. But she's young, ambitious, and . . ." This time she appeared in the doorway, her slim fingers holding some underthing he couldn't readily identify. She didn't seem to notice. "Honestly, right now she knows this case and knows about Rollins better than we do. And she wants it."

"So we let her in on the case and we'll be her heroes?"

Eleri shrugged. "Doesn't hurt anything."

He agreed with her until an hour later when they were all standing on the doorstep of a row townhouse in Los Feliz, one of the areas east of town. The place was an old, two-story with outside entrances to the units.

Donovan knocked, and the door to one unit over opened up. An older woman stuck her head out and immediately pulled it back in.

Shit. Despite the t-shirts and casual pants, the three of them practically screamed 'feds.' He'd agreed with Eleri on every point about Vasquez coming along, but none of them had thought about the fact that they were massively outnumbering a young woman with a small child.

He was hoping the woman wasn't home, that they hadn't screwed this all to hell already, when the door in front of them finally opened.

Alyssa Rollins was easily identifiable from her file pictures. Even there her expression had been wary.

It was Vasquez who introduced them. Names first, then FBI credentials, then an oh-so-soothing reassurance that her husband wasn't wanted for anything but his help.

"I don't know where he is." Alyssa Rollins looked over her shoulder, presumably at the child Donovan could hear in the background, but she didn't open the door any wider. "What is this about?"

Vasquez surprised him. She was a master in action. Her eyes darted left, then right, then she leaned forward, whispering to Alyssa Rollins. It still took a few back-and-forths to get the woman to let them come in. They could have insisted, but even Donovan knew that wasn't in their best interests.

He ended up sitting politely on an old couch that didn't quite distribute his weight and he watched the small child playing just out of reach. The kid stacked cheap plastic blocks and babbled occasionally as he threw them. *Right on developmental target,* Donovan thought.

He listened for noises coming from the back rooms, as though maybe she was hiding her estranged husband back there. But the only thing that came out was a cat. It slipped down the hallway, stopping in the door, and stared beady-eyed at Donovan, before hissing and running off.

Ignoring the conversation up until now, he was pulled back in by Eleri's voice. Less soothing than Vasquez's 'let's-be-friends' tone, hers clearly took the reins. Where Vasquez was asking open, general questions about Rollins, Eleri Eames brought focus.

"He was previously in the care of a Dr. Walton Gardiner . . ." Eleri let it hang and Donovan cringed. That name. No wonder he'd gone into psychology.

Mrs. Rollins didn't seem to notice that Eleri knew the name from memory. "Yes. But not for a while now."

"Dr. Gardiner has passed away." She waited. So did Donovan.

Nothing happened. There was nothing odd, no fear smell, no strange twitch from the wife. "I'm sorry. I didn't know him."

Clearly she didn't. The doctor wasn't an old man. His death would be a surprise. The fact that he'd blown up suddenly while sitting in his office chair was even more shocking. Alyssa Rollins didn't seem to have any idea about any of it.

Donovan took over. The wife looked like a dead end. "Was your husband seeing him regularly?"

"He was supposed to, but he quit . . . About eight months ago."

That was when it hit him. The smells here matched her and the child, but there was nothing indicating a man had been in this unit other than him. "Does your husband live here?"

"No." She looked down, "We're separated."

This time, Eleri jumped in again. "You haven't filed paperwork."

"No, ma'am." Her voice was starting to get nervous, though

Donovan couldn't read if that meant she was lying or was just a regular person unused to being questioned by three FBI agents in her own home. "I don't think we'll reconcile, but we haven't started any proceedings or even filed any papers." She looked down at her hands.

His partner offered a tight smile and leaned forward. They were almost done. One last question. "When was the last time you saw him?"

Alyssa Rollins shook her head. "I haven't seen him in six months."

Donovan shook her hand, as did Eleri and Marina Vasquez before they left. They thanked her, Eleri left their number, and it was all a very by-the-book dead end. Cooper Rollins had not been in that apartment. Alyssa and the child had lived there a while. As had the cat. He'd smelled all of it. While he could tell Eleri that, there was no repeating that kind of knowledge in front of Agent Vasquez, so he held his tongue.

Good thing, too.

As soon as Eleri pulled the rental car out into traffic, Marina Vasquez announced from the back seat, "She's lying."

3

E leri stuck her gloved hand into the box and pulled out another zipped baggie. A series of broken and re-taped seals revealed who had been handling the remains of Dr. Walton Gardiner.

Of course, a good part of the remains were already disposed of. The ME's office couldn't keep a nearly liquefied man for very long. They did, however, keep many samples. In the bags were small clear bottles filled with a DMSO and formalin mix to preserve the tissues. Tiny pinkish or yellowish blobs or even strips wafted under the surface as she looked at each.

Eleri lifted bag after bag to the light, sorting them as she went. Adipose tissue. The tip of a finger. A larger jar with a strip of skin that had survived intact. A partial lower jaw bone with a small handful of teeth still anchored. It was cleaned of any clinging tissue and sat alone in its marked bag. She set it aside and kept sorting.

Her mother, the perfect elite Southern wife, had never understood Eleri's need for the science. But after she'd been questioned repeatedly at age ten by FBI agents trying to glean information regarding her sister's abduction, Eleri had known what she would do. This was where it had all led her—holding the last piece of this man's jawbone and trying to balance dignity for him in death with justice.

Eleri didn't test the tissue samples. They'd been tested already. DNA tests had been run on the adipose tissue and matched to a sample provided by the therapist's wife.

It should have been enough. The L.A. County Coroner's Office had matched one of the pieces they'd cataloged, but they hadn't checked odontology. They hadn't checked several other things. If this was as big as her Senior Agent in Charge Westerfield thought it was, then Eleri needed more certainty than one small sample and a DNA match brought in by a family member.

More effort than that had gone into simpler things like defrauding insurance companies. If this was a conspiracy, she wasn't going to trust a lone test.

But the fingertip did look like Walton Gardiner's fingertips in the pictures she'd been given. She'd checked the face in the photos against his legal California ID. Eleri didn't doubt that could be faked—she'd heard tales of the California DMV. Right at this moment, Donovan and Marina Vasquez were at the Gardiners' home collecting more samples for their own cross check.

The match they already had was from a root ball on the end of hair plucked from a hairbrush the wife claimed was the husband's. So easy to fake.

Setting aside the fingertip, Eleri pulled the jaw out of the bag it was in, breaking the seal before signing and dating the attached record. She flipped open the file Vasquez had gotten from the man's dentist and set to work. Pulling the most recent dental x-rays, she set to matching the teeth on the side of the jaw she had left to work with.

Luckily, Dr. Walton Gardiner had fillings and some relatively extensive dental work on the molars. No implants—

which would have really helped, but she had a lot to work with.

By the time Donovan and Marina showed up with their collected samples, Eleri was convinced she was in possession of the jaw of one Dr. Walton Gardiner, psychological therapist.

She held it up as the others came in through the doorway to the lab. Donovan also showed off his baggies as he entered, but Marina gave away her newbie status by clenching a smile. She didn't seem to be able to fight turning a pale shade of green.

Eleri didn't pay much attention to her. "This is Dr. Gardiner's lower right mandible."

Marina slapped down the baggies she'd been holding as though they burned her, while Donovan came in for a closer look. At home holding portions of dead people in his hands, he almost didn't seem to notice that his partner for the day looked to be on the verge of vomiting. Vasquez's color change was growing more pronounced the longer she was in the lab.

"If that's Gardiner's jaw, then he's definitely dead."

Donovan turned to Marina, still not seeing her distress. "There's virtually no way to get that portion of the jaw from an otherwise intact head. Thus, this is evidence that his head is no longer functioning. And if his head isn't, nothing is."

As Eleri watched, Marina Vasquez turned away and started puffing short breaths through her nose. She offered a short glare at Donovan, who only now seemed to realize what he'd done. He shrugged back, like 'how was I supposed to know?'

Suffice to say, his skills lay with dead people, not live ones.

Eleri didn't put down the bone. She called out to the younger woman before she could exit the lab. "Grab some gloves, then grab a trash can to barf into. You need to come handle these samples."

"Why? You've got it covered." Vasquez started to push the door open.

Eleri stopped her. "Because you won't get far in this job if you can't handle the evidence with your own dignity intact. So come handle this now, it's some of the worst you'll see—tissue wise—and you'll barf and you'll learn."

Marina hadn't turned around yet. "Maybe I'll do it later."

"You'll do it now." Eleri kept her voice soft, but firm. "I know you want to be on this case and I know we're better with your help. But I can't have you vomiting on my evidence or ruining our credibility at a scene. There's a high possibility that we're going to come across a fresh case just like this one. "

Marina Vasquez did not leave the lab. In fact, she turned around so rapidly that Eleri was surprised how fast she'd committed. Until she realized that Marina was only committed to making sure her vomit made it into a waste bin.

Donovan frowned and looked away, finally setting down the samples he'd been holding. Maybe he was trying to ignore the heaving woman behind him or give her some space, Eleri didn't know. He snapped on gloves and took the jawbone from her hand. "You certain on these?"

She showed him the x-rays and talked over the sounds of the younger agent losing more of her lunch. She showed each of the points she'd compared and when she'd felt confident to call the odontology a match.

Just about then, Marina Vasquez reached out and pulled a pair of medical gloves from one of several handy boxes, then grabbed the trashcan and walked over.

Eleri looked at her. "Are you ready?" She didn't wait, just held up one of the bags she'd set aside. "This is skin. We're going to test it against the DNA you and Donovan gathered today."

Vasquez turned green and buried her face in the can while more sounds emerged.

"That's it." Eleri tried to be a little soothing. "Donovan and I won't tell anyone. Get it out of your system now."

Pale-faced, the other woman looked up at her, "You mean literally."

Eleri busted into a laugh at that one. "Yes, I guess I did."

"I THINK VASQUEZ IS RIGHT." Donovan bit into the burger he'd ordered from takeout, mayo and juices dripping down into the Styrofoam box as he ate with one hand.

Vasquez wasn't here to either confirm or deny his appraisal. She'd left after Eleri had made her scrape several of the tissues to gather cells. Eventually, he'd had enough of the younger agent squirming while she held the samples at arm's length and just blurted out, "They aren't going to bite you. They're dead!"

He wasn't normal. He knew that.

Eleri wasn't either. And he wasn't certain he was completely on board with his partner's 'barf-til-you-make-it' training plan. Still, she was the senior partner, even if she was a solid five years younger than him. She was also right that an agent who couldn't hold their shit together on scene wasn't much of an agent. They couldn't bring Vasquez along if she couldn't keep her lunch down.

Donovan had no such problems. He loved red meat, nearly bloody, and even rotting body parts didn't stop him from getting hungry. His sensitive nose smelled everything, but was offended by very little.

He looked up to find Eleri watching him. Her words startling. "You're like a dog."

"I'm not a dog." It felt like his lungs compressed when she insulted him that way, and he remembered why he didn't like having friends. He stared.

"Dogs have very sensitive noses, but they sniff each other's butts." She took a bite of her own burger, then said almost exactly what he'd been thinking. "You clearly have a fantastic ability to distinguish and catalog smells, but nothing offends you. Even I'm offended by some of it. But not you. It's like you have good smells—" she pointed to his burger, "—and neutral smells, but no bad smells."

"There are bad smells."

"Like?"

He sighed. Did they have to talk about this? "When I mention them, I remember them. I'm eating."

"Oh." She nodded and dropped the subject. She hadn't washed her hair this morning, he thought. He could smell yesterday's scents on it and wondered if he should tell her.

His own hair was thicker and slicker than normal and smells didn't absorb into it the way they did most people's. If he'd had Gardiner's whole head, he might have been able to sniff the hair to detect where the man had been recently. But he didn't have it. The man was mostly pink mist.

With the parts they'd ID'd and tested, he and Eleri had confirmed that the dead body and all the parts they checked had indeed belonged to the therapist. So he turned the conversation back to the documents he was trying not to drip his burger onto.

"Vasquez is right about Rollins' bank records. His military benefits are still going into their joint account, and the wife is spending them."

"How do you know it's her?" Eleri asked before spearing a spice and olive oil covered broccoli. Her own sandwich was grilled chicken on some gourmet bun. He'd quit trying to figure out her eating habits a while ago.

"Expenses at Target, Ralphs grocery store. Vasquez managed to pull her store code and got print-outs of all her grocery purchases." He pushed a list toward her. "Look, generic diapers, canned fruit, the occasional pack of disposable sippy cups. All at the store right down the street from her condo."

Eleri nodded and seemed to be enjoying her vegetables.

Her own papers were radiating farther and farther out on the table as she worked.

"Look," Donovan pushed another paper forward. "There are withdrawals for cash at regular intervals. Big sums. At least big for what she's living on."

"So? Lots of people get cash." She took a delicate bite of her frilly sandwich and waited. He liked that she asked the questions, but didn't seem to expect he'd screwed it up. She was simply awaiting details. She trusted his expertise. Maybe that was why he stayed even though she sometimes said things like the 'dog' comment earlier.

"This withdrawal is downtown." He spun the tablet he'd pulled up a city map on and pointed near the ATM address for her.

"She can move around." Eleri watched him.

Donovan smiled. "Not this fast." He pulled out her credit card records. "She checked out at her neighborhood grocery store—using her store card, just ten minutes earlier than the downtown withdrawal. The grocery purchase is for a decent sized cache, including milk. She probably went home and put them in the fridge."

"So it's definitely two different people." This time Eleri grinned. "Didn't Vasquez say she canvassed the neighborhood with Cooper Rollins' picture?"

"And no one claimed to have seen him." Donovan nodded. "So he didn't buy the groceries at the corner store. But he is taking money out of their account on a regular basis. Or someone is. He's the only one who makes sense. But . . ."

"But none of this makes any sense yet." She pushed back from the table. "What do Cooper Rollins' therapist and his old commanding officer have to do with each other?"

If there had been an easy answer to that, he and Eleri wouldn't be here. He was getting the impression that their division of the FBI—NightShade—wasn't called out unless the case was really tough. He wasn't sure yet if he liked that or not, and he sure didn't have an answer to Eleri's question.

What he did have was another question. "Why doesn't Alyssa Rollins know that her husband was Special Forces?"

This time Eleri moved forward, the last piece of her sandwich set into the Styrofoam with a thunk that said she was paying all her attention to him. "What do you mean?"

"When we talked to her, she mentioned his time enlisted. But she said several times he was a 'specialist.' That's a rank. She seemed to think he was in Afghanistan the whole time he was enlisted. But our records say he was at Fort Benning and even in North Korea for some of it."

She frowned. "Shit. We need to find out what she really believes. Why wouldn't she know?"

"So he was a Ranger, then quickly promoted and trained as a Green Beret. His unit reported to the CIA's SAD—Special Activities Division," Donovan moved his finger, reading from the notes he'd put together. He didn't know all these pieces and wasn't even positive he had it right. But it was a start. "And at the end he was discharged quickly. *Very* quickly from what I can see. That's unusual. But that's just what I put together. What gets me is that the benefits getting deposited into their account each month are for a Specialist with nine years' service. Not a former Ranger and medically discharged Green Beret. And Alyssa Rollins doesn't seem to know that."

COOPER ROLLINS CLIMBED THE FENCE. It was ten feet tall, chain link, with barbed wire at the top. Put there for the express purpose of keeping him and his kind out.

The fencing here was still pretty, clean and silver, the links still mostly intact on this side. Ozzy had wire cutters, and he'd managed to split the razor wire in one spot on each of the four sides of fence that separated this one perfect square of dirt from the streets that defined it and the cars and people passing by. Cooper gently pushed the sharp edges apart and threw a leg over the top.

This area of downtown L.A. was an odd mix. It housed various districts—a block or two of one kind of business or another. This particular block was bracketed by the jewelry district on one side and fabrics and textiles on the other.

It was a new spot for the veteran group, their old fenced-in square having recently been built on. Five blocks over, it had been next to the floral district and had smelled a bit better.

Cooper landed in the dirt with a puff of gray concrete clay rising under his boots.

"Rollins!"

He lifted his head at the sound and spotted Ozzy's hand up in the air. Making his way toward the man was a task completed by practice and Special Forces training.

The tents this group slept in dotted the ground. Some were bright and new. A small blue pop-up dominated his left, an old brown version was staked too close to the corners to gain any real stability. The ground was littered with makeshift personal areas. An old mattress covered with a smattering of dirty sheets and a blanket crossed what should have been a walking path. The owner was absent, but the things weren't touched.

Ever watchful, Cooper counted about eight people currently in the area. About forty sleeping spaces, protected from the passing business people and shoppers by the ironic chain link. Insurance companies made the property owners install it.

Though Cooper didn't live here like most did, and though he was cleaner and better fed than them, he was welcome. Almost everyone in this particular area was ex-military. They had their own code, which included greeting Ozzy upon entry. But that's who Cooper was here to see anyway.

A woman he'd never met sat next to the man, and Ozzy introduced her right away. "This here's Walter Reed."

The nickname should have been funny, but was likely a nod to her prosthetic leg and hand. It didn't seem to get in her way though and she nodded at him then went back to eating some fried chicken. She would have been pretty if she were clean.

Ozzy grinned. "Walter's MARSOC."

Cooper felt his eyebrows rise. She'd been Marine Special Forces. He didn't know a lot about it. But that lost leg and hand made more sense. It also meant she was trained in "Unusual Combat"—something he knew more about than he wanted to.

Not knowing what to say, Cooper only nodded.

It was Ozzy who picked up the conversation. "You find that fracture?"

"No. Just chatter." He'd finally gotten some of the key words he was looking for. "But it came from down here." He pointed at the ground, but meant the downtown area. He'd picked up chatter once before, but it had been closer to Alyssa and Christopher.

He *knew* that shit was all around, but it didn't make his heart race as bad when it wasn't as close to the two of them.

"Can you join up?"

"I think so." He nodded to Ozzy. "Can you keep your ears peeled?" He gave the man some information, noting that Walter Reed was memorizing it, despite looking like she was just eating chicken and ignoring the world. He decided to address that straight up. Turning to her, he added, "If you get any of this. Send it back to me? It's important for my family."

She gave a small nod, maybe assuming that if he was a friend of Ozzy's he was a friendly.

"There are two women in the group that I can tell." Cooper mentioned.

Ozzy gave a small start in surprise, but Walter didn't. Definitely MARSOC. Ozzy's reaction was the normal one. It was unusual to find women on the chatter. It made them valuable.

Walter's eyes narrowed as she figured out what he was doing. "Why would you join?" Her voice was harsh.

"It's where the money is." It was all he could say.

Walter Reed clearly couldn't tell what he was up to, but she was suspicious and right to be so. Cooper couldn't say more— not in this tiny tent community surrounded only by chain link. Ozzy's spot was near the middle, prime territory.

"Shit." Walter's voice was soft, disturbingly feminine through the swear.

Following her gaze, Cooper saw the officers, a pair in blue, coming toward the block. Ducking carefully into Ozzy's tent, the three of them moved out of sight even as the others who'd been out also quickly disappeared from view.

Inside the tent the heat became stifling. For a moment Cooper wondered how Ozzy slept in here, then he thought how much the dry heat reminded him of the Middle East. Maybe that was how.

"Hey! We know you're in there." One of the cops called out.

They didn't answer, but it wasn't a tense standoff. Walter re-settled herself but kept eating the chicken.

"You have to move from here." It was half-hearted at best. The cops didn't want to move them. No one else was using the lot. And the boys in blue weren't going to climb the razor wire fence to evict people with nowhere else to go. Especially not vets.

Case in point, Cooper heard a ratcheting noise that spiked his adrenaline. Even as he told himself he was safe—they were safe—he heard the cop take a harsh tone beyond the boundary. "Put that down, kid."

He put it together: kid with a stick, running it along the fence.

"I don't have to." The kid replied and the noise started again.

Walter had quit eating her chicken. She stared at him.

Shit. He was breathing heavily. Ozzy put his hand on Cooper's arm, an anchor to the present. The stick on the fence, the ratcheting noise . . . it sounded like the chain that opened the fence at the edge of the compound.

A loud crack split the air, and Cooper and Walter both jumped.

He told himself the kid maybe broke the stick. In the back of his head he heard the cops going after the asshole. But it didn't matter that he knew it was a stick. It didn't matter that he identified the sound as matching the gate at the base when his team returned. Or what was left of his team.

His brain looped time and when he breathed in he felt the searing heat of air on his last op. His ribs didn't want to expand because of the vest and the pack and all the weight he was carrying.

Putting his hand to his chest to prove the packs and gear weren't there didn't work. Cooper felt them. His fingers brushed the heavy canvas of the vest, the feel of extra ammo in the pockets, the wire to the radio he wore.

He watched as his best friend shredded in front of him, arms each flying into the trees, hand still holding the tactical gun. One leg pinwheeled away. Cooper tasted the blood in the air.

Cupping his hands over his ears, he breathed in short bursts and reminded himself, "It's not real, it's not real."

But it was.

4

Donovan stood on one side of the chain link fence. Ugly loops of razor wire topped it, ready to slice anyone who came in contact.

But there were people inside. People looking at him warily. Beside him, Eleri also stood gazing through the fence. He could almost hear her thinking the same thing he was: *There has to be a way in.* There were people inside. They didn't just materialize their way in and out. Then he thought of some of the things he'd seen at NightShade and Donovan fought a shudder.

Inside, the people were various shades of dirty, messy, and skittish, but they all had the same bearing, the same stiff backbone.

Soldiers.

He could almost smell it on them. The man who picked his way across the space did so unevenly, but still ready to take all comers.

Donovan was a nerd— a former medical examiner and current FBI agent. Given that, they should be able to take him, easily. But they'd never seen anything like him before, and they shouldn't ever.

"Up and over." Eleri had made up her mind. Though her voice was soft, her resolve was clear.

"I'll go first." They could only go one at a time. They'd casually checked the perimeter and found only one spot where the links had been tampered with. It wasn't clear how to get through, and the people inside could easily hold them out. So despite being counterintuitive, going over made their entrance harder to stop.

Donovan thought he could see a split in the razor wire above, but both of them going at the same time likely meant at least one of them would get caught and that stuff was nasty. So he started the climb and was at the top in no time, holding on with his left hand and carefully pushing at the coils of wire with his right.

There it was.

The barbs kept getting hung up, but eventually he got them far enough apart to get safely through. Even as he swung his leg over, he could feel Eleri mounting the links below him. He was turned around, clinging to the fence, his back to the men on the ground when she passed him going up the other side.

She didn't smile, just climbed with efficiency and determination. As Donovan hit the ground, he stepped aside and none too soon. Eleri dropped to the dirt right beside him.

This *was* the way in. These guys almost all climbed in and out, as evidenced by the packed dirt square he landed on. It was about the only place not covered by tents or bedding, about the only part of any path wide enough to land on. He looked around and thought he saw two other landing squares in the opposite corners. In and out wasn't easy, but it kept them alone.

The soldiers stared warily at the two of them. Donovan stared back, wondering if he looked like a Fed now the way these people all looked like soldiers.

An older man came up to them. "I'm Ozzy. What can I do for you?"

Donovan was starting to speak, but Eleri already had it going. After a disturbingly brief intro, she got to the point. "We're looking for this man. He's not in trouble, we're just hoping he can help us with a case." She'd pulled out the picture of Rollins and flashed it around.

A side look from her kept Donovan from reaching for the additional photos he carried. Maybe she didn't want them to know that they'd researched Rollins more thoroughly than just a quick chat would warrant.

One by one, the men and even a few women in here filed by, looking at the photo. Ozzy had said, no, he didn't know that man. Then each of the others said the same thing. Almost word for word.

Someone needed to teach them to lie better.

Donovan fought down an audible sigh and thanked the vets for their time. He wanted to ask if there was anything he could do, anything they could use, but he didn't. He'd been on the other side before, seen his father's pride and refusal to take anything even when it was sorely needed. For a while, he'd even developed some of that stubbornness himself.

There was nothing else he and Eleri could do here without alienating the people they needed, so he watched as she smiled blandly and handed out her card as though these people would up and call the FBI if they saw something. Then she calmly turned and climbed the razor wire topped fence as if that were her usual MO for entry and exit.

Donovan followed with as much aplomb as he could muster, disturbed to find he didn't do it as well as Eleri.

She gave him a moment to fall into step as they walked away back to the bank.

Before they went to see the vets, they'd stopped in and requested a video pull. So now it only took a few minutes for the branch manager to show them the clips he'd sorted out using the date, time, and card number from Rollins' bank records.

Sure enough, that was him withdrawing cash. He managed to avoid a direct shot from the camera, so it wasn't proof, but the person punching the numbers and taking the cash was definitely not Alyssa Rollins.

Aside from the fact that the branch manager was shaking in his shiny shoes over a visit from the FBI, it looked outwardly like a normal visit. They tried to leave while drawing as little attention to themselves as possible. It was only mildly successful.

Donovan had to admit that while the smells in L.A. weren't the best, the weather was pretty nice. It was seventy degrees here even though other parts of the country were already well into winter. He could wear nice shirts and pants and not sweat to death and the dry air at least didn't transmit the odors as well as humidity did.

They hit the parking garage and climbed into the car. This time he was driving, and slid behind the wheel before starting to talk.

"So we know he got money at that machine on at least two occasions. And there's no reason to believe the other withdrawals aren't him." Donovan hadn't wanted to ask the bank branch manager anything he didn't have to.

"I agree. Also, he's been down there with that enclave of vets. They know him and they aren't telling." Her lips pressed together, though if it was her thoughts or the traffic that pushed that expression, he couldn't tell.

They were only a mile, but probably twenty minutes from the rental house that was now home, when he saw a restaurant on the corner. Hungry and frustrated, he swung wide into the parking lot and handed over the keys to the valet before Eleri could comment.

"Chili?"

"I'm hungry." He didn't add that he was upset. It probably showed. "I'm sure they have something you'll eat."

What they had was a menu printed like a newspaper and about as long. He wanted a beer, but—like always—they couldn't talk in public, and he couldn't get the beer to go. He was still grumpy when he walked in the front door of the little house, but at least he could talk and he had food.

Twisting the cap from a beer he pulled from the fridge—because fuck it—he opened the containers and felt his stomach roll in anticipation of what was supposedly the second best chili in LA. He'd take it.

Two bites later, with Eleri watching him the whole time, he started talking. "We have jack shit."

"I know."

"We know he makes withdrawals within about twenty-four hours of the deposit." Though even that wasn't regular, and he didn't always use the same ATM. "So we just missed him this month. That's three plus weeks to catch him if we can figure out which ATM he's going to."

She nodded, "We're not going to get him that way. We need to go back and find out what those people know."

His bark of laughter signaled his disbelief. "Do you have any military background? Can you fake your way in there? Besides, they already saw us."

He shook his head. But his rebuttal didn't stop her.

"You can go in."

"No. I'm not any more capable than you of faking—"

The look in her eyes stopped him. Her next words didn't help.

"Well, you can't climb the fence, but you can hang out and listen without them knowing." Her fork was paused halfway to her mouth and from the looks of her, she was serious.

He almost smacked the beer down onto the table.

"No."

~

DONOVAN SAT in the back seat of the rental car, his mouth slightly open and his eyes staring at the back of Eleri's head. He could no longer make language sounds and that was a good thing or he might be saying things he couldn't take back.

She'd talked him into it.

And he'd let her.

He'd argued that Metro Animal Control could pick him up, or even shoot him on sight. She'd argued back that it was highly unlikely and she would intervene, blowing her own cover, before any of that happened.

He'd suggested they get a real dog. Put a listening device on it and use it to scout the chain-link block, but she quickly shot that down, too. A real dog couldn't follow the conversation, wouldn't know where to get the best spot. While he'd talked Eleri out of the recording device, he'd eventually caved to a small GPS.

He wanted to vomit.

Even sitting here quietly in the back of the car, the feeling of the collar around his neck was restrictive. But if something happened—if Animal Control or anyone did manage to scoop him up—he'd be up shit creek if Eleri couldn't find him.

He'd still fought against it. "I can't risk exposing myself. My people have stayed hidden for ... centuries."

She'd crossed her arms and raised one dark reddish eyebrow at him, the pale green of her eyes broadcasting sharp disbelief. "Um. No you haven't. Had y'all really stayed hidden, there would be no legends."

She shrugged at him like "beat that."

He'd nearly growled. "I'm not a werewolf."

"Fine. But you *are* the thing the legends are based on. So I argue that some of your kind *did* in fact get out and about in the past."

Then, when he'd finally capitulated, she asked if she could watch.

"No!" Donovan had exploded in disbelief. He wasn't angry so much as stuck. "You cannot watch me change. . . Ever. I don't watch you bathe!"

"It's not the same." Eleri shook her head. "I get that it's an intrusion and I'm sorry, but it's *so scientifically interesting.*"

She'd stood for a moment as though that was enough of an argument to intrude even further than she already had into a life he'd kept successfully closed for over three decades.

"Fine." He crossed his own arms, not missing that they were having a full blown living room standoff. "But I get to hand you items with horrible pasts, you even have to sleep with them, and I'll hook you up to brain monitors and I'll study you while you study me."

There was silence as he won a tiny battle in the war.

"Fine. Go change. Close the door, scratch when you want out." She'd turned away.

So somehow here he was in the back seat, wearing a collar, ready to go see if he could make friends with the soldiers. Which meant he hadn't really won much at all, had he?

They were two blocks away when Eleri found an empty spot she liked. There were plenty to choose from. Downtown LA, while bustling during the day, was a ghost town at night. Only a few people who didn't look homeless wandered around on their way from one event to another. There seemed to be a surge in new housing downtown, but the two of them had already driven past where the economic growth ended. This part of town had not yet been gentrified.

She opened the back door of the car and Donovan hopped out, the pads of all four feet making contact with the concrete. It was not the sand and reeds he'd run in at FoxHaven. It wasn't the loamy topsoil and protruding branches of his home forest. It was city, pure and simple.

Donovan loped away before anyone could see them together. He was grateful his fur was black and not a lighter color where he could be mistaken for a coyote. There was a faint trace of their scent even here.

This form opened his nasal cavities, making his inhumanly exceptional sense of smell even better. He should have found something of Cooper Rollins' to sniff before he came here.

It didn't matter. He didn't have anything and he couldn't think how to get it.

Ozzy's scent floated to him. Even though he'd only gotten a whiff of the man while in human form earlier that day, he could recognize the vet now. He was out of the compound.

Donovan wanted to get to the fence before anyone stopped him or—god forbid—tried to pet him. So he picked up his pace.

~

ELERI WALKED BRISKLY PAST, her jacket light enough to be taken for normal as the night cooled just a little. Had it been ninety, the clothing would have been more suspicious. Still, she figured she had three passes at best.

Her hair was tucked into a bun, the night hiding the red tones, she hoped. She stuffed her hands in her pockets. Looking relatively normal was harder than it seemed.

The jacket was flimsy, and if she pulled it tight, she would expose the handgun holstered at her back. She also couldn't walk like a fed, but she couldn't slouch her way around either. Getting mugged would not help their case and would definitely expose at least her when she took down her attacker. And there would be no way to retrieve her nearly two hundred pound 'dog' as she went. No one would buy that.

Best not to get mugged at all. She adjusted her stance a little and walked as slow as she reasonably could past the compound.

Donovan had beaten her there, as planned. He sat at the fence, looking in, one paw batting at the chain link as though he saw something he wanted. One of the soldiers came up and started talking to him, the way people do to dogs. She only heard snippets since Donovan was adamant about there being no recording or listening devices on him.

"Are you hungry, fellow?"

Donovan cocked his head, his ears perking.

He looked like a wolf. Just not an actual species that Eleri had ever found in nature. Then again, he was definitely part of evolution, just not the documented part.

She watched out of the corner of her eye as he was offered part of a fast food burger and took it from the man's dirty hands. Eleri fought a shudder. She couldn't look like she was paying any attention. Unsure if she was more offended by the dirt or the quality of food, she walked on. Like a dog, Donovan had a stomach that could handle anything. Probably even raw meat, though she'd never seen him eat it.

She was a believer now, that was certain.

When she was out of sight and hearing, she tucked herself into a doorway and peeled the jacket. Turning it inside out, and using the reversible color, she slid back into it. This time she added a ball cap. Not her usual style, but she couldn't blow their cover and she had to be in visual contact with Donovan. Which she wasn't right now.

Ducking out of the doorway, she let her hands hang loose and made a short loop around the block, coming to the compound on the other side this time. As she passed by, she saw Donovan was inside.

Shit. They didn't have a contingency for that.

5

Eleri spent the night in the small rental car.

After her third pass by the compound, it became clear that Donovan had been adopted by the group. That was probably the best scenario, but not one they'd planned for.

The first time they'd come, the only way in appeared to be up and over. Unless Donovan had levitation skills she didn't know about, there was an opening in the fence that she hadn't been able to see.

Donovan had clearly not levitated into the compound. She knew this only because no one made any exclamations about a flying dog. She'd seen some strange things, and she'd lived some more. Then she'd been surprised by the world all over again after joining the NightShade division.

At least animal control couldn't grab him from inside the compound. The vets wouldn't let them. So she moved the car to a nearby parking structure and twiddled away her time. She watched the GPS tracker and saw that Donovan was still inside the small fenced square. Occasionally, she managed a visual check and twice did a drive-by.

Though a few slept, most of the vets were awake when she passed. It was four a.m. before the GPS moved. Jumping up, Eleri tried to decide how to follow him without being caught. Some of these guys were ex-Special Forces, so there was a good probability that she'd already been made, but she couldn't leave Donovan out on his own.

She put the jacket and the ball cap back on and made her way out the far end of the parking structure. Managing to cross one block away, she held the tablet close to her side, needing it to be able to check in on Donovan if she couldn't see him.

From the cross street, she spotted him following one of the soldiers until the man got a few feet ahead and Donovan ducked into an alleyway.

Shit. She couldn't look like she was watching, but she needed to see if the soldier let Donovan go or tried to follow him. Eleri checked the tablet. The dot stayed motionless in one spot for a few minutes. He was waiting for her.

Turning right at the next block she made a square and headed back to the car. Less than five minutes later she'd pulled up near the dot on the map and gotten out of the car. As she watched, the 'wolf' came forward and she climbed out to let him into the back seat.

Once they were in the car, she drove off, taking a longer route out of the downtown area. Eleri did not want to drive past the veterans area again.

She could have thrown him a blanket, told him to change in the back seat, but she didn't have a blanket. In this age of cameras everywhere, someone could catch a video glimpse of the amazing transformation Donovan could make. So she drove him home and was grateful for the high fence around the back of the little house.

Once through the back door, Donovan beelined for his room and zipped back out again, still wolf. This time he clenched a towel in his mouth. He managed to close the bathroom door behind himself and as Eleri listened, she heard the water come on in the tub.

That meant he'd already changed. She wondered what had happened while he was out that had him racing into the shower, but she barely managed to eat a bowl of cereal before he was emerging from the lone bath. The towel was clutched around his hips, water dripping onto the old, hard wood floor. But he seemed to be breathing easier.

Eleri asked.

"They treated me like a house dog. Hugging me and ..." His voice was low, a bit distressed for someone usually as reserved as Donovan.

"That's bad because they were homeless? Smelly? Dirty?" That seemed odd. The man liked the smell of dead bodies.

He shook his head, affirming her theory but leaving her with nothing to go on. His shoulders pulled up in distaste, his brows furrowed. "They *petted* me. Called me *'doggy'*."

"The women?" She hadn't seen more than just a few, and hadn't seen any of them tonight.

"The men!"

That pulled her back. "It was too homo-erotic?"

"No." He sighed at her. "It was people *touching* me. I don't care who or what they are. But they *touched me*. They scratched my ears and stroked me and I was supposed to act like I liked it." His shudder was visible even as he declared the conversation over by turning and disappearing into the back bedroom.

The very thought gave Eleri pause for a moment. She'd been hugged as a child, loved, petted. It didn't bother her until after her sister had gone missing. Even then, she was still hugged—too tightly maybe, but held nonetheless.

She'd gotten glimpses of Donovan's father, seen things she shouldn't have seen. She was willing to bet that if Donovan had ever been hugged it was by his mother. And his mother had died when he was very young.

He was back out, dressed and drinking a beer, before she could finish the thought.

Leaning back in the blue painted wood chair, bottle in hand, hair wet, feet bare, he looked like a normal man. He was anything but. Eleri took in the differences.

His chest, which she'd just seen, was a bit hairy—not concerningly so, but more than normal. Even the tops of his feet had a fine coating of slick hair. His long nose looked like a normal human facial feature, but it was that length that allowed it to broaden, become the face of the wolf. She'd seen it on his father and, shockingly, later on her friend Wade, too. But she pushed the scientific curiosity aside—difficult as that was to do—and asked him the other thing under her skin.

"Did you get good intel?" He'd been in there for close to six hours.

"Yes." Tapping his forefinger against the tabletop while he thought, he laid out what he'd heard. "Most of it was crap. Probably about ninety percent was how to get a new, better tent, or where to bathe. Should they let the new lady join. . .? They talked about Rollins for a good bit before I realized it was him they were talking about."

At that, Eleri perked up. "Go on."

"They're worried about him. Think he's not right in the head. Ozzy said he felt like a traitor, but he had his doubts about what Rollins was up to. Didn't like the chatter he talked about. He set that woman 'Walter' on Rollins' tail. So Walter is going to see if she can find out what the man is up to as well."

"Wow." Eleri leaned back. Poor Donovan had to sift through loads of crap. He couldn't even steer the conversation, and he'd let them pet him. "You did good work. I'm sorry about the petting."

He shrugged as though he'd let it go, but she could tell he hadn't really.

"There's more." He took another pull from the beer, his eyes heavy. They'd both sleep deeply after this. "Walter told Ozzy that his suggestion she seduce Rollins was batshit, that Rollins was still desperately in love with his wife. There was some conversation about Alyssa after that—and they called her Alyssa the Bitch. They think *she's* turned *him* away."

"Wow."

"Yeah, the way they talked about her, it was ongoing."

Eleri felt the implication sink in. "So they have been seeing each other. We thought so."

"Good to get confirmation." He tipped the beer again, only to find it was already empty. Eleri saw his surprise, but he just thunked the bottle to the table with the movements of a man short on sleep, and spilled more information. "Alyssa *is* giving him money—there's a mutual understanding about his benefits coming to her and his taking a small part. They also said Rollins wasn't doing so hot these past few weeks and they wondered if he'd stopped seeing his shrink."

"Holy shit. You think he was seeing Gardiner all the way until Gardiner died?"

Donovan shrugged. "They seemed to think so. At least they thought he'd been seeing someone recently and that a few weeks ago that might have changed. So it's a good guess."

Another revelation, another tighter tie between Rollins and the death of the doctor. No wonder he wouldn't come in to talk to them. There was a very good chance he wasn't just someone of interest but the suspect.

Eleri's phone buzzed just then and she spared it a quick look. "It's Vasquez. Says she has something for us."

"What?" Donovan looked at her oddly. "Why is she contacting you in the middle of the night?"

It was winter in LA. While there was no snow, the morning light still came later. Eleri held the phone up to show him. "It's seven-thirty."

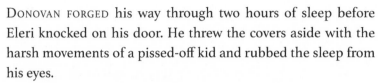

DONOVAN FORGED his way through two hours of sleep before Eleri knocked on his door. He threw the covers aside with the harsh movements of a pissed-off kid and rubbed the sleep from his eyes.

"Eleri?" He called out. "Why do we have to go?"

"Marina has something for us."

It was 'Marina' now, huh?

They'd been up until seven-thirty. The alarm clock was glaring at him, and he remembered something about live people from medical school—they needed seven to eight hours of sleep each night. He called that out to his partner who hollered back, "You aren't people."

"Neither are you!" he yelled back.

Well crap. Now he was awake.

And his mouth felt weird. It took a moment to realize that he never yelled at people. He didn't interact with them enough to get that worked up. When he did, he held it in check. He'd seen his father snarl and rage enough to scare people, enough to almost reveal what he was.

Donovan wondered now if he and his father had lived alone because no one would have them. Aidan Heath had a nasty temper. Donovan had sworn not to repeat it, and here he was, yelling at his partner as he woke up.

She must have been in the hallway, her voice sounded very close. "No, we aren't people, we're agents."

He opened the door to find her standing there, dressed, drinking something from a cup and smiling. *Bitch.* He almost growled, but as always he fought down the urge. Instead he said, "Vasquez better have something good for us."

An hour later he stood in the office, leaning against the wall because he still thought he might fall back asleep if he sat down. Vasquez didn't seem to notice. Instead she was pulling out files and opening envelopes.

She didn't mince words. "I subpoenaed Rollins' military records a while ago. With him being Special Forces, it took a while to get here."

The young agent spread several pages out on the table. "As you can see, a lot of it is redacted."

Eleri frowned and leaned forward. She was sitting at the table; she was awake. "So some of this is classified?"

"To a certain level—meaning ours. And some of it is apparently above our pay grade."

The womens' words passed in front of him and Donovan felt like he was just a little behind. Dear God, he needed more sleep. Usually, changing was refreshing to him. But usually he went for a run in his own woods or recently on the beach at FoxHaven. Last night had not been a release of any kind. His skin still crawled just a little bit, and he was afraid he was going to have to do it again.

He was thinking about that, not the matter at hand, when he heard Vasquez say, "His release is weird."

This time Donovan sat—plopped into a seat, maybe—and put all his energy into listening. "What's weird about it? It was a medical discharge."

Maybe she just didn't understand because she wasn't an MD. He waited.

"Follow me here." Marina Vasquez started flipping papers. "We can account for all his time through here." She pointed to a date barely a year and a half ago. "Clean med checks, all good. He stays with whatever unit he's assigned. He has a disturbingly solid number of missions completed."

She looked up at them. "My dad was a Green Beret. He can't tell me exactly what they did, but he did say a lot of missions go sideways. And a lot get started and then pulled back *before* they go sideways. Rollins' numbers—his team's numbers—are unusually high."

The junior agent looked up as though she expected to be interrupted or disbelieved, but he didn't have any of those thoughts. Donovan figured you didn't get into the FBI for nothing, so he waited until she started up again.

"Then, we lose him, here . . ." She showed off a series of pages that were blackened to the point of being unreadable. "All we know is that reports were filed on certain dates. But at the end, again, we get a clean bill of health. Both mental and physical. Always for Rollins. Not for all his buddies, but always for Rollins.

"Then, this one: Fallujah. I cannot begin to figure out what our guys were doing there, but I can tell you this: Fallujah has been *liberated* so many times that I think they've faced *freedom*—" she made air quotes, "the same way Americans would face a rerun of *Friends*. It's over in 30 minutes, but it'll happen again tomorrow."

Eleri nodded, her thinking frown in place as she probably tried to put the pieces together. While he'd had some geopolitical coursework in the FBI, Donovan knew he was vastly undereducated when it came to the US's foreign policies and wars.

"So we have no idea what the mission was, but this last one goes sideways. Bad." Flipping out more pages, the junior agent no longer looked at them. Her words sped up as she told them the story she'd cobbled together from redacted paperwork. "Look. Here's the mission date, here's the return. Three days they were out.

"It was so bad. Rollins and the three others who returned each dragged a dead body of one of their teammates into the compound."

Donovan felt his eyebrows shoot up.

"Yeah, *dragged*." Vasquez pointed to the type on the page and he saw it for himself. "My dad says they're trained to carry each other—"

She interrupted herself as Eleri started to give her a questioning eye. "No, I didn't divulge any classified info. I ask my Dad Green Beret stuff all the time and I couched it vaguely." She turned back inward, to her story. To Rollins' story.

"These guys are trained to carry, create sleds, you name it, but they *dragged* these bodies back."

"Does that mean something in particular?"

Vasquez nodded. "Hard to say. Maybe they were too worn out to carry them, maybe there was nothing to build a litter, maybe this was the only way to get them back. . . Or maybe it means they were traitors."

Donovan felt that sink in. *Holy shit.* These were Rollins' teammates. Special Forces. Those guys lived in each other's pockets and depended on one another to kill for them. *Shit.*

"It gets worse. During the same op, three of the guys on the team go missing." Vasquez sighed, as though she knew the implications went far beyond three missing special ops team members. "Eleven guys go out, eight return, the four dead being dragged by the four live ones."

Donovan's brain had been chewing on the ideas. "Do you think the returning guys shot the ones they dragged? Maybe some of them turned and they had to be put down?"

Finally, the missing pieces got to her. Marina Vasquez literally threw her hands in the air. "I have no idea! It's redacted!"

Eleri reached her hand across the wide conference table, even though she didn't touch the other woman. "Don't worry. You did great work."

With that, Vasquez got her shit back together. "Oh, I'm not done."

Donovan decided then that he should have taken Eleri up on a real breakfast. But it was going on noon now and breakfast had flown the coop, along with his preconceived ideas about Rollins.

"Check this: Cooper Rollins has a medical discharge, but no time in any of the hospitals. There's no record of what his medical ailment was. No diagnosis, no treatment. Dr. Walton Gardiner's records only said 'medical discharge,' too—I can't find anything, anywhere on what this medical problem was.

"So I called the military hospitals this morning, flashed my credentials. No records. None of them have seen Cooper Rollins as a patient. Not only does he *not* have a medical reason for discharge, when I looked back through the papers, I realized he *can't*. Look!"

She shoved the papers at them.

Donovan almost bonked Eleri's head with his as he leaned in to read. But Vasquez had the right of it. There was no legitimate medical discharge.

Cooper Rollins arrived at military gates, dragging a slain team member at 2100. He was discharged from the service before 0900 the next day.

6

Eleri needed food and sleep and a brain transplant. Or a good painkiller. Her head throbbed with the new information Agent Marina Vasquez had fed them at high speed after a tense night up waiting for Donovan.

She finally begged off, standing up at the table and suggesting they get food. At which point she politely asked Vasquez to get them copies of the paperwork she'd gathered. It turned out, of course, that Vasquez hadn't slept either. She'd been up most of the night constructing a timeline, but Eleri needed to talk to Donovan alone.

Then, of course, they found out there was no commissary. Too many options around, apparently there were just snack machines and restaurant recommendations. Eleri chose sushi.

When Donovan balked, she retorted, "I ate the second best chili, you can find something here."

They ended up at a hole-in-the-wall joint across from the hospital, where they checked in with a woman who spoke only enough English to seat them. Eleri ignored Donovan's raised eyebrows and asked for a table tucked against the front window. There were only a few other patrons; they should be able to talk.

It took her barely seconds to order more sushi than she could possibly eat and Donovan got a meal before she pulled out the chopsticks from their paper wrapper. She tried to seem normal, though she felt anything but. Leaning heavily toward him, she was ready to pose her question when the drinks arrived. Soda was really bad for her, but staying awake long enough to drive home was a huge perk. For a moment, she sipped her coke and forgot what she was going to ask.

Then she had to get back to reality. "Do we bring Vasquez to check out the scenes with us?"

"We're checking out the scenes?" Donovan seemed to be having a mental affair with his own caffeinated beverage.

"We need to. There's something off, and I can't put my finger on it." Eleri shook her head. It had been eluding her since last night. She'd been stuck in the car and, trying to make the best use of her time, she'd occasionally walked herself through the case.

Donovan piped in. "You're the senior agent. It's your call."

She frowned instantly. "You're just putting this off on me? I'm only playing senior agent when I have to. Honestly, being senior agent sucks, because I get the crap if things go wrong." She sighed. "Right now, two brains are better than one."

"Two?" He snorted. "Right now, we barely have one functioning brain between us."

"Probably." She almost snorted back at him. "So get your half in gear and help me make a pros and cons list."

This time he didn't hesitate. He must have already been thinking about it. "Pro—she knows the area. And she knows the culture."

That got Eleri thinking. "There's definitely a culture here. Or a thousand of them. Okay. . . Con—you can't say what you smell or perceive in front of her."

"That's only a partial con. I can hold it for later."

"Sure, but you can only be so weird in front of her." She tilted her head.

"Same for you."

"Good point." At that, Eleri welcomed the plate of California rolls that came out and set her mouth to watering.

"Oh, my God." Her hand flew in front of her mouth as she chewed and swallowed. "You have to try this!"

"I'm not a fan of fish or sushi." He eyed it as though she were offering him bugs.

"You will be." She nodded and pushed the piece at him again, then watched like a proud parent as he gingerly stuck the whole thing in his mouth and chewed. His expression changed from perturbed to pleased.

When she'd worked with Binkley—her first senior partner —she'd been very much the junior. She was younger, spanking new when he got her, and female to boot. This was better. She might barely call Donovan 'friend,' but she hardly called anyone that. Besides, she'd been around the block enough to know a good working relationship when she found it. She smiled at him.

"Okay. That is good." He conceded and reached for another piece. She should protest, but she didn't. Promptly forgetting about her list, she literally stuffed food in her mouth. Eleri told herself that sushi—along with the caffeine—was what was currently keeping her alive.

It was Donovan who resumed the chore. "Con—if you see something, will you be able to hide it from her?"

"Probably, I usually dream things."

He looked at her for a minute, chose a different piece of sushi and clearly decided he liked it, too, before speaking again. "Sure, but as strongly as you did last time? That seemed . . . *new* for you."

It took a moment to realize that he was right. "I guess it was.

Things in the past came in odd chunks . . ." She wondered if that made sense, and tried to explain. "Like, I'd see just the car, or just a portion of the living room. Enough for an impression, a bump that would send me hunting in the right direction."

"You got a lot more than that last time."

She nodded again. He was right. The dream of the truck, the girl—it had been clear, nearly real.

"So there's a possibility you might feel something there."

"True, but I'm not going to shut Marina out because of that possibility." She leaned back, suddenly more full than she could have imagined. "But you likely *will* get information that's useful. Are you okay signaling to me? Taking notes and telling me later?"

"Can you get her out or I can come back if there's something I need to do?"

"Sure. Okay, other pros, cons?"

"Pro—" he pushed another piece into his mouth like it was popcorn. "Another set of eyes and hands."

"Pro—she probably still knows this case better than we do."

"Pro—it's a nice thing to do. She wants the experience, and she needs it before they'll promote her, right?"

"Look at you." Eleri ignored the pain in her stomach. It was her own fault for overeating. "You're right. That's nice."

"Wasn't my idea." Finally, he leaned back, too. "Any other cons? Before we call this one as a yes?"

"Con—we are making this decision on a disturbingly small amount of sleep." She fought a yawn and missed. "Let's nap and then we'll meet up."

DONOVAN SURVEYED the doctor's office, trying to keep his eyes on the decor, but he could feel his eyelids clench and his eyeballs bordered on stinging. That was the thing about his sense of smell. Very few things smelled bad to him, but whatever they'd cleaned this office with was one of them.

Vasquez looked at him oddly and he just offered a tight smile in return.

They'd pulled aside police tape that crossed the entrance from the hall. The place was nearly dead at six p.m. but not dead enough.

They'd been questioned by a hallway neighbor the moment they'd touched the tape. They said they were PD, and luckily the neighbor didn't ask for a badge. Having the FBI come in looked much worse than the PD coming back. So now the three of them were closed in doing an initial survey, and Donovan wondered if he should be carrying a lab notebook or at least a recorder.

He'd mentioned that idea once to Senior Agent in Charge Westerfield, who commented in return that the memory tests they'd taken had not been without purpose. Once again, Donovan wondered just what he'd stepped into with NightShade.

The outer office looked normal, aside from having that unused feel places got, even though this one had been shut down for less than three weeks. Donovan blinked at the pain in his eyes and nose and tried to pay attention. A desk sat in the corner far from the front door, facing into the small reception. Though it was welcoming, it made a barrier between whomever sat there and the patients that waited in a variety of recliners and other assorted chairs. On one side, the chairs gathered around a low coffee table strewn with an odd assortment of magazines. In another location they faced each other, looking as though the furniture was having conversations even without people in them. Donovan didn't see anything out here that tripped any of his sensors. So, while Eleri and Marina continued to look around, he headed for the door into the doctor's office.

He'd seen the blueprints—the entire office consisted of only these two rooms. There was a suite like this on each floor, ideally suited to a shrink in solo practice. Other suites in the building had patient exam rooms and even some with operating capabilities. For Dr. Gardiner, being in this medical complex meant his patients were simply 'going to the doctor' and Donovan could imagine the psychological importance of that. He looked back at his partner and had the blinding thought that she'd spent several months in a mental institution. He'd always brushed it off as a breakdown brought on by her time in the FBI's profiling unit, but the fact was, she'd been committed. He wondered what she thought of this place. Then he wondered if he would—or even should—ask.

The second room took more adjusting. This was where the doctor had died, where the scents of cleaners were the harshest.

Vasquez came up behind him as he was working his jaw, fighting the sting that now not only watered his eyes but burned in his nose. "It was ruled an IED."

"That's a stupid term." He blurted it out without thinking.

"Have you seen what they can do?" She was obviously offended by his declaration.

But he had seen. "Yes." He'd worked on more than one patient stored in a box the way the doctor had been. "I just meant that it isn't a decent classification. It's no more precise than 'bomb.' The name 'IED' doesn't tell us whether it was made by a professional, remotely or mechanically or even spark detonated. It doesn't say what the explosive was, if it was chemical or laced with metal shards. It just means it wasn't military issue, and that's not much help to us."

Vasquez nodded—after all, he was right. She'd been right to be offended, too. It had sounded mean. He dropped it as Eleri stepped into the room.

"Oh wow. I can smell the cleaners in here. You're probably

about to . . . sneeze, Donovan." She must have turned to Marina behind his back, because he heard her explaining, "He has a really sensitive nose."

Under the cleaners he could smell the flesh. There was a mild scent of char, but not much. The bomb wasn't hot, or at least it didn't sear the man as it went off. He probably never knew what had happened to him.

The room had been thoroughly scrubbed—so as not to have rotting flesh in it—but the strong smell left it so Donovan couldn't pick up much through the harsh odors. Aside from cleaning, things hadn't been moved. The doctor's death had been enough of a mystery that the LAPD had left the room mostly alone for evidence.

The chair was heavily damaged; he'd seen that in the report, in the crime scene photos. The back had a hole almost all the way through the heavy upholstery. The place around the hole was singed but not heavily burned. The arms were more damaged than the back.

"Okay, let's walk it." Eleri declared as she went back out to the front room. "Patients come in here and wait. How many that day?"

"No one waiting." Vasquez was still looking around the back room, but answering Eleri's questions as Donovan continued to search. Her words matched what he'd read.

"Look." Eleri called from the front office and he walked out to find her at a booted laptop that had been sitting on the desk. She turned it to reveal a schedule of the day the doctor died. It was full, all the way through 6pm. However, the doctor had died at approximately 3:17pm with no one in the waiting room.

"What about the receptionist? Have you interviewed her?" This time Donovan was asking. He'd taken the police report at face value. It said she was "combative" but was ultimately declared uninvolved.

"No. They didn't really let me out of the box until you got

here." Vasquez shrugged. "The report is that she called in sick that day, and she even produced a prescription proving a doctor's visit and diagnosis of food poisoning. Dr. Gardiner was running his own schedule that day."

"And no one showed up?"

"Shit." Vasquez said it out loud. "Honestly, PD had this one and . . . I hate to speak ill of a fellow officer." She sighed. "The first detective that caught this was sharp and he started the investigation. But then it got handed off to another guy and he was a class A idiot." She shook her head. "If the patients were interviewed, it's not in the file."

"Well," Eleri tilted her head, "Want the job?"

"Sure." Vasquez seemed shocked to be offered. They really had not let her out of the box; it was like she was so unused she was still wired to the cardboard backing.

"One thing down." He thought out loud, "Let's figure out why his patients didn't show. Back into the office."

The three of them wandered once more into the doctor's space. Clusters of furniture faced each other. The seat the doctor had last occupied faced neither the long, soft sofa nor the easy chair, but a space in the middle.

Donovan kept talking through his thoughts. "So the doctor died sitting in that chair." He pointed at the central one with all the damage. "He's facing neither of the others, was he talking to someone standing? Or had he swiveled it around to stand up?"

Eleri picked up. "If he was going to stand, why didn't he? He was clearly sitting when the bomb went off."

Sometimes when he'd been a medical examiner, Donovan had put himself in the deceased's position and tried to recreate the death to better understand the wounds. Though the chair had been cleaned of the doctor's bodily tissue, which had exploded all over it in what was commonly referred to as 'pink mist', it wasn't fit for anyone to try out the doctor's last moments.

Instead, Donovan imagined it. In his mind, he sat in the chair and held the bomb. He tried to figure out where all his parts would go.

Vasquez and Eleri were already looking ahead.

"They cleaned over here." Vasquez pointed to the books on the shelves. Discoloration indicated that the cleanser had been used in a handful of positions.

"Look." Eleri pointed at the edge of the ceiling. "Up there, too, and over there." She pointed to the other side of the room.

As the women motioned in various directions, directing his attention to spots they'd found where parts of Gardiner had wound up, Donovan became more and more confused.

"Eleri—" He stopped her even though he didn't have the words figured out yet.

"Yes?" She looked at him oddly and it took a moment to realize she thought he had picked up on something he couldn't say in front of Vasquez. Ironically, he hadn't smelled anything of use. No, his problem was in the math.

At last he cobbled together some words and spoke.

"So he was sitting in the chair, that's clear. If he was *holding* the bomb, then why did part of him go that way?" He pointed to the whitish spots on the wall opposite the chair.

"So . . . He was sitting *on* it?" Vasquez frowned and looked at the spot.

"No." Eleri shook her head. "Look at the chair."

All three of them did. It, too, had been thoroughly cleaned —even into the hole that had been blown out. Which meant it had human bits in it at one point.

Eleri looked him in the eyes and Donovan nodded even as he said it. "If this is what I think it is, we need Wade."

7

Eleri was tired of this long day and its bigger problems. After gleaning what they could from the doctor's office, she and Donovan cut Marina loose and headed to the first victim's house. This scene was older, and any evidence probably less useful.

Retired Army Colonel William Ratz was the first victim. He'd lived alone, his wife five years deceased. His daughter made a checkup visit when he failed to answer the phone for several days.

Only then did she declare that her father was officially missing and there was a suspicious smell in his house. The smell was located in her father's office but she didn't check too carefully. Apparently Colonel William Ratz had been found later by officers who inspected the home.

Eleri and Donovan had technically broken into the home. Though they could flash badges and claim classified intel should anyone stop them, Eleri had spent the whole time hoping she didn't have to explain to anyone what they were doing.

Like the doctor's office, the room was cleaned but not much

more. Amy Ratz had been distraught over her father's death and hadn't done anything with the house, leaving it untouched until she could make a decision to upgrade, move in, sell, or rent. Given that the Colonel had died in the house, there weren't a lot of options. Adding that the man hadn't kept up with the times regarding the decor and anything that hadn't needed immediate fixing, Amy Ratz had inherited a very well-constructed relic.

The office told much the same story as Dr. Gardiner's office had. Once Eleri knew what to look for, the signs became obvious.

"Look Donovan." She pointed to the ceiling, to marks where some crime scene cleaner had scrubbed away human debris.

Her partner stood in the center of the room, gazing around at the walls and bookshelves, the mess on the desk, the same as her. His head tilted one way then another, checking corners, looking behind furniture, and searching out every missed or scrubbed spot. Those would tell exactly where the Colonel had gone. Pulling out her camera, she started snapping pictures for Wade, only no matter how she framed them or lit them, she couldn't seem to show the scrub marks. They were visible to the human eye only if looking for it. The cleaners had done a good job. Too good, in her estimation.

She looked to Donovan. "So he was standing or sitting when his bomb went off?"

"Yes ..."

It wasn't quite the response she'd expected. "What is it?"

Her partner started talking. They'd learned on their first case to work things through out loud, and they'd also learned they were good at it. "He went in all directions. The lack of burns on any of the chairs indicates he was standing up, *if* it was the same kind of bomb as the last one."

Biting back a sigh, because she wanted to be wrong almost

as much as she wanted to go to sleep, Eleri admitted she'd just assumed it was.

"Vasquez found the link, right?" Donovan rubbed his eyes, clearly needing sleep as badly as she did. "So I must have not been that alert, I missed hearing what that link was."

Eleri hadn't. "Ratz was an explosives specialist. Given that and the fact that he had all the necessary materials in his garage and that he was tinkering with a few novel explosives, the PD conclusion on his case is that he was holding one of his own devices when it went off. Ratz's death is still officially ruled an accident."

"So Vasquez is the only one who linked them?"

"As far as I know. The PD may have crossed checked the two —you know, two bomb deaths in close succession. You would think they would come to the conclusion that it can't be a coincidence. But officially, no, they aren't linked except for our investigation."

"And Vasquez's write up got it to us?" He still looked only three-quarters alive.

Though she was just relaying information, his question started a series of clicks in her brain. "Apparently. So something about this connection, or specifically about her report, got the case delivered to NightShade."

NightShade was a specialized division within—or rather, under the umbrella of—the FBI. Eleri and Donovan carried FBI identification, but occasionally had orders that were outside the standard scope of the Bureau. Then again, Donovan and Eleri had skills outside the standard scope of the FBI.

Donovan looked around and closed his eyes. Inhaling slowly, he spoke. "I'm getting the cleansers—bleach, something like baking soda ..." He struggled for words. "Under that ... It's like old, heated metal ... ?"

"Hot metal?" She was still examining the room. Wondering

if there was anything the detectives had missed when they first scanned the place. Having declared it an accident, they wouldn't have likely looked too hard.

"My head hurts." She let the words fall out at almost the same time he spoke.

"I have a headache."

"Let's get out of here." Eleri rolled her neck and her shoulders as though that would make up for the punishment she'd been dishing out to herself. "We are no good to anyone this way. Can you sleep?"

"No. I need food. I can't sleep with my stomach rumbling." He sighed again. "I saw a pizza place down the street. We eat first. Then we sleep 'til we wake up."

She couldn't argue with that. It was almost evening again and they hadn't slept a full night in several days. "I'm in."

She just hoped she could stay awake long enough to make it back to the small house.

DONOVAN WOKE to screams and darkness.

His eyes caught the small amounts of light that hit surfaces near him, gathering it and giving him night vision better than most people's day vision. He didn't think of this as he bolted down the hallway.

Only as he approached the closed door to Eleri's bedroom did he stop to think that maybe he shouldn't go in.

"No!" Her voice cried out. Then again, longer. "Noooooo."

Standing outside her door, he understood that she was angry, not scared. Talking in her sleep, having a conversation—if it could be called that—with whomever was in the dream.

So did he wake her and end whatever it was she was seeing? Or let her get through it? There was likely a clue in it. Then again, everyone had bad dreams, probably so did Eleri.

Unsure how long he stood there, Donovan waited. When she screamed a second time, he gave up and knocked on the door. "Eleri?"

There was no response. He knocked louder, and spoke more harshly. "Eleri!"

"Coming." The voice was fatigued and restless, but she was awake.

Stepping aside, Donovan went into the kitchen and opened a beer. This never-ending day sucked. He was supposed to be asleep.

She padded out in a set of matching silk pajamas.

He'd expected no less. "Do you want a drink?"

The sigh that came out of her was heavier than her eyelids. "Do we have anything good? . . .Never mind. Grab me a beer?"

He waited until she'd had a drink before asking, "What did you see?"

She still didn't answer quickly. "I can't tell if it's real or just my brain putting together what we saw."

"I know. I didn't ask how real it was, I asked what you saw."

"I saw Ratz, in his garage, working. He was taking apart an old bomb, not making a new one."

"Interesting." She might have made that up. Pulled it from somewhere in the back of her brain, but Donovan had seen her work before. He didn't think she was wrong. Taking another sip of the beer, he waited.

"A police officer came to talk to him . . . about the bombs. . . It seemed the ones he was taking apart were deactivated. Ratz wasn't afraid of them, even put a chisel to one part to get it to pop off."

"So you think maybe he wasn't making bombs?"

"It's possible." She continued with the dream. "The officer asked a few questions, left, came back carrying a device . . . It looked to me like a land mine.

"Ratz popped it right open. They were talking about bombs,

about deactivation, about people who build them. Ratz showed the man the inside of the bomb he'd brought, wiggled a few things, and set it down. The officer told him to keep it, and even gave him another one to look at later."

The thought hit Donovan hard. "That would mean the stuff in the garage—the evidence that Ratz was not only capable but stocked with supplies to make the bomb that killed him—was planted."

"In a way." She sighed. "In the best way. Because by handing it to Ratz, it gets his prints all over it. And he puts it away where he would file it. It doesn't look like a plant at all. But it was a police officer who handed it to him."

She squirmed. There was no reason to squirm at that point. Nor was there any reason to scream. But she'd screamed herself awake. Donovan pushed. "Then what happened?"

"The officer asked if they could go inside." She looked away. "They went into the office and the officer surprised Ratz . . . Then I woke up."

Dammit. She was going to make him ask her. He waited while she finished off the beer. Thankfully, at the end, he didn't have to nudge her further. Donovan didn't want to. He'd pushed once before and nearly destroyed their friendship. He wasn't ready to make the same mistake again.

Now when she looked at him, her eyes were clear, disturbed. And that disturbed him. "I've been in other people's thoughts during dreams. Felt their emotions, sometimes their curiosity, but this . . . I've never felt anything like this."

His own voice came as a whisper, "What was it?"

"Zeal? He was full of himself and his purpose. Like a drug." As Donovan watched, she transformed from a person telling a story to an investigator putting her pieces together. "He believed wholly in his job, that it was bigger than him. He had no compunctions about killing Ratz. The kill itself was no more to him than killing a bug in your house would be to you or me."

For a moment Donovan thought about all the times he hadn't killed bugs. An entomology course in college had left him with a soft spot for ugly insects. Follow-up coursework on his way to autopsy work had given him respect for their usefulness. But he didn't say that.

As his thoughts rolled, Eleri started speaking again. "Killing Ratz was an important task to him. There was satisfaction in completing it. It had been hard work and he was proud of it."

"So he's working toward a bigger goal?"

"I think so."

Donovan didn't say so, but noted that she was no longer speaking as though she doubted the veracity of the dream. Then she dropped something big.

"I screamed because I felt him move to kill Ratz. At first, he just seemed to be manipulating him, but then suddenly, he had everything he wanted, and he lunged. . . Then I woke up. I saw surprise on Ratz's face, but didn't see him die.

"Just before he lunged, the man said 'and they told the rest, but they did not believe'." She waited a moment.

"That's disturbing." Donovan's head hurt, there were so many pieces in so many directions. And Cooper Rollins was somehow at the middle of them all.

"This means that there's an officer involved. A police officer? LAPD?"

She paused. "I think so." Then a caution. "I don't know that this is real. I do often have dreams where I ride starfish in the ocean. Or dolphins."

He laughed. "Are you a mermaid?"

Unexpectedly, her expression changed. "Huh. I hadn't thought of that."

"What?" He frowned. She'd taken a turn he clearly missed.

"I *am* a mermaid. I wonder if that's why I dream that stuff." Her eyes were looking up into the corner of the room.

"There's no such thing as mermaids." He deadpanned. He hated mythical creatures, but she never let it sit.

"Said the werewolf."

"I'm not a werewolf. And you're not a mermaid." Though she was a fantastic swimmer, but that was off topic and Donovan decided it was time to learn more, despite only getting four hours of sleep. If he got even six in a row he'd have a party and get a damn cake to celebrate. "Well, we're awake now. Before we pursue this officer angle, let's see if it's real."

"How?"

"We were never in Ratz's garage. If you can ID things in there, that will tell us the dream is legit." He didn't like to use terms like 'precognitive' or 'psychic' as they tended to piss Eleri off. And 'precognitive' was the wrong term anyway. She didn't predict the future, but she saw things, helpful things.

Also she was way too logical and had way too good of a memory. "We saw pictures of the garage. In the LAPD report."

He shook his head. "There were just a few, only for evidence that he had the necessary supplies. I'll bet if we went, we'd find something to tell us if you were right."

Eleri protested again. "It's the middle of the night. We can't just go over there."

"It's LA. People are out and about all the time." He pointed into space, knowing his quiet would allow her to hear the cars going by right beyond the edge of the small yard. In the distance he could make out several sirens. Even their relatively quiet street got some traffic in the middle of the night. He was willing to bet no one would think anything of them in Ratz's neighborhood. He stood up, "Let's go."

"We just had a beer."

"I outweigh you by quite a bit and I only had half of mine." He pointed to the two bottles on the table, hers empty, his still partially full. "I'm driving."

She pushed herself up and chucked her bottle into the recycling bin at the end of the counter with a clunk that made her wince. Then she headed down the hall.

Presuming she was getting dressed to go out, Donovan did the same and found himself pulling into Ratz's driveway a short while later. "Holy shit, that was easy. From now on we are only driving in the middle of the night."

Her smile pulled to one side as she climbed out of the car. "If only that were an option."

They were parked in the back of the house again, but still working hard to stay quiet. As much as there was always traffic, chances were this particular house had been silent for several weeks. So he let Eleri pick the lock using the moon and the light from a nearby street lamp to help. They were in the attached garage in no time.

A car—an old, battered brown wagon—took up one side of the space, but the other spot was clearly set up for the Colonel's shop. And his shop wasn't for wood.

As Donovan looked around he saw detonators, old milk jugs of clear fluids with hand scrawled scientific names, wire on spools and in hand-wound pieces. The old man had an arsenal. When he turned to look at Eleri, she was rubbing her hands on her face. "What?"

"I remember all of this from the dream, but it's also in the file pictures."

"No, not all of it. Not the car, not even the whole table. Just enough to show their 'evidence.'" He pointed at all the pieces out and about. "Which ones did the officer give to Ratz?"

Without hesitation, she pointed to two pieces.

Nodding, Donovan moved to the bigger contraption. About the size of a pie plate, the piece sat on the particle board counter. He pointed. "What's on the underside?"

She gave him a resigned smile, "A hole. That's the piece he popped a panel off. He pulled a component out of it."

When Donovan flipped it over, he saw exactly that, and he held it up to her to see. "Are we good now?"

She nodded.

And he asked, "What's the next thing we can get from that dream then?"

She already knew. "When the officer lunged, he was holding something. It felt like plastic, but I saw metal, too. He shoved it at Ratz."

"Would it still be there?" Donovan was already moving into the house toward the office.

"Maybe." Now on track with him, she moved quickly into place. "He was standing here, Ratz there." She pointed and Donovan moved to play the part of Ratz. He did not like it.

"So, the officer shoved something at him." She mocked the move.

"Then Ratz blew up." Donovan added. "Which would send your plastic and metal thing this way—" he pointed. "If it survived."

Within ten minutes they found three pieces. Gray and thick, they looked like metal, but at their edges it was clearly revealed they were painted plastic.

"Look." Eleri held up one of them. "This looks like a lever or a switch."

"Lovely. What do you want to guess we can find something similar at the doctor's office?"

"We won't." She seemed certain, and when she spoke, Donovan understood why. "Everything there was collected and is holding in evidence."

"So the two are undoubtedly related now."

She nodded. "No question."

They had their first real link.

Donovan looked out Ratz's office windows at the sun coming up, just as Eleri's phone beeped.

"Wade."

He'd be a few hours ahead of them. Enough time for him to look at the photos she'd sent via secure email. But Donovan wondered why he'd reply in a text? That wasn't secure.

She looked up at Donovan, "He said 'It's exactly what you think.'"

Nothing incriminating there. But the words opened a maw in the ground. Donovan had never seen anything like this. Maybe that was why the FBI had called in Westerfield and his NightShade division. Things had officially gone-off-the-charts weird.

Donovan looked at her, his heart beating harder than it should. "So both men blew up from the inside?"

8

Cooper followed the woman down the street. He watched her long legs eat up the ground. Tan and lean, they moved with a rhythmic confidence that was her greatest asset.

She was beautiful, he'd seen her face—not just here, but a year ago, overseas. She had dark, round eyes. Hair so rich a chestnut that it looked like it both swallowed and dispersed the sunlight. It hung in rounded waves that gave the impression she couldn't quite tame it. She wore the clothing of any twenty-something L.A. girl. Her sneakers were cheap as a design to blend in, not from lack of resources. Cooper knew these people; they were well funded.

There was another woman, the one he'd hoped to follow today. She had lighter hair, a chemical process designed to change her appearance. Brown in color, it bore blond streaks now and she wore it stick-straight. She had green, or hazel, in her eyes. All of it was calculated to not look so much like her younger sister.

Cooper thought he'd catch Aziza today, but it was Alya that had come out, with her dark waves and printed top. He hung back, the crowd of people stretching all along Santa Monica Beach providing great cover for a covert follow. He not only paced her, he checked behind him. There was just as much a possibility that they knew about him as not.

He'd thought about this before, about what had happened on that last op. It was dangerous. If Ken Kellen were here, he would spot Cooper from a mile away and it would all go to hell. Maybe literally. There was every possibility that Kellen would shoot him on sight. Cooper was pretty sure he'd tried it more than once before.

Then again, if Ken Kellen were here, Cooper was likely already on his radar, and that was bad news any way he cut it.

His plan had been to talk to the older sister. Get his open door through her, but he hadn't seen her lately. It seemed as soon as he made his decision, she'd quit coming out—or at least she had when he was around.

Today he'd given up waiting and decided Alya was as good a bet as Aziza. He had no last names for the women, not real ones anyway. He'd been given "El Sayed"—a standard Muslim name as common as "Smith"—when he'd first met the family in Fallujah. All the soldiers had known it was a fake name; none had asked them to provide anything more. It was a reasonable way of protecting themselves from surrounding insurgents should it become clear that Americans had been harbored in their home.

Not knowing names had helped everyone. Being Special Forces, none of his people had used their real names either. He'd seen Alya before, but usually only her eyes. She, her sister, and her mother had been in full traditional garb at their own dining table because of the men they had invited to join them.

Back then, he'd been heavily bearded, his hair lighter, his eyes paler from too long in the sun. He knew his current haircut changed the shape of his face; he could only hope that it changed it enough.

Picking up his pace and suddenly believing that this was the right thing to do, Cooper caught up with her. He was just about to tap her on the arm, say hello to her when she turned and went into a store.

Shit. He'd been so close.

Right then, he determined not to give up. He would not come back another day; he would not wait for Aziza. He would try now.

So he ducked into a patch of shade and used what he knew to blend in. Without looking like he was waiting, he bided the nearly full hour before she came out with a single bag.

He couldn't get her attention at the front of the store. The employees might watch the door; they had interacted with her and would be more likely to come to her aid if she called out than the average person on the street would be.

Two blocks later, as she approached the Santa Monica Pier, he touched her arm. "Alya?"

She turned, deep brown eyes searching his face and thankfully showing no recognition. "Do I know you?"

He nodded, though it wasn't really the truth to say he knew her. "I want to help."

"I don't know what you're talking about." She didn't turn away, but she did look at him like he was crazy. It was so American. She nailed it. On the other side of the world a woman would never look at a man as though he were beneath her. It had puzzled him at first, women that acted uninterested in their own welfare. Even dogs protested a poor fate, but these women had learned not to. He wondered if she and her sister had been raised here. If Fallujah had simply been an assignment for them. Anything was possible' and he aimed to find out.

He started talking. "My name is Cooper Rollins." Without breaking cadence, he watched her face for a sign of recognition.

She gave none. "I was stationed in Fallujah. A soldier friend told me about your group. I want to help."

"Why?" She looked at him askance again. Still neither confirming nor denying what he said, she waited him out.

He looked away. It was the right thing to do. "I saw what we did."

"Who told you?"

"A friend."

"I need a name." Though she'd said nothing he could directly link to his request, the fact that she hadn't told him she had no clue what he was talking about said volumes.

"I can't give you one." The only name he could count was Ken Kellen and he had no idea how that would play out. Were they with Kellen? Against him? Cooper still wasn't sure. He only knew he was back on home soil with some crazy and unbelievable footage reeling in his head. He only knew that he'd underestimated Kellen and the others. He only knew that he needed Alya and her people to help him. So he would help them.

"Tomorrow. Right here."

She turned on a heel and walked away.

That was all.

Cooper had no idea what time the meeting would be. No clue who would come. It might even be Ken Kellen.

Donovan stood in the middle of Colonel Ratz's home office for a second time in as many days. This scene was not cleaned up the way the doctor's office had been. It wasn't considered a crime scene, so it had been cleaned by a private service that handled this kind of thing.

Donovan hoped there was more here. "Eleri, touch things, just walk around."

"It doesn't work that way." She shook her head and stood in the middle of the room, not making contact with more than the soles of her shoes.

"It *does* work that way, though."

"I get that you've been doing all this reading up, but I'm not like those people. I can't do that. The dreams are what they are." She still didn't move while he went around the room, his fingertips touching everything he could. As though she might follow along if he just demonstrated.

"El. You know it works. That's why you're standing there with your arms crossed, specifically *not* touching anything." He didn't have to look at her to know. When he thought back, she'd always been very careful, very deliberate about what she touched.

Early on, he'd assumed it was the FBI agent in her—the drilled-in belief of not disturbing the evidence, but now he knew it was *her*. She was afraid of what might come through if she touched something. And he was afraid what might not come through if she didn't.

He wouldn't manipulate this time. He had to convince her to do it on her own.

"You don't see what I see. If you did, you wouldn't ask." She sighed.

He countered. "You'll see it anyway. You know that, don't you?"

This time he stopped moving and looked at her. Concerned. He'd heard enough about her dreams, run when she'd woken screaming more than just once. Vasquez had raised her eyebrows at the thought of the two of them together, but Donovan had shut that down right away. Eleri was beautiful, and just as damaged as he was. She was also way too insightful to get involved with. Besides, he was simply trying out real friendship for the first time at nearly thirty-five. So he'd run down the hallway to screams, and he'd tell her the truth, and stay at her beach house on occasion. But nothing more.

Eleri's look told him she hadn't yet come to the same conclusion about her visions.

"You'll dream it." he said. "You'll wake up. Maybe this way you can at least be ready. Maybe if you see it now, you can sleep better at night. Maybe it won't invade you as much, make you scream. Maybe you can be alert to the fact that you're an observer."

For almost two full minutes, she didn't say anything. Just stood there in the center of the room, thinking, her arms hugged tight to her. He figured she'd tried it before. Maybe to no avail. Maybe to bad effects. But if she had, she hadn't told him about it.

"I can't do it."

Donovan nodded and resumed touching things on his own wondering what it would be like to see the history of an object. To him, the idea seemed cool, fascinating. To Eleri it was terrifying. "How did you try before?"

"With the pictures. Sometimes with the evidence. I dreamed later, but never did I see anything at the time I was touching the object. It always came later. Always a disturbing surprise." At least as she spoke, she broke form and started walking around. Maybe she'd convinced herself that it wouldn't work. But as he watched, she began touching household objects.

For thirty minutes, they walked that way—him handing her various things that it appeared Ratz had loved. She would hold the object, close her eyes then open them, and declare, "Nothing."

She handed back item after item, each of which he replaced carefully. They were missing something. And sooner or later, someone was going to notice that strangers were prowling the Colonel's house in the middle of the afternoon. Maybe they'd already called the daughter. It wasn't like the two of them could just hang out forever waiting for a touch to yield something.

Eventually, he took her out of the office and into the rest of the house. This time he stood back and didn't handle the things. Maybe his touch was obscuring something. Maybe it was all for shit and she really couldn't do it. Maybe tonight she'd dream about all the things Ratz had done. Who knew? After an hour of trying he realized he was clearly full of shit.

Donovan was ready to call off the dogs when Eleri had obviously given up on anything that made sense and was wandering the kitchen. Just as he opened his mouth, she opened the fridge and jerked back.

"Beer."

Donovan felt his eyebrows go up, but stayed silent as he watched her reach into the fridge and wave her hand through the empty space as she stared into it.

"Beer?"

"Red Stripe. The brand. He reaches into the fridge for it." She looked both shocked and pleased. But she closed the fridge, then opened it again and reached in. "When it's not here, he restocks from the pantry." She turned slightly to the right, her eyes not seeing. Or seeing something other than what was physically in front of her.

So Donovan checked. Opening the closet door, he found stale cereal, a few dusty boxes of pasta next to equally dusty jars of sauce. . . and two six packs of Red Stripe bottles.

"El." He pointed.

She looked at him, her pale green eyes wide with wonder and accomplishment. Then her wide mouth broke into nearly hysterical laughter.

Oh, fuck, he'd cracked her. He talked her through a mild success and she cracked at even that. She had spent three months in a mental institution, and he'd often figured it was more of a therapy/spa combo than a real treatment center, but maybe she really was nucking futs.

"Donovan." Her eyes were clear and focused at least. "You did it. You talked me into a psychometric moment! And I successfully identified our subject's brand of beer."

Ah. "Well, it's not the key to the case, but it's something."

"Really?" she frowned at him. "You could have opened the pantry half an hour ago and figured that out."

"But I didn't, did I?"

She laughed again. "Exactly my point. You didn't do it because it's of no value."

Donovan disagreed. It would take time and practice to hone a skill like hers. Not only had she not been working on it, she'd been actively avoiding it. "Let's go to the doctor's office. Maybe there's more there. Then dinner. My treat."

"It's an expense account." She deadpanned. She was also the senior agent and he waited for her to pull rank on him. But maybe the small success was a boost to her. "How long at the doctor's office?"

"An hour."

"Fifteen minutes." She countered.

"That's not worth the drive! Thirty."

Somehow they settled on thirty, not including however long mid-afternoon traffic took. If it wasn't for the constant sun, Donovan wouldn't even know what time it was, his schedule was so messed up. At the office, he tried again handing her things from the doctor's room. But nothing worked.

"Fail. Fail. Fail," she said with a smile. "I think a good, juicy burger is in order."

Donovan had been entertaining himself while she touched things. He was looking for a plastic piece like they'd found at Ratz's. There were a few parts in evidence with what was left of Dr. Gardiner, but Donovan was holding out hopes for more. "Give me a minute."

He heard her sigh, heard her footsteps as she walked out to the waiting room, "Fine. But just one."

It was five minutes later when he walked out empty handed and found Eleri sitting in a chair, staring into space. Eleri sat preternaturally still, her eyes wide, then turned quickly to him. "She calls herself 'Aziza'."

9

E leri felt all of it. It enveloped her. "Aziza isn't her real
name. But it's what she's used since she got to the
states."

The words fell out of her as she tried so hard to convey to
Donovan what she was seeing, hearing, feeling. "She came here
for this."

"To kill the therapist?" Donovan was looking at her oddly.
Still standing in the doorway to the doctor's patient room
where he'd stopped dead upon seeing her in the chair. The
light behind him caught his hair, the wrinkles in his shirt, put
him in silhouette. "But you said it was an officer that killed Ratz.
Male, right?"

"Yes." But Eleri only offered one word, trying to stay with the
vision. She feared if she changed her focus, even a little, it
would slip away. "She began seeing the doctor a little while
after she arrived, became a regular patient. She told him
enough truth to get by."

"Why was she coming here?"

Her head tilted to the side, but her gaze remained unfocused. Eleri could feel the overlay of what she was picking up. "She knew the doctor was treating soldiers. She followed one of them here to Los Angeles."

"How long has she been here?"

"Six months." The answers came to her, as though they were woven into the fabric that covered the chair, and she could absorb the information. "She killed the doctor. She waited here, knew his patients were canceled. She'd canceled them herself? Or . . . her *sister* did.

"The doctor opened the door and saw her. He was surprised. She wasn't who he was expecting. But she pointed out that his regular appointment hadn't arrived yet and she begged for just a few minutes. Dr. Gardiner agreed, because she seemed distressed. So he let her into the room and it went just as she planned it. She stabbed him."

"Stabbed him? Is that what happened to Ratz?"

This time Eleri really looked at Donovan, the vision peeling back as the current world came into sharp relief. "I think so. That's how they're getting the bombs inside."

Wade had eventually called her and offered a brief explanation about the explosion patterns. The tissue spatter, the direction of the explosions all led to the same conclusion. No one had come to it before, but that was because the outcome was ridiculous. Who blew up from the inside?

No one. Not even spontaneous combustion did this.

It was brilliant, really. It had taken Vasquez to even figure out there were already two cases. And it had taken Eleri's own gift to start to get at the mechanics of the bomb.

She still sat in the chair, not sure what was left to take from it, but waiting for more information to come. She focused on Donovan now.

"Why did they kill the doctor?" he asked.

"Why do you trust this information so much?" she countered. No one had before. When she'd brought hunches into her profiling team, things she'd seen very clearly, no one believed a word of it. They told her that her subconscious had put things together logically. To which Eleri had always countered, *so what?* Didn't they all rely on their subconscious? They were trained to hand write their notes because it tied various portions of the brain together. They were trained to scan with unfocused eyes for anything that popped. How was that different than her coming up with something while asleep? Had she jumped up during a group brainstorm and said "I had a thought last night . . ." They all would have listened. But her thoughts were a little too specific. So she followed them up herself when no one else would.

A former field agent at the time, Eleri had no problem unholstering a weapon and gathering real evidence. The Behavioral Analysis Unit had not liked that. She'd pushed further underground with her methods. Though she'd won cases, she'd lost herself. She did a short stint in a mental institution, then was plucked from it before she could finish getting herself together. The NightShade division needed her, Agent Westerfield said. Donovan was joining, he needed a senior partner. There was a missing child only her special skills could help find. In the end, Westerfield had been something else himself. The jury was still out on him.

But it seemed Donovan had no problem trusting her instincts. And he even had a good answer for it. "The data says that you've never been wrong."

"You've hardly been around me long enough to have 'data.'" She didn't realize her head had turned, hadn't before understood the shame she felt about her past. Eleri only saw the carpet and felt the heat of defeat in her core. "I've been wrong."

"I pulled some of the files from your old cases with the Behavioral Analysis team. Sometimes, you were late. You had *times* mixed up, but never *facts*."

Her head snapped up.

He wasn't fazed. Probably because he could take her in a fair fight. He could morph, rip her throat out with his long teeth, leave her for dead and leave no conclusive evidence . . . For the first time she wondered about that. The evidence Aidan Heath—Donovan's father—might have left behind, evidence that no one could place. But Donovan didn't have that in him. Maybe it had been bred out, maybe trained out from watching his father. Either way, he only crossed his arms with no hint of violence, and grinned. "Please, you read up on my history, too."

She had. So she kept her mouth shut.

"It's why I push you." He came over and sat down next to her. The swift intake of her breath was the result of holding back on her instinct. She almost told him not to sit, but he didn't feel what she felt. The people who came here had some serious issues. Now that she'd opened the door, she could feel them around her, almost like hovering ghosts. And she wondered if that was what it was like for Cooper Rollins.

"Eleri, sometimes you say things out of the blue that just put things together. You know about stuff from your dreams, but you would ask me things at the beach, like, 'how was the McClarty's house?' . . . You couldn't have known I'd doubled back and gone that way, but you did. And always after you touched me. This has always been bigger than you thought it was."

She nodded.

He'd cracked it. Or pushed her to crack it. It was even now mildly duplicable.

Eleri stayed in the heavily padded chair, her fingers idly playing with the piping on the seams. "I think I know how it may happen. I think I have to be *doing* what the person was doing, not just touching something."

Donovan frowned at her. He didn't understand it. How could he?

The bastard. There were others like him, his father, even Wade was like him. But her? No one was like her. Not that she'd met. Donovan said he'd read up on it, but how did she find other people who did what she did? Ones who weren't wearing gold embroidered purple turbans and reading palms...

"I'm sitting in the chair, doing what she was doing, sitting the way she sat, even. When I first sat down, nothing happened, but I shifted, and boom, there it all was. The plane seat was the same way. Then the fridge, I'd opened it and leaned down and looked inside and the cold came out and hit me, along with his memories."

"So . . . Maybe it's a combination of doing what they were doing and feeling something they felt? The chair surrounds you, the cold hit you . . . All down the front, right?" Donovan speculated. She was a mystery to him. An oddity to a man who'd been born an oddity.

Though she stayed seated, she got no more information. Even the feelings, the understanding, it was all gone. It only hovered like the memory of a book she'd just read.

Right then, her phone buzzed. Pulling it out, she checked the message. "Westerfield. He wants to check in."

Donovan shook his head. "That man has disturbing timing." Then he paused, "Do you think it's a . . . *gift*? Do you think he really does have impeccable timing?"

Sighing, Eleri stood up. "It's entirely possible. You saw the quarter. Why not also have a sense for knowing when to show up? It would be a really useful skill."

"For *him*." Donovan snorted, putting sound effects to her own feelings.

Regardless, they had to check in. And the news was likely to be disturbing.

She was reaching for the door knob when her phone buzzed again. She heard Donovan's going off at the same time.

That couldn't be good. So she closed the door, keeping them inside the office.

Eleri didn't need to say anything to Donovan; she knew he was looking at the same message she was.

"Number three."

DONOVAN STAYED quiet as they followed the directions to the new address.

It took almost an hour to get to Manhattan Beach down I-405 —which Vasquez called 'the 405.' The neighborhood was older, and by the time the two of them arrived, Marina Vasquez had been there for fifteen minutes and the place was crawling with local PD. Donovan was wondering if they figured out they had a link yet.

Probably, because Vasquez was there. But maybe she hadn't yet told the police why she'd showed up. Maybe she left that for him and Eleri. Or, for Eleri, because he would want to pass that job onto the 'senior agent' too.

As he climbed out of the passenger seat, the smell of vomit hit him.

The house sat on the upside of the street, though he thought they were too far away to actually see the water, even from the top floor. Two stories tall, the cream colored home could have fit anywhere in the US, and definitely fit into this older neighborhood. The lots were reasonably large for L.A., but not big by any standards.

Vasquez walked uncomfortably down the sloped lawn and ducked under the yellow tape a junior officer was rolling out. As she approached Donovan, he inhaled. It hadn't been her, someone else was puking at the scene here. He examined Vasquez a little more closely. She didn't even look green, just gave a tight smile and waited while he only nodded in return.

She kept her voice low. "Victim number three appears to be Victor Dawson."

"Military?" Eleri also spoke in low tones, aimed her words at Vasquez. His partner knew he would hear them.

"Not a lot of background yet. He was a teacher. English. Local high school, close to retirement. But all that's according to the neighbor there." She pointed to a stunned kid, standing alone in a crowd on the sidewalk. The girl had her arms wrapped around her thin frame and her eyes glazed. "Kid called it in. Heard an odd noise like someone had dropped something very heavy. Then knocked on the door to check on her teacher. No one answered, and she said she smelled something a bit odd. But that Mr. Dawson's car was home. So she called 9-1-1. I heard some details on the scanner, but I'm not sure yet if it's ours."

Donovan felt bad for the girl. One of the cops had come out of the house and puked his lunch up on the lawn. Now they were rolling out crime-scene tape. There was no good outcome for her teacher.

He leaned in, "What might make this case number three?"

"Someone exploded." Vasquez raised her eyebrows and Donovan nodded.

It was an odd enough occurrence that this was probably the third—provided they'd found all the ones before. "Anything else?"

The junior agent shook her head. "That seemed like enough."

"And these guys—" Eleri waved a hand casually at the cops, "—know that the FBI is on the scene?"

"Kindof." Vasquez tipped her head and Donovan waited. "I told them I was driving by and offered to help. So I held tape and stayed out of the way. But the reports from inside sound like this is possibly one of ours."

It was probably for the better. Manhandling a scene away from the cops was not a pleasant thing.

"Who are you?" A gruff senior cop spoke down to them on the sidewalk. He looked like he'd seen it all, except he somehow hadn't seen this yet. Facing to his left, he sidestepped down what was not a steep incline. He needed to get in better shape. As he approached, Donovan noticed that he smelled of baloney and onions and mint gum. Not the puker either.

By the time Donovan had made this assessment, Eleri had her ID out and he was scrambling to keep up, pulling his own FBI wallet even as she was talking. "We're investigating a case that we think may be tied to yours. I'm so sorry, but we need to see the scene to see if it matches."

She didn't flat out pull rank on the man, but Donovan knew she would if she had to.

"I can't let you do that, ma'am." The older man shook his head and planted his feet.

Donovan had seen his father transform more times than he'd like, but right now, it was Eleri undergoing a change almost as dynamic. Any politeness she had fled, her back straightened and her voice flattened. Though he couldn't see her face from where he stood, he had no doubt that it, too, had gone from gentle to demanding. This officer didn't even know that the woman before him could see into his soul if she chose. Donovan stepped up behind her, lending support she didn't need, and noticed that Vasquez unconsciously mimicked Eleri, as well.

"You don't have a choice. I have the authority to clear every last one of you from this scene and arrest you for obstruction." She paused a moment. "I only want to take a look. Because, frankly, I hope to hell this isn't related to my case. But if it is, you will step the fuck out of my way. Do. You. Understand?"

Donovan fought the smile that threatened to break their stoic line.

The officer didn't verbally concede, but he seemed to grasp that in this his rank was not equal to hers. He also didn't tell his officers that they were coming in, but Eleri seemed to have no problem turning to the nearest one and explaining that he could politely escort them in and the other officers out for a moment, or she could announce to the whole gathering crowd that the FBI was on the scene.

"Yes, ma'am." He offered a quick nod, almost too quick and did exactly as she'd asked.

Donovan was still surprised that she'd managed to speak to the second man so nicely when the first had been such an ass. That ability to turn the eye-daggers off and on at will was such a Southern thing. Eleri had it bred into her bones.

As they walked through the house, his nose picked up what they needed. He reached out to touch Eleri's arm and when she looked back, he only nodded. It saved them from stepping into the scene and altering any of the evidence. Still Eleri leaned forward, stuck her head into the room a bit and then invited Vasquez and then him to do the same.

The far wall was coated in a thin, pink slime. Chunks of what had been Mr. Dawson clung in small places. The couch showed a thicker layer, and the wall to his left was farther away and therefore less covered. As Donovan turned his head, he saw that the wall near him bore some remains as well.

As Vasquez breathed slowly through her mouth behind him, he calculated.

All four walls. Human tissue radiating out from a spot probably standing in front of the couch on the right hand side. This was definitely their scene.

Had the officer struck again? Or the young woman?

It didn't fit, not having a single perpetrator or even a single type of perpetrator for the crime. Westerfield had talked of terrorism when he called them out, but no one was claiming any of these bombings. No group claiming victory, no god, no purpose for the deaths. Vasquez had been listening to police scanners, looking for clue words. No one was afraid yet.

They might be now. The media was bound to get their hands on this.

As he turned around he saw the officer from earlier. Only now did he catalog the white shirt, the bars . . . This was the chief. *Great.*

But Eleri was already laying it out. "This is our scene. I'm sorry to take it from you, but it matches our current case."

There was nothing the officer could do about it, except be a dick—which he seemed to have a natural aptitude for. He told them they had to wait while he called it in, checked all their badge numbers, and was waiting for confirmation when another car pulled up.

As Donovan turned, his Senior Agent in Charge climbed out of the shiny new car and started up the slope. He was already talking, rattling off credentials interlaced with not-so-subtle threats.

The chief folded his arms and stared at Eleri. "Take it. What do you want me to do? Call you any time someone blows up in my district?"

Even from the back, Donovan could see that she'd snapped. Her voice was quiet. Had she been raised in the rural south, she might have said 'bless your heart' but Eleri knew how to deliver without softeners. "If you're really such a prick that a person being bombed in their own home only warrants a temper tantrum like this, then yes, please do call us the next time—" she raised her hand in air quotes that looked polite from even a short distance "—someone blows up in your district."

His face turned red, but he couldn't seem to speak. Donovan fought the laugh that was burbling up. It was wholly inappropriate.

Westerfield managed to keep his face stoic, and when the asshole cop turned to look at him as though to ask if he was going to let this woman speak to him this way, Westerfield only nodded off to the side as if to say, 'get out of my crime scene.'

Donovan almost missed the person reluctantly unfolding himself from the passenger side of Westerfield's car. He almost shouted Wade's name, but too many things happened at once.

As Westerfield began a conversation with Eleri, the police officers began filing out. Even as Wade approached to say hello, an officer stopped Donovan and handed him several pages out of a notebook.

"I was interviewing the girl . . ." He nodded his head toward the neighbor kid slightly, as it wouldn't do to openly talk about her. "These are my notes. She said someone came to the door. He had a folder in his hand. He left before the noise, so he wasn't there for it . . . That's all I really have, but it's there."

He pointed at the small, torn pages and then walked off. He clearly was on the side of justice, but also on the side of keeping the peace at his job. Donovan wanted to thank him, but a commotion proceeded just behind him.

A car was pushing its way up the crowded street, the passenger repeating, "That's my house! That's my house!"

As Donovan focused on the older man, he climbed out of the car and began running up the sidewalk as fast as a slightly-out-of-shape, fifty-ish man could. Adrenaline seemed to prod him forward and through the milling neighbors.

The high school girl, no longer being interviewed, heard him and turned. She began running toward him. "Mr. Dawson!" The relief in her voice carried across the short but crowded distance. "You're okay. I thought you weren't!"

She was hugging him, her skinny arms barely wrapping his waist. Donovan wanted to stop and savor the idea that a high schooler could feel something positive toward an adult. And apparently a teacher. Which he was just connecting in his thoughts.

He tapped Eleri and Westerfield, breaking up their conversation with Vasquez. Just as three pairs of eyes turned to him and he opened his mouth to say their suspected victim appeared to be walking up the street, the man shouted out behind him.

"Vivian?! Vivian!!!"

10

Eleri turned at the sound of anguish. Suddenly in charge of the scene, she was left with only the retreating backsides of angry cops, a loose and incomplete border of yellow crime scene tape, and a man pushing his way through, claiming to be the victim.

Only clearly he couldn't be.

A touch to her shoulder didn't make her turn. Neither did Westerfield's voice, but it did calm her. "Wade and I will secure the scene and I'll call in the CSU."

Good.

Donovan spoke in a low voice as she passed by him, "I'm on crowd control."

Only then did she notice that everyone was holding up their devices and recording. Some of it was probably already on the web. So much for keeping the investigation under wraps.

As she reached the sidewalk, the man reached her. He didn't stop, not seeing her as the authority figure here. Eleri didn't blame him. He didn't know her at all, and if he was Victor Dawson, then he was in for a horrible shock that he was no longer the authority in his own home. And someone he loved was dead. Very dead.

Somewhere off to her side, she heard the student wailing, "It was his car, I thought it was him!" But Donovan seemed to be corralling her and Eleri didn't stop in her quest to do the same for the man.

"Are you Victor Dawson?"

"Will someone tell me what's going on?" He was frantic, seeming barely able to string the words together, and Eleri understood. So the first thing she did was nod and say, "Yes."

Once she had his attention, she asked, "Are you the home-owner, sir?"

She motioned to the house behind her. This was LA, land of actors. She couldn't give this info out to just anyone. But she wasn't about to be a grade A asshat either and refuse to speak to him without ID and fingerprints.

"My wife and I. Where's Vivian?" He pushed at her, but Eleri held him back.

"I don't know, sir." It wasn't quite a lie. She had strong suspicions, but given the scene, no one would know for certain until DNA tests came back. "This is your car?"

She pointed to the one in the drive.

"My wife's car was in the shop. I caught a ride." His focus swung wildly but returned to Eleri.

She responded just as she'd been taught. Ask simple questions, give answers, establish trust. "This is your student? You're a teacher?"

His brain didn't want to acknowledge what he suspected. He was more content answering her questions and he did so, looking only at Eleri's face. "Yes, that's Hannah Gilmore. She lives next door. She's a junior where I teach ninth and tenth English. Is something wrong with my wife?"

"I don't know. Was she home?"

"I think so. She's usually at work, but she said she was headed home . . ." He shook his head. "For something. Maybe she forgot?"

"She was driving your car today?"

"All this week." He nodded, getting something out of the give and take.

"Was anyone else home?" Eleri went on with a few more questions, establishing that the body was most likely his wife and that she was Vivian Dawson. When he pushed forward, she touched his arm. "You can't go inside, sir."

"I need to see if it's my wife."

She sighed. "We can't ID the body. I'm sorry. We'll need testing. Can you come with me?"

It took a few minutes to sort out who should go to the Bureau and who should stay behind. Westerfield volunteered himself and Wade de Gottardi, the man he'd brought with him to stay with the house and direct the crime scene unit. An ex NightShade agent, physicist, and current consultant for the division, Wade was also one of Eleri's old friends and recently one of Donovan's new ones. Wade was also like Donovan, maybe he could sniff something out.

She didn't even get a chance to say hello. As much as she wanted to, it would be rude to embrace an old friend and attempt to catch up when she was trying to tell this man that his wife had probably blown up in their home.

In the end, they decided she, Donovan, and Marina Vasquez all needed to talk to Dawson about his wife. Vasquez would be able to sort out anything local he spoke of, to pipe up if anything seemed off.

It took forever to get to the Bureau offices on Wilshire, and the whole time Eleri wondered about the scene. What were Westerfield and Wade finding? Had the crime scene unit showed up? Donovan had already nodded at her, a subtle notice that something he picked up about this scene told him it was the same people.

Victor Dawson stared out the window the entire ride and Eleri was grateful that Vasquez was in the back with him. She wasn't fully convinced he wouldn't open the door and fling himself into traffic. Then again, here, he'd probably survive it. The freeways never seemed to move too fast.

Once settled into a conference room, they brought him coffee, pulled a recorder, and finally sat down. Eleri had learned long ago that her hunger and her needs were secondary to a case. So when her stomach growled, she didn't even calculate how long it had been since she'd last eaten. She just sipped at her coffee and hoped there were enough calories in it to keep her going. Checking messages, she knew what to ask when she sat down. Wade and Westerfield had primed her.

"Mr. Dawson, do you have ID you can show us?"

He easily complied. What she had to ask next wasn't so easy. "Tell me about your wife's purse."

"It's there at the house, isn't it?" But when Eleri didn't answer him, he gave her the color and a few details. Eleri's phone now had a picture Wade had sent. And when she showed Dawson the photo of the bag—sitting on the counter exactly where he'd said she often left it—he nodded and seemed to collapse.

The ID in the purse had given the name "Vivian Casper Dawson." Eleri laid out the facts. "Right now, we can neither confirm nor deny that the person at the house is your wife. We'll need DNA testing."

When he began describing her hair color, her eyes, and more, Eleri gently placed her hand over his and stopped him. She tried to keep her voice soft, but there was nothing gentle in the message. "There's nothing identifiable left. We'll need DNA. Until then, we won't know . . . but we have circumstantial evidence that it is, in fact, your wife."

Donovan and Vasquez sat back, letting her do the heavy lifting of the interview. She told the man she didn't think his wife had suffered, and that was true. Blowing up from the inside might be scary if you knew it was happening, but it wouldn't be painful. Nerves would be gone before they could even register. But she didn't give him those details. She did tell him about the bomb, because she needed him to give her anything—*anything*—that would link this to the other cases.

Mostly she needed to know before the media went haywire. With all the people posting pictures and probably video online, with the police getting kicked out of the scene and the FBI on the spot, Westerfield and Wade likely had reporters on site before they had crime scene analysts. Her own phone was lighting up with pictures and coded messages from the two of them as they found various clues and interesting evidence.

Certain suspicious things came out as Victor Dawson spoke of his wife. He was rolling from initial shock into anger and he was talking as fast as he could. Vivian Dawson worked for the Naval Weapons Station at Seal Beach. She had a high ranking security clearance, and she bought weapons for soldiers overseas. That was all her husband knew, because that was all she could say about her job without breaking federal laws.

He looked at Eleri. "Have you ever seen a military invoice where most of the information is redacted? She handled all the things under the black ink."

"Do you know if she bought supplies for soldiers in Fallujah?" It was too pointed of a question, and the man was no dummy.

"I'm certain she did at some point. I know she negotiated . . . she called it 'protective gear' for Bagram Air Force Base troops, and more. She handled some weapons claims and some vehicles. I can't tell you much beyond that. Broad terms were all she could bring home." He pushed his hands together and pulled them apart. The nervous gesture of a man whose world was tearing at the seams.

Eleri kept going. She was going to get what she could before he cracked. "Was there anything approximately nine to twelve months ago that she was upset about?"

He didn't speak right away. He started thinking about it, but his answer wasn't really an answer. "You have an idea what this is about?"

"Not enough of one." She opted again for honesty. Her gut told her that this man could be trusted, but that wouldn't fly if he spread what she was about to tell him. So she got at least verbal agreement on tape not to share what she told him. Then she let Vasquez lay out the basics of the two other cases.

As Vasquez spoke, Dawson's eyes grew large.

"Dr. Gardiner? The same as Vivian?"

DONOVAN WANTED A BEER. It had been a long day, but here he was, still working into the deep hours of the night. He wanted a cold bottle in his hand and to feel a little less responsible for the world. Instead he was drinking lukewarm water from a dish —a dirty dish—and Walter Reed was telling him he was a good boy.

Donovan considered barfing the water back up on her feet.

Only he didn't know if she had an extra pair of shoes, and she didn't even have 'feet'. She only had the one foot, as the left was prosthetic and she wasn't being mean or even condescending calling him a 'good boy.' She was a war hero and she thought he was a dog. He couldn't vomit on command anyway.

"Where'd you go?" she stroked his head and asked him.

Oh my God, woman. You wouldn't believe it if you knew. He tried to let his thoughts carry through and not shudder at being touched. Then he thought, maybe he should just shudder. Maybe it was about the same as a lot of the people here. These were war vets, most of them. They had seen things that just might make his own story tame in comparison.

Donovan was leaning down for another drink, undisturbed by the dirty dish—he had the system for it, after all—when Cooper Rollins climbed the fence.

He wished there was a way to alert Eleri that the man was here. Then again, she was surreptitiously keeping an eye on him from the dark corners of the ghostly empty streets. Maybe she'd figure it out on her own. Donovan perked his ears, aiming them at Rollins and Ozzy as they traded pleasantries.

It wasn't a surprise to find Rollins here. He and Vasquez and Eleri hadn't been able to pin down where he lived, but they'd come across him while checking the area, and Eleri had quickly put this into play. She'd raced back to the house, urged Donovan to change. They then hauled ass down here setting him free, only to find that Cooper Rollins wasn't in the block the veterans had taken over. He'd disappeared from the area in the short time they'd been gone.

Donovan had gone back and begged at the edge of the fence anyway. All the while wondering, where had Rollins been in the meantime?

"Where were you? I saw you go by about two hours ago, but you didn't come in." Walter lifted her head and her voice and said to Cooper exactly what Donovan wanted to.

"I was looking to meet up with someone." Rollins acted a bit uncomfortable answering the question and Donovan wished he could haul the man in for questioning right now. He wished Eleri could. But given that the four sides of the compound each had a spot that could be climbed, she'd be hard pressed to run the man down. And if she did, Rollins would be onto her. That was the last thing they needed.

Luckily, Walter had no compunctions about asking the hard questions. "Were you meeting that girl?"

"Girl?"

"The one with the blonde in her hair. She's actually Jordanian, you know." Walter was no idiot.

Donovan was guessing there was something up with her injuries that prevented her from getting a job. But she was bright and determined and if she knew about a girl, she'd probably left the compound and maybe tracked Rollins when Ozzy had set her to the task.

"Yeah, I know she's Jordanian." Rollins once again tried to end the conversation, but Walter was having none of it.

"She's not here for any good reason."

"I think she was seeking political asylum." Cooper shot back as Donovan fought to keep his head down, to not watch the conversation like it was a tennis match.

"That's complete bullshit."

Donovan wanted to know why exactly Walter thought that. And he wished to hell he could find out who the girl was. He was wondering if she was the same one Eleri had seen at the doctor's office.

It was then that Ozzy came up and took Rollins aside, effectively ending Walter's harassment of the man. Though the conversation turned low, Donovan could still hear it.

Sometimes Walter talked to him, or tried to get him to drink. But he only missed a little of the conversation, before he figured out to do something decidedly dog-like and put his head on his paws and feign sleep. A good animal therapist might figure out he was still listening. But no one here seemed to be paying much attention.

Ozzy wanted to know what was going on with Cooper Rollins. Rollins replied he had to "figure some things out." It quickly became clear from the tones that Rollins wasn't going to tell Ozzy what exactly he was up to, and Ozzy wasn't taking

Rollins' copout as a real answer.

"Are you in trouble, boy?" The words and the conviction behind them were serious. As though Ozzy had something to offer Cooper from here in the chain link enclave. But the fact was, he did. Ozzy knew enough people, his network might not cover as many countries as a CEO's, but it was vast. The loyalty he inspired was clearly high.

"I'm not in trouble yet." Rollins assured the older man, but it was the "yet" that caught Donovan.

He must have twitched his ears, done something, though he didn't know what. Because just then, Walter leaned down and whispered to him. "I was Special Forces, dog. You aren't asleep. And you aren't fooling me."

Son of a bitch!

He didn't move other than to breathe deeply. Any change in his stance was an agreement to something she'd said. Donovan's male brain had a moment of clarity. The only thing ugly about Walter Reed was her name.

When she pulled her hair down out of the military style and put it right back up, he got a glimpse of a woman with flowing hair, high cheekbones and a lush mouth. She was smart, capable, and determined. And she'd showered today. She was always clean despite the dirt she must actively rub on. She was always put together, and never showed anything off.

He wondered if the local men gave her any trouble, then fought a laugh at the idea of someone trying to mess with Walter. She'd kick their ass to next Sunday. Donovan felt a swift stab of attraction, and wondered if it was worth pursuing. Later.

Not this way, obviously.

When he looked up at her, checking her out as she stared back at him, a blast sounded behind him. Her reaction and his were to look to the sound, but not so Cooper Rollins.

The ex-soldier whirled to the noise, a gun appearing from the back of his jeans. A terrible place to carry a weapon,

Donovan had learned at the academy. But one far too convenient not to take advantage of once in a while.

Rollins' expression had changed to one of fear, and he gripped the weapon while swinging it at Ozzy. "Kellen! What? . . . What are you doing?"

The old man's hands went up in surrender and he seemed remarkably unfazed by the whole thing. His voice was soft, soothing even. "Rollins, I'm not Kellen. I don't know Kellen. I'm Ozzy."

"Don't do it, Kellen!" Cooper Rollins dropped into his stance, his grip on the gun unwavering. This was no dime store gang member, thrusting his piece out as though that might make the bullet go faster or his anger more obvious. Rollins was a military trained killer and tactician. Donovan was seeing it in action for the first time.

He stayed still, not wanting to get in the way of any bullets. As he'd once told Eleri, he wasn't immune. The whole silver bullet myth was nothing but a legend. He would die as surely as the rest of them.

Ozzy didn't move; he seemed to accept that his fate was not his own anymore, but it didn't appear to bother him.

Cooper scanned the area. He looked at Walter, eyes narrowing. "Aziza?"

Donovan felt his heart stop. It was the same name Eleri had given him. Cooper's voice didn't sound like he was questioning what she was doing here, he was more wondering if that was Aziza standing there.

Donovan looked to Walter. She was on her feet, the prosthetic creating a slight limp as she walked toward the man who swung faster than they could see, to aim the gun at her, center mass. *Not good.*

"I'm not Aziza. Do you know her?"

"Are you sure you're not her? Did I see you . . . in . . .?" He didn't finish, his face showing confusion.

"I'm Walter Reed. We're in Los Angeles. Aziza isn't here."

"Yes, she is."

Just then, Ozzy made a move to get the gun, rushing Cooper Rollins from the side. No dummy, he came in behind Rollin's peripheral vision, hoping to take him unawares.

He had no such luck.

Without looking, Cooper let go of the gun with one hand, lifted a perfectly timed elbow and smashed Ozzy upside the head, while side-stepping out of the way as the now limp old man fell to the ground, momentum leading him exactly where Cooper had stood a moment before. In his right hand, the gun never wavered from his aim on Walter.

Cooper's voice was labored now. His breathing ragging, coming through in the words. "Walter Reed is a hospital. Aziza is from Fallujah. That man—" he pointed to the now unconscious Ozzy, "—is Jaysh al-Islam. And I don't know who you are."

She responded in kind, slowly moving forward, banking on the fact that he seemed reluctant to pull the trigger and that he at least knew he was confused. Donovan thought that tactic could go horribly wrong at any time. He started looking for ways out and wondered if Eleri was watching.

Walter's tone was as soothing as Ozzy's had been. And Donovan began to wonder if they'd dealt with this before. Cooper Rollins wasn't *here*. He was time looped to somewhere else. Walter seemed to understand that.

"My nickname is Walter Reed. Army of Islam is out of *Syria*—"

Cooper looked at her sideways. "They are in Iraq now. Where's Kellen?"

"I don't know Kellen, Cooper."

"How do you know my name?" He was a ticking time bomb.

As Donovan stayed focused on the man in front of them, he

heard footsteps running. The pounding rhythm was one he'd
not heard often, but he recognized it.

Eleri.

She wasn't close enough.

Donovan leapt, jaws open, launching himself up under
Cooper's arm, pushing the gun up and praying as he bit down.

The blast of the gunshot reverberated in his ears.

11

E leri's gun aimed into empty air. Thank God, she hadn't fired.

Where Cooper Rollins had stood, there was nothing.

Donovan's leap had brought his mouth to Rollins' arm, pushing it upward right as the ex-soldier fired. She hadn't seen or heard any windows shatter nearby, but she checked that only after she looked at the people.

Person, actually.

Ozzy was out cold on the ground, and the other vets had somehow been sleeping through the disturbance. Some were tucked behind the illusion of walls their tents provided. Others seemed to have simply thrown their blankets over their faces to block the light and noise.

It was Walter Reed who'd been in the line of fire.

Luckily, the noise that signaled Rollins' gun discharging didn't signal her getting hit. So Walter kept walking steadily toward him, competent and unfazed. Then, with moves so fast they blurred in Eleri's vision, the woman took his arm, shaking the gun loose, then twisted it up behind his back. Controlling him now with her good arm, she pushed him face first to the ground and corralled his other arm when he expertly attempted to fight her off.

A Green Beret and a . . . Well, Eleri didn't know exactly what Walter's rank was, but she'd been Special Forces. This was definitely a fight Eleri with her FBI academy training didn't want to get in the middle of.

Thanks to Donovan's and Walter's quick actions, Rollins was down with Walter Reed on top of the pile, her face twisted in anger. Ozzy lay unconscious a few feet away and Donovan was looking directly at Eleri, his dark eyes asking questions she couldn't decipher.

"Kill me if you're going to, but you'd best make sure I'm dead this time!" Rollins shouted from under Walter's expert hold.

"I'm not going to shoot you, you fucking moron." Walter shouted back at him, then jerked her head up, looking one way then another. Her eyes caught Eleri's, and she frowned.

Yes, Walter, Eleri thought, *that gunshot and all the yelling very well may bring the police down on you.*

Shit. Now she really needed to wait around for the officers. She didn't want them writing citations to these people. One—because it was a crap thing to do to veterans who didn't even have a house in the first place. And two—because she needed this place up and running in case there was further intel coming.

Eleri sighed. She wasn't making any friends out of the departments in this town.

She knew it was the second argument that would hold sway. The first, while morally valid, didn't have any legal might. Only her FBI status and open case would help with the second. She holstered her weapon and began to climb.

She'd been tested in the Academy. She'd learned to roll and shoot, though she couldn't recall ever once using that trick.

She'd been taught to make arrests, clear buildings as part of a team, and how to always hold her gun like she meant business.

Instead, she was picking locks into the homes of people who'd exploded internally. She was dropping off her covert wolf partner and surveilling an enclave of homeless vets. She was climbing chain link fence and pushing through razor wire.

Wear a suit, keep the FBI's image professional, *my ass.*

Thankful for her informed decision of jeans and sneakers, Eleri dropped into the compound as everyone watched. Veterans had come out of tents, lifted blankets they'd used to cover their faces from the pools of the streetlights. The entire area was a nearly consistent pattern of stadium-bright pinpoints and black night between. Cooper, Donovan, and Walter occupied the edge of one of those light pools.

Eleri walked over.

"Agent Eames." Walter greeted her, but didn't move.

Eleri tried to hide her surprise that Walter remembered her name. There was a lot more going on in Walter than was obvious from the outside. Right then, Eleri decided that she was bringing the woman in for questioning, too. She was far too useful to let go. "Walter."

Seeing that Walter had a handle on the fading struggles Rollins put up, Eleri checked Ozzy. Donovan was already there, nudging the man and sniffing at him. She took the deliberate downward movement of his snout as a nod that things were okay; Ozzy was just out. Her own check confirmed it and her small hands were able to smack at the man's somewhat dirty cheeks and get his eyelids to flicker open.

She wondered for a moment if Donovan should have just licked his face.

Walter seemed to have assessed her situation and decided that Eleri was her best bet. So, despite the fact that Walter was sprawled on the ground using martial arts to pin down one of the best-of-the-best, she struck up a semi-casual conversation that Eleri hadn't seen coming.

"So, where's your partner tonight?"

Right beside you. But she didn't say that. "On another assignment."

Walter offered a nod, but was clearly playing a hand she'd carefully laid out. "What brings you by?"

As though Eleri had stopped in for a drink.

Deciding that Walter was too smart to manipulate, Eleri gave her the truth. "I'm actually following that man you have face down in the dirt."

"Fuck you." Rollins muttered up at her while Walter smirked.

Shit. Bad play. While she was making friends with Walter, she'd pissed off the man she was after. Eleri might find Walter useful, but Rollins had been her primary target. *Rookie mistake.* She wanted to kick herself.

"Sorry, Rollins. You know where you are?" She squatted down to get a good look at his face and saw him roll his eyes at her.

"Los Angeles." He offered up with a side of pissed-off right-eousness.

But Eleri understood. She'd seen a lot of this in the hospital. A lot. While she had no formal training in therapy, she did have a psych degree, with plenty of work in abnormal and trauma psych. Bread and butter to someone in her line of work. She had him diagnosed the first time she'd seen him. "Rollins, where were you just a minute ago?"

He didn't answer.

"Fallujah?" She offered.

His eyes flickered and she could almost see his brain register the surprise then write it off as a good guess. He was ex-military, a lot of them had been through Bagram and the area.

She tipped her head a little farther to the side, glad that

Walter was working with her, sensing that Eleri wasn't ready to let this explosive man up yet. "It wasn't a guess."

His slight nod was the only acknowledgment.

"Do you know why you're on the ground?"

He nodded again.

"I want to have Walter let you up. You can't go for a weapon again. You know who Walter is?" She needed to be sure. There was no telling how many weapons these soldiers had stashed here. While she thought most of them were perfectly safe in the hands of trained servicemen and women, she didn't want Rollins getting his hands on them. And he probably knew of several within reach.

"She lives here with Ozzy. I don't know her real name. She's MARSOC." He sighed again, maybe because no one had let him up.

Eleri cataloged that he only said he didn't know Walter's real name. Maybe he knew Ozzy's. But she went on. "You have a diagnosis on file?"

This time, his eyes flashed quickly to hers. Not afraid, not angry, but warning.

No. He did not have a diagnosis on file.

Eleri pushed.

"Dr. Gardiner helped you?"

"Yes." He gritted his teeth but stayed still on the ground.

Looking up at Walter, Eleri gave a small nod. Walter slowly eased off, letting up pressure, and only releasing Rollins' hand at the last minute. Had he done anything sudden, she could have easily regained control.

He stood, brushed himself off, and was careful to make no sudden movements. First, Cooper Rollins turned to Ozzy, once again sitting in his chair, keeping watch over the proceedings, just like he'd started the night.

"Ozzy, I'm sorry man." Cooper's stance, his flitting hands, his tone, all told the same thing. The apology was sincere and his actions truly regretted.

Ozzy had none of it. He waved a hand. "We've all been there. One way or another."

Rollins nodded toward Walter, but she didn't get the same apology and Eleri took a slow deep breath in without looking like it. Everything came to a head now and she was out here apparently alone. Donovan *couldn't* be her backup. It would blow the singular best cover in the world.

So Eleri Eames, senior partner, was trying to haul in a Green Beret and a Marines Special Forces Operator, by herself. The only way was to secure their agreement. She would not win against two of them.

If she failed, Cooper Rollins would be in the wind and there wouldn't be anyone on the inside to tell them what was under all that black ink in his files. Why the Fallujah mission had gone so bad, so fast. And who the hell was blowing up people with a tie to the military in general and to Cooper Rollins specifically.

Eleri had to talk them into it.

"Rollins. I came here to find you."

He stiffened and she changed tacks.

"You're the only one who can help us sort out what happened in Fallujah . . ." His shoulders ticked again, and she softened her voice, if not the words. "And who killed Dr. Gardiner. We need your help."

He wasn't convinced. His stance radiated his military training and his reluctance to move.

Want to get something? Give something.

The words radiated through her head. Her Academy trainer had made them put the phrase at the top of every written test in negotiations training. She'd had to mutter it before going into live action scenarios. She now heard that trainer's voice in her head and she handed over a piece of intel to Cooper.

"There are three victims now. The third happened earlier today."

This. This had his eyes locking on hers, and in her periphery Eleri could see she held Walter's rapt attention, too. "We have suspicions, but we don't *know* anything." Eleri looked briefly at Walter, wanting the woman to know she was in on the conversation.

"You know, don't you, Cooper, that we can't ID anything they leave behind without DNA tests." And she took a wild guess, something coming to her. "You were there, right? After Dr. Gardiner died."

His head jerked toward the side, but his eyes stayed on her and she pushed with nothing behind her reasoning but a feeling in her gut. Donovan would be proud.

If it went well. If Rollins ran and Walter pummeled her to the dirt, Eleri would blame her pushy partner into perpetuity.

"You saw what was left of Gardiner—his office—before the police came."

His eyes flickered once. Twice. He nodded the slightest amount and Eleri knew it was the only admission she'd get.

For a moment she took stock. Her back was tense, her leg muscles ready to pop into action at any second. She wished Wade were here as backup. But he and Westerfield had worked the crime scene and maybe gone to bed. Donovan hadn't wanted to share their undercover plan until it was completed. He really did not like running around as a wolf in Los Angeles. While Eleri agreed that the fewer people who knew the better, right now she wished someone understood.

Then she lied. "We know you're one of the good guys, Cooper. Can you come in and tell us what you know? Help us save people?"

12

Donovan showered quickly, once again the feeling of being in the confined square of the compound lingered long after the experience. Maybe it was Walter petting him constantly, or being called simply "dog" by most of the men. He wasn't sure; he was just glad to be out.

It didn't help that when Eleri finally showed up, she spoke to Cooper Rollins and then to Walter Reed and walked away. Simply leaving Donovan there.

She'd let Walter lead Rollins through the nicely concealed hole in the chain link. It was generally kept jammed, so that it didn't appear broken. But with a single tug at one of the sides, two curtains of chain link opened, allowing a person to hunch over and push through.

It wasn't beautiful, but it did seem big enough for the guys with arthritis and bad knees. There were two that Donovan had met in his few trips 'inside.' The second, younger man was ravaged with cancer. Donovan could smell it on him, hovering under the lingering odor of cheap whiskey. He probably drank like a fish to subdue the pain. He wasn't long for this world by either estimation.

As he watched Eleri walk away, pointing out the car to Walter and Cooper, she flashed the numbers '4' and 'o' back at him. Forty minutes to get out of here. To get to the meet-up point they'd pre-designated.

It had taken an hour.

During that time, he'd whined and been let out through the break in the fence. This time, no one followed him; they'd simply watched him walk away. He'd turned the corner, arriving where he could hop into the back of the car unseen, and waited.

When she finally picked him up, she was all apologies. "I had to get Walter and Cooper settled. Separately. And then get Marina in, and explain that she was to keep them there while I ran an 'errand.'" Eleri made air quotes, taking her hands off the wheel for a moment. He was almost afraid, but he was too ready to be out of this shape to start anything.

Eleri just kept chattering. "I almost said I had to 'pick up Donovan' but that would have led to too many questions. Like, why can't Donovan drive himself?"

Yeah, no opposable thumbs. He sighed.

She heard him. "I know. But we're on it, and I'm trying to get you home."

"Home" was a loose term. He hadn't had any real time at 'home' in a while now. To be fair, he wasn't sure it really was his 'home' any more. But he owned it and it was generally where his mail went. For now, 'home' was temporarily in West Hollywood, in a bungalow designed for a family.

So he showered, trailed water through the hallway just because, and he put on slacks and a shirt that buttoned then thought better of looking too nice. He'd just been in there with these two. Though they didn't know it, he'd learned a lot. He'd even bitten Cooper.

While he changed, he thought about telling Eleri to dress

down, but then thought better of it. Her changing her clothes would be more telling than anything else.

She was waiting in the car with the engine running. As Donovan climbed into the front passenger side this time, he saw she was eating a sandwich and his stomach growled. He was starving. Changing was metabolically taxing. He'd studied it.

He'd studied himself.

It took only a moment of looking at the sandwich as Eleri pulled out of the driveway and into traffic before he remembered he could speak now. It turned out he didn't need to. She reached into the middle console and pulled out a waxed-paper wrapped sandwich for him, too. He almost wept when she pointed to the can of soda she'd stashed for him. "You have to be hungry."

He answered by chewing.

They arrived at the Bureau building on Wilshire just before midnight. When they entered they found Cooper Rollins cooling his heels in one of the many chairs in an otherwise empty conference room. He'd already been left for an hour. A soda can sat crumpled by his hand; a bag of Doritos had obviously been bad and lay shredded around the table, the chips long gone.

Eleri stuck her head in and managed a supremely apologetic look. "I'm so sorry this took so long, but I wanted to bring my partner by." She stepped into the room, motioning to Donovan, who put his hand out while she spoke. "His name is Donovan Heath, and he'll be doing some of the interviews. We just need your statement and I can't tell you how sorry I am that you had to wait."

It was one of those things people didn't think about, and something Donovan was just learning. Sometimes you found what you needed and logistics got the better of you. Thank God

Vasquez had come in and at least done the initial intake, checking backgrounds and such.

Eleri interrupted his thoughts and Rollins' growing surly mood, "We'll be back as soon as we can."

Then she took him across the hall and did the same with Walter Reed, this time finding Marina Vasquez still in the room, her laptop in front of her. But the other agent popped up and followed, the three of them convening in the hallway, deciding how to split things up.

Vasquez, still holding her open laptop, was the first to volunteer information. "I checked both of them against ID. That is Cooper Rollins, or someone who looks very, very much like him and knows his military background. Walter," she said it with the kind of question one would of a woman named Walter Reed, "is actually Lucy Fisher. Her ID matches as do her injuries. I'm confident of ID on both of them. Do we make one of them wait?"

Donovan shook his head. "I don't think we can. If either of them waits longer they'll be a wasted witness. They'll hate us and start the interview even angrier than they already are."

Eleri nodded and Vasquez failed to vote. For once he wasn't the lowest man on the totem pole. In fact, "I should interview Walter and you two should interview Rollins."

Though she was bottom of the voting barrel, Vasquez had learned she was free to speak with the two of them. Donovan still got the impression that the L.A. Bureau didn't think much of her. Which was their loss. "Do you really think a full cross-gender interview is the right way? Two females interviewing Rollins?"

It was a consideration. Donovan could see Eleri thinking it over, too. She turned to Vasquez. "Did you get the impression that Rollins was misogynistic? Or that Walter might not take to a male interview?"

"No, it's just that you usually aim for something familiar.

Like we did with Alyssa Rollins. There's almost zero familiar in that interview set up."

"Ah. But I have some insight on Walter." He tipped his head to Eleri a little, indicating that she should listen to what he didn't say. He'd had literally hours with the woman. The trick would be not to reveal anything she'd told her dog friend; Walter was sharp as tacks.

Eleri nodded back at him and he saw Vasquez was no dummy either. She picked up on the exchange, but just as wisely held her tongue, just stood there looking back and forth, waiting on a decision.

Eleri asked him if he needed any help with Walter, because she thought having Marina in with her, checking out local info, etc, was helpful.

"I agree with that. I think Rollins is the more important witness. Hence, he should get two interviewers, and he should get the person who knows the case best. That's the two of you. Vasquez, do you have anything special on Walter Reed that I need?"

"Oh yeah. You should both check out her record." With that, she hit a few buttons and turned her screen to them.

Well. He knew his face reflected the new information, but he didn't say anything. Just saluted the women, gathered the recorder Vasquez had already started with Walter, and a pad of paper, which was always kinder for notes than typing away. He figured Walter would be a paper girl. And he pushed his way through the door.

"Walter Reed?"

She nodded at him, her space cleaner than Rollins' had been. She looked not to have eaten the offered vending machine fare, or if she had, she'd cleaned up. Then again, she'd eaten while he was with her earlier in the evening, and given her service record, he'd bet she could turn her need for food off and on as a situation dictated.

For a moment, he forgot she didn't know him and he awkwardly introduced himself. Donovan hoped it was endearing rather than off-putting. It was possibly the first time in his life he'd ever hoped he was endearing.

"Your real name is Lucy Fisher?"

She nodded, treating him as a stranger though she'd scratched him behind the ears just a few hours ago. He wanted to shudder all over, the feelings of being there coming back in a wave. But he was getting good at bottling it up. Again.

Donovan fought a sigh. He'd worked so hard to get a life in which he didn't have to stifle these things. Yet, one call from the FBI and here he was again. He tamped it back down and focused on the woman across the table. "I've seen your record. It's quite impressive. You lost your hand and your lower leg to an IED?"

She nodded, and though her tone wasn't arrogant, her words were proud and a bit ironic. "I'm a combat medic. A combat communications specialist. And a combat helicopter pilot. I'm combat injured. The only thing I'm not is a 'combat veteran.'"

∾

ELERI WALKED INTO COOPER ROLLINS' conference room with Marina right behind her. "Hello, Officer Rollins. I'm so sorry we kept you waiting."

They took a moment to sit down and while they did, she watched him. He didn't squirm or act nervous in any way. In fact, he didn't act anything at all. She wasn't used to interviewing people as well trained as she was, or better. He might see right through everything. Or he might turn the tables on her and she wouldn't even know it. Eleri was grateful that Marina was in this with her.

She got right down to it. "I'm not sure what Agent Vasquez

has told you, but we're grateful you came in. We need any information you can give us regarding a series of murders. Anything will help."

He paused, letting the room go silent. Eleri knew that trick and she waited, too.

"Am I under arrest?"

"Of course not." She answered quickly and with as much vehemence as possible to convey believably. She just hoped he didn't decide he needed to leave.

Cooper Rollins only sat back and nodded, leaving Eleri faced with the decision of where to start. She rarely went into an interview without a game plan. But she'd been shoving food in her face, because going in with low blood sugar was worse.

"Let me first tell you what we know. Then I'm hoping you can fill in some gaps." She leaned forward, trying to look as desperate as she was and trying not to look as though she were sizing him up to be the criminal at play.

In short order, she walked through Ratz's assassination, then Dr. Gardiner's, followed with sparse information about Vivian Dawson. Ultimately, she pointed out that they weren't sure Vivian Dawson had in fact died. But she was missing, and there was a person splattered on the inside of the Dawsons' sitting room.

"I knew Dr. Gardiner. I saw him for a while after I returned from Afghanistan." Cooper spoke the statement calmly.

Eleri nodded and asked him for dates, which he readily supplied. She quickly realized she was going to have to call bullshit if she was going to get anything. It was a gamble, but she took it.

"You continued seeing Dr. Gardiner after he supposedly discharged you, didn't you?" She tipped her head, asked it as though it was just another question. She was up against a trained interrogator and Green Beret. She had nothing on his skills and she knew it.

"I don't understand." No expression.

"You continued to see Dr. Gardiner. I don't know if he charged you or not, but you had regular appointments with him . . . under another name."

For a moment his expression stilled and she could tell he was deciding what to tell her. "Yes."

She let it go, didn't act as though he had conceded anything. "You have a diagnosis of PTSD?"

"No." He didn't move.

"You don't have an *official* diagnosis?" Eleri waited while he shook his head. "You do have it, though."

It wasn't really a question. He didn't answer.

"It's severe, if intermittent," she commented. He couldn't really deny it. She'd seen it. Either he had PTSD so bad that he was pulling a loaded Army regulation handgun on his friends, or he was an Oscar-quality actor and a grade-A asshole.

This time he nodded.

Why wouldn't he be officially diagnosed? Why wasn't he getting real treatment? Giving in to her desire to understand, she just flat out asked.

Folding his hands in front of him, Cooper Rollins returned fire with a question of his own. "What do you know of my military history?"

Eleri threw that one to Marina, who could probably recite it from memory. And she did, right through to the end. "Though, as you know, a good portion of your raids, or assignments, are redacted in your paperwork, we do know that you returned from an assignment that went sideways and were medically discharged with no diagnosis within ten hours."

Right as Marina rolled it smoothly off her tongue, Eleri regretted it. She'd just tipped her hand that Cooper Rollins wasn't as casual of an interview as she'd wanted him to seem. She was going to have to play it off, but he spoke up.

For the first time his face offered some level of expression.

His mouth twisted down at one side, up at the other. "That's the military for you. Years of service to get in, just a few papers in as many hours to push you out."

"I'm sorry." It rolled off her tongue sincerely. He'd loved what he did. He'd clearly felt he was part of something bigger than himself and that the work was important. Then he'd been betrayed by his colleagues and screwed over by his government. Now he was becoming the prime suspect in a disturbing set of murders. Eleri didn't envy him at all.

"I know you served under Colonel Ratz, and that he wrote your recommendation letter into the Green Berets. And I know he did it right when you had the minimum number of years of service to qualify and that he gave you highest marks." She paused, "So this wasn't just your commanding officer. You had a solid relationship with the man." Another pause. "Did you keep in touch with him? Or get back in touch with him once you returned home?"

"No."

Marina's foot tapped the side of hers under the table. And Eleri agreed: he was lying. But she let it go.

This time Cooper Rollins volunteered something. "I didn't kill Ratz. And I didn't kill Dr. Gardiner either."

Marina's foot didn't tap hers. Eleri spoke quickly. "I know that."

"How do you know it? You don't know who did kill them, or you wouldn't have me here." He looked hard at her, his eyes narrowing as he tried to figure out what she was about. He was no longer hiding it.

"I don't know who did it. But I do know it wasn't you."

Marina Vasquez didn't comment. Probably thought Eleri was playing him. It seemed Cooper did, too.

"How?"

"I can't disclose how I know." Not if she wanted Vasquez—or anyone really—to think she was sane.

He was clearly unsatisfied with her answer, but before he could say so, she threw him another question.

"Did you know that your alias was on the appointment list the day Dr. Gardiner was killed?"

He nodded. "I got a call cancelling my appointment. They said the doctor was sick. But that's happened before. Usually Katie stays and answers the phones, handles the records, even if he's out." He paused, maybe wondering what he should tell, or maybe feeling something at the loss of the man who had helped him. "I went over later to check in with Katie. Get out of the house. Katie wasn't there and his office door was closed. So I opened it and checked."

He looked away, and Eleri got the distinct impression he was telling the truth and that the truth hurt him.

"It was stupid. I smelled it. I shouldn't have opened the door." He brought his eyes up to meet hers. "I did exactly what Dr. Gardiner taught me to do. I closed my eyes, breathed in through my mouth and reminded myself that I was in CONUS." When Marina frowned, he added, "Continental US—Stateside. I told myself it was all in my head. Then I turned the knob to his office and saw it. So I told myself that it was nothing and that I was just seeing things. But nothing made it go away."

Eleri nodded at him.

PTSD was a disease of time loops. A trigger could take a person back to a traumatic situation. Apparently Cooper Rollins had a buttload of them to draw on. Once in the grip of the trigger, the loop would continue until it played out or was dislodged. A man who'd seen colleagues blow up before his eyes, a man who had lost a third of his command never to be seen again, and the living third helped drag the remaining third, dead, back to base, could easily have thought what was in Dr. Gardiner's office was really in his head.

"Knowing no one would believe me," he offered that first line with a challenge, but Eleri didn't rise to the bait and

Marina stayed silent. "I wiped down the door knob and left. I know I destroyed evidence, but I destroyed it when I touched it in the first place."

He was obviously ashamed of his lack of forethought and at the same time defending what were actually perfectly reasonable actions.

"Whoever it was," Eleri didn't say 'Aziza' though she knew, "wiped down all the knobs and desk surfaces before they left. It wasn't you."

Then she asked another question. "Did you know that all your files are missing from Dr. Gardiner's office?"

13

D onovan was having no real luck with Walter Reed.

What she hadn't volunteered was that she'd been given a medal for the incidence that cost her hand and leg—a Bronze Star—for bravery in combat. Though, as she'd pointed out, technically she wasn't listed as having been in combat because she was female.

She'd showed off her prosthesis, or really just held up her lower leg. The leg of the camo pants was tightly tied around the metal of the flexible scoop. It wasn't designed for show, it was for speed and balance, like what the paralympic runners used. That completely meshed with what he knew of Walter.

She wasn't used to being called Lucy, and hadn't answered to it in almost a decade. She'd been "Fisher" in the service and "Walter Reed" since she'd finished rehab.

Yes, she understood there were programs for vets, to help place her in a job and a home. And, no, she didn't really give a shit.

She'd held up her left arm, the shirt sleeve pinned up in place of the missing hand. "They wanted me in a desk job, which I'm obviously not suited for. It would be a pity position anyway, it's not like I'm a fast typist. And I refuse to answer phones. I'm good where I am, for now."

When he'd followed the thread of her "for now," Donovan learned that she was pursuing a PI license, and he tried to use that as an 'in' to get her to talk about Cooper.

She only knew him through Ozzy and the 'square'—as she called it. She'd been in the Middle East, but as there were tens of thousands of US troops there, it wasn't surprising that they had been at some of the same bases, maybe even at the same times, but never met.

Then things finally got interesting. Walter started volunteering information. But Donovan had to pretend he hadn't heard it before and he spent most of his time not really listening but dissecting. He needed the things he didn't already know. And he needed to pluck it out of her speech so he could ask the right questions without seeming psychic or like he'd planted a bug—or a dog—in their compound.

"Ozzy asked me to follow Cooper, and I decided I should. Something is up with him, but I can't figure out exactly what." She leaned back in the chair, looking lazy, irritated, and a little jumpy. Donovan was confident she wasn't actually any of those things.

With this case, the people who might help them out were vaporized or had Special Forces training. Donovan was smart enough to know that he couldn't play games with Walter. His six months in the FBI Academy had left him as no match for her MARSOC training. So he did the only thing he could. He quit writing, leaned across the table and started a real conversation.

"Why did Ozzy want you to follow him?"

"Honestly, he suggested I seduce Rollins or something like that." She waved her good hand and erased all possibility of that thought. "I'm not a nineteen-sixties spy girl a-la Bond. I'm recon trained." She shook her head. "Normally, Ozzy doesn't come across as sexist, but sometimes his age shows."

Donovan nodded. "I find that to be true in an older population. How do you respect them without telling them off?"

She laughed. "It's a fine line with Ozzy some days. He just didn't like that Rollins disappeared sometimes, thought it was suspicious that he wouldn't talk about it. So I did some covert follows on Rollins. Let me tell you, that was fun. Except for the part where he might kill me or whatnot if he found me. And the fact that the dude has some bad-ass PTSD."

Donovan knew that already, but he wondered what Walter had seen of it. He was getting ready to ask when she started talking again. "I saw him have two full blown episodes, not including the one your partner came in on tonight. Was she following him?"

Donovan nodded but went after the PTSD, hopefully brushing off Eleri's amazingly timely arrival. "We've been trying to find him for about a week. When we find him, we lose him— or probably, he loses us. We weren't sure about the PTSD though. What did you see?"

"Once, a slamming door set him off. I watched him deal—or *not* deal—for twenty minutes. He hightailed it down the street, blending in, but ducked into a doorway on the first empty shop he found. He picked the lock and hid behind the counter in what was left of the old store. Tactically, it was a good move. But no one was after him. After about half an hour, he crept out and went on his way."

Thirty minutes? Donovan thought. That was a long episode. Then again, no one was helping like they had tonight when just about everyone had tried to talk him down. "Did he pull a weapon?"

Quickly, Donovan backtracked, trying to figure out how he legitimately knew that fact, but Walter passed it off. It probably

made sense he'd gotten a rundown from Eleri while Walter and
Rollins waited.

"Maybe?" She shrugged. "He was hidden—and well—a lot
of the time. He was carrying though. So it's entirely possible."

Shit. The man was dangerous enough when he was stone-
cold sober. In a full-blown PTSD episode like Donovan saw
tonight, he was insanely deadly. From Walter's comments, it
wasn't as rare a happening as Donovan wanted to believe. They
would have to get Cooper Rollins off the street before he killed
someone. But they needed him on the street to see where
he led.

"Here's the thing." Walter interrupted his thoughts. "The
reason I'm in here talking is that Rollins has a problem, and I
don't know if he's working a black ops case and we shouldn't
get in his way, or if he's turned and we need to shoot on
sight."

Clearly, she was conflicted. "Tell me what you know."

It was a broad statement, and she didn't have to do it, but
she did. "Tonight . . ." She looked out the window briefly at the
sun coming in through faint rays, "*last night* he said Ozzy was
Jaysh al-Islam and he called me 'Aziza'."

Donovan waited and Walter didn't disappoint.

"Jaysh al-Islam is one of the many rebel factions over there.
It roughly translates to 'Army of Islam' but they're in *Syria*.
Cooper seemed to think they had infiltrated Iraq." She paused.
"I have an idea what he did over there, though only an idea.
The problem is he could be hallucinating a bunch of mixed up
shit or he could have some real intel the rest of us just don't
know yet. I can't tell the difference."

"I'm having the same problem with him." Donovan sympa-
thized, though not because it was an interrogation tactic. He
really felt for her trying to figure out just what the hell Cooper
Rollins was up to, and she'd been doing it with far fewer
resources than they had.

"Also, Aziza is someone he met. She looks like an American college kid, and I followed Rollins to her and her to a ... group."

"Describe the group?" Walter didn't look comfortable with this, and that just made Donovan more interested.

"It's a variety of people. But two are Aziza and her sister Alya. They're from Fallujah and they've got an axe to grind with the US. The others were harder to trace."

Holy shit. Walter was a fucking gold mine.

"Rollins was in talks with them, on several different occasions. But they seem to want him to join. They're trying to get him to be the blond-and-blue."

ELERI STUCK her head into the room where Donovan was supposed to be interviewing Walter Reed, a.k.a. Lucy Fisher. But it looked like they were just having a casual conversation.

She wanted to ask about it, but couldn't. Right now she couldn't help it, she had to interrupt and derail him. At least she wouldn't question him.

"Agent Heath?" She used the formal with him in an attempt to maintain any authority he needed in the situation.

Donovan brushed it right off. "Eleri, are you finished? Come in." He gestured for her to sit at the table with them. So she joined, not knowing where this was headed but figuring she'd find out soon enough.

He tapped his hand on the table then looked up at Walter, who had been talking when Eleri opened the door, but had stayed silent since. "Walter, you have to be hungry. What can we get you?"

The woman almost snorted. "Breakfast. But I'd love a diet Coke."

Donovan turned to Eleri, "Can we make that happen?"

She knew that by 'we' he meant her. He was into something,

that was for certain. "Of course." She looked at the soldier sitting across from her, more stoic now than when she'd first walked in. "We can't take you out anywhere, but I can get the diet Coke. Later, when we're done here, we can definitely feed you."

Shit. That came out wrong.

Walter, like the rest of them, was proud of her self-sufficient status. It wouldn't be a problem except that she spent a good part of her day with people telling her to get off their sidewalk. The "we'll feed you" comment may have come across as demeaning, though Eleri hadn't meant it that way.

Donovan shocked her by catching the gaffe and saving it. "That would be great. I'm starving." Then he suggested a place he'd seen nearby, and asked Walter if she knew if it was any good. She relaxed again, but didn't resume her chatty nature.

"Donovan," Eleri touched his arm. "Can I talk to you in the hallway for a minute?"

He looked to her, then to Walter, then back to Eleri, though she couldn't read what he was trying to convey. She was going to have to ride this out in front of Walter.

"Eleri, Walter was telling me that Jaysh al-Islam is a rebel group out of Syria, but that Cooper seems to think they are—or at least *were*—in Iraq."

Eleri raised her eyebrows, looking between the two. She'd heard that earlier, when Cooper Rollins had his gun on Walter. She turned to the woman and asked directly now. "And Aziza? Do you know her?"

Donovan nodded to Walter in a small gesture and the gates opened. Her face grew more animated and it became clear she was repeating what she'd said to Donovan earlier. Eleri listened to how Walter had followed Cooper on more than one occasion, that she'd seen Aziza, Alya, and a few others.

Donovan added in, "She was just telling me that they want Rollins to join them."

"Shit. That's not good." She normally didn't swear in interviews. Just like when she was a kid and she had friend-language and parent-language, but it had slipped out. Rollins' past could have him on either side of the game, and after a few minutes she had Walter saying the same thing. Despite having followed the man several times, and thinking she'd managed to stay off his radar, Walter couldn't say for sure one way or the other.

Donovan had been right. Walter was the resource, not Rollins. So Eleri took a chance. "Rollins just left. We can't hold him for anything. He's just a person of interest."

She didn't say more. Didn't know what Donovan had told Walter about the bombings, about the suspicions of terrorism.

Donovan picked up on what Eleri hadn't said, and he laid it out there for Walter. "We need to follow him." Then he turned to Eleri, "Tell me you bugged him."

She let out a bark. "Yeah, I successfully placed a device on a Green Beret! . . . I didn't even begin to try."

The bugs she had access to, he would find. Cooper Rollins had probably stopped within the block and checked himself. Or he was good enough to know she hadn't tagged him.

Donovan leaned across the table, clearly having made friends with Walter. "If we give you the information, can you get his phone? Download an app to follow him?"

"Won't he find that?" Walter said it but Eleri had the same question.

Donovan answered them both. "It doesn't matter. If we get even a day or two of info out of it, it will be beyond useful."

"He can't know it was us." Eleri cautioned.

"Walter here is studying to become a PI. I'll bet she can find us something."

Walter nodded, then added. "Maybe I can tack a listening program into it. See if he really is becoming the group's blond-and-blue."

Eleri jerked back and both Walter and Donovan leaned forward to her, speaking over each other.

"You know what that means?"

They said the words almost in unison, but Donovan's revealed that he didn't, while Walter's tone showed that she was pleased that Eleri did know.

Eleri turned to Donovan, her heart beating faster. "A 'blond-and-blue' is a white, American-looking person on the side of a non-white, non-American terrorist group. A 'blond-and-blue' can move freely throughout the US— easily fly on planes, carry guns and other weapons—without all the racist profiling that occurs."

Eleri blew out a breath and hoped to expel her growing terror with it. "A blond-and-blue is an enormous benefit to a terrorist cell."

14

Donovan sank into the seat at the small, chipped blue kitchen table. It had been painted long ago and aged into a shabby chic finish that was legitimate rather than created. The chairs matched, though they showed traces of a pale peach paint underneath.

He never knew if the colors he saw were the same as everyone else's. He knew his night vision wasn't anywhere near the normal human spectrum, so it stood to reason his day vision might not be either. So he stuck to 'blue,' 'green,' 'red' and the basics when he spoke.

Mostly, right now he thought the chairs worked because they held him up. Because the table held a beer Eleri had popped for him, and it was from a local brewery. He saw some posh, hand-bottled cider in front of Eleri, and Marina Vasquez was sitting down with a store-bought hard lemonade.

All three were at the table, all three were drinking, and all three had finally, blessedly slept. For the last one, Donovan was the most grateful. He remembered long nights from their last case, but not so many of them. Then, they'd been working in a small town, where being out and about at two a.m. was frowned upon. He remembered being up all night in med school. He also remembered it was working with live patients that bothered him far more than the hours. He'd counted down until he got into the morgue, knowing the day would come, that he was paving a job that suited his particular needs.

Then, he'd wound up here. Up all night, surrounded by people, and having early evening meetings in rental houses on the opposite side of the country. Suddenly, he craved a run. Deep in the woods, with no people around, no one who would care anyway. Sadly, he knew that was a long way off.

So he sipped at the beer, unable to hide the sigh at finally getting a cold one. Finally being rested enough to do his job. And just for being in jeans and barefoot in a homey kitchen, instead of in work clothes in the stuffy, orthogonal Bureau building.

"You look like you're feeling better." Eleri grinned.

"You slept fewer hours than me. You went out and got beer, arranged a meeting . . ." He held the bottle up, tipping it and his head towards her as a thank you. "You were awake just as long."

She lifted her shoulders in a shrug. "Maybe you need more sleep than I do." Her eyebrows indicated what her words allowed to stay silent—that she understood the change required food *and* sleep. He'd sacked out cold without even undressing when they'd finally arrived.

Beer aside, it was time to get back to this case. They'd started with two linked deaths, and a third person had died already.

Donovan knew that more deaths were inevitable. While he didn't know Vivian Dawson personally, didn't grieve her loss as her husband would, he felt the weight of the failure on his shoulders. Life was precious. He'd felt the deep cuts that loss left when his mother died, and he'd lived with the pressing sensation brought on by the shadow of his father's deep disrespect for all life.

That Mrs. Dawson had died while they ran down Cooper Rollins didn't help either. He drank more of the beer, not that it would make him feel better about her, but it felt cold, and it tasted good, and it was a small comfort in a fucked up case.

"Anything new about Vivian Dawson?" He looked at the two women sitting at the table.

They looked about like he imagined he looked. A little disheveled, a little down-hearted, a lot determined.

Marina put down her lemonade and nodded. "I have more about her work. Obviously not the full story, but her death and the manner of it, caused them to release more information about her. She definitely bought supplies for troops in Fallujah." Marina sighed and Donovan had learned that was a sign that something was bad, but it was good for the case.

"I don't know why I followed it, but I did. I found someone at her office, an assistant willing to talk to me. Maybe because I'm FBI. It was off-the-record and I'm currently protecting my source like a reporter. So only the two of you know about this. I haven't written it up yet." She fortified herself with another drink, the level in her bottle dropping faster than his or Eleri's. Donovan thought that spoke of the nature of the issue.

"According to him, the requisitions she handled were for large numbers of weapons for the troops. Often for more weapons than needed. There was an internal investigation that's still ongoing about munitions disappearing. No one knows where they went, only that the numbers were off. The requisitions seem to have normalized, but Vivian's department was in on it."

"What does it mean that the numbers are off? Where do the extra weapons go?" Eleri frowned.

"I can't say for sure, but my guy is pretty convinced that there are factions over there, selling them or outright giving them to militant groups."

"Is that supposed to happen?" Donovan had his own frown

now. He felt it in his chest. "I mean, it makes sense that we'd help arm allies, right?" He looked around the table but didn't get the easy response he'd hoped for.

Marina outright shook her head at him. "According to my guy . . . and this is all according to he-who-shall-not-be-named, but no. Maybe groups that we think can help, but not formal allies at all. Weapons were turning up in the hands of militant groups that were turning on soldiers. There was plenty of evidence that soldiers were being killed by US supplied guns and ammo."

She drank again, though it didn't improve her mood. "A lot of people are arguing that this is due to insurgents pulling weapons from dead or incapacitated US soldiers, but the numbers don't hold up for that. The numbers apparently only work if we're supplying relatively large quantities of arms—far more than go missing from our dead. There are a few higher ups being investigated, but it looks like it was working at all levels. A network of officers and soldiers and Iraqis. It wasn't all about just arming the right people either. There was a lot of money changing hands."

She tipped the bottle up, not finishing it either. "The three whistleblowers have already been found dead or declared missing. One of the guys was mutilated and left for carrion just beyond the base fence. Troops found him the next morning . . ."

Donovan leaned back. "That alone almost speaks to the accuracy of the information. Whistleblowers suffering repercussions is usually an indication of someone's guilt and desire to keep things quiet."

"It's worse," she said.

"Well, shit." Eleri's response.

Donovan stood up for another beer, hoping Eleri had gotten him more than one. He pulled open the older fridge and saw that yes, he was at the beginning of a six pack. He felt like grabbing two so he didn't have to get up again, but didn't feel like looking like an ass, or taking any steps toward becoming his father. Donovan had always been a responsible drinker after seeing what unchained alcoholism had done to his family. But now his main concern was making very poor decisions in front of Marina. His bad choices could scare the shit out of her.

He hid a chuckle in the fridge as it was totally inappropriate to the conversation. But she didn't stop talking because he wasn't far enough away. His faint smile died on his lips as she said, "Some of the higher ups over there and over here are trying to shut down the investigation."

"Holy shit." This time Eleri had more emphasis. "In the states, too?"

Vasquez shrugged. "Sounds like." Then she stood up. "I have to use the ladies." She headed toward the hall before anyone could say anything else.

Donovan set his beer down trying to avoid a telltale thump. His frustration was edged with fear and he leaned across the table, whispering loudly, grateful again that he was not the senior partner. "This is so beyond our scope! This is an international terrorism plot with US military involvement!"

"We don't *have* a scope." Her voice was flat, her face completely devoid of his welling anger.

"The FBI functions within the borders of the US—"

Eleri leaned forward this time. Though her words were not soothing, it was comforting that she was upset, at least a little. "NightShade isn't really FBI. We know that now. We have to shut this down." She shrugged, as though she knew no other way. "We're brought in when other organizations can't fix things."

His breath huffed out. "I wish I'd known that when I thought I was joining the actual FBI."

Her brows quirked, her mouth turned down. She hadn't known either. Eleri had been what he now thought of as 'real' FBI—under the standard umbrella—for years. Now their pay came from the Bureau, they had all the badges and ID, but Donovan had learned the diamonds on the borders of their ID cards and at the bottoms of their badges signified they were NightShade Division . . . and it was just as dark and underground as it sounded. Maybe even more so.

He looked to his partner for answers again, "What about Vasquez?" His whisper was harsh, cutting through the air between them.

"We'll leave her behind if we get into something we can't explain."

He snorted. He was so far into what he couldn't explain, he didn't understand how anyone could even see him.

A footstep on the hard wood behind him let him know Marina Vasquez had returned from her restroom break, and he had to wonder how much she had heard.

ELERI WATCHED Marina come back into the eat-in kitchen and she scrambled to cover for the conversation she and Donovan had just bitten off. Vasquez would not understand getting dumped mid-case and left behind. Nor could she; it wasn't something Eleri or Donovan would be able to explain.

The woman's face didn't give away that she'd heard anything, but she was clearly confused as to why the conversation had stopped. She didn't ask though.

Eleri didn't volunteer. "I don't have any new intel to add. Honestly, I would say the interview with Rollins was a bust. Marina?"

Whether it worked at steering the conversation, or if Vasquez just let it seem that way, Eleri didn't know. "He didn't want to tell us much." She turned to Donovan, giving a quick rundown of the brick wall Rollins had presented. "He refused most questions, citing that if he wasn't under arrest we couldn't demand answers. And if he was under arrest, he wouldn't answer until his lawyer was present. He wouldn't tell us where he lived, or how he was getting his money. We asked if he was in contact with his wife and son, but he said no. Seemed like he was lying though. But maybe I only thought that because I already knew he was lying."

Donovan nodded, the conversation starting to wind down with all of them a little wiser. "There's more from the Dawson house, not sure if you heard it from Wade or Westerfield?"

"I heard from Wade." Eleri spoke up. "He sent me a bunch of documents, crime scene photos, early lab results." She turned to Marina who wasn't getting a second drink. Unlike Eleri and Donovan, Vasquez had to drive home. "I'll share with you as soon as I sort it out."

She meant, *as soon as I make sure you can see it all,* but she thought maybe Marina was already onto that. As NightShade agents, they were allowed to interact with other FBI Agents, but they weren't to let anyone know what their directive was or that NightShade even existed. Eleri knew that firsthand; she'd been friends with Wade for years, having no idea he was Night-Shade. All along, she'd believed he was just a senior investiga-tor. She'd been right, but so wrong. Now she was keeping Marina Vasquez in the dark just like Wade had done to her. Only, Eleri thought, Wade had done it better.

Donovan's voice broke into her thoughts. "Victor Dawson said something interesting in his interview the other night. He didn't know if it was pertinent or not."

Donovan wouldn't have said anything unless it brought something up. "So?"

"There was an Indian man who came by in the evening several days before. Vivian answered the door and let the man in, as he was preaching some door-to-door religion. Victor called her 'Viv'—he said 'it wasn't like Viv to let anyone in the door that she didn't know. She wasn't a 'serve you lemonade' kind of woman.'"

Eleri frowned. It might be nothing.

After another sip of his second beer, Donovan spoke again. But Eleri was watching. She'd seen his father, seen what he could do on a bender. She needed to be sure Donovan didn't go for a third, or more. Besides, the ready excuse was they had to stay sober in case a call came in.

"According to Dawson, Vivian let the man into the living room—the room where Vivian was actually killed. And he said the man seemed startled to see him there." Another sip. Eleri didn't want to count, but she was counting. "I asked him why he thought the man might not have expected him and the only thing he could think of was that Viv's car was the only one in the driveway."

Donovan was drinking and referring to the victim with the husband's pet name. The case was getting to him more than he wanted to admit. And Vasquez' own info-bomb about military involvement was making him squirrely.

It was Vasquez who asked the pertinent question. "That would mean the Indian man not only knew that they had two cars, but that he knew whose car was whose. That's a stretch for a door-to-door guy. . . unless you don't think he was."

Eleri was shaking her head already. "Wade's notes. There was an Indian man in the neighborhood yesterday. The canvass brought it out, several neighbors mentioned it as the only thing out of the ordinary. They all found him sweet and not pushy at all."

"So the Dawsons have a different perspective of the man?" Marina asked. "Okay, that is odd. Not sure it's relevant."

"The neighbors said he hadn't been there before." Eleri filled in. "So he went through the neighborhood this afternoon . . . and he was gone before she died. But he'd been to only their house before?"

"Not sure." Donovan answered, leaning back in the chair. "The description is 'Indian man.' It's not very clear."

"Native American? Or India Indian?" Vasquez asked, not seeming to recognize Donovan's own Calcutta heritage.

"India."

"Are we sure he went to the Dawsons' house yesterday?" Eleri asked filing the pieces and looking for gaps.

Donovan nodded. "The girl next door who called it in? She said he went there. Also, another odd note: Victor Dawson says Vivian was mugged recently. Downtown. They took her purse. It's why he knew exactly what purse she was carrying and what was in it. He had to go shopping with her for the replacement."

Eleri was ready to rattle her head and see if that made some of these odd pieces go together.

"Too much coincidence." Marina's voice took on an ominous tone that Eleri didn't like. "So someone had their home address, her keys?"

They had so many pieces, but as of yet none of them fit. "Was the mugger Indian?"

Again, Donovan shook his head. "Muslim."

"How would they know his religion?" Eleri asked. 'Muslim' was not a race.

This time her partner held his hands up. "His words, not mine! When asked, Victor Dawson clarified 'Middle Eastern'."

That's not good either. Eleri almost said it out loud, then she catalogued what Marina knew and what she didn't. The agent knew of Aziza and Alya, and the cell, if not that Aziza had killed Dr. Gardiner herself. "We already have people of Middle Eastern descent in this story."

Donovan looked at her. Though he didn't say it, she could almost hear his thoughts. *And a white police officer.*

"Oh!" Eleri jumped up. The pictures. She grabbed her tablet and started sorting, not ready to show Marina everything until she knew exactly what was in them. But she pulled up one and flashed it around. "Look."

Donovan and Marina both squinted at the picture of the couch, the mess that had been Vivian Dawson, and a coffee table with magazines.

She pointed. "The pamphlet?"

Marina squinted and Eleri enlarged that portion of the photo allowing Marina to read it. Donovan could see it with an easy clarity, but he let Marina say the words out loud as though he needed her to. "Jesus' lost years—the Best of the Sons of Men." Then she looked up. "It's a religious pamphlet. Do we know if the neighbors got anything like it?"

"Not yet." But it wasn't the pamphlet itself. "Jesus' lost years were supposed to be in India. It makes perfect sense that this is what he was handing out. And if he is linked to this stuff, that paper may have answers or at least leads."

Jesus' lost years . . . it wandered through her head and linked up with something she'd heard before. The kills were connected. They couldn't *not* be. So the words probably were, too.

Then she remembered.

And they told the rest but they did not believe.

15

Donovan smelled Westerfield before he saw the man, and he wondered if his boss knew he could do that. Probably he suspected—Westerfield had worked with Wade for years. What had Wade told the man about their kind?

Donovan was still getting used to the idea that there were more of them out there than just his family. Wade had been an anchor of sanity linking Donovan to a past that was more due to his father than his breed. He hadn't realized until he met the other agent/wolf that he'd carried a heavy burden for a long time, wondering if he would turn out like his old man.

He'd been hoping Wade would be here today, expecting it actually. As Donovan and Eleri walked into the conference room, he saw that it was just them.

Eleri seemed well put together, but she was in full-scale professional mode. Donovan couldn't quite put his finger on it. He didn't think she was ever really unprofessional in a work situation, but there was something about Westerfield that Eleri seemed to answer to. She was more than happy bossing Donovan around, easily fulfilling her position as the senior partner, but she was all business in the meetings with West-erfield.

They hadn't seen him face-to-face since the day he pulled the quarter trick and Donovan wondered if Eleri was going to ask him to do it again. She might even demand.

Westerfield only nodded at them to take their seats, and both obediently sat. He didn't move much, except for the quarter that nearly always walked across his knuckles. Back and forth. Donovan had initially thought it was a fidgeting thing. He'd been wrong. "What have you got?"

There was a pause, a gap in the silence as Donovan thought over the real answer to that question. He was still checking through it in his head when Eleri said, "Nothing of value."

This didn't faze their agent in charge. "What do you have not of value?"

"Too many things." Subtle differences in her carriage showed defeat. Not deep seated, nothing she couldn't over-come, but right now Eleri was feeling the burn of the pieces not coming together.

Westerfield waited them out until Donovan started throwing out some of the bits of information and evidence they had amassed. Eleri chimed in then, listing more that didn't connect.

Westerfield only nodded when they mentioned Donovan had gone into the square and listened in on conversations. Donovan told how Eleri had seen the police officer with Ratz and Aziza with Dr. Gardiner.

Cooper Rollins had confirmed that he'd been in the office after Gardiner had died, but there was no remaining evidence and other than his own statement, there was nothing to tie him to the scene.

They tossed out fact after disconnected fact, until Wester-field finally leaned forward. "What actions have you taken?"

Donovan wasn't sure what it was, but he always felt judged

when speaking with Westerfield. Westerfield didn't offer indications of approval or dissent, and it made Donovan squirm. He hadn't squirmed under anyone's scrutiny in a long time. Donovan decided to make it end by telling. "We're investigating Vivian Dawson and canvassing the neighborhood for the Indian Man. We're following the pamphlet, since we now have confirmation he was handing them out. And we're hoping to get a GPS tap on Cooper Rollins' phone."

Was that enough? He wasn't sure.

"Do you think she can do it? Get to the man's phone and get it set up without getting caught?"

Eleri spoke up this time, resuming the lead role. "I don't know if she can complete the task. I believe she can save herself from getting caught, but as far as making it work, I think she's the only one who possibly can."

Westerfield nodded. Sometimes he added ideas, brought new intel to the table. Last time, Westerfield had given them curveballs and intel, but that's all there was. Neither Donovan nor Eleri had been with the unit long enough to know what normal was. If he paid attention to her experiences, 'normal' was different all over the FBI.

"So put it together." Westerfield's voice cut his thoughts.

"I'm not sure we have enough yet, sir." Eleri's voice was firm. It wasn't that she doubted herself, it was that she was scientific. Donovan knew this about her without a single thought otherwise. She was happy to speculate when it was called for, but she didn't seem to want to do it now.

"Guess."

"Do you have more intel for us?" she asked Westerfield, and Donovan almost smiled. "Are we missing anything?"

He'd never worked with anyone like this before. Never been part of a group other than for track in school, and that wasn't a team sport, not really. He and his dad had not only not been a team, they'd been at odds. But having Eleri put voice to what was in his head made him feel connected, a symbiosis he'd never experienced until now.

He pressed his hand flat on the table between them, hoping she'd understand that he meant he had her back.

A waft of air brought a faint scent he recognized. *Wade.*

The other agent must have been shut out of the meeting. He was in the hall or had been just a moment ago. Donovan tried not to let it show on his face.

"No more intel. In fact, I'm disturbed by the chain leading into the military." Though his voice didn't level any tonal change to indicate his perturbation, the quarter stopped walking. "Do you think it has to do with the black op that Rollins was discharged for?"

"I have no clue, sir." Eleri told him, sitting up straight, but when he didn't respond, she added, "But if it did, it would sure tie everything together neatly."

"Keep going." Westerfield prodded. "What would you guess if it were a game and it was 'guess or forfeit'?"

Eleri looked to Donovan and he spoke up. "The officer said 'and they came back and told the rest, but they did not believe' before he killed Ratz—"

"And you know this how?" Westerfield interrupted.

As Donovan's own anger flared, he watched Eleri's teeth clench. She'd been in the mental hospital the last time the burden got too great. Even Donovan himself had been pushing her, but the difference was he *believed* her. Every word. "Eleri."

Westerfield only nodded.

Apparently, that was good enough. But that judgment had come through again.

Donovan took up the slack, wishing he could pat his partner on the shoulder or give some sign of comfort, but this was neither the time nor the place, and he really had no clue how to do it. So he talked. "Aziza was quiet, but the Indian man was proselytizing 'The Lost Years' when Jesus was in India. So it would seem there's a religious angle to it."

Westerfield sighed. "There always is."

Eleri spoke up. "Are we the Religion Based Crimes Against Humanity division?"

This time Westerfield barked a short laugh, finally seeming human. "No. It's just turning out that way. You want a break from the zealots next case?"

"Yes, please." Eleri slumped.

Westerfield's quarter started moving again, a sure sign that his brain had turned to a different direction. "Which side do you think Cooper Rollins is on?"

"I have absolutely no guess on that one." Eleri shook her head. "He's a slippery bastard. Won't tell anything. Excellent at evading us. And he's totally under the gun of some serious PTSD. To the point where Dr. Gardiner was willing to treat him off the record. I think just to keep him off the streets."

Their boss stayed silent for a moment and Donovan waited for the next question to pop, but it didn't.

"See if you can get ahead of the next one. Let's see if we can get a handle on this before it becomes a media circus. So far no group is claiming this. I'm hoping to God it's not US military folks covering tracks on a deal gone bad."

You and me both, sir. But Donovan didn't say it.

"You want the good news?"

Eleri said yes, but Donovan just wondered what the hell the 'good news' could be. And would it only be 'good' by Westerfield's standards?

"You're in. You're unified and the two of you are staying together."

"What?" The word fell out of his mouth. Unprofessional. He might as well have said, "huh?"

Westerfield stood. The leaving part was good, but Donovan wanted to understand what the man had said. "You didn't know that you were on probation to this point. But you've been cleared. You're both going to stay in the NightShade division, and you've shown you can work together, taking advantage of each other's talents and, shall we say, 'special skills' to bring a case to its conclusion."

This time he managed to keep his mouth shut, but Donovan's brain was going. They'd been a probationary team? All this time?

Westerfield must have caught his confusion, or maybe he just read Eleri, whose look was plain as day.

"It's standard for a division like ours."

A division like ours? There were other divisions like NightShade?

"You waited this long to clear us?" Donovan didn't mean to seem ungrateful, but he was ungrateful.

"Not me. The higher ups."

"Who?" Eleri pushed as Donovan frowned.

"Trust me, you don't want to know."

COOPER ROLLINS WALKED the streets of downtown Los Angeles, checking the square corners for enemies, looking into store fronts for shady deals, and wondering what he'd come to. Though he had a solid sense of purpose and a deep-seated belief in what needed to be done, he did not have a good grip on who he really was anymore.

When he was in the teams, he'd been the guy you could count on. Even among the guys you knew had your back. He was smart, though not the smartest. He was good with languages, though he didn't have Kellen's gift there. He was decent with creative wound care—the only kind in the field a lot of the time. He was passable at making friends. He was the non-specialist. Never the best, but good at all.

And he always had your back. He was always mentally and physically strong.

Until the last mission.

Cooper hadn't realized that PTSD could come on like his did.

He'd been in so much combat, seen so much. He'd watched towns get bombed, seen people he didn't know run screaming. He'd killed more than just one of them. He'd seen a friend die from an IED: one second he walked along, the next he flew in more parts and directions than was human. He'd seen a friend get shot while they'd been talking. Cooper still didn't know why it wasn't him. And he'd held his friend, unable to stop the bleeding from the artery, unable to hold his life inside him, and he'd humped the body back home for the family Cooper had never met. For the people he'd never seen, who loved his friend as much as he did.

He'd never lost it.

But that last day he'd cracked wide open. Some of his men had turned on them, and he'd shot some of his own. A few had disappeared into the surrounding landscape. And Cooper suddenly realized just how serious it had gotten.

He was pinned under fire with dead friends and live traitors. Disturbing as it was, he still didn't really know which was which.

Did the guys who fled do so because they thought *he* was the traitor? Did they flee to cover their own transgressions? Were they dead? Several of them had hiked back to base—the only course left—not knowing who was traitor and who wasn't. Had he shot his friends and helped his enemies?

And he didn't know if he'd been on the right side of things. That wounded him even deeper than the bullet had. They'd dug the metal out of his side and stitched him up. No organ damage, just a scar. But no one had been able to dig out the damage to his faith.

Cooper Rollins had always been a believer. He'd joined because it was a good fit for a patriotic adrenaline junkie. Always the smartest and the noisiest in his classes, he'd been excited to no longer be outstanding amongst his new peers. He'd learned to be quiet, too.

So he went down the paved sidewalk purposefully making noises. It wouldn't do to stay silent when no one else was. Blending in wasn't about not being seen; it was about being seen and then forgotten as quickly as possible.

He'd come here two days ago, talked to the man Aziza had sent. This time he was supposed to meet with Alya. Unfortunately, he had to appear at the meeting site and wait.

Cooper wasn't right on time. He was early with plenty of time to check the place out. But if he wasn't in place when Alya came by—if he wasn't clearly visible—she wouldn't stop. He wouldn't get a second chance.

Turning into the front of one of the old edifices, Cooper entered as though he knew what he was doing. The desk guarded the stairs, but it wasn't much of a task for Cooper to stride into the restrooms at the back of the lobby, then wait for a moment when the desk agent had his back turned. Cooper was climbing the steps silently, looking like he had permission.

On the fifth floor, Cooper finally found an office where he could get over to the corner and look down on the meeting site.

Fifteen minutes to meeting time. Seven minutes until time to head out. Standing at the plate glass window, his arms folded across his chest as though he were simply thinking, Cooper counted and cataloged the people he saw.

Given the corner, he had a view down each of the streets, and on the third one he was analyzing he saw Alya. She hung back, walking slowly, her non-distinct brown backpack slung over one shoulder. She was ready for his meeting, but she was talking to a man with dark red hair.

The jolt to his system surprised Cooper. The low pull of

base fear tugged in his gut, and he felt his insides start to collapse with the pull of the episode.

No.

He would not loop.

He was *here*. Now.

His jaw clenched and he pushed his lips together before remembering to purse them and push air out. He concentrated on his breathing—in, tight, through his nose, out with pressure through those pursed lips. He reached out, tapping nearby objects until his hand slapped one that had a distinctly non-military, non-Middle Eastern shape. The curve of the polished wood ladder-back on the chair he'd grabbed anchored him in the US. In downtown Los Angeles, looking over the street corner that he now had four minutes to get to.

Still fighting a past that wanted to take him over, he told himself no one was shooting at him as he raced down the stairs. He reminded himself that the enemy wasn't present. But he wasn't very convincing. If the redhead was Ken Kellen, then he didn't know what was happening.

The steps flew beneath his feet, as he never considered waiting on an elevator. He dashed past the guard at the desk, only seeing that he elicited strange looks. Stealth was not his strong suit right now, and his priority was twofold: find out if Alya was talking to Kellen, and stay in the present. An episode now would ruin everything.

He fought to hold onto his sanity as he ran.

Hitting the warm air as he pushed out of the building onto the street, Cooper let the heat resist his forward momentum and bring him to a slower pace. He let the humidity remind him he wasn't in Bagram or Fallujah. His breathing slowed, too, no longer the deep inhales of a man who'd run three flights of steps with the devil at his heels.

A message dinged his phone and he pulled it from his back pocket. *Alya.*

"R U ready?"

He hated the text-speak, thought German swear words were a prettier language, but none of that registered in his features.

"Y" He could speak the ugly language like a native teen. And he only briefly stopped to consider that this shorthand was native to neither him nor Alya.

He looked down the street, but she approached alone.

Wanting to look like he was doing nothing other than checking his phone, he hit a few buttons and once again had to push his emotions down.

Son of a bitch! His brain took off, a string of swears rolling but not released. *How had he missed this?*

His phone had a tracking program on it. It appeared to be broadcasting to somewhere. But there wasn't time to fix it.

If it was Alya and her people who put it there, he had to leave it.

Shitshitshit.

But he smiled slightly and nodded as they passed on the street slowing just enough for her to look up and raise her eyebrows in question.

Cooper answered in low tones that no one around them would hear.

"Fracture Five."

16

E leri watched the square, waiting for Walter. Walter stayed inside the chain link, oblivious to Eleri's presence or at least putting up a good show of it.

Eleri didn't know what to make of it. She thought she and Walter had garnered a good rapport during the interview and the subsequent breakfast on the FBI's dime. But she hadn't seen nor heard from the woman in a few days. Walter wasn't specifically supposed to check in, so maybe she should set up something a little more formal.

But this morning she'd gotten a ping on their tech. An email with a link from Walter Reed Medical Center, in Bethesda. Somehow Walter had managed to create an email that was from the actual medical center or at least she'd made it look that way. Given their conviction that it was from the veteran, Donovan had clicked the included 'your medical records' link and been directed to a map that tracked Cooper Rollins' whereabouts.

Eleri had struck gold, and she wondered if she could thank Walter and ask for more. But she couldn't if she couldn't contact the woman.

Walk right up to the square and rattle the chain link? No. Word would get back to Rollins and that would be the end of it. So Eleri had to catch Walter when she was out and about. But it had already been about four hours of daylight and Walter hadn't moved.

Eleri sighed. Why hadn't she given the woman her number? Gotten a number? She could have been napping, drinking, or at least helping Donovan and Vasquez research past local deaths.

No. She was sitting in her car, feeding the meter and watching a group of homeless vets like a perv, or like the FBI. At least she actually was the second. She put her book back up in front of her face, remembering to turn pages so she didn't look like she was doing what she was doing.

It took another hour in a car that she wasn't able to turn on, reading a book she couldn't read. Eleri at least had the windows down and the weather was nice. That was L.A.for you, the temperature was perfect, but you couldn't see very far with the pollution. It sure didn't have a clean air smell like FoxHaven or Bell Point Farm.

Eventually Walter left the square, heading in the opposite direction from where Eleri sat. So she jumped up, left the car and attempted to look casual as she tried to figure out where to go to cut Walter off.

Though Eleri made it to the next intersection with amazing speed, and she should have seen Walter down the street, the woman was gone. Jesus, Eleri was good at what she did. She could sneak through the woods and raid a home as part of an assault team. She could crack a suspect with a cup of coffee and a well-timed question. But clearly she could not tail a Special Forces operative.

Eleri gave up and headed back to the car. Half a block away, she spotted Walter leaning against the driver's side door, her arms crossed as she waited. Eleri asked, "So, did you make me wait four hours on purpose?"

It wasn't what she should have said, but dammit, that had been a long time.

"Four hours? No." Walter shook her head. "You weren't here that long, were you?"

"Yes. This spot." Eleri pointed, and Walter seemed to take the hint and move out from in front of the driver's door. "Come with me?"

A nod, and Walter gracefully made her way around the front of the car, all economy of motion, despite the missing limbs. As Walter slid in and buckled herself, she commented, "Well, you're better than I thought if you were here that long. I only found you an hour ago."

"And you made me wait?" Eleri now found it comical rather than rude. Eleri now had the air conditioning on and was on the way to the Bureau office. That definitely made a difference.

"Ozzy was talking crap. If I'd interrupted him and acted like I had somewhere better to be, he would have been suspicious." Walter looked out the window, seeming to note that Eleri hadn't driven her back by the square where someone might see. "So what's this about?"

"I need to hire you." Eleri heard her own voice and found it too blunt. So she started over. "The FBI would like to hire you—"

"Oh, I'm no agent." Walter shook her head.

The laugh that came out of Eleri's mouth surprised even her. She really liked this woman. "You'd have to pass classes at Quantico first. Not that you couldn't. No, we're looking to hire you as a consultant. You got the tracer app onto Cooper Rollins' phone—great job on the email, by the way."

Walter only nodded.

"We'd like you to do some more, but at this point, we have to actually hire you. I can't report that I used a civilian for favors."

"I'm hardly a civilian."

Eleri grinned again. "Though I whole-heartedly agree with you, the Bureau does not. You are not employed by the Feebs, nor agency-trained, thus you are a civilian and I cannot keep asking you to do possibly dangerous tasks for us."

"Tagging a phone isn't dangerous."

"Tagging Cooper Rollins is." Eleri countered. "Clearly, you're better at following him than we are. We have a situation that may be terrorist linked—" normally, she never would have said that, but Walter had figured that part out long ago, so it wasn't news. "And you have a decent idea about Cooper. We need to know if he's with them? Infiltrating them? We have three dead already. Once some group claims it, it'll become a media circus. Honestly, I'm surprised it hasn't happened already."

"Oh, no worries. We're currently electing a new mayor, and thus the PD is all screwed up. A corrupt election is a good lead story, so no one is really digging for more. You lucked out, there." Walter looked at her hand, not as a nervous gesture, but almost to focus her thoughts.

"Oh. That's good to know." But she steered the conversation back. "I can take you to the office and fill out the paperwork now. You'll be on a need-to-know basis, so you won't be in on the whole case, but we'll have assignments. And you'll be paid."

Walter smiled. "I don't need to be paid."

That gave Eleri's heart a little shove. Walter was good. As a wounded vet, she could have wound up in a bad way. But she was still capable, and at this point the handicap was hardly even that. Walter was just a little different than before.

"You have to be paid. It's a legal thing." Eleri liked that. "Maybe you can put it toward opening your own PI business."

Something in the tilt of Walter's head made Eleri think the woman was surprised she'd remembered.

They pulled into the Bureau with Walter agreeing to the deal, then seeming pleased with the pay rate, then trying to hide that smile. Inside of the hour, they had paperwork filled out and Lucy Fisher was the newest part-time, need-only consultant in the L.A. branch. Donovan shook her hand and welcomed her to the position. Then they immediately set her to task tailing Cooper as much as she could without getting caught, or having the others around her become suspicious of her missing time.

She refused a ride back downtown and headed out the front of the building with nothing more than she'd come in with, except a job.

Eleri watched her go, then joined Donovan and Marina digging through local death records. Four hours later, she got a text from Walter. Eleri looked up at the other two.

"Cooper isn't carrying his phone everywhere. He knows."

DONOVAN GROWLED low in his throat as he padded down the street after Eleri. It wasn't a real growl, not indicative of anything other than that he didn't want to be walking down the sidewalk at Eleri's side like a good puppy. Once in a while, random people tried to reach out and pet him, but not often— he was relatively menacing looking.

The pavement was rough under his paws, his fingertips sensitive like a human's, thus his front feet in this form were more sensitive than the hard pads of a wolf's. Maybe that's why he was so keen on running in the woods. There was something about the variegated feel of dirt and branches, crunching leaves and soft loam. Here, it was just rough concrete square after square.

She paused and looked down at him, questioning.

Donovan understood, *where had Cooper Rollins gone?* He stepped forward, letting Eleri pace him, but taking the lead at the same time.

The view of her from down here was interesting. Her posture was straight, he'd noticed that before when he was upright, but from this angle it looked more like something she worked for than something that came naturally. Her shoulders appeared broader from this angle, her cheeks and lips rounder. For the first time, Donovan noticed that she wasn't completely Anglo.

It startled him. He knew she was Kentucky blueblood. Hell, she had more than one family home and they all had names, like "Patton Hall" and "FoxHaven." So he'd just assumed she was about as white as Wonderbread. But from here, he could see she wasn't, and it startled him a little. The color in her skin wasn't a tan, but a tone. His eyes blinked. The straight, reddish-gold hair and the pale freckles made people assume what wasn't really there. Eleri was part African American. He blinked again. A good part, if what he was seeing was true.

She tapped him on the shoulder, breaking his startled forensic musings.

He had work to do; he'd have to ask her later. He inhaled, taking in the scent of metal from the jewelry shop they'd passed. There was a food truck around the corner, selling questionable pizza and hoagies. The man walking about three people in front of them hadn't bathed in over five days, not shocking though, given his attire. And Cooper Rollins, who exuded alpha hormones he probably didn't know he had, had been here just a few minutes ago. It didn't hurt that he was eating a sandwich he'd bought from a different food truck a few blocks back. The scent of shawarma made him easier to track.

Donovan turned his head, so Eleri could look like she was walking her dog and not the other way around. She took the hint and the corner and quietly said, "Got him."

Though Donovan wasn't tall enough now to see very far, Eleri had the man in her sights. *Good.* They padded along, hanging back, wondering what the hell he was up to.

Thanks to the newly hired Walter Reed, they had a lot of intel on Cooper. Within twenty-four hours, she'd located his apartment—a tenement not far from downtown and shabby enough for him to keep odd hours and odder friends. Walter also followed him once while his phone stayed home. Then tipped them off this morning that Cooper was on the move, though once again his tracker was not. He was only carrying it sometimes, so he looked like he hadn't discovered the tap, but clearly he had.

Eleri and Donovan had come quickly, and Eleri had tagged out with Walter. Then Donovan easily tailed her and joined up several blocks later. There was always the chance that Walter would follow them and find Eleri and the new "dog" clearly working in tandem, but it was a chance they had to take. Eleri couldn't track Cooper like Donovan could. And Donovan couldn't wander downtown midday like this without a clear human escort. It was bad enough to feel like a pet dog. It would be worse to know what the inside of animal control was like.

Cooper was on foot, walking the route. It was lucky for them, and according to Marina Vasquez, unusual in LA. But given that Cooper appeared to be tracking Aziza today, and this group seemed to be localized here, foot traffic was easier. Donovan recognized the irony of tracking someone who was tracking someone else.

While Aziza wandered in and out of various shops, Cooper waited her out. Then Cooper would duck in or follow her. Eleri made notes, texting Marina the names and locations of the buildings and periodically getting messages back from the other agent. She would softly tell Donovan what she heard back, after the first time where she started to hold the phone down to him. He could read it, but that would draw some disturbing attention if anyone noticed. Luckily Eleri caught herself before he had to try to point it out. She'd put her hand over her mouth as though coughing and said, "Sorry." Then she'd laughed outright.

Cooper turned another corner, and Donovan caught Aziza's scent closer. He wondered if she had any clue Cooper was following her. Or that they were here.

If the young woman was smart, some of her stops were random. If anyone in her unit was smart, they'd taught her to do that. If she was meeting contacts at each of her stop points, then they were all in some deep shit. Even if she wasn't, he could actually smell Eleri's growing concern as Cooper ducked up a set of hidden stairs to another tenement.

Donovan sniffed the doorway and gave two short grunts. One for Cooper having been there, the second for Aziza. Both were up the stairs, and Eleri and Donovan couldn't follow. This wasn't a business, it was housing. That meant some kind of private meeting, likely more than just a passing of information.

Cooper probably wasn't meeting Aziza, since it seemed he was furtively trailing her. Walter had assured them that though he had figured out his phone was tapped; he probably hadn't traced it to Walter or to the FBI. Even though he was Special Forces, Rollins would have to have put a lot of little pieces together for that one. Thus, he probably suspected Aziza and her group. It was reasonable to think he would carry it to meet with them, if the meeting were legit. That way they wouldn't know that he knew his phone was traced.

At the least, it was a mess, leaving Donovan with nothing more than some good logical speculation.

The two of them wandered the block, waiting. Eleri bought a corner sandwich—one that Donovan had to approve. The carts were hit or miss. She fed him half of it in bites and scraps. So they waited nearly an hour before Cooper came back out first. No sign of Aziza.

They were taking up the tail, far enough back, when Donovan smelled it.

No!

He growled, low and even, getting Eleri's attention.

"What?" she looked down at him, her brows pulled together, the gravity of the situation not clear to her yet.

His nose was going off in a way he'd never felt before, and he didn't know what it meant exactly, but it was bad.

She started to follow Rollins, still looking down at Donovan.

He didn't want to bark. He growled at her again, and was reaching for her pants leg when he caught the faint scent again.

Fuckfuckfuck.

It was everywhere. Down each of the side streets. It wasn't just that they were close, they were closing in. They *knew* he was here, and they were coming. It wasn't a welcoming committee either.

At least Eleri had stopped, her head leaning down, her look now very concerned. "Donovan?"

She shouldn't have used his name. God forbid someone wonder why her dog and her partner shared a name, but that was not his primary concern right now.

"We're going to lose Cooper." She whispered the last part, shaking her head.

Finally, he remembered. *The kill switch.* They had a kill switch.

Donovan pressed his paw down on top of her foot. Hard.

Kill. Abort. Now.

He did it again.

Suddenly, Eleri got it. She turned, then turned again, "Where? Which way?"

He turned a short circle.

"Anywhere?"

Nowhere.

He moved his head slowly side to side. It didn't do any good to look like he was saying 'no' and the smell was overwhelming now. The shit was about to hit the fan. Only he didn't know how. He tapped her foot again, once, twice, until she looked up and started scanning the area for threats. She didn't see it, but she did reach back and almost casually unsnapped the holster on her weapon.

Donovan turned and saw the man coming down the street. He was headed right for them. Donovan gave a small growl for Eleri. She looked. "Him?"

Donovan was already looking another direction, another man, thinner, scruffier, same direct gaze. Another growl, another turn. People on the street were starting to give the two of them a berth. Probably a good idea.

From the third direction, a woman. Her gaze was more serene and more deadly. Donovan could smell her; she was the alpha. By the time she arrived, three other men were flanking the two of them and Eleri was on high alert.

Bless her, she looked cool as a little southern cucumber, but Donovan could smell it on her.

So could they. She wasn't fooling any of them. And Eleri was the only one who didn't know it.

17

E
leri paused for a moment, her whole system alert. She very calmly looked each of them in the eye, except for the man who was now squatting down next to Donovan. In the periphery, she could see the man smiling at her partner, and her partner baring his teeth, but making no sound in response.

Donovan no longer pushed on her foot—their agreed upon signal for danger. It was too late.

This was one of those situations most people would be uncomfortable in, but might have a hard time pinpointing exactly why. Eleri had no such problems. She and her partner were surrounded. The four had come in from different directions, targeted the two of them, and neatly boxed them in. All four managed to be just inside the boundary of her personal space at the same time.

She had a gun, training, and a partner who would bite the shit out of them. Eleri waited.

Sure enough, one of them spoke.

"That's a nice dog you got." It was the woman. One woman, three men.

Eleri nodded, but didn't speak. Something was very off here. These guys looked more like street thugs than terrorists.

Her initial thought had been that she and Donovan had been made. Aziza had spotted them, or the group was smart and tailed their own people to be certain no one else was. So she'd initially figured this for backlash.

But if that were the case, why not mug her like someone had done to Vivian Dawson? Just shoot her on the spot. No one should pay that much attention to Donovan.

The man squatting on the ground was still staring at Donovan as though studying him.

Eleri breathed in deeply.

Dog. She smelled dog. Clearly, she didn't have anywhere near the sense that Donovan did. Just as she thought again, *no one should pay that much attention to Donovan,* the woman curled her lip, revealing a long canine.

Holy shit.

This was a pack.

With a slow movement of her head, the lead female let her short, gorgeous gray hair ruffle in the wind. Her nose flared as she inhaled the scents in front of her. She knew Eleri was human, and she was simply letting Eleri know that she was 'lesser.' Her voice was butter and gravel. "You walk him like a dog?"

"Sometimes." Eleri shrugged, playing it bold. Not sure what else to do, other than stay very alert.

The man still at Donovan's eye level glared at him. "You let her?"

Donovan growled. Eleri wondered if they could understand that as a yes or no answer.

Without moving her eyes, Eleri checked the group. The woman was clearly the alpha. *Interesting.* She seemed the most aggressive of the pack, too. She leaned forward, showed her teeth. She was the one Eleri had to watch.

Eleri switched tactics. "What's your name?"

Her pale blue eyes bore into Eleri. "We don't let your kind rule us."

A threat? More than they'd already done by holding her here?

"We're just out today. He's his own person." *Person* might have been the wrong word. Eleri had harbored hopes that they just wanted to know that Donovan was okay and not some dog-slave. That was silly. They didn't ask, they demanded, they threatened first. She tried again, "No leash or anything."

The bitch licked her teeth. "So give him to us."

Oh, no way in hell. Eleri just smiled and shook her head.

Before she saw what was happening, the two men beside their woman closed ranks as the woman's face pushed forward. Her teeth extended even further from her jaw and her shoulders rolled back, her neck growing thicker.

This was the transformation that Donovan hadn't wanted her to see. This was what she'd observed in his father, the speed and aggression of the change, fueled by rage, the night she'd dreamed of Donovan's past. This woman was getting ready to bite Eleri in the face.

The quick action was punctuated by an attack growl from Donovan that was sharply truncated. The man on the ground had wrapped human arms around him and was effectively holding him back.

The two on the sides were blocking people on the street from seeing what the woman was doing. They'd created a system for Eleri to be effectively attacked by a wolf while no one saw anything.

For a moment, her brain flashed forward. If she died of a bite, Donovan would go down for it. His only hope would be to run, and these people were holding him there. This was no longer a fight. It was a murder.

And it wouldn't be Eleri's.

The gray-haired woman's teeth came out further. At her sides, her long fingernails blackened into claws, ready in case the teeth weren't enough.

Holding still until the last moment, Eleri flung her left arm up, smashing her elbow into the side of the woman's changing face.

Though "Gray's" cheekbone took the hit painfully, so did Eleri's arm. Bitch had a thick face. The men closed ranks, grabbing at her, but Eleri was ready.

She dropped to the ground, out of the air they grasped at, and as their hands quickly followed her down, she took advantage. Grabbing each of them by one arm, she yanked as hard as she could and scrambled the fuck out of the way as the two came crashing down into each other, their momentum their own enemy now.

Facing the now exposed half-wolf, Eleri popped up, rushing her, the only option to take the offensive. Stepping hard on the back of one of the downed men, she launched herself at Gray, one hand out, the other behind her, under her jacket.

The momentum gave her power. Gray outweighed her, but she was starting to stumble backward even as Eleri came forward. Maybe she was afraid because she'd been exposed, but Eleri was pissed as hell and not to be messed with. The fingers on her outstretched hand reached Gray's neck, but she didn't squeeze. Dog necks were thick; dogs were hard to strangle. Eleri had been reading up.

Instead, Eleri dug her fingers into the muscle, pushing on nerves and arteries. A gurgle escaped Gray's mouth, even as her face and neck pulled back, became human just in time for her head to bounce off the pavement. Eleri switched grip and just used the hand to hold her down.

Gray got mad—or frightened, or something—and popped her shoulder, using her greater weight to advantage and rolled Eleri off. Now she was the one with her back on the concrete, with Gray's hands on her shoulders, pinning her to the sidewalk.

That was stupid. Clearly Gray liked to dog fight, rather than human fight. And, exposed, she didn't have the option.

Just as the woman growled again, Eleri brought up her free hand, the one that had reached behind her and now held her gun. She pushed it under Gray's chin, then smiled at her own advantage.

Gray grinned back. Her men towering over them again, guarding the fight and their leader. Off to the side, the other man still wrapped his arms around Donovan in a hold that was effectively chaining him.

The woman didn't budge from the gun under her chin, but commented slickly, "You need silver bullets for me."

Jabbing the gun harder, Eleri countered, "No, I don't. *Bitch*."

Gray glared, but Eleri kept going. Though her shoulders were pinned, she could move her arm, and she reached into her pocket before the woman could stop her. The woman was growling over her when Eleri flipped open her leather wallet with practiced ease.

"I'm FBI. And so is he." She moved her eyes to Donovan. "We know exactly what you are. And now we know *where* you are."

It didn't work. It only made Gray angrier. "I will kill you!"

She reared back, twisting her head away from the barrel of the gun, ready to shred Eleri in her nearly defenseless position on the ground.

Eleri was fucked. She didn't want to show the gun to the people around them. It was bad enough she was in the middle of a scene like this while she was trying to be covert, dammit! She was pissed as hell, and this breach was going to cost other people their lives even if it didn't cost Eleri and Donovan.

Something snapped in her, and she reared up off the pavement, her own primal growl coming at the woman.

Gray must not have expected it, because she leapt back of her own accord, her face twisted in fear. The two men blocking the women in also abruptly stepped back, as though the sight of Eleri mad was scarier than anything they were. The one effectively caging Donovan dropped suddenly back onto his butt and he scrambled to join the others.

Donovan rushed to her side, making a line of defense the best he could and growling at them. The two groups faced each other, the dog pack suddenly wary.

Eleri stepped forward, into Gray's space, and for some reason, they let her. For a moment, their eyes darted to each other, questioning. She locked her gaze with the leader and heard her own voice, deep with anger and the gravel of her convictions.

"Run along, *puppy.*"

Slowly, they stepped back, then one by one they turned and began walking away, the encounter ended in the same almost-casual fashion in which it had started.

Shaken, Eleri held herself together long enough to look around. Several passersby watched, but none had stepped forward. Probably a good thing. Not a fight a random hero would want to get involved in. Besides, it had been a disagreement to start with, she'd been caged, but not hit. Then, when moves were thrown, it had probably all been over with faster than anyone else could have jumped in.

The few people who paid attention waited for her to nod that she was okay. Her gun was no longer in her hand and, reaching back, she felt that she'd automatically reholstered it. Good for her.

Turning, she made sure Donovan was at her heels, then blended back into the crowd. Cooper Rollins was gone; Aziza was gone.

Hopefully none of them had seen that clusterfuck.

Her day was screwed. She now knew there were wolves everywhere. And apparently, they didn't like her.

DONOVAN HAD BEEN ITCHY. Inside his skin. He'd been twitchy, frustrated, and needing to get out. He'd known what he needed, he just hadn't known how to do it.

While Eleri walked into the kitchen and started on a hard cider, she called Westerfield and asked what the protocol was for writing up such an incident.

Donovan only twitched more.

Sure, they'd been assaulted. Not by anyone related to their case. Still, the idea that there might be a registry of his kind? That did not sit well. So while Eleri unwound with the odd combination of alcohol and paperwork, Donovan did something he'd never done before. He called a friend.

Wade answered on the first ring. "Thought I'd hear from you soon. Didn't know if you'd ever had that before."

"What was that?" Donovan shook his head as though that might settle the swirling parts. It didn't. "That was a *thing*?"

He could almost hear Wade nodding, adjusting his glasses. While Donovan was as much into science as anyone could be, it had been a haven maybe more than a home. Wade had embraced it all the way. The man loved Minecraft, comic cons, and Star Trek—though only certain portions of the series. But for all his differences, Wade was also Donovan's only sane source of information. "Around the world there are solo folks like you and me, and then there are some . . . packs, for lack of a better term."

"Are they all judgmental assholes?" That had just slipped out. Maybe these were Wade's people. Maybe Donovan shouldn't latch on too tightly, too fast to his new friend. He'd done that once in middle school and it had backfired badly. Most of his attachments had.

"The packs? Yeah, mostly. They're like gangs, but with teeth instead of guns." Wade was pacing; Donovan could hear it through the line.

Inside the house, Eleri's keyboard clacked softly, making a white noise to his sensitive ears. He didn't mind the sounds. For a long time, he'd just assumed the other kids could hear what he could. That they could tell what he said from two rooms away, or down the hallway. It had taken a while to shake the paranoia. Today, it had all come flooding back.

He felt bad for stealing Eleri's friend. She and Wade went back almost a decade, as far as Donovan knew. But she'd only just recently learned that Wade was something more like him.

"Are there a lot of these packs?" *Was this going to be a likely occurrence?* Going undercover as his wolf-self had seemed obvious, relatively easy once they worked out a few logistics. He couldn't ask questions, but no one worried about what they said in front of him. This new problem—that others would sense him and come after him—it wasn't anything he'd even considered a possibility.

That they would come after Eleri was something he wasn't ready to deal with. She was small and lacking teeth or jaws. Although, today, she'd surprised both Donovan and the others.

"The packs are more prevalent in big cities and out rural where they're the only ones." Wade was explaining. "I think in the cities they seem to be in the poorer areas—forming for the same reasons other gangs do. No money, no prospects, and too much power."

Donovan didn't like that idea.

Wade continued, "Not a lot of lobomau in the suburbs."

"A lot of what?" Donovan wasn't sure if he'd heard correctly.

Wade laughed, and Donovan could imagine him in his plaid button down and khakis, somehow far more comfortable with what they were than Donovan had ever been. "*Lobomau.* Sorry, it's a Portuguese term, literally 'bad wolf.' That's what I've always heard the gangs referred to as: Lobomau."

His head swam. There was so much more out there than he'd imagined. He hadn't even known it went beyond his own family. There was the legend of the werewolf, and his father had embraced it, but never said anything about others. Aidan Heath wasn't the kind of man you asked questions. He was the kind of man who picked his son up in the middle of the night and said they had to move. New town, sometimes a new name. Donovan didn't ask. To this day, he'd never gone back and investigated. What he already knew was enough to make his sleep uneasy.

In college, he'd come to realize that the legends didn't have anything to do with his father. He made the logical leap that the legends existed for people to explain odd people like him. But he never bothered to seek any others out, and he wouldn't have imagined getting assaulted by a full pack on the open streets in Los Angeles.

"Are you squirrely?" Wade asked. "Do you need to run?"

"Yes." It was a relief being asked, not having to ask. It was a relief to know that it must sometimes happen to Wade, that maybe it didn't make Donovan inferior at the thing he'd thought for so long only he was. "But how? It's a city."

"There's always a way. We'll get Eleri to drive us up to Griffith Park. She can stand guard. It's good to have a normal standing watch."

Donovan snorted. Eleri was hardly what he would call 'normal.'

"I'll check." Donovan put his hand over the mic on the phone, as though that made a difference. Just another thing he did in the guise of 'normalcy.'

Donovan made his plans and Eleri popped up, wearing jeans and a jacket, the hood pulled up, her hands shoved in her pockets, the outline of the Bureau issue firearm plain as day along her back.

Wade showed up about half an hour later and the itch still had a good control on Donovan. He couldn't explain it or reach it; it was just a desire to change, the need to run, to stretch. And doing so in this form was helpful, but not really what would help. In the end, they wound their way up the hill, Donovan getting closer and closer to wanting to crawl out of his own skin as they approached the observatory. At least there were trees here. Not his South Carolina national forest, not his miles of space, but something. Dirt, shrubs, animals.

They parked, stationed Eleri at the edge of the woods, and thanked her for waiting. The two men wandered a short distance into the trees, each heading a separate direction, Wade seeming to understand that Donovan was not, and probably never would be, a pack animal.

Donovan yelled back, "El, if you hide our clothes, I'm going to . . . well, you won't like it."

He heard Eleri shuffling around at the edge of the woods. She'd done this for him before—let him run. Last time it had been with a purpose, he'd even been wearing a GPS. This time, he cocked his neck, popping muscles with practiced ease.

His shoulder blades flexed upward, the muscles there were morphing his ribcage, slightly altering its shape. He rolled his hips, repositioning the femurs in their sockets and stretched his limbs out, letting them pull back into their new form. That was all just contortion. Some people could fold their legs behind their necks, he could fold into a wolf. But the flood of hormones that came with it was unique to his group—or maybe just to him.

It felt like relief. Like cold, low level adrenaline. It made his hair stand on end, and when that happened, it ruffed up like fur.

Taking a deep breath in through his now expanded nasal

chamber, he could smell oxygen from the trees. The sharp grade of sulfur products in the air. Faint overlays of the people who tread here earlier in the day, and Wade, off to his left, giving off his own burn of adrenaline.

Donovan padded over to see his friend. His mouth was now locked with his mandible and maxilla pushing his face out, speech no longer possible.

Wade looked at him for a moment through dark hazel wolf eyes, then turned, running headlong into the woods. Stretching for the first time in too long, Donovan followed, running until his breath was heaving, and odd muscles burned with new use. They explored the edges of the area, never venturing too far out of the trees.

In some places, the woods provided cover right up to the backs of houses at the edge of the suburban sprawl. It others, the ground ran dry, leaving wide gaps between them and the human population. In some directions the space went on nearly forever, trees growing farther between, gullies waiting to be crossed. And everywhere, the low tang of coyotes.

It was a few hours later that the two returned to their original spots. Despite the time, Donovan found his clothes untouched. Suddenly thinking of Eleri, waiting on them, standing guard with nothing to do, just so he could burn off the itch, he changed quickly. Shaking out his pants, he pulled them on, then popped into his shirt. He was sliding now-dirty feet into his shoes when he emerged to find Eleri standing against a tree at the edge of the woods, her arms crossed, her thoughts clearly far away.

She turned, shaking away whatever she'd been musing as they emerged from the tree line. For a moment, her eyes caught the light, and he saw it again. She'd seemed far away.

"Did we leave you too long? What were you thinking about?"

"That encounter today, the whole thing just made me mad."

Again, the light caught her eyes and Donovan stilled, wondering if Wade saw what he did.

Standing there, at the edge of the woods, his need for freedom finally sated for a while, he broached another concerning topic.

"Eleri, what did you do when that woman had you pinned?"

Frowning suddenly, she turned to him, clearly confused. "I kicked her ass. What do you mean?"

He shook his head. "No, you were good, but she had the advantage, then you got in her face and they all backed off. What did you do?"

She laughed. "I got mad as hell. Showed her I wasn't going to back down. She understood that, I guess."

Donovan took a deep breath and looked to Wade. Their friend had a look on his face that told Donovan maybe Wade had seen the glint in her eyes, too. Like a lingering remnant from the fight.

"Eleri, I don't know how to tell you this, but . . ." Donovan let the words trail off. He really didn't know how to tell her. "You scared them off, because when you got good and pissed, well your eyes . . ."

"My eyes?" She looked at him oddly. She really had no idea what she'd done.

He tried again. "El, your eyes went bright . . . black."

18

E leri was grateful they were men now and she wasn't stuck with two dogs, the only conversation one sided. There were words swimming in her head, needing clarification. But not quite yet. She started her conversation more casually. "Did you have a good run?"

Donovan looked lighter, more tired, but less stressed. It wouldn't last long. She'd just been standing here, waiting, daydreaming, and the words had just come to her. Since they could have come from no other place, no other connections, she had to assume that they had something to do with Cooper Rollins.

Eleri sat in the back seat and waited quietly as they wound their way through streets that were miraculously clear. Despite the dead of night, there was still traffic. People walked the sidewalks, though they were few and far between. Some slept in the nooks of business doors, others worked the corners, the warm night letting them all stay out.

As they crossed Vine, she finally spoke up. "What's Fracture Five?"

"*What?*" Apparently Wade's mouth and feet worked concurrently, because he hit the brakes despite the fact there was no real reason to stop.

Eleri threw her hands up to keep from slamming into the back of Donovan's seat. It was only okay because Donovan was doing the same thing to the dash.

With the car completely stopped in the middle of the street, Wade turned and looked into the back at her. "I'm a *consultant*. I'm not supposed to be involved in this shit any more. Is that what this is?"

As the lone other vehicle on the street honked at them, she wondered if he was going to put them out of the car. Eleri eyed the neighborhood. Relatively clean during the day, it looked less than stellar at one in the morning. Looking back at him, she repeated, "What's Fracture Five?"

Wade started driving. He muttered under his breath, but he didn't answer. He bitched about answering Westerfield's call. He let roll a soft string of swear words, starting with the usual and getting downright creative as he went.

Donovan looked over his shoulder at her, then back at the road as though checking that they were still headed in the right direction. By the time Wade pulled his car into the driveway of their tiny rental house and turned the engine off, he still hadn't answered them.

Eleri was starting to climb out, but finally Wade stopped her. "Five Fractures?"

She shook her head and switched the words back. "Fracture Five."

They sat in the car for a moment, Wade trying to figure out what to say, Eleri and Donovan waiting.

"I got out of Terrorism for a reason." Wade's words seemed resigned. Like cops, they often referred to their units by an incomplete but understood name. Eleri hadn't known he was ever in the Terrorism division. And she hadn't been entirely confident that's what this case was about.

Up until now, they had been questioning terrorist activity. They had illegal arms deals, but no one to pin it on. They had American soldiers involved. And people of three nationalities. But Wade seemed convinced now that it was, in fact, terrorism.

"A fracture is a way of keeping the top level coordinators from being found out if a low level terrorist is caught. That's why it's so hard to pin these guys down. The fracture is whatever they put in place to keep the lackeys from having names they can hand over." Wade sighed. "It means if they're captured, they can't talk about anything but their own assignment. Even if they wanted to. It's that in each cell, someone communicates with the higher ups, but even they often don't know who they're talking to."

She absorbed that, her brain turning it over. She also absorbed all the things she had learned about Wade since rejoining the FBI. She'd always thought he was just a senior agent who knew his physics well enough to pinpoint a shooter or unravel an accident in under two minutes. But despite the fact that the man had hidden wells she'd never even known about, she had to stay on task.

"So does this organization have five of these 'fractures'?"

"That's what it sounds like." He sighed. "Most have two or three."

Donovan joined in then. "That's what I was about to ask. So we not only have terrorism, we have some of the worst."

Wade was nodding but Eleri was filling him in. "We were pretty confident there's a terrorist cell here when we started hearing mutterings of a 'blond-and-blue'."

"Oh, God." He shook his head and started swearing creatively again.

Eleri climbed out, and so did Donovan. "Thank you Wade. For all of this. Get some sleep."

He cranked the engine hard. "No way in hell can I sleep now. Good luck."

With that, he reversed out of the driveway and drove off. Eleri was pretty certain she could see him muttering more swear words as he passed by.

DONOVAN SAT at the conference table the next morning nursing a paper cup of coffee. He played with the sleeve as though that would somehow keep him awake. Instead, though his eyes lolled and tried to shut, his brain wouldn't turn off. It was exactly the problem that got him here in the first place.

Up until about two a.m. washing the dirt from the soles of his feet and the palms of his hands, his brain had raced with Wade's information.

Five breaks in command from the top of the organization to this point.

If that's what "fracture five" truly meant. Wade said it like "five fractures" and Eleri later told Donovan that she'd heard it, spoken clearly in Cooper Rollins' voice, while she'd stared into space waiting for them while they ran. She'd promised she was alert, watching for anyone and anything that would be a threat to two wolves running roughshod on Griffith Park land, but she'd seen nothing.

She'd been contemplating the write up on the pack. She didn't like having government information on the whereabouts of certain kinds of people. The database she was contributing to all felt very Nazi Germany to her. Donovan agreed that it was first seeds of the same and all. But Eleri also had an opposing point. They'd been attacked, by an organized group. In any other instance they would have written the attack up and included any identifying characteristics of both the individuals involved and the group. This was nothing more than that, except for the fact that it turned her stomach.

So she'd been standing there, leaning against the car, arms

crossed, sorting all that out in her mind. She told him the words came to her so clearly, she turned to see if Cooper Rollins had followed her. She'd recognized his voice immediately. She'd talked herself down, told herself it was stupid, and that if Rollins had followed them why in hell would he approach her and say something so out of scope as "Fracture Five"? But then she heard it again.

Donovan, unable to sleep, had rolled out of bed and gotten online. He'd searched the term but the only hit he got was some book.

Now Eleri sat beside him, looking slightly more chipper than he did. He wasn't sure how she did it, but there were a growing number of things about Eleri that he didn't understand. His brain became more alert as he remembered the shade her eyes had become as she'd stared down the lead wolf.

Taking a sip of coffee as rich as it was expensive, Donovan hid his thoughts. No plain Bureau coffee today; Eleri had pulled up to the shop without asking him and he'd been too half-dead to say anything one way or another. He'd simply followed her inside and grunted a few words before letting her pay for everything.

Marina Vasquez walked into the room just then. The woman they'd been waiting for had her arms full of files and her clothes a little rumpled. "Is that for me?"

She almost dropped the papers and the tablet to reach for the cup Eleri held out.

Eleri had been awake enough to not only stop for better coffee but to pick one up for Vasquez.

"Thank you." Vasquez appeared inordinately grateful over the coffee.

Donovan knew he was fully lacking whatever it was he needed this morning. His brain was so many different places. Wade's comments about the wolf packs. That the women were rarer and often either incredibly passive or highly aggressive.

That matched what Donovan had seen. Was that aggression pushing them into pack leader positions?

"—the origins of the term 'fracture.'" Marina had obviously been talking and he'd missed it.

Pulling himself from the depths of his musings about the gray-haired wolf-woman who looked too young for that hair color, and the things Wade had told him about 'their kind' and the fact that there actually was a 'their kind.' He again forced his thoughts back to the point at hand. They couldn't afford to have him not here. Three of them against this. It wasn't enough.

"So a 'fracture' is exactly what I thought it was—a disconnect protecting the upper echelon of a terrorist organization." She expertly thumbed through a few pages while sipping from the coffee, leading Donovan to believe it was a relatively common state of being for her. "But I couldn't find anything on 'fracture five' specifically. Though I did fall asleep on my keyboard last night, so there might be something out there that I *couldn't* find, but I obviously didn't find it."

Eleri finally spoke, her voice not giving anything away about the fact that these were nearly the first words she'd uttered all day. "Is it a code word for the group?"

"Maybe," Marina looked thoughtful. "I've heard of the branches being referred to as 'fractures.' That would indicate that it's a splinter group, getting intel and probably instructions from a senior level member—whose name they probably don't know. They may not even know his location, or maybe only think they do."

Donovan added his first helpful thought of the day. "I would guess they don't know who it is—if they're using the term themselves. Either they understand the meaning like we do, or they're really in the dark, believing they know everything and not understanding that their passcode is calling them idiots." He took another sip as the coffee cooled. "I'm guessing it's the former. I don't see Cooper as the idiot passing his information off while in the dark about what he's saying and doing."

Marina shrugged. "I don't see Cooper joining an organization where he doesn't understand the orders coming down the pipe and follows them blindly."

"So you're on Cooper's side?" Eleri asked. "Think he's infiltrating the group for his own purposes, rather than just joining?"

Marina was nodding even as Donovan asked. "Wait. He was in the military. Didn't he spend his whole career doing exactly that? He took all kinds of orders and blindly carried them out. This would just be more of the same, but for the other side. I'm not sold on the American Hero aspect."

Marina seemed to think about what he said for a moment, while they all drank their coffee and each tried to put all the pieces together. None of them succeeded.

Marina opened a different folder. "Here's more. I think there may be a fourth death. I didn't find it before, but now with three—"

She trailed off and Donovan saw her worry take over. He filled in the space, hoping to make her feel better. "Each one sucks, but each one gives us more information to help solve it. What did you get?"

"Missing Person. Another woman with a military connection."

"Any link specifically to Cooper Rollins?" Eleri asked before taking a drink of her coffee and seeming to realize it was gone. Barely even looking, she chucked the cup over her shoulder directly into the trash. A calling she'd missed? Or had she also been the star forward on her women's basketball team?

"Not directly yet. But enough overlapping places and times that it's concerning." Marina closed the file as though it could offer nothing else of use. "There's no body or residue that's suspicious though. Nothing about her. Just disappeared."

"So what grabbed you? The military?" Eleri was leaning forward now, awake and fully involved.

Just then, a knock came at the door. As the one closest to it, Donovan peeled himself from his seat. Standing was more effort than he was truly excited to make. But it was on him. The three steps to the door felt rough, the interruption rougher.

He found a man in a cheap white shirt with a cheaper tie and a rolling cart. To some extent the old ways were still the best. It was safest to have the mail delivered by a person. People could make decisions, look for anything odd. The mail boy didn't look like he was any more alert than Donovan, but Donovan could hope.

The kid glanced down at the puffy brown envelope. "Eames, Heath, Vasquez?"

Donovan leaned his neck out and read the address. Exactly as the kid had said. No "Agent," no first names, just the three surnames in that order.

"Heath." Donovan said and held out his hand for the envelope. He signed for it and the kid let him take the package before closing the door. Turning back to the two women, he held it up. "Go on."

Marina did. "There's just one comment from a neighbor that grabbed me. He said when he went on the back porch to knock the day before, the porch was slippery and there was slime in a few places on the railing."

Donovan frowned at her. "No one tested it?" The PD should have tested it; this shouldn't have gone unchecked.

Marina shook her head. "The neighbor commented on it as something weird. He saw that the first day. But didn't think anything of the neighbor not being home. He didn't report the neighbor missing until three days later when he realized no one was feeding the cat. By then it had rained and there was nothing on the porch. It's just a side note."

Donovan was surprised she'd even found it, and spent a

solid minute telling her so. He was beginning to pick up Eleri's desire to help the woman get ahead. Even though he found it funny. Vasquez had probably been in the Bureau longer than Donovan had. She smiled and thanked him for the praise anyway.

Pointing at the envelope, she indicated she was done with her part.

Indicating the envelope, he asked Vasquez. "Has this been tested?"

"If it's in the building, yes. You can open it."

A small burner cell phone fell out. The old flip kind.

No one touched it.

Thirty minutes and a trip to the lab revealed nothing. Not only did the envelope reveal too many fingerprints to count, the phone revealed none. The one thing the lab tech did point out was a mar in the plastic. "See this? It's where someone wiped the phone with a solvent powerful enough to partially melt the plastic. You can leave it with me to test, but I'll be at least a day, maybe longer. Or you can take my best guess, that there's nothing on it."

So they took the phone with them and powered it on, the screen popping right up with no need for a password. Donovan started hitting buttons. The call log was empty. He'd get that checked.

It seemed the phone hadn't been used.

But then, in the picture file, he hit the jackpot.

leri's phone rang and she considered ignoring it. Standing over one of Donovan's shoulders, she was pressed full side to Marina Vasquez as all three of them tried to view the pictures on the tiny phone.

They'd voted not to plug the phone into any kind of screen or projector for the sake of time. But the picture size and the attempt to view them on the phone screen, which was low quality by available standards anyway, might have been a bad choice.

So she was focusing on recognizing faces—Aziza, Alya—and cataloging those she didn't already know, while her phone buzzed at her hip. When it immediately buzzed again, she decided to look at it. Because it was Wade, she excused herself for a moment.

Just heading to the other side of the room, so as not to talk over Donovan and Marina, she was speaking in a low voice before she remembered that it didn't keep her conversation private from her partner and his wolf-ears. "Hey Wade."

There was a brief silence on the other end of the line. "Heath is there. Who else?"

She stopped herself before rolling her eyes. Wade had it too, of course. She lowered her voice further, suddenly wondering if Marina had any strange secrets she was keeping from them. "Agent Vasquez, you met her briefly."

"No one else?"

"No." Eleri frowned. It was a bit much on the cloak-and-dagger for Wade. Or had he always been this way and she was just a lowly field agent before and so he didn't let her see any of this? "What did you want?"

"I'm heading out of town." It was a simple statement, though there was a gravity behind it that she could pick up on but not understand.

"New assignment?"

"No. Just getting out. I'm already unhappy that my name is on a report associated with this case. You called me in for a consult on an explosion. That's not what this is."

Eleri frowned again, her chest tightening by a degree. He sounded upset, and she couldn't put her finger on why. "Are you mad at me?" Then before he could answer, defensive words rolled out of her mouth. "I thought it was just a bombing case when I called you."

"I know. I'm not mad. I'm *worried*." He sounded tense. In a layer of sound behind him, she could make out grinding noises, soft purrs, the occasional odd musical note.

"Are you on the freeway?"

"Yes, I'm literally getting out of town. And you should be, too."

She'd never heard him like this before. Previously, when Wade gave her advice, it was always mellow, take-it-or-leave it, just-so-you-know kind of stuff. "I can't get out. It's our case."

From across the room, Donovan looked up at her, his eyes questioning. She shook her head and shrugged, having no clue what Wade was really getting at yet. Looking to Marina, she saw the woman hadn't overheard the conversation, that was just the two men and their supersensitive ears. Unless Marina was playing them.

God, she'd gotten suspicious as hell in just the past thirty minutes.

"Hand it off." Wade's sharp tone pulled her back to the phone in her hand and the tension in her ribs.

"To whom?" It was her case. Westerfield wasn't communicating much. They had sent the information they had up the pipeline to him and he'd said he was 'working on it.'

"Terrorism. Give it to the task force. This is either a terrorism case or a military treason case interlaced with terrorism."

His words hit her like a truck.

He was right. Though they'd said 'terrorism' a few times early on while talking about Cooper Rollins and the case, it had been very slim speculation. Then they put small pieces together and slowly built the information they had. But they hadn't stepped back to look at the big picture. There was an FBI group already in place—several in fact—with the training to handle exactly this kind of thing.

Protocol said they had enough information to share. "I'll loop them in. You're right."

"No." His word came down the line and smacked her before she even finished the sentence. "Don't loop. *Hand it off.* You don't want to be in this."

Marina's voice, open, excited and unaware of Wade's ominous suggestions, called to her from across the conference table. "Come look at this!"

"I'm not a rookie agent, Wade." Her voice was soft but firm as Eleri worked to not be insulted. She'd been handed this case. Westerfield believed they could handle it. Her boss was up to speed on everything they recovered and even on their speculations. He had not once suggested they hand it off. Even if Wade was right. She should discuss this with the Terrorism Task

Force, loop them in, listen to them, act accordingly. But she didn't need to hand the whole case over.

"I can't stop you, El." He sighed. "If there's anything I've learned about you in all the years we've worked together—in all the time we've been friends—it's that I can't stop you from doing anything."

What was she supposed to do with that? If she let him stop her to prove that she wasn't illogical, then she was a pushover acting on non-logical suggestions. If she stood her ground, then she proved him right. Eleri held her tongue.

Wade continued, probably realizing that she wasn't going to answer the challenge he'd thrown out. "I'm getting off the case. I can't consult any more. I think you should, too."

Another pause. This time she had no idea what to say. So she tried to reassure him. "I'm okay, Wade. I will be."

"I don't know about that, El. I'll be there to pick up the pieces if it all goes to hell. But you've seen what's been happening. There may be too many pieces to put anything back together." He paused. "Or no pieces at all."

The click of the line told her that was all he was going to say. He'd hung up and probably pressed the gas pedal. But as Eleri stood there, holding her silent phone, a chill ran up her spine.

DONOVAN WAS CONCERNED about the look on Eleri's face. He couldn't hear the entire conversation, but he knew that Wade had not been happy, and that his wariness had transferred to Eleri.

Marina was pointing things out in the photo now. "Is that Ken Kellen?"

Eleri shrugged as she returned to the conversation. They'd never seen the guy but had heard of him through both Cooper

Rollins and Walter Reed. Donovan and Marina had agreed that the photo matched the description.

So did Eleri. "Let's pull a military file."

"Hahaha." Vasquez's response was dry and humorless. "His file is buried. Where Rollins' records were redacted, Ken Kellen's are stuffed under so much red tape that I only got them yesterday."

Eleri looked at the other woman, and Donovan wondered why she hadn't already at least scanned the file. Vasquez stared back at him, clearly understanding what he was thinking.

"I got three hours of sleep last night. There was no time."

He'd slept more than three hours last night and hadn't realized what Agent Vasquez was doing outside of working hours to keep this going. Eleri had seen it. Knew Vasquez was hungry, ready to get out and be tried in the field. Unfortunately, they weren't the ones to do it. They couldn't bring her along on half their ops, and while he knew NightShade division was different, with different boundaries, the lines sometimes got fuzzy. Donovan was far too new to push any envelopes.

Still, she'd already hopped up far too willingly for someone with so little sleep and volunteered to run back to her desk to get the delivered documents.

As soon as she was out the door, Donovan rolled his chair next to Eleri's, "What was Wade about?"

She spoke over him. "Wade says he's getting out of town."

Donovan pulled back. "Why?"

Eleri sucked in a breath. "He says we need to hand this up to the Terrorism Task Force."

"Oh. Yes, we do." Despite being in NightShade, they'd both been through the same training at Quantico as every agent. Donovan remembered the protocol for things like this, but he sure hadn't remembered before Wade had suggested it for them. They still weren't even sure what they had was bona fide terrorism. But since all the signs pointed that way, the rules were that the TTF was to be alerted and they would make the call on whether or not they should handle it.

"But he also seemed really anxious to get out of town and to keep his name out of the files." She sounded as worried as the words did.

"Did he say why?" That was odd. Wade was a solid investigator. At least everything Donovan had heard about him said so. Wade had even made their raid on a Texas compound possible in their first investigation, proving himself steady, solid, and invaluable. None of this clicked.

"I didn't really get anything except the idea that he thinks this is headed sideways and he can get out, so he's going to." Eleri shook her head, her eyes in the distance, her thoughts processing Wade's words but not coming to any obvious conclusion.

Donovan held up his phone. "Then let's do it. Let's call Westerfield, then hand this up to TTF."

Eleri nodded in agreement and let Donovan ring up their boss. Once he started the conversation she chimed in.

Donovan expected Vasquez to come back with the file on Kellen at any moment, but protocol was important—he understood that logically, even if he didn't have an attachment to order in his own life. He didn't want anyone accusing them of causing more problems by holding the investigation for themselves for longer than they had to.

Westerfield's answer was not what he expected. "I just fought for full ranking for both of you. Are you suggesting that you're not up to the task?"

Donovan almost recoiled away from the phone. "Shouldn't we at least consult the TTF?"

Her ear pressed nearly to his, the phone not on speaker in case Vasquez did come back, Eleri turned her eyes sharply to meet his. At least it was comforting that she didn't think that was their best course either.

"You're NightShade. We're a special division. We *handle* our assignments. Unless you're resigning, this one is yours." Their boss seemed almost disturbed that they had called. He was overseeing their case, was supposedly still even in the area, but his reaction concerned Donovan. "Follow your leads. Solve it."

Eleri spoke up then. Her words more general, her thoughts probably just as convoluted. "So do we come to you before we follow protocol in general? Like if we have a child kidnapping do we not alert that task force? Or if we have a suspected international event, we keep it to ourselves?"

"That's exactly what you do. We can call in backup as needed, but the second we do our hands are tied." He sounded gruff, almost parental.

Eleri turned her head so her frustrated sigh didn't broadcast into the phone.

It made an odd kind of sense. They had special skills and special directives. Even working with Marina was a balance between how much the other woman helped and how much they had to hide. But it didn't make sense not to at least alert the appropriate people, to get help of exactly the kind they needed.

The silence on the phone was broken by the sound of footsteps coming down the hallway. Vasquez was coming. Donovan opened his mouth to speak, letting both Eleri and Westerfield know their privacy was about to shift, but Westerfield managed to be a microsecond faster. His words traversed the air before Donovan could make his first sound.

"You work it the way we discussed. Find them, figure out who's on what side, and remember that you have permission to remove someone if you have the evidence." Then he hung up.

That was the NightShade directive: Use whatever you had. Donovan hadn't really been let in on that in the beginning. Neither had Eleri. But Westerfield had followed her 'hunches' when no one else had. He'd also encouraged them to make use of Donovan's abilities. Then he'd told them to take out their target rather than aiming for an arrest. NightShade had that umbrella directive, too, apparently.

Though Donovan as a medical examiner had been much more comfortable with dead people, he'd never been comfortable with the idea of making them dead. His Hippocratic oath had been just as sincere as his classmates' had been, even though they fought cancers and delivered babies and treated ear infections in the living. None of this sat well in him.

Just then, Vasquez entered awkwardly, unable to open the heavy door and keep her freshly topped coffee from tipping while clutching the packet of info on Ken Kellen in her other hand. She came in with a smile on her face. "There's a lot here. It may take us a bit."

Their conversation about Westerfield and their directive cut short, Donovan and Eleri turned to the paperwork. Vasquez divided it and they spent an hour wading through, grabbing stacks of pages then resorting them. Eventually they made it to an incomplete set of data that was still partially redacted.

"Most of the redacted stuff is the same as for Rollins." Vasquez mused. "I wonder if that's important?"

"Probably is." Eleri muttered. "If it weren't, they wouldn't have hidden it from us. Twice." She was still looking down at the last pages in front of her.

Donovan knew that look. Wondered if she'd gotten something. While no one was watching, he palmed the small headshot of Kellen, wondering if his partner could get anything from a reprint of a photo. A thought flitted through his brain about religions that didn't allow photos, about witches not showing up on film, about pictures stealing your soul. While he didn't believe any of it outright, he passed a musing thought that maybe there was a grain of truth in there, and that maybe Eleri could latch onto that grain and use it.

Despite her insistence that he didn't want her 'skill,' he still did. It would be so much easier to handle it himself, tell her later what he'd found. He didn't like pushing her, and she didn't like being pushed. Still, Donovan couldn't deny the results, so he shoved the picture down into his pocket and turned his thoughts back to the present.

"So Kellen is older than Rollins, definitely been in the army longer. It seems like it took him longer to get into Special Forces than Rollins. He's a languages expert . . ." Vasquez sighed. "Which makes him a perfect candidate to turn."

Donovan frowned, and she seemed to pick up on his need to hear more.

"It means he could converse with any of the locals, probably already understood their customs and values better than the other soldiers. He could also possibly have private conversations in the open and not have anyone understand. Not any of his fellow soldiers." She shrugged. "We need our troops to comprehend the other side, but not too much. It's always a risk. The more they blend in . . . the more they *can* blend in, the more they can change their minds."

Eleri pointed to her page. "He also doesn't have Rollins' commendations. That could make him bitter or just an underachiever."

Vasquez shook her head. "There are no underachievers in Special Forces. And they don't have underachiever kids either."

"Oh." Eleri's mouth went round with understanding, followed quickly by what was probably sympathy. Donovan remembered the junior agent saying her Dad had been Special Forces, too.

Vasquez waved her off. "So there's no real overlap between these two until they're assigned to the same team in Fallujah."

"The team where the op went to shit." Donovan supplied. "Was he discharged around the same time as Rollins?"

Eleri nodded and held up her stack of pages.

Donovan was so used to e-copies from his old days; he still

hadn't quite gotten used to Eleri's love of dead trees. But he had to admit that she retained so much more when she had her papers. Reaching into the stack she deftly pulled one out. "Same day. They went out on the same mission and were both discharged after returning from it. But get this, Kellen was not one of the four who returned together. I don't have anything on how he came back to the base, or even if he did. You?"

Her eyes searched them both. Both shook their heads.

Asking what he really wanted to know, Donovan looked at her pages. "Bogus medical discharge, like Rollins?"

Nodding, Eleri added, "Within the same hour."

"Wow." It was Vasquez' only comment. She was opening her mouth to say more when she startled.

Donovan was about to ask what it was, when the other woman jumped up, pulled out her buzzing phone and sighed, "I have to take this," before wandering out into the hallway.

Apparently, it was just the gap Eleri had been looking for.

Her suddenly worried eyes rolled right to him. "Wade has me concerned. I don't like what Westerfield said about the TTF or how he told us to handle this."

"Me, either." Donovan shoved his hands into his pockets, frustrated at his inability to act in the way he'd been taught, and the way he truly believed was in everyone's best interest. For a moment he remembered the windowless rooms in the medical examiner's office in Columbia. He remembered just how little he had to answer up the pipeline. It hadn't been never, but he couldn't recall feeling like this. He wondered if he'd regret joining the FBI.

Eleri's next words didn't help.

"Do you think he's setting us up? Do you think this is all going to go to hell and he's throwing us under the bus?"

20

Cooper fought the sensations swarming him. He wanted to sit on the curb and put his hands over his ears. Instead he had to stand, listen, even occasionally speak in coherent sentences.

He swallowed but didn't let it show. Then he did it again.

Ken Kellen knew exactly who Cooper was. They'd traded stories about home, talked about women and kids and family. Kellen knew about Alyssa and Christopher. He even had a good idea where they lived. And if he didn't, Kellen had the chops to get into the network—the same as any of them did—and find out exactly where Cooper's family was.

Cooper didn't put it past the man to do something to them.

Still he had no clue who Ken Kellen really was.

He'd been there the day it went to hell. But he didn't seem to have any bad side effects from it. Cooper had PTSD—developed after years of being in war, but all from that one mission turned rancid. Cooper had no wife or child anymore. Not really. He'd come home to them, but he'd not been fit to live with a family. Alyssa hadn't wanted him. Not like he was. She pushed him into counseling. He did it.

And now Dr. Gardiner was dead.

Gardiner had to die. Cooper could see all the strings, leading out away from him, as well as the ties between the people in front of him. Sometimes they spoke English, keeping him in the loop, but every now and then someone lapsed into Farsi, or Pashto, and he was left with fragments of words that embedded themselves like shrapnel. He didn't understand what they said, only bits and pieces.

He also understood that Kellen understood everything. The man laughed with the others and turned to Cooper, translating. Though Cooper offered a conciliatory smile, the joke wasn't funny anymore.

He laughed with them again. A false front of humor even when the joke was in English. They planned a meeting for the next week, then they split up.

As he headed back home, he felt Kellen following him. Was he trying to finish a job he hadn't completed in Fallujah? Was he watching out for his friend, making sure that Cooper was okay? Or was he just suspicious of the new guy?

Cooper never actually saw the other man behind him. So he went home, and waited. Only then did he see Kellen pass by on the sidewalk about five minutes after Cooper was safely inside.

On a whim, he turned the tables.

Placing the phone with the tracker on his nightstand, he pushed another phone in his pocket and headed down the stairs. He still didn't know who was tracking him, but if it was Fracture Five, they'd hopefully believe he'd stayed home.

This time, he followed Kellen.

The redhead went straight back to the apartment where they'd had the meeting. That was actually quite good. While he'd been in the meeting, Cooper watched out the windows, looked for vantage points to see inside. So when Kellen went in, Cooper went past. Into the next building, he wound his way up the stairs, and picked his way into the empty unit he'd spotted.

Field glasses revealed something surprising. Everyone was there. Except him.

Shit. He was still the new guy. Hadn't done enough to earn their trust yet. He wasn't all that surprised. He'd hardly done anything. Just moved a few pieces here and there. He wasn't an idiot—he hadn't opened any of the backpacks. That was not appropriate for a first run, or a second, or even a third. But while he made one of the trips, he had held the backpack he carried out a bit, pushing it near the noses of the dogs he passed. Most turned their heads, indicating that whatever he carried was something they didn't like the smell of.

He'd waited to get tackled. To get taken down by the police, or the FBI people who kept trying to follow him. It hadn't happened, and he'd delivered the plain, almost too-normal looking backpacks several times.

Still, the cell didn't trust him. They had deliberately broken up the meeting, dispersed and regrouped once they believed he was home. Kellen was on the inside. But Cooper wasn't.

He couldn't hear what they said, but the conversation seemed more intense than the one he'd been part of—or almost part of—earlier.

Several hours later, the meeting ended and Cooper found himself following Ken Kellen again. This time, his ex-team member headed a long way down the freeway, and Cooper barely managed to keep up. Stealing a car was a bad but necessary tactic. He'd return it later.

It was a good call, as Kellen met up with another group. These guys looked like they were meeting for poker. Only when Cooper got a view through the window in the unassuming home, they sat around the table, no cards, no chips. Instead they were having a deep conversation.

Several of the men pounded on the table. Several women refilled glasses and brought small amounts of food but stayed part of the vehement conversation. Kellen fit in here as well as he did at the other meeting.

Only this time, the members clutched Bibles. Cooper could have sworn he saw several mouths say the passcode "Fracture Five."

~

ELERI'S HEAD HURT. She'd slept with the picture of Ken Kellen despite the fact that she hated that stuff. She did it despite the fact that she was rolling into old habits—putting the job before her own needs, pushing herself to squeeze everything she could out of any gifts she might have.

Those old habits had gotten her four months in the looney bin, and she'd only gotten to stay for three of those months. Westerfield had yanked her from her cocoon before she'd been finished. While inside, Eleri tackled her treatment with the same gusto and desire for success she brought to everything. Something her therapists pointed out was maybe not the best idea.

They wanted her to do things like 'take up a hobby' and 'find a romantic attachment.' So, ever the achiever, she'd taught herself to knit with a pair of chopsticks from the cafeteria. Apparently, actual knitting needles could fall into the wrong hands. Eleri bit her tongue to keep from pointing out to the kindly staff exactly how much damage she could inflict with chopsticks. And how much easier death would be from a pointy object.

She'd also developed imaginary relationships with fiction-alized versions of several actors. Why settle for just one boyfriend? It wasn't as if there were any real prospects at the hospital. Just other patients and the staff. All inappropriate. And out here? Donovan was her partner and she didn't think of him that way. Wade was gay. Westerfield was her boss, and everyone else was a suspect.

The man she was currently sleeping with was Ken Kellen—in photographic form. All she'd gotten out of it was waking cranky, unsettled, and with no additional information.

Now she was topping off her night with a very early morning ride out to the home of the fourth missing person. Donovan was driving, which was a good thing. She was downright pissy.

The sun was barely peeking over the horizon. They were heading out without Marina Vasquez, on purpose. Yet another thing they couldn't tell their junior agent. And for some reason, L.A. was cold. Eleri almost hadn't thought it could happen.

She was naturally warm blooded, but this morning the cold got to her and her hand lifted to her upper chest, touching the lump under her shirt and the jacket over it. It was probably pretty obvious, but Donovan hadn't asked.

Another mysterious package, this one just for Eleri, had been on the dining room table this morning. Eleri told herself that Donovan had brought it in with the mail. Didn't let herself even think back to whether it had been there the night before, or that mail didn't come between the hours of eleven p.m. and five a.m. She ignored the fact that it was addressed simply to "Makinde" in Grandmere Remi's loopy scrawl. And she didn't let herself think that Donovan would have no idea that her Grandmere called her by that name. It had somehow been waiting on the table.

Inside she had found only the *grisgris*. No note, no warning other than the beautifully worked leather pouch strung from the gorgeous ribbon. This one had no scent.

Eleri had learned long ago that a love spell smelled, a keep-away smelled, the pouch to be worn next to the skin in order to bring harm to another smelled. This one had no odor. This one was for protection from the darkest of human hearts. Grand-mere believed fully and deeply. Eleri didn't know what she thought of it herself.

But it didn't stop her from wearing it. She'd slipped the ribbon over her head and shoved the envelope down in to the trash.

The pre-dawn light cast the city in shades of gray and blue, matching the bleakness of her thoughts. The place was, at its heart, a party town. Inside were enclaves of neighborhoods mostly made up of various groups. West Hollywood was best known for its gay population, but what people didn't seem to realize was that the area had been settled by Russian and Jewish families long before the fabulousness had arrived.

As Donovan aimed the car up the highway, traffic built up heading toward them. Their lanes stayed miraculously clear. Quickly the city gave way to bedroom subdivisions, inter-spersed with clearly older small towns that had been swal-lowed by development. Their strip malls still standing in testament to the sixties and seventies when they'd been sepa-rate places.

"Old" out here had an entirely different meaning than where she'd come from. At home, "old" meant several hundred years. It meant deciding to air condition a house was a huge deal, as it would damage the history. Here, it was all in varying shades of recent and even that managed to be less well cared for than much older structures back home.

The home Donovan pulled up in front of was nearly iden-tical to the ones on either side. The only real difference was the feeling of emptiness.

A car pulled out from the garage on their right as they passed. The houses in this subdivision were garage-front, the drive heading right under the massive, roll-up door they didn't have a clicker for. They were mostly interested in the back porch, but they'd have to leave the car somewhere. "Walk in."

It was the only two words that Eleri had spoken since they left the house that morning. Once again, her hand reached up to clutch the grisgris, but she stopped herself just shy of touching it, leaving the movement as stilted as her day felt.

Donovan nodded and parked two houses over. Luckily, the lights were still off, and before she could think otherwise, Eleri opened the door into air that didn't feel right and headed for the neighbor's open side fence.

Hastily, she tromped through grass turned brittle and brown. Even she could hear Donovan behind her, crunching with his booted feet. In moments, she was face to face with a pink cinderblock wall about six feet high. She was just reaching for the top, when she felt hands close around her calf and boost her up.

Grateful, Eleri pushed up onto her palms at the top of the 'fence' and threw one leg over then the other. She was dropping down on the other side when Donovan appeared to pop over the top all by himself. Well, he was tall and had upper-body strength.

She looked across into a back yard in nearly perfect reverse of the one she'd just come from. The sun was hitting a higher note, the air charging and warming around her as she softly made her way to the back porch. When she stood at the base of two cement steps, Eleri paused. Behind her, Donovan remained silent. Good thing. She didn't want to do this.

It was never just a movie in her head. When she was honest, she admitted it never had been. In her dreams she'd stood in killers' homes, seen their magazine collections, checked out their kitchens. But she'd sometimes also felt what they felt, her gut had churned as her chest tightened with desire so strong for small children, for women who fought, for the feeling of someone's life slipping away through your own fingertips. It wasn't her desire, but theirs.

Though they faded, the feelings never completely washed away.

Donovan didn't understand that. And she didn't know how to say it.

Part of that was because she didn't want to. There was no one else, and she wouldn't say *no*. What if someone else could have seen Emmaline? Eleri would have given anything —*anything*—to get her sister back. So she walked up the steps, knowing this was someone's daughter, sister, mother, *someone*, and she started touching things.

She trailed her fingers along the railing, but it held no memories for her. She touched the door. The window sill that might peer into the kitchen had the blinds been up.

From behind her, Donovan's voice gave her information. "She was fifty-four. A mother, but her children were grown. A widow who lived alone. She was home midday from work. I don't think she would have trailed her fingers along the railing."

What would she have done? But what Eleri asked was, "Why was she home?"

He shrugged. "The work report said she called in sick. So they didn't think too much of it when they didn't hear from her the next day. Maybe she was actually sick."

"Pretty convenient that she's home sick so our bomber can get to her." Eleri kept her voice low in case the neighbors were up.

Donovan thought for a moment. "Maybe it wasn't convenient; maybe it was *contrived*." He stood at the base of the porch, all two steps below, the railing hardly necessary. "Maybe they made her sick, to keep her home. So they could get to her."

Eleri leaned forward, planting her hands on the railing, looking down at him. Suddenly, a fever washed over her. Her joints ached. Her stomach churned. Then her head jerked back as she heard a knock at the front door.

Eleri was looking at Donovan, starting to sweat, to breathe through the pain of the illness, when she heard the knob turn as the person let themselves into the house, calling out her name.

21

Donovan stared at Eleri as she stood with her hands braced on the railing. At first, she paled and headed quickly into a cold sweat. Just as he was about to ask her what she saw—and it must be bad—it got worse.

Her head snapped around, and she focused at the door into the house. Donovan stopped dead. His blood cooled at the sight.

Her body changed, Eleri looked both taller and frailer, and not like Eleri. Even her facial features seemed to have moved so she looked more like the older woman who owned this house. It must have been his imagination. He'd seen pictures of the woman, so he was overlaying her face now as Eleri walked to the door and opened it.

But was he overlaying the odd movements?

Donovan knew, better than anyone, just how much a face was capable of change in the right circumstances.

Eleri walked as if her knees bothered her; she breathed as if the movement took more effort than it should. Then her body lurched, just as she reached for the door handle. Donovan lurched, too, thinking to grab her, stop her from falling when he realized it was a cough. A hard cough.

Simultaneously, Eleri opened the door and looked down at her hand.

Clearly, she saw someone in the doorway; Donovan did not. His chest clenched. Did he stop her? Or did he let her get more information? Was the decision even his?

His own breathing was faster than it should be. His worry skyrocketing as he fought all sides of the issue and still didn't know what to do.

Eleri—or whoever she was now—seemed happy to see the person at the door. But whatever was in her hand made her afraid. Very afraid.

Once again, just as he was getting ready to ask her something, to pull her from the vision she was caught in, she jerked again. This time she stared at the person she saw in the air before her. Donovan's breath caught.

This was so much easier when it was him.

But what had he done lately? He'd gone for a run. When the lobomau had come, Eleri fought them. She'd slept with Ken Kellen's picture; she was on the porch now, seeing what the old woman saw. His 'special skills' hardly seemed special in comparison to hers. It seemed all he could do was get close enough to help if he was needed.

Just as Donovan hit the steps, he heard and saw Eleri inhale deeply. She seemed surprised, then she scared the shit out of him, by lolling her head back and simply collapsing.

Gravity was faster than he was, and he didn't catch her. He could only leap as he watched her fall like a building imploding, like everything holding her up snapped piece by piece.

Her legs buckled, making the fall awkward and leaving her in a pile of her own bones. The odd angle served to keep her head from cracking against porch boards.

Donovan didn't hear his knees smack to the deck. He couldn't hear her breathe or if she moaned; he couldn't hear anything over the sound of his own wild heartbeat. Over the roar of the unknown.

The older woman had died out here. He was convinced of that now.

Would Eleri die if she lived through the death of another? Why hadn't he gone into emergency medicine? It would be so much more useful now.

Things ran through his brain. *MASH IITT.*

No. That was the acronym for taking patient histories. *ABCs.* Yes. But despite 'Airway' being A, he pushed his fingertips to her neck and checked for C—Circulation.

It took three frantic tries, as his own pulse raced beneath the pads of his fingers, and each time he couldn't feel hers, he grew more worried, his breath more labored, his thoughts more scattered. Once he did find a pulse, he turned his attention to her breathing. Luckily, the small bump of whatever she was wearing on a ribbon around her neck made it blessedly easy to spot the rise and fall of her breath.

He felt his shoulders drop suddenly, relief replacing the support of his muscle tension with limp worry. Now, he needed to get her awake, get her talking. Make certain she was still Eleri. Donovan was tapping her cheek before he thought better of it. He was a trained physician; he should do better than this.

Eleri's first move was to push his hand and simultaneously turn her head away from his obnoxious touch, but she wasn't fully awake. Her eyes blinked. Her mouth worked but no sound came out.

He worried about brain damage. Had she hit her head and he hadn't seen?

Though her words were clear, they made no sense. "Emmaline? Grandmere?"

"Do you remember where you are?" he asked. He was getting ready to ask her for the date, to ask who was president, when her head snapped toward him and she stared.

"They're coming." Her now lucid eyes looked right into his as she pushed one hand behind her and the other grabbed at his arm. Using him as an anchor, she was upright before he was, steady on her feet, all Eleri again. Her gaze swept the back yard as she tried to decide which way to go.

"Who's coming, El?" He breathed it out, the words low in his chest. He heard things on the other side of the house. One car, doors opening and closing, feet on the ground. More than one.

She was already down the steps, ducking through the back yard, aiming to launch herself over the six-foot, cinderblock fence as though her adrenaline could make it happen.

He wanted to call out, but instead he leapt from the porch himself, his feet landing in soft grass, his toes curling in his shoes at the impact, his ankles flexing, stronger for their size than a normal human's.

His muscles wanted to change, even more than they did most times he ran. Now, his body was actively trying to transform. The need to flee triggered it. He'd noticed that before— adrenaline pushed the change. Donovan pushed it back.

He was halfway through the yard when he heard it. Eleri's hands had just grasped the top of the fence and she was using fear-fueled strength to haul herself up.

"Wait, El!" He said it loud enough to make her stop and soft enough to not alert the people out front that they were here. "Wait!"

She paused, awkwardly looking back over her shoulder as she hung there at the top now, perched on straightened arms, ready to throw her leg over and disappear into the neighbor's yard.

He sniffed the air. He felt his ears twitch. And he couldn't help turning his head toward the side of the house. The squawk and buzz of the radio was as distinct as the tone of the voice issuing information in lock-step fashion.

"El." He turned his face back to her, wondering if he'd transformed a little bit. "It's the police."

She shook her head and dropped to the ground, her knees taking the impact and making her wobble a little. His first instinct was to race for her, grab her, hold her upright. But she managed it on her own.

He couldn't protect her, it seemed, though he felt he should. She didn't need it, that was certain, but every time he pushed her to do something like this, he felt purely responsible for the outcome.

She dropped to the ground and turned back, looking right at him, her green eyes worried. He still had no clue what she'd seen, and there wasn't time for her to tell it. She shook her head. "It's them."

Just then there was a banging on the front door. Her head snapped up, and something about the way it happened, about the way she held her shoulders, focused her eyes, had him asking, "Is it the same person you saw?"

"This is the police." The voice spoke loudly, clearly, just shy of yelling. The obviously male timbre had Eleri jerking back as more words came. "Is anyone here?"

She shook her head at Donovan, confused, but still started walking toward the small porch. She reached around her flank, but not for her sidearm. Instead, she pulled her small, rectangular leather wallet that held her ID.

Donovan reached for his, too, the movement not as ingrained in him as it clearly was in her. It was a security of some kind for her, a natural move in times of stress. He hadn't realized quite how much Eleri identified herself as an FBI agent until this moment. And he flashed back to her claims of spending three months in a mental hospital, and thinking she'd never work in the Bureau again. It must have been hell for her. More so because she'd broken down in the first place doing exactly the same kinds of things he was pushing her to do now.

How was now different? Was it enough that he and Westerfield knew what she was doing? That she could tell people when it went sideways on her?

He hoped so, because it sure as hell didn't seem to be any easier on her. Holding his own wallet flipped open and ready to flash, he heard her plant her feet and prepare to identify the two of them through the door.

She was cautious, the last thing any of them wanted was to make the police upset. They sometimes came with guns out. A finger at the ready was also a finger ready for a mistake. That had been drilled into him at the Academy. As though the gun itself hadn't felt foreign enough to him.

"FBI." She spoke loudly, the sound carrying the three identifying letters first. They never said NightShade. Aside from the diamonds on the border lines on the badges, there were no marks, nothing to associate them with a division of the FBI that most didn't even know existed. "We're in the back yard. Our badges are out. Please come back."

Eleri stopped moving. She stood in the middle of the grassy space, her ID raised for whomever might see it, though no one but Donovan was back here yet. Slowly, Donovan raised his own badge, though he heard the two men at the front door. They tried the knob, walked across the front porch, probably looking in the window, then went down the concrete steps heading toward the side.

Two of them. Medium build, boots. Small sounds of weapons jangling on full utility belts. Then the voice again.

"We're coming around the side."

"Okay," Eleri called back and turned toward her left, toward the brief wooden fence that separated the front yard from the back.

The fence swung open and as the first man walked through, Eleri angled herself, but stayed put. "Special Agent Eleri Eames, and this is Special Agent Donovan Heath."

The officer looked from one of them to the other, hands resting on the weapons hanging from his utility belt. He was relaxed, his hands positioned in the threat of a threat, but nothing more. Nodding sagely, he didn't move his hands, but tipped his head as he said, "Officer Harding. This is Officer Davies."

The second man moved out from behind the first as he, too, came through the tall gate. Donovan nodded a hello to each of them. Only then did he notice that Eleri had frozen where she stood.

ELERI STARED at a face she'd seen before. Now she had a name. Officer Davies had appeared in the scene she'd witnessed of Ratz in his garage. It had been Davies who had visited Ratz, bringing him the bomb makings, and eventually plunging the knife into him and leaving before Ratz's final moment. Davies had walked away clean.

She was standing in front of a man she knew to be a murderer and suspected to be a terrorist, and she had absolutely zero proof. She was also standing like an idiot, staring wildly at a man she should not be giving anything away to.

Almost able to feel Donovan's indecision about whether he should take the lead, Eleri shattered the chill holding her back and slapped on a false smile. Luckily she had years of practice.

Putting her foot forward, she still held her ID up as she approached Harding. "Do you need to see it?"

"If you don't mind." It was a good response. He shouldn't

trust people he found in a missing person's back yard and she liked him better for it. Though she wasn't sure if his association with Davies was because he was assigned to the same car, or because he was more deeply associated with the cell. She and Donovan waited while Harding looked at each of the IDs, though if he knew what he should be looking for, she couldn't tell.

"Thank you." He handed both of them back and Eleri pocketed hers, just as he spoke again. "Can you tell us what you're doing back here?"

Eleri nodded her head, but her voice said, "Somewhat. We're simply following up to see if Mrs. Sullivan is associated with a case we're working."

"Is she?"

She could have told him it was classified, or she could have been a bitch and said it was above his pay grade. Instead she said, "I'm pretty confident."

It told them that she and Donovan would be here longer, or more often. But she continued. "Agent Heath and I need to conduct a further search, and I could request police help, but unfortunately, it needs to be FBI." As though she would want Officer Davies—the murdering asshole—anywhere near her investigation. She tried to look frustrated with her fakely tied hands. "Do you maybe have spare keys? Or have a record of who does?"

Change the subject, ask for help in a different way than the one they're offering.

Donovan didn't say anything. Just stood by, looking official. Though Eleri knew he was waiting for her to explain what the hell had just happened. Why she'd run. If she was even okay after passing out on the porch. Given the way she'd felt so sick, so fast, and that she'd come around to find herself lying on the back deck, she was quite confident that's exactly what had happened. Donovan needed an explanation. One he wasn't going to get until she was good and confident that Davies and Harding were long out of earshot.

Harding put his hands back on his belt in that casual way that officers had of resting them there. It was authoritarian, but not immediately threatening. "I don't know that we have a copy. But I can call in."

"That would be wonderful." She smiled at him as he and Davies stepped back through the gate, into the tiny front yard as though they were getting out of the way. She could hear him radio in for information on the case—or lack thereof as best she could tell from the files Marina pulled.

As their backs finally disappeared from view, Donovan turned to her, laser-sharp eyes questioning her health.

"I'm fine." She mouthed it to him. No need to give the officers any indication that she was other than spot on. If they didn't know what they'd almost walked in on, she wasn't going to tell. More loudly, she said, "We'll need a search of the house. You and I should start."

She said the words in an even tone, not wanting to shout them, but not wanting to sound like she was hiding anything from the officers, either. No need to make them suspicious. Though, chances were good that Davies already was.

When Donovan wandered over toward her and asked what they needed to do to get things started for the search—clearly having picked up on the 'be casual' directive—she turned to face him, thinking to let him read her lips.

Then, almost laughing, Eleri turned away and spoke in a very low voice, knowing Donovan would hear it. "Davies—" she pointed at a window while she looked at the back side of the house as though making decisions, "killed Ratz."

She looked up at him casually, finding his eyebrows raised and his mouth nearly open. He didn't have the same opportunity to talk to the grass and have her hear it. Donovan was reduced to hand gestures and crudely over-emphasized mouthed words. He pointed to the back porch. "Did he kill her?"

She shook her head. They didn't need to search the house. They needed to search the grass. The yard had been pretty before the woman died, as best as Eleri could tell. Watered, mowed to an even height, then left to whither when Mrs. Sullivan went missing. It would be harder to find what she was looking for in the tall, dead grass.

She tried not to look at it. Didn't want the officers to see that what she really wanted was on the ground when she was supposed to be requesting access to the house. Eleri had just tipped her head to see Donovan checking out the detached garage at the back of the property when Harding and Davies came back through the gate.

"I'm sorry, ma'am." This time it was Davies. She hated the sound of his voice, and hid her bristle at his slight. *Ma'am? That's "Agent" to you.* But he wasn't just an asshole. He was a murderer. "We don't have any access to house keys."

"No worries." She smiled at him, but wished he would catch a venereal disease. "We'll contact the family. Thank you."

It almost hurt to thank this man, but she reminded herself that she was going to take him down. And now that she was with NightShade she didn't have to say exactly where she got her information.

She would double-check. She would be certain that she hadn't simply had a dream that happened to have his face. Then she would shut down the whole damn cell.

A clean feeling of liberation washed over her suddenly, as Davies nodded at her and said, "We'll leave you two here unless you need anything else."

Donovan told them "No, thank you," and watched as the two headed out through the front yard. Eleri stood there, breathing in air that she knew wasn't quite clean, but cleared her out nonetheless. There, in Loreen Sullivan's tiny back yard, a weight lifted from her shoulders as she realized that her NightShade directive set her free more than it tied her down.

"Eleri." Donovan's voice broke the spell but didn't bring her back to full gravity. Maybe nothing could. "Are you all right?"

22

"I'm fine." But she wasn't, Eleri knew. "I'm okay." She didn't say it a third time. The third time indicated the lie. And she knew better.

"You look off."

She shook her head, because she couldn't explain it. Couldn't explain it to herself.

Donovan waited, his head tipped toward the front of the house. For a moment, she wondered what he was doing, then she realized he was listening for the police car. "They're gone."

Implicitly, that meant they could now speak freely. And he did. "What happened?"

"I had my hands on the railing, and I guess it was the way I placed them—"

He didn't let her finish. "I mean: you passed out. You asked for Emmaline. And 'Grandmere.'" He looked confused, but Eleri felt her hand reach up for the grisgris around her neck. Had she seen them when she was out? She'd seen Emmaline in her sleep numerous times before now, though it had been a while since she'd dreamed of the sister she'd lost so long ago. And Grandmere?

Eleri shrugged. "I don't remember seeing either of them." Donovan knew a good bit about her sister. Though she hadn't really sat down and poured her heart out—didn't even know if she could where Emmaline was concerned—Donovan knew more about her sister's kidnapping, and Eleri's subsequent dreams, than anyone else. Though he didn't know much of anything about her grandmother, she must have muttered the name or he wouldn't even know she used the French, or actually Acadian, term in that case.

He brought her back around. "Are you physically okay? You may have hit your head."

Eleri reached up, her skull throbbing slightly now at the mention of the possibility, but with no single source of the feeling. Her hand wandered, the bones revealing nothing as Donovan shook his head. "Let me."

That was almost weird. But he was a physician. It took a moment with his fingers carefully sorting through her hair, checking for cuts or bumps. He didn't push or massage, probably in case she did have some damage, but he quickly came to a conclusion. "I don't see anything. If you don't feel anything, you probably didn't hit it."

Shaking her head slowly, Eleri denied the slow creep of tension through the muscles, it was at such odds with the feeling of lifted weight. But whatever she was feeling, Donovan didn't see it. He simply kept interrogating her now that he could. Her small epiphany was not the order of the day.

"What did you see when you touched the railing?"

Now that she was deemed physically whole, her mental issues, visions, could be addressed. He was such a doctor; she almost said so. Instead, she gave him the story. "She was really sick. Fever, stomach upset, joints hurt. I could feel it all."

He nodded, "You looked like it. Your stance changed."

That shocked her a bit. Had she become Loreen Sullivan

just for a minute? "The person at the door knocked and came in. In this neighborhood, that would mean she had a key."

"Why 'in this neighborhood'? This is a decent place."

Eleri shook her head. "No, I mean, L.A. In general here, people don't talk to their neighbors much. Maybe they're just too on top of each other. The one older gentleman next door is the only one who noticed something was up. No one else did, or else they didn't think it was their business. So you can bet, around here, doors are locked."

Donovan nodded, then his eyes popped. "It was a woman? Did she stab you—Sullivan—while you were seeing it?"

He became more frantic as he spoke and Eleri worked to calm him down. "No, she didn't stab me, Sullivan passed out when the girl told her she'd been poisoned with ricin. The girl pulled the blade and said it was kinder than letting her die in pain."

"Ricin?" Then he paused, "You coughed and looked at your hand. Did you see something?"

It took only a second to think back to what he asked about. "Yes. The cough was painful and there was a spatter of red on my hand. She didn't realize quite what it was, but she was afraid." Eleri looked off to the side, her eyes not focusing as her brain worked.

Donovan nodded again, his brain obviously churning too, and when pieces fit together, the next question would come out of his mouth. "Girl? Aziza? Alya?"

"No. Someone different." She purposefully lowered her voice. Just because the neighbors didn't check on each other didn't mean they weren't above listening in over the wall. "The thing is, we have four murders each performed—nearly identically—by four separate people."

He nodded again, his eyes wandering a path similar to his thoughts. "It does make it really hard to track. I don't think they even know each other. I mean the murderers. Do you?"

"I don't even know if they know *about* each other." She shrugged again. It seemed to be her rote response to this case. "This girl was white, blonde, blue-eyed, maybe early twenties, and said Mrs. Sullivan was the very devil that needed to be eradicated from this land before she triggered the end of days."

"Those words?"

"Pretty much." Eleri looked at him, "Can you hear the neighbors? Is anyone snooping?" She'd given up trying to figure it out herself. Might as well use his super-powers. She almost laughed.

"No, no one's there. I made sure the officers had driven off before I started talking." Then he thought for a moment. "The wording sounds very Christian. So we have a Muslim killer— Aziza, and an Indian killer—the unknown man at Vivian Dawson's, and this Christian girl?"

"Don't forget that Davies killed Ratz."

"Jesus."

"Literally." Eleri sighed. "So we have what? Three different 'fractures' all carrying this out?"

"That's what it sounds like." Then he finally looked at her. "Why are we still in the back yard? Shouldn't we be on our way to the office and getting Vasquez on some of this?"

"Not yet. We're here, and we need to do what they didn't do the first time. We need to search."

"Okay. What am I looking for?" He scanned the yard, looking way too high up for Eleri's purposes.

"The grass. Bone fragments. Teeth. Any small part that might have survived a blast."

He nodded, not any more disgusted by the thought of finding tiny bits of body parts than she was. It took a certain kind of person to go into a forensic field and for all their many differences, they were both it.

She was getting ready to suggest they grid the place, or at least sub-divide it, when he walked back up onto the porch. He stood, facing the doorway. "So she was here when she was stabbed? Facing this way?"

"I don't know. I passed out at the sight of the knife." Then she perked up. "The knife! I saw it." Excitedly now, she started to describe it. The metal blade that scared the shit out of Mrs. Sullivan, but that Eleri recognized as a little too wide. "I think it was hollow. The explosive was likely inside it. So there might well be metal fragments from the blade exploding. We need to look for that, too."

She told him of the handle, that it was dark in color. That was the plastic, with a button that she assumed was a timer trigger. "That would mean that a smart person—or a psychic one who knew the knife would blow—could pull it out and throw it and maybe survive the stab wound."

"Would anyone know enough to do that?"

Her breath soughed in and out. "I doubt it. I don't think anyone really even has a clue people are dying this way. And the standard treatment for a stab is . . ."

"Don't pull out the blade." He finished for her. "In fact, you should bind it. At which point you are sure to blow."

"I don't think there's enough time between trigger and explosion for any real first aid. I get the feeling the victim staggers back and it's just long enough for the killer to get away."

Again, he looked up at the house. "So, we're assuming she's facing the killer in the doorway. And it's someone she knows. She's what? Shocked?"

"Betrayed." The word rolled out of her. Eleri had felt it. Mrs. Sullivan had trusted the girl, and only in that moment had she realized that every move between them had been a ploy by the girl to get to this point.

Donovan seemed to understand, but kept mapping out what happened.

"She would have blown up back this way." He gestured behind

him, out into the yard. "Some will go up," but there was no awning over the deck, just a small one over the door. "Maybe something up there?" he pointed to it, but continued talking. "Some will go out. Maybe even as far as over the fence, but definitely into the grass in whatever the radius is." He turned and looked over the yard.

"I doubt anything specific got over the fence. If a neighbor found pink mist or a tooth in their yard, they'd complain."

"Are you sure?"

Her smile was grim. "I'm sure the homeowner's association would frown on that kind of thing."

She could see he almost laughed, but he kept going. "And some would go down." He pointed to his feet. "Between the slats."

"Lovely." She sighed. This day just kept getting better and better.

DONOVAN LOOKED AT HER. Eleri seemed okay. More importantly, she seemed like Eleri. He was still concerned, but he was starting to breathe easier.

Oddly, she seemed a little lighter, didn't smell quite as stressed out. It wasn't a bad smell, not like full stress-sweat, which he could never actually imagine the Southern, money-raised Miss Eames smelling of. No, it was just a warning, like a person snapping at you, only it came right before that part. The stress of this morning had clung, even after she'd come around and leapt from the porch. But then, after the officers left, it was suddenly gone.

"How do we get Davies?" He asked her.

"We're NightShade." She smiled as though that solved everything.

He was concerned by that, though he did his best to make

light of it. "If you were grim, you could have said that like 'We're Batman.'"

At least she laughed. She'd sure looked at him like he was nucking futs when he said some of the human debris from the explosion would have gone under the deck. It was going to be the most likely place it would be preserved too.

"No, we're not Batman. But we have a directive to do what we need to."

Almost like adrenaline, alarm shot through him, starting in his chest and spreading through racing tendrils until it hit his fingers and toes. "We can't just kill him. We need evidence."

"Actually, we don't." She returned the volley quickly, and though there was no malevolence in her voice, his blood ran colder. "And that's the problem."

He sighed out relief as the tension left him. "So what do we do about it?"

"We have to fully agree before we order anything. Before we pull any trigger in anything other than flat-out self-defense. And we—you and me—we never operate from my dreams alone. We go for arrests rather than kills, if possible. You got me on that?" She stared at him, as serious as he'd ever seen her. She had good cause, too. There had been no arrests on their first mission. Apparently, she wanted some this time.

"Of course. So we have a lead on Davies—a good one." Though they would never do anything based solely off her dreams, they'd proven to be nothing but solid. "How do we track him?"

"Let's put Walter on him." She grinned.

Oh shit. He nodded. Walter was good. "Can we give her a pay raise?"

"Sadly, no. The rates are set by the Bureau, and we already operate outside the norm. I don't think we should raise any flags we don't have to." She headed for the corner of the yard, just to the side of the deck. "We can contact her later today.

Give her intel and set her on her way." Then she slid right into the next topic. "I'm taking this area. You can pull up the deck if you want."

He tried. He knelt down, and worked to get his fingers through the spaces between the wood. Only it wasn't wood. It was pressed, hard plastic composite with wood-grain etched on it and it had zero give. So he went to the end of the deck, away from Eleri and tried to pry it up. It did not give. There was no way he was getting under here on his own. Wolf, yes. Superhuman strength? Not at all. He might want to consider working out a little more.

"I'm checking over here." He announced, pointing away from the stupid back deck. But Eleri barely nodded at him and didn't look up from the grass she was leaning over.

Standing again, he started looking at the ground, actually the driveway. This entire side of the yard was paved. Just slightly wider than the average car, it reached from the edge of the house to the property line. If the police had driven in here, they'd likely inadvertently picked up, crushed, or otherwise ruined any evidence. He didn't blame them. They'd been investigating a missing person, not a death, and certainly not a person who exploded from the inside.

Very quickly, he finished his spot—meaning he didn't find anything. When he looked up, he saw Eleri almost on her hands and knees on the other side of the yard. "Should we bring in a cadaver dog?"

Almost instantly, she shook her head at him. "He'll alert everywhere. If she exploded—" Eleri cut herself off, seeming to realize what she was saying. "I don't think it will find what we need. Just reaffirm what we're already certain of enough to start looking." She turned back to the grass, pushing her flat hand over it, bending the blades this way and that to see if anything was covered.

His stomach growled at him, but Donovan ignored it and

started on the ground at the edge of the driveway. The grass was disturbingly uniform, probably sodded—the yard was small enough that it could be done on the salary of a working woman in L.A. His eyes crossed as he searched for any changes in the pattern, anything that might be useful. He was hungry, and finding a scrap of a candy bar wrapper and a bit of foil didn't help.

By the time his search area met up with Eleri's he had five small pieces of trash and two bits of plastic—which might also just be trash. He held them out to her.

"This!" She picked up one of them; the timing since the incident was too long to be worried about fingerprints or chain of evidence. "I think it's part of the knife."

Grateful to have been of use while growing his own headache, Donovan held onto the plastic but dumped the trash into the bin at the side of her yard. It didn't look like anyone was taking it out to the curb anymore. It was as good a place as any to keep stuff. Eleri bagged what she thought was a knife shard then held up her own finds.

Donovan looked on, impressed. "What? No trash?"

"I left it." Instead she held out a piece of plastic that matched his in color and texture and thickness. Only hers had some tissue dried on it. He was grateful right then that he was a trained medical examiner, otherwise it might have turned his already unhappy gut. She also had part of a molar and a piece of bone. She pushed them toward him. "Human?"

"Looks like." He picked them out of her hand and examined the pieces. "This is skull." He held the one piece out. It had fluttering edges where the head had blown apart at the suture lines or been cracked into pieces after hitting something. Bone often came apart where it had grown together in the first place.

Donovan turned over the other. "This is definitely human." He held the tooth up. "Given the fences, the likelihood of a non-human animal of the right size or even anyone else getting their bones back here is relatively small."

"I concur." She took them back and put them in the bag with the plastic. "Let's get in the house and get some of Mrs. Sullivan's DNA to match."

They let themselves in the back, Eleri once again picking a lock. The house felt still from disuse, the dust having settled into the cracks and crevices even if they couldn't see it. Eleri didn't seem to like being in the house, and as she'd pointed out earlier, they were really more interested in the forensics of the backyard.

Donovan tried for conversation, thinking to take her mind off things and wondering if she was becoming afraid to touch things that belonged to other people. It had not occurred to him before now that if she got better at it, she might not be able to turn it off. She'd had that episode on the plane coming out here . . .

"Should we set a team up to come take apart the deck? The best evidence is probably under there. Anything that went through the cracks is likely pretty well preserved."

"True." She climbed the steps, looking in doors until she hit the bathroom. "If we don't get a hit off the tooth or skull fragment, we'll send in a team. But hopefully this will be enough. We just need to confirm that she's dead."

Eleri found a hairbrush in the main bedroom and Donovan just grabbed it. They needed hair with root balls. It was best to get the whole thing. They had to assume it belonged to Mrs. Sullivan.

This time, they walked out the front door, locking it behind them. Donovan wondered who was watching. If Davies was back, he'd see them come out the front and hopefully mistakenly conclude they'd searched the house. If he knew the case, then that would make him falsely relieved. But Donovan didn't see him. He only saw Eleri, casually scanning the street the same as him.

They walked down the sidewalk, not hopping over the fence again, and were almost back to the car when her phone rang. Eleri spoke for a few minutes, looking exasperated but faking a smile and a happy tone. When she hung up, she turned to him. "Can you take care of things tonight? My mom and dad are having an impromptu thirtieth anniversary celebration this evening."

"Where?"

"In Vegas, of course." Eleri gave him the same false smile. Debutante. Belle. Mainline matriarch. He couldn't quite tell. But on his friend it looked a bit scary. She sighed. "They want me to fly in this afternoon. Look, we're running lab tests now. I'll work from there and it's less than an hour away by air, in case something goes wrong. Otherwise, I'll be back tomorrow morning."

23

D onovan was on his own for the first time. It took all of fifteen minutes for Eleri to explain to him about her parents. About the fact that they could decide to fly to Vegas—some business her father was dealing in—and then decide, since all their friends were already there, they needed to host a party.

It would be small. Then Donovan almost snorted his coffee at the seventy person catered affair she mentioned. And that she had to get to town in time to get a gown.

Donovan didn't know what to make of that. He'd been to impromptu parties, but they involved beer and pot, not champagne and shrimp. He didn't buy last minute plane tickets. If he went anywhere it was usually on someone else's dime. He didn't travel for vacation; he usually just stayed at home, ran in the woods and did nothing. The idea of a hotel room in a strange town was too reminiscent of an unsettled childhood to be anything like fun. To think that's what people did when they had extra time and money was beyond him.

But Eleri handled it like a pro, packing her things at the house even while she explained, making certain that he had the evidence bag from Mrs. Sullivan's back yard and that he was ready to head to the Bureau to talk to Marina and get Walter on track. She promised she'd be available by phone and that she'd be working the majority of the time she was out.

Eventually, he pushed her out the door, saying, "Yes, Mom. I have my lunch packed, too."

She'd laughed at him, missing the clench in his chest.

It was a funny thing he'd heard people say in college. He'd never really felt comfortable enough to repeat it, and now he wished he hadn't. Donovan wasn't a man for memories. Only now did he understand why.

He was swamped with thoughts of his mother. Of her face, her hands, her smell. Suddenly he remembered curries simmering on the stove and scenting it from down the street before he walked in. He remembered the tiny white house with the loose screen door. His breath came fast from the sudden and clear image of her smiling face. He'd loved her, and never doubted she'd loved him. His father had himself together back then.

Donovan had forgotten that.

He mostly remembered Aidan as the man who pulled him from bed in the middle of the night, the smell of alcohol stumbling into the tiny homes before the man did. He remembered his father as the one who took them from place to place, from house to trailer to cheap apartment, each one worse than the one before. By the time he'd graduated high school, they lived in an area where used needles often were easily found in the gutters.

But Donovan had managed to make that his entire history. He'd forgotten that he'd once loved his father. The memory of that better time hit him like a Mac truck. It took him apart like one, too.

On the drive in, he nearly passed the exit for the Bureau,

despite the fact that the morning traffic was barely crawling. Any faster and he would have missed it.

Taking the ramp down into the surface streets, he made several turns and waited through a few lights, using the time to push away the tidal wave that had hit him. He hadn't seen it coming.

He believed when he went into the Academy that he'd learn how to use a gun and interrogate a suspect. The intellectual and academic side of it seemed enticing. He'd needed something new. He hadn't thought they'd want him to make friends or at least alliances.

Then they'd thrown him at Eleri, and he had probably the closest thing to a friend he'd had since grade school. Since his mother died and the easy, comfortable world he'd known had been plucked away from him one feather at a time.

Pulling the evidence bag from Eleri's empty seat and tucking it into the satchel he carried, he parked the small car and headed from the garage into the Bureau. Unlike the warren of halls he'd been in in Texas, this building was laid out in grids, easy to follow, each floor nearly identical to the one below. A person need only make sure they hit the right button on the elevator panel and all was well.

As he'd suspected, Marina Vasquez was already at her desk. He knocked, only just then thinking he hadn't brought coffee or anything—clearly not his strength to think ahead or make those nice friendly gestures that seemed natural to Eleri. "You ready for this?"

She grinned. "You got something good? Because I'm in the middle of some damn dreary paperwork."

He always forgot that she had other cases. Other people asking her for help, backup, support. But she seemed to want to do this, so he smiled and said, "Yes. Come on down to the conference room when you're ready."

"One minute." She turned her head back to her screen and

typed again into whatever she was working on, as Donovan turned and realized that the conference room might need to be reserved. What would happen if someone was already in it?

Luckily, no one was, and he set his things down. He'd just come up with a plausible lie about the information when Vasquez arrived, carrying a stack of papers of her own. "Whatcha got?"

Donovan grinned, excited about his first almost solo assignment, as small as it was. He shouldn't have felt so very off-the-leash, but he did. "Well, Eames was called out to a family event, so she'll be back tomorrow morning."

"Oh." Hand flying to her mouth, Vasquez looked stricken. "Is everything okay? She can stay as long as she needs."

Donovan almost laughed. "No, it's not that kind of a family emergency. It's her parents' thirtieth wedding anniversary."

"Why didn't she say anything before?" Vasquez now looked confused rather than concerned.

"Apparently, it's a 'small,' impromptu thing in Vegas with seventy of their closest friends. And caterers." He grinned at the silliness of it, until he realized that he may have let a cat out of a bag he hadn't thought about.

Shit, was quickly followed by, *too late now.*

"So it's spur of the moment and in Vegas and they want Eleri to fly in?"

So Vasquez didn't come from money either, or she would likely have understood the hop-on-a-plane-darling mentality. She wouldn't have said 'spur of the moment' either. More ordinary turn of phrase. Well, Vasquez was an investigator and was going to figure it out one way or another. So Donovan just said it. "Eleri comes from money."

"Money? Like a lot of money?" Vasquez tipped her head down and eyed him from under her brows, apparently not quite expecting this new line of information. *Interesting.*

He hadn't guessed Eleri's background either. Though he hadn't been surprised by it, it wasn't the one he'd mentally generated for her. "I don't know an amount, but it's of the equestrian-competitions and three-homes-with-names variety."

"Well, holy shit."

No. Marina Vasquez was not another trust fund baby working her way through the FBI.

She surprised him by following that up with, "You?"

"Oh hell no. I come from a variety of trailer parks, student loans all the way, and I've never even ridden a horse." It would just be too weird.

She looked at him more closely. "I wouldn't have guessed that either."

Maybe that was a good thing. He didn't want to cart that around with him. Instead of addressing it in any way—he'd had enough of that just on the drive back—he said, "Don't worry, she'll be back tomorrow morning, and you and I have some fun work to do."

"Then let's get started." She smiled despite the fact that he hadn't brought her coffee. He'd brought her meaningful work, and that trumped all else apparently.

"So, Eleri and I hit the Sullivan house this morning, cased the neighborhood, checked it out a little more."

"And you got a hit." She could see it on his face.

"Several, in fact." Then he lied through his long teeth. "A neighbor gave enough of a description to make a match on a visitor. We headed back to Ratz's house later for more info. I'll explain that in a minute." But could he? It was taking one lie on top of another to make it work. Then he would have to tell all his lies to Eleri so they'd line up. He veered back to the truth. "With the tip, we searched the back yard, on the assumption that Sullivan was in fact dead and from the same method as the others."

Vasquez nodded until he held up the evidence bag. Then her eyes flew wide.

"We recovered this—"

"Is it human?"

Always a good question to ask when a person recovered bones. As the Medical Examiner, he'd sent students out to ID bones as non-human more times than he could count. On the first few requests he'd gone out himself, thinking people had interesting finds, only to discover what they thought was a human skull was a wild pig, or something else so clearly not human, that he'd quit going. "Yes. I'm board certified in pathology, and Eleri has a forensics background. In fact, it's a human maxillary M2."

She frowned.

"Second molar, top of the mouth."

"Oh! So we'll test it then?"

He nodded again, grinning along with her pleasure at the evidence. Maybe she wasn't turning green because this was dry? Still, there were only so many people you would please by bringing them a broken tooth from a dead person's mouth. He was one of them. Good thing she was another. Then he pulled out the rest of it. "And we have her hairbrush to compare DNA from the root balls."

"Excellent."

Yes, a brush filled with someone else's hair was "excellent." He was in the right job for him, despite the fact that there were days he very much doubted it. "There's more. The reason we checked Ratz's house is because two local PD showed up on the scene at Sullivan's. Harding and Davies. Write that down."

She did and he kept talking.

"While we were there, Davies said something about bombs." Donovan lied through his teeth again. "Since we hadn't mentioned it, and she was just a missing person, we found that odd. So we flashed his picture around Ratz's house, and we got a hit."

"You have a statement?"

And this was exactly why you didn't lie. "No." He thought fast. "Neighbor wanted to remain anonymous. Wouldn't give a formal statement since it's against an officer."

Vasquez nodded as though he made perfect sense. So Donovan pushed forward before anything could enter through the massive holes in his lie. "Even without the statement we have enough to check up on Davies' background. And Eames and I are going to make that happen. We'd like Harding checked, too. Is he usually with Davies as a partner? Or was that just a daily assignment?"

She nodded, "You want to assess whether there's any reason to believe that Harding and Davies are working together or if Davies is going it alone."

"Well, probably as part of a cell." Donovan inserted, glad that she'd taken his change of track away from the odd path they'd taken to almost opening a formal investigation of a police officer. Then he wondered why she hadn't suggested they contact the Terrorism Task Force yet. They should have. Was she just following their lead? She shouldn't. Even as a junior agent, she'd gone to and graduated from the same Academy as both of them. Probably in a class or two right before or after Donovan for all it was worth. She should know. Why hadn't she said anything?

"So," Vasquez interrupted his thoughts. "You want to me check in on him? Put a tail on him?"

"Yes, check in on him, paper check only." Then he grinned. "We want to put Walter on his tail. He'll never see her coming."

～

COOPER LOOKED OUT HIS WINDOW. The downtown apartment was one of three he maintained, even though he only paid for one. This one was an empty unit. The owner had committed suicide, and the case remained open. In the meantime, Cooper had a very nice living room and bed room. He simply didn't go into the master bedroom and deal with the mess that was in there. It had been cleaned so it didn't smell, and that was enough.

Death didn't bother him the way it had when he was younger. The way it had when he first entered the service, where every death was in his face and each one rocked him to his core. He'd learned to put it away. To remind himself that death for country and freedom was an honor and that the brave men and women he'd seen die had chosen it. He'd been good that way for a long time.

Then he'd joined Special Forces and had to deal with the odd deaths. The necessary ones—the people who didn't have to die because of themselves, but had to go because they were in the way of something that had to happen. He'd talked himself into accepting those deaths, too.

Deaths overseas were somehow okay. As long as deaths at home were safe. Old people, stupid people, awful people. Everyone needed a category in his mind that made their death okay. Then Cooper could go on with his day, which often involved sitting around waiting for something to happen. It involved playing a stupid-ass game of cards while speaking only Pashto. That thought alone brought him around to Ken Kellen—languages expert. He could insult them in any language at all, it seemed. He even had a grasp on a few African dialects.

Barner once asked—actually harassed—him about it once, but Kellen had grinned and said, you never know. That day, he'd laughed and agreed with Kellen. That day, Kellen had been his friend.

But the deaths by betrayal, Cooper couldn't handle them.

The deaths that he couldn't categorize brought on the headaches and the voices. They screamed for redemption, for forgiveness, to be believed as the good men they were. But Cooper didn't know if they really were what he'd thought. He'd come to the conclusion that he might never know. If he couldn't tell, how could he sort them? How could he justify it? How could he quiet the voices and go home to his family?

As he looked out the window, he spotted two of the agents in an apartment across the street. Watching him. Watching more than him.

He gave them credit. They picked a good spot. View from one window of the apartment right into his living area. They'd found an apartment that he didn't have any paper trail to. That indicated the tag on his phone was most likely from them.

They watched from several stories higher, and while that limited their scope into his place, it looked like it gave them a straight line of sight over the building beside him and into the windows where Aziza and Alya were holding their meeting.

As far as Cooper could tell, that unit served no other purpose besides being a meeting point. Though some of downtown was gentrifying, this particular area was still held by landlords who didn't care what you really used the apartments for, as long as you paid on time.

Cooper paid a few days late every month. Didn't want to look suspicious. If he was too perfect a tenant, he might stand out. He wondered if the cell did the same.

The problem was that he'd spotted the agents with no real trouble. He did daily sweeps. When he saw a window he couldn't account for, he paid a little extra attention, and boom, today, there they were.

A little ways back, in the shadows to be sure, but watching his window. He headed into a different building and used his scope to watch them watching him. Only they were watching the jacket he'd stuffed and set into his one chair—a rolling desk chair, not a coincidence. Then he'd rolled Fake Cooper in front of the computer and left.

Sure enough, they watched Fake Cooper while Real Cooper watched them. A little too easily.

While Ken Kellen was the languages expert, he was no shit-for-brains when it came to surveillance either. So he would find the agents, too, and it wouldn't take him too long. If he connected them to Cooper, then Cooper might be well and truly fucked. He'd never get into the cell.

Heading home, he snuck into his own apartment, and wondered if the agents had figured out that "Cooper" had been sitting at the computer for over thirty minutes and hadn't moved. But he had to come back. He'd left his regular cell phone, the one with the tracking app, here at the apartment.

Though Cooper had previously been relatively convinced that the FBI hadn't tagged him with that weird app, now he leaned the other way. He just wasn't entirely convinced they needed it. If they didn't really need it, why risk him finding it? Because he would. Maybe they were just tapping his line or triangulating him every ten minutes. He could cloak the phone, but that would be even more suspicious if they were onto him. So he'd left it, then snuck back into his own place to pick it up.

Not a problem, he knew five points of entry and egress here. He looked around before peeking out a side window. Seemed they were still there.

They were going to fuck everything up.

His only real problem was the little redhead. Where was she today? Was she on his tail and he didn't see her? Cooper didn't think she was that good, but he'd been smacked and smacked hard before by underestimating people.

So he picked up the tracked phone off the small cardboard box he used as a bedside table in the second bedroom and called a number he knew. As he stared through the slit in the curtains from this room, he watched as the tall, Indian-looking agent picked his phone out of his pocket. Did he frown at the number?

Cooper hoped so.

"Hello." There was a question in the voice, but Heath recognized this number.

"Get the fuck off my tail."

He could see the movement in the other apartment. *Yeah, I know you're there. I see you. And you only think you see me.*

Then he added the part he needed to. The part that wanted to get out of him. "Or people will die."

24

E leri sipped champagne as she stood in an alcove, the party in one ear, her phone to the other. "He said what?"

"Or people will die." Donovan quoted. "Exact words."

"Geez-es." The most she could swear at one of her mother's precious soirees. "I'm not positive it's not a direct threat, but I don't know where to report it to, either."

"Anything good on your end?" he asked, knowing full well where she was.

"The turbot with artichoke was fantastic as were the escargot." She smiled faintly at the wall in front of her, thinking that she was still following her mother's party dictates—find something nice to say—and wondering if Donovan had ever eaten either turbot or escargot. She'd mapped the cells and what they knew, and tried to work. But she hadn't been able to make heads or tails of any of it.

"Well, I'm glad you're enjoying the party." The tone in his voice indicated that, no, he'd not had either and might vomit if he was offered them.

"I didn't say I was enjoying it." She offered with the lilt that always crept back in when she was around her mother.

"Eleri, there you are." As if summoned, her mother materialized by her side, a smile wider than normal plastered across her face.

"I have to go." She nearly whispered it, as though she could keep Nathalie Eames from seeing the dreaded device. Eleri pushed her finger on the button then shoved the phone into her small handbag that matched her dress and pasted on her own smile as she turned to face her mother.

Nathalie Eames was a vision, dark hair, dark eyes, round features, half African American and as beautiful as people of mixed race often are. Eleri knew where her mother came from. New Orleans to be exact. Eleri had spent time with Grandmere Remi, actually her great-grandmother. Nathalie's own mother Emmaline Remi, had been a wild child and eventually a drug addict who disappeared. To this day Eleri had no clue why her sister had been named for the woman.

Her own Emmaline long since gone, her mother's smile reached higher these days, but still not quite to her eyes. Eleri was the only one left to be the dutiful daughter. So she stood here in enough make-up that the quality of her gown was the only way she was distinguishable from a high-priced call girl.

"You must meet Wilson Canders, dear."

Ah yes. Wilson stood before her with a smile and a subtle pass of his gaze. Did she muster up to his expectations? His wishes? Her mother was sure hoping so.

Eleri fought the sigh and the urge to ask exactly which prominent family did Wilson hail from? And why did it matter to a woman who'd grown up in a small row house in New Orleans? Then Eleri reminded herself that was probably exactly why it mattered. But it didn't matter to Eleri.

With her own wide smile and proper tilt of her head, she held out her hand, fingers together and forward, as regal as she'd been taught as a child. "Special Agent Eleri Eames at your service. Wilson, was it?"

The last few words came out over his sputter.

She smiled. *Question answered.*

Eleri would attend the parties and go ball gown shopping in Vegas and listen as her mother told the seamstress all the last minute hemming and tucking that must be done to make the gown perfect. But she would not date any of the men her mother had thrown at her.

"And you?" She cued the man who was still stuck with his tongue somewhere on the roof of his mouth. Her mother's fault, Eleri thought. If she'd thought to mention the most important thing in Eleri's life along with the introduction, it might not be a surprise. But here stood Wilson trying to remember what he did for a living. Her mother was long gone, having done her usual introduce-and-ditch.

"I'm a VP at a software firm."

She didn't care but smiled anyway, and exchanged her champagne glass as a server went by with a tray. "How exciting. What exactly do you do there?"

"I procure funding for research and development." He grinned, having said the words *research and development* as though he were talking about cancer treatments or reducing global warming. She reminded herself that the champagne was good and the dress was gorgeous, though it was out of the price range of her FBI salary.

Eleri was taking a rather full sip when he asked, "So how does a trust fund baby wind up as an FBI agent?"

Before she could answer, he added, "Are you active or is that a fun title?"

She pulled her leather wallet from the small bag, reminding herself that you just never knew when you might need your credentials, but she hadn't thought it would be to impress the men her mother constantly dragged past her. None stuck. This one wouldn't either.

Holding up the wallet with the only ease she felt tonight, she then watched as he inspected it with a grin. She felt compelled to add, "I don't touch the trust fund." And though she also felt compelled, she didn't say, "Because half of it belongs to my murdered sister."

There were too many questions generated by that one sentence, and not even the obvious ones. Unfortunately, he was now a little too enamored with her status, and she took a moment to assess if it was her. Surely one of these days, her mother—even if purely by accident—would throw an interesting man her way. It hadn't happened yet.

She smiled at him just as she caught the end of his sentence.

"—would you put me in handcuffs?" His subtle leer made her regret her own smile.

No, she had not been too uptight. Eleri grinned wider. "I don't carry handcuffs. I carry a tazer." Then she leaned in and whispered in his ear, "A good number of grown men piss their pants when they're tazed."

Then she stepped back, let loose a grin she learned from a girl on some disturbing meds in the hospital, and polished off her champagne. Surely this shit had to wind down soon. Weddings, funerals, and her mother's summons could not be missed.

Eleri turned to find her parents on the dance floor, her father gazing into her mother's eyes. They seemed good together, despite the fact that they'd lost a child young. Despite the time they'd spent apart because her mother couldn't deal with the loss and her father wouldn't.

Though she'd grown up in their house—or houses—she'd never understood how her parents lived their life. From the moment her sister had disappeared, they'd all had different reactions. For a long time, her mother lived in a pretend world where Emmaline was just a little bit lost and would be back in a short while. Her father had thrown himself into his work. He couldn't save his daughter, but he could build an empire. And Eleri had needed to be useful.

She'd been on the fast track to the FBI since age ten. Wanting desperately to be like the men and women who'd searched for her sister. Somehow, she'd wanted it deep in her bones despite the fact that those men and women had failed. Or maybe because of it. Even though she'd known for a while what no one else knew—her sister would never be found alive.

"Hanging out at the edges, are we?" Haley Jean Bellamy sidled up to her, a rounded glass of warm red wine in her manicured hands.

"Nice fingernails." Eleri replied with a genuine grin. "Did your momma take you out for a manicure?"

"You know she did." Haley Jean laughed. A PhD botanist, Haley Jean dug into her trust fund with as much joy as she dug in the dirt. She owned a wooded property with three greenhouses. The houses had some kind of distinction that Eleri could never keep straight, even with her own biology degree and Haley Jean's ever enthusiastic descriptions. "Should we kiss, so our mommies think we're gay and stop trying to set us up?"

"Tempting." Eleri replied, wanting to hug her friend and catch up, but a school girl display was frowned upon here. "Sooner or later doesn't she have to throw me something decent?" she asked, echoing her own earlier thoughts.

"Given her taste, no." Haley Jean plucked a chocolate from a passing tray and ate as though her own mother wasn't watching. "I saw she threw the young Canders buck at you. Do not go there. It's disturbing."

Eleri couldn't hide the genuine laugh as it burbled out. "He asked if I'd use my handcuffs on him and I told him I'd taze him . . . and that he'd piss his pants."

"Oh, good for you." Haley Jean, like Eleri, maintained a passive smile and smooth lilt to her words. "I threatened him with a variety of botanical poisons."

"Nice one." Canders had clearly not been the lucky shot her mother had to someday take, and Eleri wondered exactly how much longer she would have to stand here in this whale-bone supported gown that flowed around her ankles and made her look like a slim goddess with class and a bit of sugar. It so wasn't her. "Want to meet up at the bar later and have something without a French name and catch up?"

"Love to. What's the time frame on this shindig?"

"Oh honey," Eleri mimicked her mother. "There is no time frame on class."

Haley Jean's laugh covered the sound of Eleri's phone at first. She had it on silent, but she felt the buzz of movement tug the strap to the small purse at her wrist and she pulled the phone out to check it.

Donovan. But she'd just talked to him. Turning sideways again, she let Haley Jean shield her from the guests. It was just so tacky talking on her phone all the time. "Donovan?"

There was no preamble, nothing. Just, "We just got pictures from Walter. She tailed Davies to the Calabasas group. Where he met up with Kellen and opened a duffel bag of guns and distributed them."

"She has photos of this?"

"We do. Now." His voice was tense. No wonder. Terrorism, illegal arms distributions to probable terrorists. Her heart rolled in her chest.

"How is she transmitting?" Surely she wasn't using her cell phone. "If it's radio frequency, get her out of there now."

They would sweep. The cell wouldn't last long if they weren't regularly sweeping for spyware. Ken Kellen or anyone who'd been special ops would know better, and Walter herself would know better. The tension Eleri felt let go as quickly as it had gripped her.

"Cell phone."

It popped back into place, the bands that tightened her chest, and she reminded herself that Donovan was new, but he should have learned from the Academy—

His voice interrupted her thoughts. "FBI issue, set solely for transmission."

Her shoulders relaxed, probably obviously to everyone around her. The pale russet gown her mother had chosen was gathered and twisted in a slim strip over one shoulder only. Leaving the other bare to be seen as she tensed and relaxed each time.

She went for a more important topic, glad she hadn't accused Donovan of being a dumbass. "So Kellen just armed the entire cell? Handguns?"

"Only a few. Bigger game hunting."

He wouldn't list the makes and models over the phone, it wasn't like this call was secure, but he did say, "Three long range, with scopes."

His voice was somber. He knew what that meant. So did Eleri. Sniper rifles. "I'm on my way."

"See you." He knew she was a few from being there, but it was better than coming back tomorrow. Even before she turned to tell her friend, Haley Jean was on it.

"Give me your room key. I'll get your things. You get a flight and kiss your momma goodbye."

Eleri handed everything over and held onto the thought that while she didn't need a boyfriend, she did need her friends. She made a mental note to call Haley Jean soon and see her after the case was over. It had been too long. Then she wound her way into the fray for the first time tonight and found her mother.

The woman was a master of social cues, but somehow managed to miss that Eleri was running down an emergency. Or the woman had caught the hint and was actively ignoring it.

"Mama, Daddy," She broke into the conversation with another older couple. "I'm so sorry, I've been called on an emergency and I have to go."

"Oh baby, not tonight." Her mother then turned her frown to a grin in a way that Eleri always thought would make her highly suspicious if she were interrogating the woman. "Just tell them no." When Eleri started to shake her head, her mother put up another front. "Let someone else handle it tonight. It's not like no one else can do what you do."

Eleri felt her head snap back. It wasn't intended as an insult, and it wasn't even the value judgment that got to her. She was used to them from the mother who hadn't understood a single one of Eleri's life choices since the day her sister had disappeared. It was that Eleri suddenly realized that her mother had it all wrong. No one else *could* do what she could. With her appointment to NightShade, that had actually been recognized.

"Mother, this is my case. I have to go handle it." With that she took a page from her mother's book and kissed the woman on the cheek as polite as could be, but brooking no argument.

Her father was another story. He'd accepted a long time ago that his girl wasn't going to live the life he chose for her. Still, he inserted his choices wherever he could. So after a short, strong hug, he told her, "Go get'em, Cupcake."

As if Eleri was anyone's "cupcake." She smiled and turned away, weaving her way out through the partiers, casually brushing off anyone who tried to stop her, congratulate her on her parents' long marriage, or ask about her work. In deference to her mother she waited until she hit the doors leading through the maze into the hotel before she pulled out her phone and started looking up flights.

Shit. She could barely make it if—

And there was Haley Jean, sitting politely with the bag Eleri had brought and hadn't even really unpacked. Her friend looked ridiculous, sitting on a lobby couch in her long, deep red dress, her pearls around her neck and dripping from her ears, and Eleri's plain black bag sitting next to her. Eleri was about to look even more ridiculous. "Thank you so much." She hugged her friend, "But I need to get a car and there's a flight—"

"I already got you one, Sweetie. It will be here in two minutes." Haley Jean hugged her back and said, "When you get done with this, just show up at the farm. We need a girls' week."

The grin came easily. The lapse since she'd last spent time with Haley Jean suddenly unimportant in the way of real friends. "You know I will."

The car pulled up and Eleri climbed in, pulling her gown behind her as Haley Jean loaded in her bag. She tried not to fret her way through the drive, traffic was going to be what it was, and it was Vegas, there would always be another flight to LA.

She must look ridiculous, but there hadn't been time to change.

The security agents were ready for her, but not the discrepancy between her looks and her ID. "I came directly from a party." It was all she said, not wanting to protest and cause suspicion. Eventually they let her and her bag with her gun tucked inside through into the airport proper. She wheeled the plain black duffel down to the gate, once again looking horribly out of place in a party gown, spiked heels, and jewels that she only just now remembered she'd borrowed from her mother. But she didn't lift her hand to check them. The movement had been trained out of her during her teen years.

Instead, she explained the necessity of her bag to the flight attendants and whisked her way into first class where she said no to more alcohol and yes to ice water. With lime. Because she was in a party gown and still wearing that whale-boning and a color of lipstick that said she belonged in noir film. She had her water and her skirts tucked up around her while she tried to get intel from Donovan on her phone.

Not much they could say, but she managed to convey she barely made her flight and, so far, was on time.

Just then, someone slipped into the seat next to her. Thankful for the first class opening and debating if she would catch any sleep on the short flight, she wasn't prepared for the resonant voice and the introduction.

She was looking up and taking stock before her brain cataloged his words. Dark jeans, a belt, a pressed white button-down shirt. She was taking his outstretched hand by habit before she felt the jolt of his too-blue eyes. He was just a little too rugged to be pretty with his neat brown hair. His voice almost lulled her. "Avery Darling of the South Georgia Darlings."

The words registered.

Lord. It must be because of the dress, the hair, the makeup. She couldn't take it again. Though she was on duty again with the Bureau, she was damn well off duty with the pageantry, dress be damned. She smiled sweetly back. "Eleri Eames of the Federal Bureau of Investigation."

He blinked.

She tugged her hand back and turned her attention to her phone, alerting her partner that they were finally taxiing.

Just then, Avery Darling of the South Georgia Darlings busted out with the laughter he'd apparently been trying to hold back and nearly choked on his beer.

25

Donovan watched as Eleri exited the town car in front of the small house. It was nearly three in the morning but she looked like a million bucks. Red lipstick, bare leg leading the way out of the back seat of the car, foot encased in a heel the likes of which he'd never seen on Eleri's feet before.

He wouldn't have guessed it was her if he hadn't known she was coming, known she'd had no time to change and would have worked instead of changing anyway. If he hadn't seen her face, he might have thought someone else had taken her car from the airport to here. But it was Eleri in the long, sunset colored gown that swirled around her ankles and bared a shoulder to the cool L.A. night air. It was Eleri who laughed to someone in the car, then stood and talked over the hood as the other occupant stood, too.

A man. Donovan smelled him as soon he saw him. A sniff, a slow inhale, and he got a few assessments, none of them worth anything. He was a guy. He bathed regularly. Before Donovan could figure anything out, the man headed around the back of the car and knocked on the trunk that popped open even as he did it.

Though Eleri reached out for the bag, the man slung it over his shoulder and his voice resonated through the air.

"Well, I must admit that I'm disturbed that you're involved with a case right now and I won't get to see you again."

She was facing away from him, but Donovan could hear the grin in her voice, and he took another sniff of the air as she spoke. "Who knows when it will wrap up? But you could give me your number?"

Her hand was out, and Donovan ducked back inside, not sure exactly what he was witnessing, but as they came closer he smelled the pheromones between the two of them and it was best he get out of the way.

"Donovan!" She called to him, stopping his retreat. "I'm so glad you're still up. As soon as I change . . ." She pointed a finger up and down her form. She was severely overdressed compared to both her date for the evening and needs of the situation.

"Yes. Vasquez is here and we're on it."

She turned to him again. "Donovan, this is Avery Darling of the North Dakota Executioners."

The porch light must have lit his face up, that or Avery Darling had superior vision. Because he immediately caught Donovan's confusion. "Professional Hockey."

He almost said, "Looks like you still have all your teeth," but bit his tongue. Instead he said, "Nice to meet you."

Then Eleri continued with her introduction, telling Avery Darling about her partner. The man laughed at her, then whispered.

Donovan turned away, trying not to hear, but he did.

"I can have your number, too?" Even the words had a goofy grin in them.

Words sang in Donovan's head, *someone's got a boyfriend*. He shut the door behind himself hoping not to hear more. A moment later, they came through the doorway, Avery Darling still carrying her bag which he set just inside the small entryway as he looked at Donovan for the first time in the light.

Should he growl? Play the overprotective friend?

But Avery's smell changed. *Oh shit.* Dude was threatened by Donovan. So he overplayed it. "I'm heading into the kitchen to catch up with Marina. Let me know if you need anything."

It was for show. He'd hear the two of them just fine from in here and Eleri knew it.

But Eleri was Eleri. Inside of a minute she'd exchanged numbers and shuffled Darling boy out the door, back into the waiting town car. She passed by, bag in hand, her body tilted away to balance the weight, quite the feat on the heels.

"Holy shit." Marina finally chimed in from her post at the small kitchen table. "You are all dolled up. Didn't change for the flight?"

"No time. I boarded in full regalia." She disappeared down the hall and was back far too quickly in jeans and a t-shirt, but still with the hair up and makeup on. She turned to Marina, who appeared both captivated and confused by Eleri. At least Donovan had known for a while what her background was. Marina had only a few hours to deal with it.

"He sat next to me on the plane and introduced himself as though he was from an old money family. Which he's not. He just did it because he thought I was overdressed for the plane. Which I was."

Marina stifled a small laugh. "What did he say when he found out you actually are from an old money family?" Then she stuttered, "You are, right? Or do I have that wrong?"

"Oh no, I am. I'm Eleri Grace Eames of the Virginia Eameses, who came over on the Mayflower. My father is Thomas Hale Eames of the Massachusetts Hales." She gave them her best classy background recitation.

"And your mother?"

"Oh, she's Nathalie Beaumont, of the New Orleans Remis. A family from the wrong side of the graveyards and the levees." She grinned just as wide at that.

Donovan hadn't known any of that. But Marina was nodding and getting straight to the point. The two of them had been up, talking with Walter and organizing what they had. But Eleri was the senior agent and Donovan didn't want to move forward without her. He didn't want the responsibility, especially after Westerfield told them to handle probable terrorism themselves. Whatever this was, it was already going to have his fingerprints all over it.

Was it cowardly? Possibly. But he also reminded himself it was smart. Two heads were better than one. Marina was great, but couldn't factor anything of the NightShade directives into her advice or decisions. And Eleri was the senior agent because she'd been out in the field before, worked various units in the Bureau. He was on his second case, not a lot to recommend him there. Pretty much zero experience.

She was picking up the tablet they had out and flipping through the pictures they'd collected from Walter. "Is she still out?"

She meant Walter and Donovan shook his head. "The group disbanded about an hour ago," He checked his watch, "Shit. Two hours ago. And she followed Kellen back to his place and we told her to call it a night."

"Did she have any idea if he knew he was being followed?"

Good. He was doing the right things. The pride in his chest was that of a self-pat-on-the-back. "I asked specifically that question, and she said she didn't think so. It's always possible he knew and wasn't letting on."

Eleri thought for a moment and again came to the same conclusions he had. "But if he'd known he was being followed, he probably would have called off the dogs and not distributed the guns."

Donovan nodded at her. "I agree. He would have to know the images we have are grounds for arrest and questioning. If we can locate just one illegal gun, then we can convict him."

But conviction wasn't their job. He looked to Marina who was nodding her agreement. She was agreeing with the idea that Kellen probably would never have done what he did had he known about Walter. She probably thought they were leaving smaller fish in play as bait for bigger ones. If only that's truly what they were doing.

He interrupted the thoughts that were rolling over Eleri's features as she looked through the pictures and notes. "It gets worse."

She looked up at him.

"I told you on the phone that he said people would die. That he caught Marina and me in the adjacent building watching him. And we were dumb."

"What do you mean?" She squinted a little as though that would help her sort out his dumbness. Beside him Marina sighed, obviously feeling as stupid as he did at getting caught by Rollins.

"He set up a dummy at his computer. Back facing us, and we watched it for a while. He then called and issued the threat and the dummy didn't move at the computer."

She fought a grin. "How long did you stake out the dummy?"

"Twenty-five minutes." He looked at the ceiling as though it would forgive him when even she wouldn't.

"Seriously, the guy is special ops. This had to happen sooner or later. If it makes you feel better, when I was just starting, a perp once came up behind me and tapped me on the shoulder at a stakeout. Total rookie mistake. Didn't account for a second guy."

"Were you okay?" Marina jumped in. Donovan wanted to know, too.

"Yeah. He tried to jump me, but the tap on the shoulder gave him away, and I managed to get the better of him. The gun helped." She shook her head, her eyes far away as she recalled her own stupidity to help ease their frustration. Then she came back to the pictures in front of her. "What do we have on each of these guys?"

"Wait. I didn't tell you how it gets worse."

"Oh, staking out the dummy wasn't it?"

Shamed, he shook his head again. "No, that was stupid, but with no consequences beyond what we already had. No, when we left, we passed Aziza." He sighed, then continued before Eleri could prod him. "I think she knows who we are."

"Why? What do you mean?" The string of questions tumbled over each other as she fought for some level of clarity where there was none.

"I can't say for sure." Donovan turned to Marina who shrugged her shoulders even as she agreed with him.

"It was the way she looked at us." Marina filled in. "She didn't say anything, but as she passed us on the street she paid too much attention. Examined us just a little too closely to be casually passing by someone she didn't recognize in some way."

ELERI FELT FRAZZLED. The one time she'd taken a break from the middle of a case! She'd never done it before. Never let her mother browbeat her into these things when she was working. She'd always managed a solid "no" before.

Honestly, she expected the anniversary party wasn't as last-minute as they'd said, still she'd been suckered. The gown, the champagne, the flying, it had all been useless by nature, and she'd missed an important development in the case.

Currently she was helping Marina sort through individual pictures Walter had sent of each of the participants. Though the previous meeting had been more male, this one had almost half the attendees as women. The way people sat, leaning toward someone, a hand on a shoulder, or just the position at the table, led her to pull her old psychology training out of the back closet of her brain. She was pretty convinced there were maybe two or three singles in the group, and the others were couples. Husbands and wives most likely.

Despite the fact that she'd gotten dressed yet again to head into the Bureau, and despite the fact that she sat at the conference table, her brain kept pulling to the side. She was trying to play catch-up here and trying not to think about the benefits of flying to Vegas. She'd seen Haley Jean and she wanted to visit her friend's farm in her downtime. Grab some wine and eat vegetables Haley Jean had cross bred and grown herself. She wanted to relax. But that wasn't coming soon; she had to live through this case first.

Certainly it wouldn't happen with Avery Darling on her mind.

Eleri told herself it was stupid to think of him. But he'd already texted and wished her luck with the case and said he hoped he could see her again. She reminded herself she was not a schoolgirl with a crush but a special agent with a gun and badge and a werewolf for a partner.

She turned her face back to the pictures as Marina started talking.

"This looks like Warner Salling—the owner of the house." Marina pointed to a government ID shot on the tablet as Donovan leaned over Eleri's shoulder to see.

"Lord. Warner Salling sounds like an evil name. If we arrest him, he'll never get a fair trial." Eleri sighed. He even looked determined and rigid, like part of a terrorist cell.

Marina held up her own tablet with the man's driver's license picture enlarged. Visually, he looked a few years older, and Eleri was confident of the match. Next Marina pulled information on his wife, and they quickly found her face at the meeting too.

Warner Salling's son was not present at the meeting, but his twenty-three-year-old daughter was.

Donovan finally spoke. "The family that slays together, stays together."

"Oh, not funny." Eleri cringed before turning back to Marina while Donovan shrugged. Morbid humor was not uncommon in medical examiners, cops, or agents. Donovan was now two out of three. She should have seen it coming, but instead of saying anything more, she turned to the other woman, "Do we have any intel on the missing son? Let's find him and see if he's just absent from this meeting or if he's not part of his family's regime."

As Eleri flipped through the pictures one by one, she was more and more impressed with Walter's skills. There were dead-on pictures of each person at the meeting. There was not a single back of a head anywhere that didn't have a corresponding clear shot of the face. She'd also managed as many shots as possible of people standing.

It was something Eleri hadn't thought about until she'd made it through the Academy, but knowing how tall your perp or suspect was changed the game in finding them. Facial recognition was great, but you wanted whole body stats if you had to run anyone down.

Walter had given them everything. She hadn't just hidden in the bushes below one window, but must have stayed for hours, changing locations and knowing what information to get. Eleri wanted the woman at Quantico, but didn't think Walter would agree. Instead, she'd be an investigator for hire, and soon enough Eleri wouldn't be able to afford her.

"Give me a minute." Marina started tapping away at her keyboard while Eleri examined the pictures for any additional clues. Walter had them time-stamped and Eleri hoped something more might be found.

Once Eleri had come back, she'd moved the meeting to the Bureau building despite the late hour. Had anyone hacked the modem at the small house or anywhere down the line, the results could have been disastrous.

Eleri was considering moving them entirely. They'd been at the house for a while. Timing was an issue, but Marina and Donovan getting caught by Cooper Rollins and warned off? Then having Aziza seem to recognize them? For a moment she wondered if it was because she'd been gone . . . But that was insulting to both the others. As though they needed her to do the job correctly.

Almost as if he'd read her mind, Donovan leaned over and said, "It's probably a good thing you weren't with us yesterday. Rollins and Aziza may recognize us, but as far as we know, at least she doesn't recognize you. . ."

As his voice trailed off, there was a look in his eyes; Eleri recognized it. They didn't know the wolf either. There was still hope. They hadn't been completely busted.

Also, there was now a good reason they couldn't bring Marina along on surveillance. Eleri had wondered how long they could keep that ruse up. But she nodded at him and turned back to the pictures while Donovan checked out the weapons, trying to see if any makes and models pinged anything useful.

The sniper rifles bothered her. When she let herself trail that thought all the way through, the understanding that several of the members recognized Donovan's and Marina's faces made her afraid. Again, she pushed her thoughts to the task. From the pictures, the people in the house either were Oscar-caliber actors, revealing pertinent and almost definitely illegal information, or they had no idea they were being watched.

Go Walter. At least that much of surveillance had gone right. Donovan set his tablet down, his expression not good.

"I have a link to one of the victims: these guns—the makes and models—exactly match some of the supplies missing from Vivian Dawson's records."

26

Once again, Donovan was both exhausted and itching to run. The run wouldn't happen, and he set his mind to accepting that. The morning had been busy, and the day was nowhere near over yet. In fact, he had to get his shit together since Westerfield called and let them know he'd just parked and would be "attending the conference room" any moment now.

Donovan figured they had the length of time of an elevator ride, because the man would not stop, since he wouldn't drink the coffee here. "Marina?"

"Yeah, I get it." She was gathering her things. "Your SAC called and I need to get out of here for your meeting."

At least he didn't detect any bitterness in her voice. Then again, if it were there, would he? He could hear so much, but unlike Eleri, he'd never listened. Not to people. He'd had no desire to understand them or get closer or be anything other than a voice of reason from beyond the grave. He found himself now looking at his special talents and realizing he was still at a distinct disadvantage.

"We'd keep you. It's a Westerfield thing." Eleri lied convincingly, with a shrug and a half smile as though 'what could you do?'

Marina nodded, still stacking reports, tablets and more. Then she shocked them. "I don't know your SAC from anywhere before. I thought I was keeping better track than that." She looked at them expectantly.

Eleri kept her cool. "Hmm. He's been with the Bureau quite a while."

That was all she said, and she left Marina Vasquez probably on her way to investigate the mysterious boss of her team members, and Donovan wondering just what—if anything—she might find. It was possible Westerfield's entire record was redacted.

Even though she was halfway out the door, Marina Vasquez wasn't done with them. "I'm going to see if I can dig up anything indicating when or how Cooper Rollins might have sent that phone with the pictures."

Donovan smelled Westerfield before he saw him, and heard him just at the same time Vasquez did.

"That's a dangerous assumption—that Cooper Rollins sent that phone. We don't yet have any evidence that he did, do we?" With the last two words, Westerfield turned his attention from chastising the new girl to looking expectantly at Donovan and Eleri.

As Donovan opened his mouth to say no, there was no new evidence, Marina straightened. Though she was behind Westerfield, she spoke solidly and without hesitation. Odd, since she often looked to the two of them for lead. Maybe she just didn't like his insinuation.

"No sir, we don't. That's why I'm on a positive/negative search. If it's not possible that Cooper Rollins sent the phone, then we can start looking other places." Her gaze was steady as she stood up to an agent clearly her superior. "Right now, we need anything we can get, and we have nowhere else to look."

She waited a beat, her eye steady on Westerfield's, not defi-
ant, but standing her ground. She was afraid—the light but
sharp smell coming from her Donovan's only cue, but one he
believed.

"Good point." It was all Westerfield said before offering her
half a nod of dismissal and turning into the room.

Behind his back, Donovan caught Eleri giving Vasquez a
thumbs-up signal, then he followed the two of them somberly
back to the seats. He was far too uncomfortable to make this
report. So far they had managed to tie everything in the past
together relatively neatly. Eleri had fleshed out who had killed
whom. They had eyes on Rollins, they knew the Indian faction
existed, even if they didn't know where. Now their job was to
use that information to predict the future, and on that front,
they had exactly jack shit.

Westerfield closed the door on Eleri and Vasquez'
exchange, appearing not to see it. But Donovan didn't put
anything past the man. Eleri might give hand signals behind
their boss's back, but Donovan didn't think that was necessarily
off his radar and Donovan wasn't about to do it himself.

As per usual, Westerfield seated himself and began asking
questions before either of them was fully settled. Donovan
hadn't yet figured out if this was a good thing or not. Sometimes
the man waited; it seemed to mean the news was bigger, but not
necessarily better.

"Cooper made you?" He looked at Donovan.

"Yes, sir."

"Did he see your faces?"

Donovan hadn't seen that coming. He'd just assumed
Cooper had. He'd called them after all. Though they'd given
him the number, in case there was anything he'd wanted to
share—despite the one time he'd sat down to speak with them
and repeatedly said there wasn't. "I have to assume so. He
called me. I supposed it's possible that he called three other

people who might have been surveilling him and said the same thing. I didn't actually admit that I was doing it. However, he has spoken to me before and operating under any lesser assumption is probably foolhardy."

With effort, Donovan made himself shut up. Time to stop talking about what an idiot he'd been.

"Has he seen the wolf?"

Both of them shook their heads and Donovan wondered if Eleri was sticking up for him or just trying to get into the conversation.

Westerfield breathed in and out, not slowly, but audibly. This time he looked at both of them. "Have you had any more run-ins with the local lobomau?"

Donovan tried to hide his shock at the use of the term he'd only ever heard from Wade. Then again, Wade de Gottardi and Westerfield went way back themselves, and apparently Donovan was pretty late to his own game. He shook his head.

"Then you'll go back in that way if it comes up?" Westerfield looked between them, and it seemed they weren't answering fast enough. "Sounds like Eames here shut them down. I don't think they'll give you more trouble."

That seemed to be enough for Westerfield. They'd been attacked, they'd made it out, therefore all was well. Eleri had written up the incident, and Donovan signed off on it, though they both agreed there was a certain element to it that left a sour taste, they had reported only the facts and had to do so. What was missing was how Eleri won.

The report said she'd drawn her gun, that she'd placed it under the chin of the lead female. While that did somewhat coincide with the wolves backing off, Donovan was very certain that wasn't the actual cause. He'd seen Eleri's eyes. And they still hadn't discussed it because she'd redirected the conversation with her insight of the words "Fracture Five."

Westerfield must have ducked his hand into his pocket,

because a quarter now walked across his knuckles. It roamed, flipping slowly and very controlled from one end of his hand to the other. Donovan was never sure if it was just a habit, or if it was intended as a warning.

"Who are you following?"

That was the big question. Eleri clicked on her tablet as though she needed to be reminded of the names. "Cooper Rollins still—through his phone tracker. Though we aren't sure he doesn't know about it. Also via Walter."

"Walter? I don't recall that name on the reports." Westerfield looked confused for the first time. Usually he just made them tell him things he already knew from their reports.

Donovan fielded this one. Give Eleri some time to think, if she needed it. "Lucy Fisher. The PI. Her nickname in the square—where the vets are, and where Cooper Rollins sometimes hangs out—is Walter Reed."

Westerfield blinked. Normally. That was probably the only acknowledgment Donovan was going to get.

Eleri picked up the slack, even though he could see she was getting a bit stressed. She wasn't even supposed to be back in town from her parents' party yet. Donovan was betting she was supremely grateful she'd come back early.

"We're following the cell in Calabasas. Checking names. We're running down the son of Warner Salling. Salling and his wife own the house where the meeting was held. His daughter was attending, the son was not. We're trying to find Jacob Salling and determine if he's a detached part of the group, no help at all, or if he has any insights into his parents."

"What about the Indian man?" The quarter kept walking.

"Nothing." Donovan reported, pissed that he'd been forced to say it.

"But what kind of nothing?" Though Westerfield's eyes turned to him and bored in, Donovan knew what he was being asked.

"We checked the pamphlet. No church exists with that name. The website has only the one page despite the menu at the top." Donovan took a deep breath and kept going. There was a lot of nothing there. "The physical address listed on the pamphlet is phantom."

There was "non-existent address" which could mean anything from 441 wasn't a viable house number—there was a 437 and a 443 but no 441. To the street ended with home number 350—didn't have any block on the 4s. Or even that the home address led to a non-home, something like a factory, school, business complex, or some other non-residential type building. This one was category: phantom.

There was nothing. No street that matched the name, though it sounded like it could exist. In L.A. it was probably harder to make up a street name that didn't actually exist. You'd be more likely to discover there was a "Morgan Street" in Calabasas and a "Witson" in Culver City. This one didn't exist at all. The zip code started with 913. That was LA, but once again, they'd managed to get one that wasn't real.

The problem was "non-existent" was helpful. People tended to build fictions from things or places they knew. You just had to figure out why your perp was listing X office building as his home address and you could maybe find him. "Phantom" led nowhere.

Donovan picked up the thread with more bad news. "There's nothing to tie the printing of the pamphlet to anything unusual. We can't find a print shop that remembers printing it. We ran a few partial fingerprints but got nothing useful, there were no fulls."

"Paper can be a bitch to recover from, too." It was probably the best encouragement they were going to get from Wester-field today.

"The only thing we do have," Eleri picked up, seemingly as pissed off about the nothing as he was, "is the phrasing."

Westerfield waited.

"The phrase, 'the best of the sons of men' has been linked back to India and the belief that Jesus spent his middle years there. Ages twelve to thirty." When Westerfield paused again, she filled the void with more words. "They believe in and revere Saint Issa—believed to be Jesus, traveling through India."

"Jesus, huh?" For the first time Westerfield looked like he was absorbing information rather than just cataloging it and judging them.

Nodding, Donovan picked up the thread. "Many Hindus, Muslims, and even some Buddhists refer to Jesus as 'Saint Issa.' In some sects of those religions it's simply accepted as scripture. That's where Jesus was and how it went."

"So we have three deeply religious sects?"

Donovan sighed, having learned not to answer before he was certain. He could see Eleri doing the same, but she let him field the question. "We have two seemingly deeply religious sects—the Christian group in Calabasas and the Muslims in the downtown area. The Indian man was in the Huntington Beach area, and the quote makes him *seem* like part of a deeply religious group, but we don't have the evidence to back that statement up yet."

For just an instant Eleri looked put out. Then the words out of her mouth confirmed it. "Can we not be assigned to religious nut-jobs next time? Are we the 'Crimes committed in the name of God' unit?"

Well, well, she'd managed to startle Westerfield. Then he laughed. "No, you are not the 'Crimes committed in the name of God' unit. It's strictly coincidence. But extremists are your criminals. 'Extreme anything' is often criminal related."

That was all Westerfield said, but Donovan started tying in his FBI Academy training, finding a lot of it matched. Extreme wealth was often gathered criminally or at least through unethical loopholes. There weren't that many incredibly wealthy people who were completely ethical. Extreme poverty often caused criminal activity. Extreme religion led to extreme actions . . . He could keep going.

Eleri seemed to accept that, even though their boss hadn't said they wouldn't get assigned to the same kind of thing next time. "Because I believe in things, and I'm personally offended that these nut jobs do this in the name of an otherwise peaceful religion. How do they all link?"

Westerfield knew this. Donovan wanted to frown. Was this his version of brainstorming? As though if they all sat down and recapped it they might see a new connection? He wasn't presenting it that way. He was still lording the "In Charge" part of "Special Agent in Charge" over them.

Ultimately, Donovan knew his role. Though this boss was more overbearing than the administrator at the medical examiner's office, Westerfield was around a damn lot less. Thankful for that, Donovan answered the question. "Right now, the link is the term 'Fracture Five' and the fact that Eleri can connect each group to a specific murder with an identical MO."

She didn't wait for him to think of the next one. "And the murders' all link back to Cooper Rollins."

"And the military." Donovan finished. He didn't know what to make of Rollins' yet. He could be the mastermind or an entry level anti-American soldier or just a guy with PTSD and bad taste in friends.

Okay, he was in way too deep to be the last one, but he was hard to place. Donovan said so.

"I don't know." Eleri replied. "He's intricately linked to each of the four victims."

"How is he linked to Mrs. Sullivan? I know she had a military connection, but what specifically?" Westerfield watched the quarter.

Had they not included that in the reports? Donovan almost rocked back. No, Marina had brought them the information, just a few days ago . . . Yesterday? *Holy shit*, he couldn't even tell anymore. "Her husband was Ken Kellen's superior officer. And she was a secretary on base during her husband's appointment. She retained the job even after he died, having cleared her own security checks. She left the job suddenly, and it was rumored that she'd gone whistleblowing on something."

"So she's linked to Kellen, not Rollins?" Their boss squinted and the quarter stopped. Now he looked from one to the other.

Shaking her head, Eleri filled him in. "We found indications that Rollins may have visited the Sullivans. She sent both of them . . . Not *care packages* per se, but stuff through military channels. It seemed to start when Kellen joined the Green Berets. Before Rollins met and married Alyssa, before Mr. Sullivan died."

"So she went to the secretarial job after the army?"

Eleri nodded.

Now Westerfield was leaning over the table, his elbows splayed, the quarter finally disappearing into his pocket. "So all the murdered have ties to what we have to assume are the missing munitions. Which ties them to both Rollins and Kellen."

Eleri shook her head. "Just Rollins. Dr. Walton Gardiner has no ties to Kellen. . .Well, that we know of."

She looked to Donovan. "He did work with vets a lot. And we know he saw Rollins for a while under an assumed name. It's not that far of a stretch to think he might have seen Kellen, but . . ." He let it trail off.

Eleri got it. "But we don't actually have that. Just the possibility."

Donovan agreed with her. A nod all he was able to give. "With Sullivan, everything has some kind of tie to Cooper Rollins."

"So we keep following him." Westerfield said. As though that changed anything. They were already all over that like bacteria on a corpse. "So, the Middle Eastern group has two blond-and-blues now—Kellen and Rollins."

Donovan and Eleri nodded in tandem and he couldn't decide if he liked that or was perturbed by it.

"The Indian group, we don't know, but—" Westerfield continued. "People don't seem as afraid of Indians as of Syrians and Iraqis. And we have the white, very Christian group. Anyone else?"

"Not that we know of."

This time, Donovan could see the man was pondering. "Three distinct groups that are carrying out the same crimes. They don't seem to know about each other, but they use the same passcode. A passcode that hints that they are a cell and far removed from the person or group issuing the orders. But they believe and carry out the tasks. Each group seems to have enough information or impetus to murder someone they are not associated with."

"Ken Kellen has been seen with two of the groups." Eleri supplied.

Westerfield looked at them, from one to the other. "So what would they do next?"

"We don't know." She shrugged. Shook her head. Like Donovan, she ran on evidence, but Donovan understood what Westerfield was saying before Eleri made him say the words.

"You've got all that in place, what do you think would be the purpose? What would you be doing if you'd set all that up?"

Eleri said it. She didn't hesitate. The words came out of her mouth exactly as Donovan thought them.

"I'd be planning a massive, simultaneous, multi-point strike."

27

E leri hated the words even as they rolled out. This time she didn't stop her hand as it reached for the grisgris Grandmere had sent her. She would need all the protection she could get, and she would take it from any angle. Besides, Grandmere believed, wouldn't that be enough?

Eleri didn't miss that Donovan saw her clutch the talisman even if Westerfield kept talking, oblivious. "There's your path. Get in and stop it."

He stood, placing his hands on the table and exiting as though he'd said they should research cell phone plans or figure out where to get the best sushi. He then left before she could muster up the courage to shout, "*How?*"

Stop a multi-point terrorism attack? Without the Anti-Terrorism Task Force? What if they were wrong?

She wanted to scream. Her eyes watered from the stress of holding it back and it took her a moment to realize that she and Donovan had lost whatever cool mental communication they'd had going. They'd been finishing each other's sentences, and she'd felt like it was solidifying into a real partnership, not just two people working together. But as soon as Westerfield had dumped the shit pile of the mother of all responsibilities on them, it was gone.

Donovan was still sitting in his chair, whereas she found herself having already leapt to her feet. He looked shocked. As in 'medical shock' and she wondered if she should find him a blanket and hot liquids.

His eyes not quite focusing, he rolled his head around to her and in a faintly confused voice, asked, "Did he just tell us to stop a massive terrorist attack and then mosey out the door?"

"Yes." She stared, unable to reconnect to him, to figure out what he needed.

But Donovan supplied a slightly dazed answer. "I need chili. Can we go back and get some of that chili? And something good on draft? Just a little."

It was three p.m., really too early for dinner, but she didn't care. "Of course."

Grabbing her jacket, which she didn't need other than as a part of her uniform, she headed out the door, figuring he would follow.

Inside fifteen minutes she was sitting at a scarred wooden table with a pool table at her back. In another two minutes, she had a pear cider in her hand. And it didn't seem to do jack shit for her mood.

Somehow, she'd thought it would.

Donovan looked much the same. Leaning forward, he looked at Eleri and managed to push out a few words.

"Are we really . . ." he trailed off.

"Yes." *Fucked.* That was the word she would use, but instead of saying it she sipped at the cider in her glass. It wasn't often one found pear cider on draft. She decided to enjoy it.

It wasn't often one met a professional hockey player with a decent sense of humor or a seemingly solid understanding of her dedication to her job, either. One with all his teeth. But that had happened, too. And the guy really floated her boat.

She'd even managed to text him back a few times. Though he was almost always prompt, he didn't seem at all disturbed by her poor response time. Eleri wondered if Avery Darling would miss her when the city blew up around her.

Surely it would. Surely the whole city exploding would be her fault, too. Not able to stop what she'd seen coming. This time she interrupted her own slow sips of cider. "Is there anything that would even indicate an end date?"

Donovan breathed in, out, and she wondered what he smelled. Did he like all the things he could pick up from the kitchen? He seemed to like the beer. "I don't think of anything. Except that someone has to be smart enough to see that the murders will eventually get linked."

She blinked, nodded, and understood where he was going. "So even though each group doesn't seem to know about the others, and each may fully believe there are only one, maybe two murders—"

"If we have them all." He interrupted.

"Good point. But let's say one—maybe two—then the groups may believe they're in the clear at least for a while. But someone higher up the chain knows what's going down, and has to understand that someone *will* put murder and murder together." She leaned back. "That means someone up top knows that the timeframe is getting shorter."

He seemed to agree, if taking a sip of his cider indicated agreement. "And that means whatever the endgame is, it's getting closer."

"I don't think that's a 'whatever.'" She thunked her glass onto the tabletop. Had she not already drunk more than she intended to, it would have sloshed.

This was the part that disturbed her the most. Until this morning she thought she was the only one thinking that. "If three of us independently put the pieces together to make up the same endgame, then it's not a *whatever*. That's what it is.

And God bless us if we're wrong, because if we are then it's even worse than we think it is."

Donovan had seemed startled; he leaned forward, then back. Almost as though he were going through all five stages of grief in a single minute. When he hit 'acceptance' he spoke. "What exactly are we tasked with?"

"We have to stop it." How could he not see that?

"Obviously, we do. But I was under the impression that the general goal was to hang out and see if we could get bigger fish." This time it was Donovan plunking his glass onto the table. "But if we wait for bigger fish, people could die. Hell, *we* could."

"Oh." He was right. They had been tasked with that. If they stopped this attack, but not the attackers, then the top brass could come back and plan it all over again. "Then I guess we're really fucked."

She'd finally said it out loud and it felt good.

"Why?" he asked, tipping his head as if he had no clue.

"Seriously?" She blinked and wondered just how fast the alcohol had hit her. Was he that dense? Or was she that drunk? Peering into the glass at the pale colored liquid, she didn't think that was possible. But then again she was investigating a pear cider instead of a bombing.

"Yes, I'm serious. I want to know why you think we're fucked and if it matches with my ideas of why I think we're fucked."

"Oh." That did make sense. She set the drink away from herself, deciding she'd had enough. Obviously. "I think we're fucked because we have to find the big fish and take him/her down. And the chances of doing that, within a timeframe before everyone—" she looked around the restaurant and saw that it was virtually empty, but she still whispered the words, "*blows up*, are just high enough to make us believe that we might stand a chance. So when it all goes sideways, we'll be as guilty as we possibly can be."

"Yeah, that's about where I was." He leaned back. "If it was truly impossible, I'd consider getting out of town and handing it over to the task force. Screw Westerfield's orders. I'd just like to be alive later to have him yell at me."

She looked at him for a moment. It was a bad day when you considered that your best recourse involved Westerfield yelling and probably pulling your badges. She'd never even seen Westerfield yell, but she didn't doubt he could do it or that it would be bad.

So she did what she did best. She thanked the waiter politely for her salad—it was kind of anemic—and her bowl of chili—which was piled high with rice, sour cream, cheese and olives and definitely not anemic. Then she waited for him to leave and got down to brass tacks.

THIS WAS THE BEST ELERI, Donovan thought. This was the Eleri who would help him be his best and maybe even lead them to solving the case.

"So we have Cooper Rollins that we can get our hands on pretty quickly."

Donovan felt the thread, and followed along. "And we should be able to find Ken Kellen and detain him—"

Eleri interrupted. "You think we can find him? He's way too weasely."

"That's a word?" Donovan heard himself say it before he pulled back onto track. "We can't find him, but Walter sure can. So, yes, we can bring him in."

"But will it stop the attacks?" Eleri asked the pertinent question between bites of chili. She seemed at ease to anyone casually observing her, but Donovan understood. Westerfield had lit a fuse, and no one knew how long it was.

Donovan shrugged. That was the problem. "We don't have

enough intel to know who's our keystone. And we sure as hell don't know if we pull that keystone if everything will crumble or if someone else will slide right into place and keep the gears running."

"They won't keep the gears running." She shook her head. "They'll ramp up the speed. It's like standing over a bomb. Do you pull the blue wire or the red? Which one will stop it and which one will make it blow up faster?"

There were no good answers and they both knew it. "So the next question is," he said it while he thought about how much he'd really like another cider, but this was probably the last one for a while. Until the case was solved. While it had been fast before, it was in hyperdrive now. "How do we get the information we need? And what exactly do we need?"

That seemed to turn Eleri's gaze inward. "Get the check. We're getting out of here. In fact, we're getting *out* out."

He didn't know what that meant, but he knew she was onto something. Since he'd triggered it, he pulled out his wallet and paid the tab while she started talking on the phone.

By the time he made it outside, she was already waiting in the passenger's seat. Not her usual spot. Eleri liked to be behind the wheel. So that meant she was more in control from the other side talking on her phone. As he headed toward the house, which she'd mouthed to him, he got the gist. They were moving.

Job one: don't be a sitting target. They'd hauled Rollins in, and they'd had Kellen followed and at least Rollins, if not also Aziza, had made them. They needed to get the hell out of that house. While she talked to Marina about very rapidly locating a new place for them, with secure internet—very secure—he pointed at the steering wheel. "Get a new car, too."

"Shit, yeah—No, sorry, not you." She turned her attention back to the other agent on the phone and explained about the car.

It took an hour and a half. Too long. But necessary.

They cleared out of the little house, whatever the payment was, it wasn't worth quibbling over. Let Westerfield and his secretaries handle that. Eleri packed faster than he did, a fact that never ceased to amaze him as he was pretty damn quick.

While he finished up, grabbing all the toiletries—his and hers—from the bathroom, she cleared the food stock from the kitchen. It would have been domestic. A couple packing after vacation. Except they weren't a couple, they weren't on vacation, and the only thing domestic was the location of the possible terrorism. What they were was a team. Even in this.

Ever efficient, Vasquez met them at the car rental return in their new rental car, a smallish SUV from a different company. It blended into the L.A. landscape perfectly. "Here's the keys. Wanna drive?"

"Nope."

Vasquez blinked, almost as used to having Eleri behind the wheel as he was. "I'll drive then."

She headed straight back to the Bureau office building. Inside, on the top floor were four suites for exactly these purposes. They would have FBI internet, supposedly unhackable, though Donovan was as clear as everyone else that an 'unhackable' net was about as real as a unicorn. But it was the best way to be as secure as was possible.

He couldn't have said just how much it hurt his chest to be living inside the Bureau offices now. Suddenly the tiny house seemed open and airy in comparison to bullet-proof windows and thick walls. According to Marina, all the units were empty and they could even choose separate ones if they wanted.

Eleri said no, then looked to Donovan, who agreed. Then she gestured for him to pick one. Donovan pointed left, thinking it aimed their windows away from the main street.

They needed separate bedrooms, but Westerfield had put them together to be a real team, not just two agents working a case. If they were going to succeed on this, they needed both their brains at full tilt and Marina's to boot.

"Come on in." Eleri walked in the door of the unit he chose, heading straight back into the bedroom on the left as though she'd known it was there.

Donovan was emerging from his own room—he'd only set the bag on the bed and moved the second bag of toiletries to the bathroom counter—when Eleri came out from her room with a puffy, manila envelope in her hands. "Look what was waiting for me."

Vasquez looked up from the box she was unpacking into the fridge and the few cabinets that existed over a subsistence level kitchenette. "What?"

Her tone conveyed the complete confusion she felt. After all, Donovan had just picked out this suite, right?

He had, but he'd seen that envelope before. He'd seen the loopy scrawl and now knew that "Makinde" meant Eleri, that it was a pet name her Grandmere used. He also knew that it held meaning for them, but not for the population at large.

"My Grandmere sent them." She opened the end of the packet as though finding something waiting for her in her bedroom of a randomly selected safe house didn't surprise her. After everything else Donovan had seen Eleri do, it didn't surprise him either. In fact, he was beginning to wonder if her skills were genetic in origin rather than some random luck.

"What are they?" Marina Vasquez seemed to think that if Eleri was handling them, she must investigate.

"It's a grisgris. My Grandmere sent them for you and Donovan."

He almost smiled, "Did she leave a note?"

"No."

"Then how do you know?"

She pulled them out. His was on a black leather cord and the pouch had a wolf drawn in loose ink.

Marina's had two ribbons, one exactly matched the color of her blouse, the other the color of her pants. "Wow. It's perfect. How could she have known?"

Eleri didn't answer that question. Instead she said, "Grandmere believes. And Grandmere clearly thinks you two are in grave danger."

onovan looked at the weird little pouch and wondered how Eleri was going to explain the wolf on his. How had her Grandmere known that? What had Eleri told the woman?

He was giving her a sideways look, asking just that, but Eleri was paying no attention to him. She was fielding the oohing and aahhhhing from Vasquez over getting a baggie to wear because it matched her outfit so closely.

"How could your grandmother have known? What did you call her? Grand-mar?"

Eleri answered the easier question. "Grand-mere. It's the French, or in our case, Acadian."

That was an excellent topic change, and as Donovan watched, Marina Vasquez started coming to the same conclusions he had a few days ago. Only he couldn't be smug about being first. He'd known Eleri for several months before he figured it out. But then he'd had no one telling him her origins either.

"You're Acadian?" It was a question, but filled with both gravity and surprise.

"Partly. Mostly African American and old Massachusetts founding family." She looked to Donovan, only just then eying the wolf on his grisgris. "Put it on. Grandmere wants you to wear it. And you don't mess with my Grandmere." She grinned at him as though that said everything.

Unfortunately, her comment pulled Vasquez right back around to the topic he didn't want to discuss.

"So why the wolf?"

Eleri caught his expression and casually waved it away. "It's like his spirit animal or something."

Eleri steered the group where she wanted them, just as both Vasquez and Donovan were settling the odd little voodoo talismans around their necks. She'd even pulled hers out—loud and proud now that she wasn't the only one. "Our talk with Westerfield gave us a direction: We're looking for multiple strike points for a simultaneous attack."

"Not more individual murders?" Vasquez looked at her.

This time Donovan jumped in. "It's not ruled out. But if we assume we have time to figure it out, we won't. We have to work this as though the attack will go down in a manner of days. Because if it does and we miss, we're all screwed."

He didn't just mean out of a job, either.

"But what's the tipping point?" She looked from one to the other of them. And Donovan honestly couldn't answer that.

Their conversation with Westerfield changed where they were headed, but unless their boss was in the cell himself, that decision of theirs wouldn't change anything the groups were doing. Was there any indication lately of a change of plan?

Eleri looked at him. "I think Cooper Rollins is the tipping point."

Vasquez frowned, but Donovan got it. "They've targeted enough people around him that if the link comes up in the investigation, he may turn on them. It could be used as leverage to get him to roll."

"How long has he been in the cell?" Vasquez asked. "Because the Sullivan death was months ago. But I guess he was discharged before that. Did he come right back to California? I mean, was he even here for that death?"

Donovan looked at her, not comprehending, before he realized she was working from a Cooper-Rollins-as-the-killer template. At least for one or two of the murders. That theory made sense, if you hadn't seen what Eleri had, if you hadn't heard her name each of the killers. She'd seen the Gardiner murder, the Sullivan one, and the Ratz case. They had the Indian man associated with the Dawson case, but the fact was, there was nothing tying him to that exact murder, and Rollins sure could have come in after him. In fact, Rollins conceivably could have perpetrated each of the crimes.

Except Eleri had seen otherwise.

Dammit.

He was starting to see why NightShade stuck with their own and why they only called in special teams when necessary. Why Westerfield had said they could use Vasquez, but they should just *use* her. Instead, they'd adopted her and Westerfield hadn't stopped them.

Was he letting them flounder? Letting them learn and grow? Donovan wondered.

But this was no cut-your-teeth-on-it case. This was getting bigger and bigger, which was leading Donovan down a darker path. What if Westerfield expected them to fail? What if he didn't even so much expect it, but was making contingency plans in case they did? Eames and Heath had been handling it. Would they take the bulk of the blame? Would their boss turn on them and question them as to why they hadn't called in the Terrorism Task Force? Would he lie?

Donovan felt Eleri looking at him. What should they do about Marina? He could see it in her eyes.

He didn't know. But he did try to find a way to ask the junior agent to leave so they could figure it out. "Tell you what, why don't you let us get settled in and then we can convene and do some real digging. But think on that multiple point attack idea. Where would the points be? Who might carry them out? That kind of thing."

Unable to tell if she thought that was a great idea or if she realized she was being shooed out and simply handled it with grace, Donovan watched as Marina accepted the suggestion and gathered the few things she'd brought. As she headed out the door, she looked around the place, "Is there anything else you need? Food? Computers? Paper?"

He shrugged. No clue. Eleri at least gave the place a good scan before saying, "I think we're set, but we'll let you know if we think of anything." Then she jumped onto her own words. "You don't have to get things for us."

Vasquez only smiled, and the two women seemed to communicate the level of 'okayness' between them. He saw it happening, but he couldn't read it other than that it was 'okay.' This case, the Vasquez-Eames connection, was giving him some disturbing insight.

He could smell how people felt sometimes. He should have a much better than average ability to read and react to people, instead he lagged far behind. He was a second-grader to their advanced level understanding.

As Vasquez disappeared and closed the door behind her, he turned to Eleri. "Did she understand that she was getting shooed out? I couldn't tell."

Eleri almost laughed at him. "She could tell, and she honestly didn't mind. She seems to understand that a good portion of this case is above her paygrade. I think she's just having a good time getting to do something important. She's happy to be out of her cube."

He eyed his senior partner. "And you know all this because you had a discussion with her about it?"

This time, she really did laugh. "No, that's body language. That's me bringing her coffee as a gesture of consolation when I can't give her more information."

"Or you're psychic." He went to his fallback position. Maybe he wasn't so far behind, she was simply way ahead.

"I'm not psychic." She raised one elegant eyebrow at him.

"I'm not a werewolf," he responded.

All he received in exchange was the other eyebrow climbing to match the first. Yeah, well, that one stayed at the impasse. "So what do we do now?"

"What do you think of Westerfield?"

Not what he was expecting, but Donovan answered her honestly. The way he figured it, Westerfield was at one level and he and Eleri were a unit at least one—if not more—levels down. "I'm not positive he's trying to set us up. But I think it's becoming pretty inarguable that we are, in fact, positioned to take the fall should it all collapse."

"So it can't collapse," she said. As though that solved everything.

"Are you seeing the future?"

"If only." She made an odd sound in the back of her throat, but Donovan couldn't interpret that either. Instead he moved a little closer, her scent faint but there. She was nervous. Tense, low grade vibrations seemed to emanate from her and her smell was just a bit sharp. She wasn't as at ease as she appeared. "I'm just saying, if we fail, we don't just fail ourselves. This is a big enough burden that getting thrown under a bus may feel really good—almost deserved."

Another angle he hadn't considered. "So let's sit down and get started. That way, if it all goes to hell, we can at least say we gave it everything we had."

Donovan had to wonder when he'd given everything he had. If he ever had before.

She grabbed a box of crackers and popped the top on a

coke, asking him if he wanted one. Somehow the girl who grew up with cooks and maids never seemed to have a problem serving others. For a split second, he wondered about the mother she complained about and where that humble ability had come from.

From inside his head, he was listening to the noise of his own crackers being chewed, and from outside, he heard Eleri munching through hers. They thumbed through the papers, the pictures, the names and tried to come up with whatever they could.

But Fracture Five was good.

Too good.

He and Eleri had pieces. So many pieces, so many links, and no way to put them together to form any kind of concrete answers. Ken Kellen went from one cell to the other. Cooper Rollins was at least in one cell and tied to all four murder victims. They had Aziza and Alya, who were in on student visas and whom Ken Kellen and Cooper Rollins had first met in Fallujah.

They had the cell in Calabasas, who now had guns and sniper rifles. Another tipping point, though not one that pointed to mass terrorist attacks but another kind of singular assassination. Unless...

"Do you think they're planning to blow people up? Or snipe people?"

Eleri's head snapped up at the words. "You mean because they blew people up in situations when other killers would have used hand-to-hand methods? So they might be doing this somewhat backward. They might then do a mass attack that's not a bomb per se?"

He nodded at her, his head moving and his brain on one track while his mouth tried to explain what the rest of him was doing. "I think what we're missing is the 'what are they going for?' question."

"So we assumed they're aiming for mass casualty, but what if instead, it's straight up terror?" Her eyes didn't settle on him, or on anything in particular, instead they roamed, an outward mirror of her inward thoughts. "Give me the paper?"

He handed her a legal pad Vasquez had left behind as though knowing they would need it. Maybe she was psychic too. He brushed that off, knowing Eleri's list even before she started it. "Options: mass casualty. That could be bomb, biological, poison, etc. *Shit.* Too many ways to do that. . . . Option 2: Terror, and there are options within that, too."

He frowned until she explained.

Writing furiously, she didn't look up at him but seemed to read him just as clearly as if she'd looked. "Short term terror. The clock tower, Paris."

"Paris lasted a while," he pointed out.

"It's still short term. Ongoing, until it plays out. There's instantaneous, too. Where the act is singular—not like Paris, more like Oklahoma or the Boston Marathon."

"So what's long term?" He asked.

"The Unabomber. Anthrax in the mail. Multiple point acts with no one claiming them. No way to find the perpetrator, or perpetrators, and a nation waiting to see who and where will be next."

"Charleston? Columbine? Where do those fit?"

She shrugged as though they weren't talking about terrorism on home soil. As though she were giving tennis tips. Only she didn't play tennis. She rode fancy horses and she fought terrorist plots. "Those walk the line between mass shootings and short term terrorism. The difference is sometimes subtle, sometimes in the intention. I'm not entirely up on Columbine, but if I remember correctly that wasn't about fear but about actively killing people. Charleston was about removing a certain kind of person and starting a war. Not quite the same thing."

For the first time it occurred to him that Eleri felt some of this much more deeply than he thought. She'd begun her long journey to this table with her own terror. He'd only been asked to the table recently, and he'd agreed because he was bored with his job at the ME office.

Well, he wasn't bored now, was he?

"What do you think is the case here?" He asked.

"That's the problem. I think they're perfectly situated for any of the three. If they are placing bombs, they have independent groups ready to move in unison even if they don't know it. Thwart one and the other two get through—"

"If there are two others."

"There are." She looked up at him finally, her list paused for the moment.

"No, what if there are *more* groups? Four? Or five? And we just haven't found them yet."

For some reason, it seemed she hadn't thought of that. She paled just a little under the fine mocha of her skin. "So we could stop everything we have, everything we see, and still come up short."

Yup. That was the big picture problem: they didn't yet have a big picture. "Let's start figuring out how to do these," he offered, wanting to be working rather than soaking in the likelihood of failure. "We might at least get rid of some as implausible. Do we call Marina back? Three heads are better than one."

Eleri looked at him. "Yeah, but first how do we tell her what we know? She needs to be playing with a full deck and she's not."

"Let's just tell her." He shrugged and only as he said it did he catch Eleri's horror.

The sheer shock was another wake-up for him and he was getting damn tired of having them. What it must have taken for her to trust him, when she looked so utterly disgusted and even betrayed at the very mention of telling a woman she obviously liked and respected.

"I didn't mean 'tell her' tell her. I just meant give her the information."

"But how do we say we got it?" Now she was frowning and it felt disturbingly good to be the one explaining for once, for making a solid positive contribution.

"You said yourself that she understands part of this is above her pay grade and she's just happy to help. So tell her that we can't tell her. We give her the intel, but not how we got it." It made perfect sense to him.

Nodding slowly, Eleri seemed to absorb that. "In fact, we could develop some kind of code, just something to say, that lets her know she won't know where or how we got it, but that she should work with it." She was warming way up to the idea. "That way we can easily get rid of her at any point when we're out if we need to. Makes our job easier."

She was looking up at him now, and Donovan nodded back. "Exactly. We just tell her we have a series of inside informants, and we know that Cooper didn't kill Sullivan, etc."

"I love it. . . .and honestly, she probably will, too. It's kinder than acting as though we just need her to leave for a minute."

Donovan actually smiled. In the middle of trying to sort a terrorist plot, he grinned and he wondered if that would always strike him as weird. "She's a big girl. She'll like it. Call her back."

Eleri had just stuck a cracker in her mouth and she motioned at him to do the honors. So Donovan rang up the woman stuck in the tiny cube office downstairs and invited her back up. He figured she'd probably just gotten into something important, but she didn't complain. He was about to hang up when he added, "We have snacks, but feel free to bring your favorites."

Sure enough, Marina Vasquez showed up seven minutes

later with all her papers, her phone, her computer bag, and four bags of vending machine chips along with three cans of some cherry drink they must stock in the break room. Donovan almost laughed as she stuck two in the fridge and lined up the chips along the counter. She popped the tab on the drink and yanked the first bag open. "So what's new?"

They explained the 'non-identifiable informant' to her and left it at that. Then they dropped all the information they'd been holding back and watched as she scrambled to re-organize it all.

"So each killing was carried out separately? Like we thought, but worse. Because it wasn't Cooper Rollins. Is he even involved, really?"

"Doesn't he have to be?" Eleri countered, but Donovan knew that really was a question and she would take 'no' for an answer.

"I'm not sure any more." Vasquez pondered it. "Honestly, looking back it doesn't make a lot of sense. He may be responsible for the murders—they are all connected back to him—but the cells were here before him. He didn't form them. He joined later."

Donovan took that in. An excellent point. The signs had all pointed to Rollins, but he might be no more than a side challenge. "In order to do what we now know happened, Rollins would have had to have his hand in all the cells—or at least all three that we know of—since right after he got home."

Eleri picked up his thread. "Otherwise, how would he have convinced other people to kill for him? And, as far as we know, he's only just now getting into the cell. They aren't even letting him into everything from what we can see."

Donovan took a deep breath. "So he's joining them, but he's a scapegoat, too?"

Marina was tapping her finger on the tabletop. A chip remained in her other hand on the way to her mouth, having stopped its motion when Eleri asked her question. "So we really have two separate problems. The cells can't be dedicated to bringing Cooper Rollins in for a string of murders he didn't commit. It's too many people with too much organization for that. The murders are one thing and the terrorist activity is another."

Donovan was glad they'd brought her in. She had a sharp mind and a keen sense of people. For a moment he almost thought they could get out of this intact.

Then she asked another question, "So what made the two things intersect? Why are the cells here? And why are they killing people associated with Cooper Rollins? And what if they don't actually all connect to Cooper Rollins?"

29

Cooper Rollins jerked his right arm up to stop the attack, but wasn't fast enough.

He hadn't seen it coming.

"Give me the damn phone, asshole." Kellen squeezed Cooper's wrist in an attempt to make him drop the disposable cell. Cooper tried to hold out, willed his bones and neurons to withstand. The beauty of the move was that it wasn't about pain, it was about physiology, about neural signaling. Though you might withstand the pain, your hand would still open, and his did.

He heard the plastic clatter to the ground and he aimed his free fist for Ken Kellen's midsection, hoping to stop the obvious next step. But Kellen stepped on the phone even as Cooper's fist connected with the solid muscle he'd been expecting.

His right hand was useless, Kellen still held it tight, the bones crushing together under his grip. Kellen also used the hold to pull at Cooper, but the problem was, they'd trained to fight under the same guys. Been given the same techniques—moves that were never meant to be used against each other. Cooper knew Kellen was going to use the wrist to his advantage, and he already had his weight over his front foot, throwing himself forward as the other man pulled.

Though Kellen let go of his wrist, Cooper made the split second decision to twist, grabbing the other man's light jacket and managing enough of a fist full to pull him down, too. They hit the pavement with Cooper blowing hard just before he hit and half a second later hearing Kellen do the same thing, too. Both men gave up their breath before it could be knocked out of them, allowing for a faster re-set, no phase-period, just like they'd been taught.

Because he'd hit the ground first, Cooper had a momentary advantage—*finally!*—and he used it to turn and aim while Kellen was still busy landing. Curling his fingers, he took advantage of Kellen's exposed neck and aimed for the spot just under his jaw. Like Kellen's move to his wrist, a shot here couldn't be countered once contacted. And this one could knock a man out. Use the enemy's body against him, he'd been taught. He just hadn't quite gotten the lesson on how to fight another soldier. How to fight the one who was supposed to have his back. How to hit the guy he'd once have died for.

They also hadn't taught him that when he got here, he'd mean it.

Cooper meant that hit in a way he'd never meant anything he'd done to any other enemy. Maybe it was PTSD. Maybe it was actually a tiny war here on an empty side street not far from the square, so maybe he was wasn't over-reacting this time.

As he rolled for the hit, his knuckles connected. But since he was going for the close side of Kellen's neck, the exposed side, he couldn't get the good cross swing he wanted and the hit hurt—he could see that—but it didn't take his enemy out.

Kellen let out a bark somewhere between a yelp of pain and a growl of anger. Somehow he jumped up from flat on the ground, but not to his feet. On his knees now, Kellen came at

Cooper, putting him back on the defensive, and for the first time, he raised his arms to protect his head even as he scrambled to get out.

He'd banked on that last shot.

And it hadn't paid off the way he wanted it to.

Deflecting a few hits as the other man tried to straddle him and keep him down, Cooper jabbed both his elbows forward at the same time he brought up his knees. It protected him and bumped the other man back just a bit. Just enough to make a move. Cooper was taking aim on a new target and finally hearing that Kellen was talking to him.

Talking wasn't the right word. He was forcing out words as he swung repeatedly. Still keeping his arms up, Cooper tried desperately to listen.

"Get out . . . Mine . . . Phone."

He couldn't put it together.

Though he wanted to listen, he had to fight back. If he didn't, he'd get his ass royally kicked, in public, by a man he hated more than anything. Kellen was part of what had broken him. The main part of the mission turned rotten in Fallujah, the PTSD, the reason Cooper couldn't live with his wife and young son. He gathered his hatred.

Taking a breath without looking like it, he prepped for a hit, only to have Kellen yelp and go flying off him just as he was ready to strike.

In the rapid aftermath of his surprise, he saw a shoe swing by, finishing its arc. It must have connected with Kellen's side, kicking him off the way one might do to a dog.

"—and my foot is metal, asshole." He heard the words before his brain placed them. "So don't think I won't do that again. It didn't hurt me at all."

Walter.

Cooper could see her standing over a downed Kellen now, as he looked up from his spot on the pavement to Kellen's spot close by. He grabbed his side, but didn't fight back. Only stared at the woman.

She wasn't done. "I have a metal hand, too. And you probably have some deep-seated psychological aversion to hitting a woman. I will use that against you. I am the fucking Terminator. Now get out of my sight."

Kellen rose to his knees, then his feet, unable to contain the fact that his ribs clearly hurt him. No wonder, bone could do some damage, but at least bone against bone was fair. Walter was right, she was the fucking Terminator, and Kellen's ribs hadn't stood a chance. The medic in Cooper looked for signs of Kellen's having punctured his lungs, but didn't see any. He wasn't glad.

He rolled easily to his own feet, his own side having not been kicked in, and faced Kellen.

"Don't come back." Kellen said.

Cooper just stared.

"Fracture Five is mine. I made it. I'll see it through." His stare was glazed, maybe with pain, maybe with hatred, maybe with something else. Cooper couldn't tell. But he shook his head anyway.

If the others let him back in, he was in. He'd worked this hard to join, he wasn't backing out now.

"WHAT DO YOU MEAN?" Eleri asked, confusion everywhere in her system. She felt it, that hum right before they figured something out. She also felt the confusion that often happened at that point too. Where nothing fit and it looked like nothing ever would. The hum was the only clue they were headed in the right direction. She clarified, "What do you mean 'what if it doesn't all lead back to Cooper Rollins'? It *does*."

"Yes," the other woman was speaking faster, connections forming that Eleri and Donovan didn't see yet.

Looking to him, Eleri found Donovan shrugging back at her with an I-don't-get-it-either expression.

"It does all lead back to Cooper Rollins, but what if that's not the point?" Marina paused, and when neither responded she fleshed out her answer more. "What if it happens to point to Cooper Rollins because he's connected to all of them, but the connection to him isn't the reason they were targeted?"

Eleri was starting to put it together now and as Marina kept talking, it made more and more sense.

"We've been following the Rollins thread because it's the easiest to pull. But it's not him killing people, right?" She looked to both of them, to confirm what intel they could share, if not the origins of it.

Eleri nodded quickly at her. "So it's not Rollins that's the common thread, but there's a common thread between the four dead people *and* Rollins that's something entirely different."

"Exactly!" Marina smiled.

Donovan hopped in then, when Eleri's brain was trying to sort all the things they knew that tied Rollins to the dead people and what might be that thread—there were really a good handful of options—when Donovan turned her thoughts.

"What if he's a target?"

"What?" she asked. Rollins had been a suspect for so long, joining Fracture Five, hooking up with Alya and Aziza and the group. It didn't compute for a moment. "He's in it up to his neck. Are you saying he just happened to join a group that's actually targeting him?"

Despite the clouds parting a bit when Marina had thrown the other option out there, Eleri was now confused again. How could Donovan think that?

"No, he didn't just happen to join. He's Special Forces trained. He's moved out from his home, seen the people he knows from now and long ago die in mysterious bombing deaths, and that's a man who goes on a hunt." Donovan had one hand resting on the tabletop while the other sorted through the pictures laid out on the table. He pointed one by one at the pictures they had of the targeted victims. "Sullivan, someone he may have known personally. Ratz, a mentor he definitely did. Dawson, a woman he probably never met, but he communicated with her about munitions orders, right?"

He looked up at Marina, who nodded, pulling a few pages of her own. She pushed printed off e-copies of forms that were highly redacted but bore Rollins' signature. Then she pushed a few others over.

Eleri looked at them and recognized Ken Kellen's scrawled name along with a few others she didn't recognize. "These are claim forms for munitions that Dawson sent to them in Fallujah. Is that odd?"

"A bit." Marina shrugged, "Special Ops guys spend a lot of time waiting around. They're trained to keep track of their supplies, guns, food, everything. It keeps them alive. Regular infantry would never sign for these things. They have officers who handle that. But the teams do everything themselves."

Eleri was putting more pieces together. "So someone wasn't just sending the guns to Fallujah, they were sending them specifically to special ops?"

Marina nodded. "Had to be. These signatures are other guys in their unit." She pointed to the mostly black ink pages. "Look, Dawson sent them all."

Eleri looked it over and Marina was right. Vivian Dawson was shipping large amounts of arms to the special ops guys in one unit. "Is this an abnormal amount to send to this one unit?"

She didn't expect Vasquez to have the answer to that, but she did.

"Yes, it's unusual. I think the real question on that is, was

Dawson doing it? Or was she following orders from someone else?"

Eleri asked again, "Can we get that information?"

"I've requisitioned it, but don't have it yet. They're balking." She offered a shrug.

"Do you ever sleep?" Eleri asked her. Honestly, she didn't sleep much herself, but Marina was making them look like slackers.

"Not lately," she admitted.

"You need to. But this is awesome." She pointed back to the pictures. "Victim number three, Dr. Walton Gardiner, who was seeing at least Cooper Rollins as a patient."

Donovan joined back in, this time having scrambled through for the file they'd found on Rollins in Gardiner's office. "I finally found a moment to go through this while you were at your parents' party."

Though he hadn't said it with any rancor, didn't seem to mean it as anything other than a fact, Eleri winced. Donovan didn't notice.

"Rollins told Dr. Gardiner some of the things he saw. Gardiner's notes are not redacted. You should read this, El." He held the plain file folder out toward her. "But it's not an easy read."

She took the file, looking at him. "Should I read it right now?"

"I don't know." He looked at her a moment longer than necessary, and it seemed he was conveying that she might pick something up. "It's some seriously strong stuff. Rollins goes into detail about some of the things he saw. And he indulges in fantasies about revenge at the doctor's urging. He's a trained killer, they aren't pretty. But I flagged some stuff that seems to be from Fallujah."

She looked down at the torn orange post-it notes sticking

out haphazardly from the edges of the thick file. Before she could make a decision, Donovan spoke again.

"I put the two files together. That's why there's a piece of red cardstock in the middle. It's what I could find." He pointed as she thumbed through to find it. "What's before was filed as Rollins, what's after was under the fake name."

"Gotcha." She looked back and forth between the other two. "So maybe we don't need to find the tipping point so much as we need to find the ignition point. Maybe that will lead us to the purpose here."

Donovan nodded cleanly, but his words were muddy. "I guess. We don't seem to have anything else to go on. I think we need to dive into what happened on that last mission in Fallujah."

Marina spoke up again, drawing Eleri's attention her way. "We need to do that, but I'm guessing that was a blow-up too, and not really the start point of all of this. We need to go back further."

Eleri agreed. Going back was the only way to predict the future. Unless someone wanted to just walk in and hand them a packet with intel. Or a phone with pictures. "We don't even know who sent that damn phone still."

"Rollins? Kellen?" Donovan posited.

"Walter Reed?" Marina asked.

"Not Walter." Eleri commented. "She's working PI for us. I can't imagine she sent us the phone and didn't say anything."

"That makes sense." Marina agreed. Then she sighed. "So, Rollins, Kellen, or any of the other players who want to talk to us anonymously. Yeah, that's no big deal. None at all." Then she looked up. "Can we safely rule out the people in the pictures on the phone? I.e. if they sent a picture containing themselves, they would have to have at least one accomplice. Someone else who wanted to communicate with the FBI. That seems like too much. Don't you think?"

Then she yawned. Eleri wasn't surprised.

"That's where we have to start. Do you want to do that? Scrub the pictures and rule out anyone in them. See who's left as a suspect?" She looked at Marina closely. "After your nap, of course."

"Yes, to all of it." Marina started eating the chips again. She slugged the last of her soda, having only made it through the one, then she slammed the can back on the table as though doing shots. Eleri had to laugh.

"Just go. You've done so much." She smiled genuinely then. "Come back when you're ready. You've been a lifesaver."

When Marina went out the door, Donovan looked to her. "What do we do?"

"I think I have to read this. At least the flagged parts. See if we can put anything together from his past."

Donovan grabbed her arm. "Have you ever picked anything up from something like this? It was bad enough that he lived it. You shouldn't have to too."

"I haven't before." But she seemed to be getting better at it. In all her years, ever since Emmaline had disappeared that day, she would never have said she had a talent. She'd dreamed things, and they'd been accurate. Still, she'd always believed that was just her brain putting the pieces together with her subconscious. The only difference she had from her fellow profilers was that she remembered her dreams. And they were clear enough that she'd acted on them.

But now, it was much stronger than that.

She had to admit she'd always seen Emmaline. She watched Emmaline grow up, somewhere far from home. She'd fully believed it was a dream, until the day she felt Emmaline die. Then it had been too late and she hadn't acted.

It wasn't her fault her sister had been kidnapped. It was her fault her sister stayed kidnapped and had died at the hands of her captors ten years later.

Eleri had never failed to act again. Even when it cost her. Even when the 'hunch' was a slim thread she pulled at. Now, she was having waking visions. Clear movies playing in her head as though she was in the garage with Ratz. In the office watching as Dr. Gardiner was stabbed. Then she'd *been* Mrs. Sullivan.

There was no telling what she'd get from Cooper Rollins' chart.

But she had to read it.

leri's dreams were rough. Probably six different times she'd woken up during the night, her chest heaving from rapid breathing. Her heart pounding at dreamed-of terrors. Her brain scrambled from the disturbing dreams.

Unfortunately, they were useless.

The dreams were exhausting. Along with the lack of sleep, she wasn't getting any rest when she did sleep. She was inundated with warped tales right out of Cooper Rollins' already warped imagination as per the files from Dr. Gardiner.

In her dreams, she fought insurgents riding a variety of animals. In the rainforest. She saw rebels holding guns stamped "U.S.A." shooting dogs and kittens as they sat astride rhinos and giraffes. Then she sat at a low dinner table, eating the most wonderful Indian food, even as she wondered why they would eat that in Pakistan? One of the diners, Ken Kellen, with his red hair and his American accent, ate pasta. He used a fork and spoon to twirl the ribbons in a classic Italian style. He spoke Italian, gestured like an Italian, and pushed aside the family's pet sloth as it tried to nudge its way to the table for scraps.

When she asked why Ken had pasta and red sauce, they all turned on her. She would sneak out, duck between trees, hearing gunshots in the distance as the family closed in. Hunting her for some slip in etiquette.

When she tripped over a tree root and hit the dirt, she jerked herself awake, where she lay gasping softly at the ceiling once again.

She rolled her eyes at the moonlight. Or maybe it was just city light pollution coming in around the cracks of the curtains. There were blackout shades—after all, Agents might need to catch their sleep when they could—but she hadn't pulled them.

For a moment she thought she should. That if she got up and got the room good and dark, she'd feel more at home. Then again, if this was what she was dreaming in the light, what would she dream in the pitch black?

Instead, she stared at the ceiling. Wishing something in the file had connected. Wishing that if she was going to suffer she would at least earn something for it. If she were dealing with this crap, then she'd like it to mean something. But these were ordinary bad dreams. And she was tired.

So she didn't close the blackout curtains, she just straightened the sheets and pulled up the blanket for weight if not warmth, then she rolled over and closed her eyes. She took slow deep breaths until she drifted off again.

She didn't know how long it took before she woke up, sitting bolt upright in the strange bed, the light still coming in around the curtains even though her clock read sometime after three a.m. Her breath was labored again, long and slow and deep, and she was almost in tears.

The dreams kept coming, each one different from the one before, but always the same theme. For a slow, sleep-fogged moment, she wondered if she 'got it'—if she figured out what the dreams were trying to tell her—could she get some real damn sleep?

Well, she wasn't getting any rest by going back to sleep, and she threw off the covers thinking something to eat might wake her up. Get some fuel for staying up, since sleeping wasn't an option.

Padding into the kitchen area, she poured herself a bowl of disturbingly expensive cereal. The cost of the upscale granola, combined with L.A. prices, had given her sticker shock, and she vowed to enjoy every bite. But she didn't.

She chewed while musing. Then, even before she finished eating, it occurred to her that she was eating, and in each dream she was eating. And in each dream Ken Kellen had been eating food of a different nationality. Grabbing a pad of paper and a pen, she returned to her spot, trying to eat with one hand while writing with the other.

In the dreams they all ate the same food. Even Cooper Rollins. But never Ken Kellen.

Did it mean that each person was doing what he believed in —except for Kellen? Or were they all doing the same thing, except Kellen?

The danger always came when Eleri pointed out that Kellen wasn't eating what the rest of them did. Only then did the dream turn threatening.

"Is that a reason list for us to bring Kellen in for questioning?"

Eleri startled, only barely saving herself from choking on the last bite of her cereal. She managed to chew a bit, shaking her head at either Donovan's ability to sneak up, or her own ability to get lost in thought enough that she didn't realize a six-foot man was walking up behind her.

"No." She swallowed. "I think it's saying that we *don't* bring him in."

He leaned over her shoulder, looking at the words she'd

scratched onto the legal pad and he frowned. "One of your dreams?"

"Not one of those. Just ordinary dreams." She shrugged.

"You don't really have ordinary dreams, do you?" He stood up, scratching at his chest through the t-shirt he must have slept in. She wondered why men did that or if women simply couldn't do it, and that's why it was such a 'man' thing to do. Then she realized she was really incredibly sleep deprived if she was contemplating the gender bias of scratching.

"I do have ordinary dreams." She brought herself around to the conversation, even as she peeked out the window at the timeless, odd gray light that came around the curtains. "I see one person morph into another. I dream of peas for odd reasons. Some of the insurgents were riding zoo animals in the rainforest in one."

"That sounds like way more fun than what we have going on for real. Did you grab a hippo and charge one of them?" He pulled out the seat opposite her. Grinning when he sat, Donovan quickly changed his expression. "Did you sleep at all?"

"No and no." She answered, realizing that it didn't matter which came first. "I mean I must have, because I kept having these wild dreams. But I didn't get any real rest."

"You look it." He turned his head one way, then another, and she decided to take it as a medical assessment. As long as he didn't say she looked like one of his former patients, she'd be okay. Eleri was always one to accept the truth of things. She probably looked like utter crap and he was being nice.

Turning the conversation back to what she'd scribbled, she told him, "In the dreams, the common thread was we were all eating dinner each time. And Ken Kellen was always eating something different."

"So he's doing something different than everyone else? But

you don't want to bring him in?" Donovan gave her a slight frown, not understanding.

"No. Each time I pointed it out, my life was suddenly in danger."

She was shaking her head, still trying to make sense of it, when he asked, "From me, too?"

"No." She thought back. "You and Marina were always there. And you were never running with me, but it wasn't you I was running from. It was *them*." She put her fingers up to do air quotes right as she stifled a yawn. "It makes me afraid that if we bring him in, it will all go to shit."

Donovan nodded at her, just as the light began to change.

Holy shit, it was morning already.

Then she sighed. "Or it just means that's what I'm afraid will happen."

DONOVAN HAD MANAGED another hour of sleep after Eleri had wandered back off. It had seemed inappropriate to open her door and check in. She was a grown woman after all, and not his girlfriend. He learned about normal by reading books. So how would he even know if he was doing it right?

Instead, he listened at the door. When he didn't hear anything, he assumed she was doing better than she had been. He wasn't going to wake her. Not on purpose.

By accident might happen, though.

He'd fielded a call from Vasquez, and she'd come in through the front door of the suite, coffees in hand, along with all her other necessary crap. She looked as bad as Eleri had, only she wasn't going back to sleep. Donovan at least knew better than to say that to her. He just kept that to himself and thanked her for the coffee.

He held it under his nose while he chatted, the aroma

drifting through his sinuses and making him want to sigh and shift his face a little to get more. He did it sometimes when he was at home. He'd never done more than a nose flare in front of Eleri. She'd seen the beginning product and the end, but never anything in between. At least not that he knew. He wouldn't freak Vasquez out by morphing in front of her, and not over a cup of coffee. "What do you have?"

"So much. So very much." She smiled through the smudges under her eyes, against the gauntness of her skin. It had all set in since he and Eleri had arrived with their NightShade case and their "can't tell you" intel. But the woman seemed happy, and Eleri assured him that she was.

"That sounds promising."

She sighed. "I have no idea. But it's something. Which is so much better than when I work and work and come up with nothing." Then she sat down and pushed her tablet toward him, even as she opened a program from upside down.

"Okay," she started, "these are the photos from the delivered phone. Cooper Rollins is not in any of them. I'm thinking he sent it. I have zero actual proof, but everyone we've seen from the downtown cell, and even a few we didn't know about, show up in these pictures."

Donovan flipped through them. She was right. The universal missing constant was Cooper. "But you're not calling it?"

"Can't." She was frank about it. "There are people in there that we don't know about. People I had no clue were in this cell." She pulled the tablet back a little and, leaving it oriented toward him, scrolled through to one picture after another, pointing out a few unfamiliar faces. "Who is this man? He's here . . . and in this one . . . and here. Not a leader, but definitely part." Then she pointed out another person. "What about her? She's in this picture, too, which bears a different date stamp, and she's wearing different clothing. Just like the man. So they met with the downtown cell at different times."

"These are unknowns and we'll find out about them." Donovan said. He didn't say, *you'll* find out about them, though he suspected Vasquez would be the one to dig it up in the end. "Why does that rule out calling it as Rollins?"

Maybe his brain wasn't working. As soon as she spoke it seemed so obvious.

"Because, we are obviously missing people. If these people were in the cell and we didn't know, then maybe someone else is, too. They could have sent us the phone." She shrugged. "Just as easily as Cooper Rollins."

"Not as easily as Rollins." Donovan corrected. "We brought Rollins in, we talked to him." They hadn't questioned him, really. There was nothing more to do at that stage of the game, and sadly there still wasn't. "So whoever else might have done this would have to find us and get our names."

She shook her head, and just then Donovan heard Eleri stir in the other room. He hoped she was rested now, but he didn't say anything to Vasquez. He'd learned long ago not to make random comments on what he heard. He didn't want to open any of those cans of worms.

"We followed Rollins." She pointed out. "Rollins followed us. He made you and me. So it stands to reason that anyone following him could make us, too."

Donovan was nodding even as she finished her point.

"We'd be fools to assume we were safe as long as you and I stayed out of Cooper Rollins' line of sight. With this cell, with what we think is going down, that could get us killed."

"And a whole bunch of other people, too." Donovan murmured as he took a sip of the coffee. It didn't taste as good as it smelled, but he drank it anyway.

Eleri emerged from the back room looking rumpled and much younger. She managed a nod and a hand to her head before turning and making her way into the bathroom. Even Vasquez had to hear the shower running. El would be out in a bit, and it looked like no one would want to talk to her until she was ready anyway.

Vasquez' voice brought him back around. Her eyebrows were up and he realized that most people didn't see the early morning Eleri. The one who blinked and looked rumpled. The one he'd really gotten a good first glimpse of at her beach house at FoxHaven. The first time he'd realized there was more to her than just the agent. More than just the older sister, still avenging the younger sister, even though the time for that had long since passed. Vasquez hadn't seen this before. "Bad night?"

He nodded. "Nightmares?" He said it as though he didn't know. "She got up in the middle of the night, and woke me up, too. Finally went back to bed." He shrugged as if it was nothing too serious even though he'd never seen Eleri have nightmares —regular nightmares—before. There'd always been a tradeoff, something good in return for the bad. This time, it was just a hunch. A real hunch. Not a good Eleri one. "That's why I let her sleep in."

"Good thing." Vasquez seemed to have real sympathy for his partner, even though she herself hadn't been able to sleep in. Maybe not once since they'd arrived. She turned back to her task. "We don't know about the Calabasas cell, either. I mean, we know names, but none of them are in these pictures. If they found the other cell, linked them, they might turn. Maybe someone would send us a phone?"

He hadn't considered that. His brain mulled it over next to a dozen other thoughts and the beginnings of a rumble in his stomach. Eleri would be out soon. "It's possible. But the same thing could happen from the other group. The one the Indian man is from."

"Yeah. It could." She pulled the tablet back. "I think it's Cooper. But I can't pin it down."

Donovan tasted the coffee again. It had cooled a bit and without the heat didn't mask the undertones as well, but he could use the caffeine. He sipped at it while he mused. "There are a small handful of women in the downtown cell."

"I've been thinking about that." This time Vasquez looked at him instead of the tablet. "I don't like where it's going, but I think it's genius."

He did not like the sound of that.

"Islam—strict Sharia Law Islam, the kind that may produce a terrorist cell—forbids women the activities these women are doing. These women show their hair. Hell, they color it. They wear pants and wander around outside the house, alone—"

"Maybe they aren't that strict then." Donovan interrupted.

"But I think they are. Each group seems to be strict. Think about what Walter got on the Calabasas cell: they're sitting around their group with Bibles in hand. The Indian man? That pamphlet? That's a sect. He's described as wearing traditional garb and telling people about his religion, hoping to get them to join. That's a serious involvement in your faith. Most of us don't go door to door professing our creed and suggesting others join us." She made a solid point, and Donovan tipped his head in agreement. Then she brought out actual evidence.

"Look at these pictures." She held out the tablet again, this time with the L.A. cell pictures pulled up again. "There are only two of them praying, but the time stamps match the right times of day, and I checked. They are facing Mecca."

It started to sink in. "So the women are breaking their religious law to do whatever they're doing?"

Marina nodded. "It gives them the perfect cover. In extremism, it's almost always the men who commit the crimes. Send in the women, and who would suspect them?" She sat back, the implications of what she proposed settling uneasily.

"But it's completely against their doctrine."

She argued back, literally the devil's advocate in this situation. "God will forgive them. They act in faith."

Shit. The same could be said of the Calabasas cell. What they might do? If it were what his team suspected? It was against the faith as well. But if they thought it was necessary, if they thought God would forgive them, there was no telling how far they would go. He closed his eyes.

Vasquez' voice brought him back. "If you want some good news, there's this."

She pushed the tablet back at him. A name and address shone up at him, next to a California Driver's License picture.

"There's good news?" Eleri stepped up beside the table, her clothing impeccable but her hair wet, one hand rubbing it with a towel.

"Apparently." Donovan answered her, looking at the tablet, even though he didn't process it. Jacob Salling?

"That's the son of Warner Salling, the homeowner of the Calabasas meeting site. I have his full name now and he appears to be at that address." She grinned and Donovan now figured maybe she hadn't slept at all last night. In which case she looked damn good. "I pulled his phone records. There's no break in service for that land line, not since the date the license was issued."

"So he's likely still living at that address." Eleri added her first two cents of the morning.

Vasquez nodded and handed Eleri up the coffee she'd brought. *Multi-tasking until the end,* Donovan thought. "And there's no record of him speaking to either the Sallings' home land line or his father's or mother's cell phones in the last year. I'm working on finding the sister's. She's on a separate plan."

"Holy shit." He'd thought it several times since she'd shown up, but this time he said it out loud. Mostly as a sign of respect. "That's impressive. So what we think is that there's no evidence the son is in contact with them."

"That's what it looks like to me." She looked from one of them to the other. "I think it's worthy of a trip up to Ojai to talk to him."

Eleri agreed, a sweet smile on her face. It was sincere, but Donovan couldn't quite interpret it. "Do you think you can handle that? On your own?"

Vasquez was thinking it over, and as Donovan was starting to suggest she at least get some sleep before taking the trip solo, Eleri gave him that look. This one he knew.

"Donovan and I need to do some recon."

She tilted her head. And this he understood.

Are you ready to go out as the wolf again?

31

Eleri hung back, following Donovan as he followed Ken Kellen. They'd shifted their focus today from Cooper Rollins to Kellen, trying to see if they could solidify the link between the cells. Marina headed north trying to see if she could locate Jacob Salling, pull him from whatever he was doing today, and get him to roll on his parents. No small task for a new agent on her own, but no one else could follow Ken Kellen but them. And no one else was on this huge case that kept getting bigger.

They'd been talking about how to get to Kellen, since they didn't have a home base for him. His driver's license led to an address he hadn't been at in over three years, and even then, he'd been deployed. So Eleri wasn't surprised when no one in the house had ever heard of Ken Kellen even though the place was out near the base and was being rented by four soldiers.

She sent out word. That meant Walter. The only feet they had on the ground in this thing. Then they got lucky. Their PI sent notice that Kellen passed by the square just an hour after Eleri asked. She turned to Donovan and let out a string of curse words.

"What?" He'd pulled back, not used to her swearing that way. She did try to be a lady . . . Most of the time. It was ingrained. But this. . .

"I am so fucking stupid."

He blinked as she explained. "We need you downtown as the wolf." She looked around the apartment, out the tenth floor windows that overlooked a city that managed to mostly stay just a handful of stories tall. It sprawled, wild palm trees and tame, square buildings. "How in hell are we supposed to get you out of here? Marina will figure out what you are if she even *hears* about me walking a wolf out of this damn building. Where are you going to change?"

It hadn't occurred to him either. She could see that in his eyes.

Donovan shook his head but looked like he might have an idea.

"What?" She prodded. She hadn't thought ahead. Just figured things would be the same—but safer—at the Bureau apartment. Maybe this was exactly why Westerfield had them 'off-campus' to start with. Now she had a bead on Kellen and no way to track him. And she was feeling stupid.

"I was thinking Griffith Park is a good place for a change, but it's too far away."

He said the last part just as she thought it. Plus, she figured there were cameras up there. Last time, when Donovan and Wade had run, three people walked in and three people had walked out. This time, she'd go in with Donovan and walk out with a very large dog. If anyone found that on security footage, she'd ruin a people who'd spent centuries if not millennia successfully hiding. It wasn't her place to out them. "Shit, shit, shit."

He sighed. "I have an idea. But you don't watch."

"Why can't I watch?" She didn't know why she latched onto that like she did. She had plenty of science in her education background, a lot of bio, the whole thing fascinated her, but she wasn't allowed to look.

His expression told her that wasn't going to change. He frowned harshly. Glared. Opened his mouth. Closed it. Then managed words. "Because this is the closest I've ever come to living with anyone, and I'm not using the bathroom with the door open, or clipping my toenails in front of you, and I'm sure as hell not doing this."

She had to say he had a point on that one, and she was going to have to just get over it. She deferred. "I won't look. What's the plan?"

"There are corners in the parking garage not covered by cameras. We have an SUV with dark tinted windows. So we back it into a corner," He used his hands to explain, "and you get out while I change in the back. You hop in, drive away."

She nodded, talking through as she worked out the details in her head. "No man in/wolf out on camera. Only if someone can tie footage from the Bureau lot to downtown and be certain we didn't make any stops. You won't be found." Eleri thought it through. "Yes. That can work. You're a genius!"

Then she sighed again. "The next big question is: can you get a tracking device into Kellen's pocket?"

"I can try."

This time he shrugged, but she felt better having a semblance of a plan. She felt better since her stupidity had hopefully been solved.

So they'd done it exactly as he suggested and found a corner of the parking structure without camera access. The tinted windows lent Donovan another layer of security. She hopped out, stood in front of the car while he climbed into the back, and when she pulled out of the lot, there was a stack of neatly folded clothes in the one remaining back seat. The other had been folded down and away, and the wolf sat there, almost grinning at her.

She'd driven, texted Walter—it wasn't like Donovan could do any of that in his present state—and she'd caught up with the PI on foot. They passed each other on the street subtly, changing out positions as Kellen's tail. Eleri did the job solo for a few blocks until Donovan traded out with her, once he was certain Walter was out of the way.

It had almost hurt Eleri's head, the number of switch offs. Then again, if you were going to successfully track a covert operative, that was probably the way to do it. It would be second nature for him to check his surroundings. If he found the same person behind him twice, he'd make a mental note. Three times, and he'd ditch them.

So Donovan followed Kellen. It was unlikely the man would think the animal was tailing him, but that animal was doing far more than that. As Eleri watched, Donovan ducked and bobbed, staying out of sight. Occasionally letting a person pat him on the head and compliment him, which made Eleri want to laugh.

It was fine until Kellen headed into a parking lot, clearly aiming for his car, and Donovan hadn't gotten close enough to drop the tracker into a pocket. Not that that would be easy, or even possible. Still, they'd decided to at least try.

But as Kellen stepped over the curb into the lot, keys in hand, Donovan turned back and ran the short distance toward her.

What was he doing? She squinted at him as he looked left, then right.

Hair raised on the back of her neck, even though she knew that was his territory, not hers.

He growled. Too far away for her to hear it, she saw the way his lip curled and she began to understand.

"Go." She mouthed it as carefully as she could. It wouldn't do to look like this was her dog; she couldn't appear to have any connection with him. It was probably unavoidable, but they couldn't afford to have Kellen catch on. So she turned away from her partner, hoping he could do his job while she tackled the new one facing her.

Lobomau.

Bastards. Couldn't they just leave her alone? Was the last time not enough? They'd held Donovan back and she'd still held her own. Then again, he'd said something about her eyes and she wondered if it was real.

The two of them hadn't talked about it again. Now there wasn't time. The silver-haired woman walked right up to Eleri, holding her attention. Eleri was still aware of the two men coming up beside her. Where was the fourth?

Was four even their limit? There had to be more, right?

Shit.

"Hello." Eleri made a point to speak first. "Nice day for a walk."

She stared the leader in the eyes, trying to read what was going on in there and not give away anything of her own. She didn't reach for her gun, though it was tempting. She was the officer here; she had her badge in her pocket, and NightShade or not, she wasn't supposed to start a gunfight on the street.

"Not on a leash." Gray responded and Eleri definitely wanted to know this woman's name. For a flash of a moment she almost laughed. Marina Vasquez could probably find it out, but then she'd have to know everything.

"No one's on a leash here." She kept her cool. She wasn't afraid, but she was wary. This woman or either of these men could spring at any time. They could close ranks like they did during their first meeting. At least she was better prepared this time.

The one on her left looked at her like she was cake, and he brushed against her in a way she couldn't tell was sexual or just meant to be imposing. She pushed at him, not bothering with any etiquette where he was concerned. He backed off, probably not wanting to tangle with her after the last time they'd all met up.

Behind her, she heard growls in the distance, and Eleri fought hard not to turn around and look. Donovan was back there and by the sound of it he was tangling with a real dog that caught his scent and didn't like him. Or maybe one of these guys was running interference.

Eleri's money was on the second option. Now, she tried not to be afraid. She didn't know what Donovan's fighting capacity was as the wolf. He'd been trained in weapons at the Academy, but now he had no weapons other than his teeth and paws. He'd been trained in hand-to-hand, but he didn't even have hands now. And Donovan was not the violent sort.

For the first time she actually hoped he had a little of his father in him, though the thought—and the memory of what she'd seen—made her shudder.

"Nervous, Red?" Gray tilted her head.

"Only for your guy." That was a lie. She was nervous for Donovan, and afraid that these shits had blown their op— again. The nervousness gave way to being pissed at that thought. "You need to stand down."

"Listen, Red—"

"No, *you* listen, Bitch." Eleri leaned forward, feeling her blood surge. "You have no clue what you're playing with. Do you really think the FBI doesn't know what he is? Do you really think your kind are the biggest, baddest asses in the gene pool? Because you are in for a rough lesson. So I would get the fuck out of my face if I were you."

The woman pulled back, not liking what she saw.

Eleri wanted to believe it was just her own bad-ass-ness, but she *felt* it this time. Donovan had tipped her that there was something there, and she wasn't shocked when Gray whispered one word at her.

"Bruja!"

Witch.

"You'd better fucking believe it." Eleri stood tall and unmoving, and she heard several things simultaneously. The dog fight was over and Ken Kellen was saying something about 'get off' and 'down.' She wondered if he'd shoved Donovan off him. She wouldn't doubt it. That sucked, but it kept up the realism.

She also caught a glimpse of Walter Reed coming up on her right. Leaning in toward Gray, Eleri took advantage. She pitched her voice low and spoke succinctly, "Do you smell her? She's half metal. Go on. Sniff the wind, Bitch."

As she watched, Gray's nostrils flared, and from the corner of her eye, Eleri saw the two men do the same. A wolf she didn't recognize walked up beside the one man and stood patiently, but even he sniffed.

"Do you smell it? You do not want to tangle with me. Or her. So crawl back into your little kennel, and if you come near me again, I will shoot you on sight. I'll claim you interfered with an ongoing investigation and that you were a threat to the population at large."

Gray whispered the word again. "Bruja."

"Don't you fucking forget it." Eleri stood as tall as her small frame would hold her until the four walked away, three of them on two feet, one of them on four.

"That was pretty bad-ass." Walter commented.

"Yeah, they're awful. Don't mess with them if you see them again. Gangs." She added the last word, hoping it would make everything seem as normal as possible.

Walter laughed. "No, I meant you."

"Oh, thanks." Eleri was taken aback, finally startled from her anger. Walter managed to take advantage, explaining what she was doing there before Eleri could ask.

"I hope I didn't mess anything up for you. I was actually running an errand, and saw you with them. I knew you were tracking Kellen, and this looked more like a random situation than anything." Walter seemed apologetic.

"No, you did exactly the right thing. We ran into that group once before, and they are starting to piss me off." She watched as they turned a corner, disappearing from sight, and she wished she could smell them the way Donovan did. "I lost Kellen a little while ago, so no worries. I was trying to see if I could catch up, and I almost did, but these guys interfered and . . . Well, I think he got in his car and left."

Walter nodded. "Looked like it to me. I'd offer to trade off and see if I can catch up to him, but if he saw us together, I may have blown the cover. I'm sorry."

"Not your fault. Theirs." Eleri pointed to where the lobomau had turned the corner. She really hated them for a growing number of reasons.

As she swung around to check the parking lot about a block over, it looked as though Kellen's car had disappeared. She also saw Donovan, loping back toward her, but he stopped when he spotted Walter with her and he turned another direction.

This time she faced Walter as though she didn't know anyone else on the street. "I'm sorry. I really appreciate your help, but we shouldn't be seen together. Not any more than we have to be."

Just a nod, an informal handshake, and an "Anytime, ma'am, I'm just glad I could help."

Walter was dressed in camo today and looked like a soldier helping a civilian in a street altercation. Eleri loved her and tried not to smile as she walked away.

"Are you okay?" A man walked up to her, his suit clean and pressed. "I saw what happened." He reached out for her arm, a little over-forward.

"I'm fine." Her words were clean and Southern, the belle brushing off the problem. Inside, she was pissed. *Really? Where were you when the shit was going down?* But she reminded herself that any human who got involved with that fight was risking more than they knew. "I'm good, thank you."

He was so late to the damn party, but then he nodded and seemed to understand she wasn't going to faint into his arms, and he backed off. Right as she decided to memorize his face. Why had he come forward? So late in the game? And he touched her. People who touched her always made her wary, and she was no less so after that brush with the lobomau.

He had a round, clean face. A gentle smile. Straight teeth. Brownish hair, short, parted, a slight curl to it. She smiled a little, hoping he wouldn't see that she was cataloging him. "You're so nice to offer to help."

She cataloged his height, approximate weight, and shoe size before extricating herself from yet another involvement in this one cursed, square meter of pavement.

Donovan couldn't join her now. She made her way back to the car, thinking she'd have to pick up her partner at their designated back up location. The car was in gear and rounding a corner to take the long way, when she had the thought.

Too many people had touched her. Gray, the one lobomau, Walter, now this man.

Shit, shit, shit.

She was sitting at the third stoplight when she finally found it stuck under the hem of her jacket.

Sonofabitch! She'd been tagged. Just like they were trying to do to Kellen. But this wasn't one of their pieces of tech. The only one she could be relatively confident that it wasn't was Walter. To be honest, that was just her gut, not entirely supported by fact. She breathed out and removed the tracker, wanting to throw it out the window but knowing that was the opposite of what she should do.

Turning off her blinker, she headed straight, away from her meeting point with Donovan. She'd just have to be late.

It took her five minutes and help from the onboard GPS to

locate a gas station, and when she did, she managed to go into the store, buy a coke and put the tracker on a man who looked like he was putting on a lot of pounds via Twinkies and soda. She hoped he gave whoever was running the tracker a very boring, useless day.

When she was certain she wasn't being followed—and she'd watched her car, making sure no one put a tracer on it while she was inside—she finally headed back to pick up Donovan.

He wasn't there when she pulled up. Then again, he couldn't be seen sitting on the corner waiting, then hopping into a car that pulled up at exactly that spot. There were too many homeless people down here, waiting in the corners, watching everything. So Donovan was likely tucked away nearby.

Eleri made the pass without seeing him, then went back a second time about five minutes later. No Donovan then, either. Another ten minutes. Another check of the rearview, making certain she wasn't followed, that no one was watching. No one was in the buildings overhead, not hanging on what were probably the only fire escapes in LA, checking out the goings-on below.

At the third pass, when Donovan still didn't show, she picked up the phone. But then, who did she call?

Not Marina. She didn't even know Donovan like this, and looking for the man would be a waste of time. Eleri was wondering if he'd been captured, was hurt, and whether she could dial up Westerfield—seemingly her only option—when he appeared out of a corner, a slight limp slowing him down.

She was so glad to see him, intact and at least mostly okay, that she popped out of the car and opened the back door for him.

When he climbed in, she gave him the good news. While

she'd been waiting to circle back, she'd checked the tracker. "You got the tracker on Kellen. It's working."

He gave a small nod as she smiled.

"We got him. He's on the move." Then she put the car in gear and headed out. "Do you need any medical attention?"

She was worried and wondered if he could smell it on her. But his head went side to side, a clear motion now that it was only the two of them. Eleri aimed her second question. "Can you change in the car on the move?"

Even as she said it she took it back. "I'm sorry. I won't ask again. That was stupid."

She wanted to follow Kellen, but she needed her partner back. And he might have twisted an ankle or something worse than she thought. The drive back to the Bureau lot was long and her heart beat hard in her chest, wanting to know what was happening. Wanting to check the tracker on Kellen, but she couldn't in this traffic. That was dangerous as hell and an accident with Donovan in the back was the last thing they needed.

Instead she bought time, telling Donovan about what he might not have seen with the lobomau. About Walter, the man with the sweet smile, and the tracking device that had been placed on her.

They pulled into the lot, parking in the back corner as a matter of course now, the back of the car facing the cement wall. She hopped out, waited, her back to the car, until Donovan emerged too.

There was some dirt on his arm, a scrape, a scratch.

"Holy shit." Her voice echoed back to her in the horrible acoustics of the cement square. "You got bit."

"It's nothing." He flexed his arm, but the hesitation revealed that it wasn't quite nothing after all. Dirt snuck out from beneath the edge of his short sleeved shirt. When he spotted that, Donovan pulled on his jacket to cover it, not needing to be told that they were entering a building of very observant people.

Moving in here had been a mistake. But how else could they keep everything they needed at their fingertips and secure? It was a no-win situation.

They made it to their suite on the top floor. Though Eleri half expected it, no mysterious package had arrived from Grandmere today. She found herself a little grateful for that, though she couldn't place if that was because she didn't want to have to explain Grandmere again, or if it was because she was glad that Grandmere didn't see the need for more voodoo. In no shape to sort it out, Eleri peeled her jacket and waited while Donovan took a shower.

She changed her own clothing and curled into the corner of the couch where she logged in to check the tracker. She wasn't sure if it was still with Kellen or not, but she was going to find out.

It took a while to load everything. When it did, it revealed the device had already been disabled.

For a moment, she wanted to cry. How would they get anything done if they couldn't follow the people they needed to? At least Cooper didn't drive much, but Kellen just hopped in his car and went. Maybe they should trace the car.

Then again, he'd found this piece inside of two hours. He was no dummy, that was certain. She pulled up data. Looked at where the tracker had been before they'd disabled it—possibly under the heel of someone's shoe. The trail led into a neighborhood marked on the map as "Valley Glen." She grabbed a second tablet and pulled up a map and a street view.

Small, neat homes lined two lane streets. Sidewalks fought with old growth trees and most of the yards had charming fences and too-green sod. Cute places. Kellen had exited the freeway, taking Victory Blvd and turned south on Ranchito Dr. After a few more turns, he'd parked and gone up to a house. She pulled the address, wondering what was special about it. Or maybe it was special simply because it wasn't.

It meant nothing to her, though she took note of the picture of the front of the house. Eleri headed to her next bit of intel as Donovan came out of his room. Dressed, his hair was still wet and he rubbed a towel over the short ends, nearly drying it. She hid her jealousy and reminded herself she'd never survive with hair that short. Then she turned on the sound from the tracker.

It should have recorded and broadcast up until it was disabled. But there was nothing.

"What's that?"

"Audio loop from the tracker." She looked up at him, even as she fast-forwarded it to almost chipmunk speed. "It recorded and transmitted until it was disabled—" she checked her watch, "forty minutes ago."

"Crap."

She shrugged. Her mood lifted a little as she watched him hobble ever-so-slightly into the kitchen area. Coming in had been the right thing to do. They'd lost the tracker, but she still had her partner. Hopefully he'd walk fine on it tomorrow.

Voices cut the audio in high pitches, and she jolted back to the task at hand, running a quick rewind and playing it back at regular speed. It wasn't English, though that did sound like Ken Kellen's voice.

She frowned at Donovan as he frowned at her. They listened again, trying to place the words. "Is it . . . Hebrew?"

Neither of them knew, but she added a layer to her map. "Look." Six synagogues ringed the house. "It's a Jewish neighborhood."

"Holy shit."

"Literally holy. They all are." She let the air out of her lungs wondering what other surprises the day could hold. It was only four o'clock.

Donovan spoke the new conclusion even as her phone rang. "So Fracture Five has another branch?"

She answered the phone, Marina Vasquez not even taking the time to listen to Eleri's hello. "I found Jacob Salling. He's in the car with me, coming back to headquarters. He has a lot to tell you."

32

It took two hours for Vasquez to bring Jacob Salling back to Los Angeles to talk about his father's religion and zeal. Donovan tried to use the time wisely.

Apparently, "wisely" included letting Eleri badger him into wrapping his ankle in a bandage on the hope that it wouldn't get any worse. He'd managed to put her off until she went with the guilt play and told him if he twisted it again when they needed him at full capacity, how would he live with that?

So now his ankle was fat with elastic bandaging stuffed into a lace-up shoe. He grudgingly admitted that it did feel better and yes, doctors were in fact the very worst patients.

He filed a report on putting the tracker on Ken Kellen. Eleri filed one on running into the lobomau again, and Donovan added to it. One of those bastards had been in wolf form and tried to start a damn dog fight with him on the street. He'd bitten at Donovan's front leg, and Donovan had given him the what-for. He'd been pissed as hell.

He needed to bump into Ken Kellen well enough to get the tracker in a pocket. Not the best place to hide one, but who would suspect the big dog they sometimes saw wandering

downtown of something as nefarious as laying tech on someone? No one in their right mind, that's who. But as soon as the
fight broke out, Donovan became a 'dangerous dog' and it got
harder to 'bump' into Kellen.

In fact, it had been Kellen who knocked him over and
twisted his ankle. He hadn't mentioned the bruised ribs from
that fall to his partner, but in the shower he'd seen the purple
start to bloom on his side. In his wolf form, he didn't have the
flexibility to reach out and stop a sideways fall. Advantages and
disadvantages to everything, he supposed.

He and Eleri had listened to and gotten interpretations of
the last bit of the audio-recording since neither of them spoke
Hebrew. Once a translator was located—not a hard job in the
branch office in Los Angeles, apparently—the interpretation
came pretty quick. It was less than two minutes of audio.

It entailed Kellen and the other man greeting each other
and a version of "you know the drill." At which point Kellen
must have been wanded or something for radio trackers,
because there was a loud beeping and they found the tracker
with no fanfare whatsoever. Kellen was accused of tracking
himself. He cursed and commented that he wasn't so stupid
and someone must have put it on him. He didn't seem to
suspect the dog he'd knocked back when it tried to approach
him and Donovan never commented on what a punch Kellen
packed.

There were a few moments of undecipherable murmuring,
followed by, "Is that a microphone?" Then the sound went off
and fifteen seconds later the entire tracker stopped relaying any
information at all.

So it had been pretty much what Donovan and Eleri
suspected from their first listen, given the tones of the conversation. The translation itself was relatively useless, but all
together the information told them a lot.

One, Kellen was going to a place where he was getting

checked routinely for tracking and signaling devices. Two, it was a different cell—which made Eleri shake her head as though she might explode. Donovan thought this was bound to happen, there had to be more than just three. But Eleri had had enough apparently. Too bad, she didn't get to decide when the terrorists were done building cells. And three, it gave them a location to start.

They had the homeowner's name and info within a handful of minutes, though they couldn't drive by, the cell would be on high alert. They'd probably move their location first thing—at least they would if they were smart—so a visual check wouldn't give any information other than what the roses smelled like. But they had a thread to pull.

Somehow they still had an hour before Marina Vasquez arrived with Jacob Salling and Donovan ordered in food and tried to catch a quick nap before they headed into yet another interview. The sleeping part didn't work.

His brain boiled with ideas. Questions with no answers. Problems with no solutions. When Eleri knocked on his door to tell him food had arrived, he jolted awake, apparently having fallen asleep after all. Instead of feeling rested, he felt only the effects of having been pulled from deep under.

She had everything laid out on the table and he ate without tasting it until the call came from Vasquez. She was downstairs with Jake Salling. Donovan wondered if he was trying to shake off the biblical times with the nickname. Three more bites went into his mouth with rapid succession before he grabbed a shirt that said "interview" more than "I've been asleep for the past thirty minutes" and tried to get ready.

Eleri didn't finish her food either and they didn't even talk as they rode the elevators down to the third floor and the conference room. As usual, when they walked in, Vasquez had everything in place. She'd gotten Salling a drink, there was fruit on the table, and it all said "thank you for talking to us." Most likely so he wouldn't think he was a suspect, though Donovan and Eleri hadn't taken him off the list yet.

He stood up, held out his hand, and shook each of theirs. Donovan noted that it didn't tremble, the hold was firm, and Salling looked them each in the eye.

Then he shocked the shit out of Donovan.

"I always thought I'd end up here." He sat back down, leaned back in his chair and took a sip of whatever was in his cup.

Finding himself settling into a seat, Donovan mirrored the man's position as he tried to garner what he could from the looks of things. It appeared Eleri was giving him the same once over from the seat next to him.

The man wore jeans, relatively plain, which had been obvious as he'd stood. He wore hiking boots, much the way his parents had. His hair was cut short, but not military tight, and a variety of holes could be seen in his ears—and his upper and lower lips when Donovan looked close enough. "Why is that?"

"My parents taught me a lot of things growing up. I'm still trying to sort the good and bad out. But I've learned since leaving, that my father is a radical. Someone, sometime had to come asking after him." He sighed. "Agent Vasquez tells me you're worried about my parents and my sisters and would like anything I can give you."

Eleri's hand slipped down between them and her finger motioned in a circle, like 'keep him going.'

But Donovan didn't have to. Despite being hauled in across the state and plopped into an FBI conference room, Salling held his own. "It would take years to tell you what my father thinks, what he truly believes. I really don't want to be here. I prayed and hoped this day would never come, that Dad would quietly preach his caustic gospel and this would go away. But clearly, it's gotten worse." He stopped a moment but Donovan didn't interrupt. It seemed he was the star of this one, with Eleri directing, but he couldn't ask why she didn't jump in.

Salling continued. "Probably the most important thing you should know about my father is that he truly believes what he does is God's will. He's not afraid to die for that. He's convinced it's a ticket into Heaven. So don't ever look at him and think, 'He won't really do that.' He never speaks without meaning. If he said it, he most certainly will do it. What do you want to know?"

At last, Eleri jumped in, picture in hand, "Is this your sister?"

Three hours later, Marina Vasquez ushered Jake Salling out the door and back into the car. She was going to put him in a hotel for the night. Take him back the next day after he tried to ID some of the people in the Calabasas group. Donovan walked calmly out of the room and into the elevator before he turned to Eleri.

"Holy shit."

"Holy is right." She shook her head, looking defeated, when Donovan thought they'd likely hit the motherlode of information.

"What?"

"I need a good serial killer. Maybe an old corpse." This time she looked up at him. "I cannot take another case of zealots."

"Sounds like an old-timey disease." He pitched his voice a little lower. "I see you've got a full blown case of zealotry."

"It'd be funnier if they weren't trying to blow up the city."

"But they aren't!" He grinned. "They're just trying to take out the Godless."

"I can't believe I'm saying this, but that cult in Texas was way better than this." She looked up at the lights and stepped out on the top floor and into their apartment.

Suddenly bone tired, Donovan followed her into the living area, knowing he had to stay awake until Vasquez came back.

"The arsenal he said was under the house is not on any blue-prints or any city documents. That's pretty interesting."

She kicked off her shoes and sank into the couch, curling her feet up under her. "I find it more interesting that they hate Muslims and Jews and Hindus."

"Well, they hate everyone except themselves." Donovan mulled it over. "There's like a bullseye of hate with them. The closer you are to their beliefs, the less hate you get. The further your beliefs, the greater the hate. Wonder what they'd do with an atheist?"

"Asking for a friend?" She quirked part of a smile then checked her phone.

"Anything?"

"Nothing." She sighed again and he felt it in him.

He was at odds. The case sucked and he was pretty sure there was a reasonable possibility they were all going to die. But they'd worked like a well-oiled machine in there. Eleri prompting and Donovan asking the next question. Vasquez diving in at the right time, playing good-cop.

Salling had even waved her off, suggesting he knew what they were up against and he would help however he could. He was even admitting to participating in some relatively rough stuff as a teenager. Though he'd come close, he hadn't cried, and he'd said he'd understand if they prosecuted him for what he'd done when he was with his family. He just wanted to call his fiancée first. Vasquez had assured him he wouldn't be arrested for old crimes. That his help was appreciated.

"Did you believe him?" Eleri asked, even though she looked like she was about to drop into deep sleep at any moment.

"Honestly, yes. He didn't do anything that indicated he was lying." Donovan was no lie detector, but he was pretty good at spotting shit when it came out of people's mouths. Maybe it wasn't smell or anything, but just from having grown up with his father and the kind of people that came around when he was a kid. "Which means Ken Kellen is new to that group, and that he must have done something to make them trust him."

Which made the "nothing" from her phone even more important. Eleri had set Walter Reed on Kellen's tail. She'd funded two rental cars and an assistant. It was that important that they know where Kellen was heading. Donovan had listened as Eleri had asked if Walter knew anyone who qualified to tail Kellen.

It was then that Walter proved her worth yet again. Her voice came over the phone speaker loud and clear. "This isn't a cheating husband. This is a terrorist cell, right?"

Eleri had looked at Donovan. They shouldn't tell that. Walter was to be given an assignment and carry it out. Eleri spoke toward the phone. "Yes. That's exactly what it is."

"I know just the guy."

~

ELERI NEARLY PASSED out curled in the corner of the couch.

Marina Vasquez appeared at the apartment door, startling both her and Donovan awake with a quick knock. Eleri had popped up guiltily as though she had fallen asleep in class.

As soon as she let Marina in, she grabbed a coke from the fridge and quickly began guzzling it, letting the fizz open her throat and her eyes. "What did you get?"

She watched as Marina's eyes flicked beyond her to the couch where Donovan was coming around, though not quite as fast. Eleri guessed that was a remnant of being a medical examiner. In the FBI she'd learned that sometimes, for weeks on end, everything was imminent. For a medical examiner, aside from a few high profile or particularly pressing cases, you could work a reasonable schedule. After all, the person was already dead. He hadn't lived for the FBI like she had. Maybe the Academy hadn't had quite the same effect on him.

Settling herself at the table, Marina first asked them, "What did you think of him?"

Eleri shrugged. "He seems stable. Didn't see any tics like he was lying. It really did seem like this day was almost inevitable for him."

Marina nodded as Donovan pulled out his chair and sank into it a little too languidly. They were all exhausted and it was nearing the end of a long day. If only crime understood the need for a good night's sleep. "My background checks all seem to support that. I can't say for sure."

"So we're running in part on gut instinct?" Eleri looked at both the others and saw Donovan giving her a pointed stare. As though she would just know whether Jake Salling was truly trustworthy.

"Most likely." Marina shrugged. "He's settled in the hotel. I have his cell phone . . . Well, tech does. They're going through it for all previous GPS locations, to see if he's in with any of the cells. To see if he's been talking to his parents. He handed it over with no problem. I gave him unlimited access to the hotel phone, but it will alert us to all his calls and record them."

Donovan blinked slowly, as though he were actively trying to fall asleep. Still, he spoke coherently. "If he's smart, he wouldn't ever contact his family on this phone. He'd assume the hotel phone is bugged and not say anything that sounds even remotely suspicious. So none of that is anywhere near definitive as a positive recommendation."

Eleri sighed, the caffeine in the coke not even working a little. She set the can down half full and forgot about it. "So let's sleep on it and see if we can come up with any way to verify whether he's on our team by morning."

Then she leaned forward. "If we can tell him what's going on, can he be of more help?"

Donovan thought about it. Marina didn't.

"That's a massive violation of protocol." The junior agent frowned at Eleri.

"I'm just throwing it out as a hypothetical." She wasn't. "If there was someone who had inside information, and we could trust them, would that help?"

Donovan leaned back. He'd clearly considered the option, and forgotten that one of the people at the table was not operating under NightShade directives. Eleri was still wondering if it was a good idea or if her brain was too damned fogged from lack of real sleep.

But Marina Vasquez had a real answer, and Eleri was beginning to wonder what the woman was taking.

"As of right now, it appears none of the cells know about each other. Only Ken Kellen has been verified as a link between them."

"And we have someone on Kellen right this very moment. Hopefully we'll have more by morning. Maybe we'll even find out where he's living." Eleri shrugged at that one.

"But if the cells don't know about each other, how could telling Salling tell us anything? Even someone on the inside, what could they know about cells they don't know exist? Isn't that the whole point of the fractures?"

Her brain was sluggy. Eleri felt her lips twitch with her thoughts. "But if they could tell us how those in the cell would react—say, if they found out they weren't the only ones—that might be very useful. I.e. do they know about the others? Like Jake Salling says his father is the group leader. Which means Ken Kellen isn't. Right?"

Donovan shook his head. "No, it just means that if Ken Kellen is, he's persuaded a very set man to allow him to do it. Which means he has something in his back pocket. Something he passed to the elder Salling that's very powerful probably."

Her brain hurt and Eleri changed the subject. "Marina, do you have any paperwork on Jake Salling?"

"Sure." She turned to the tablet and started typing something in.

Eleri put her hand on the other woman's arm. "No, I mean anything on actual paper? I can't look at a tablet tonight. I'm about to pass out."

"I can print—"

Eleri shook her head. "Too much effort. Anything already on paper?"

Marina shrugged and leaned down, reaching into her bag. "Just this. A few pictures. A few things the local PD pulled up for me when I inquired after Salling at the local station. By the way, they'd never heard of him. To their records, he's a model citizen. Not even a speeding ticket."

"Hmm." It was all Eleri could muster. That could mean he was a good guy. Or he was another terrorist, simply doing a good job of flying under the radar. But she took the file. In it were several photos of Salling with friends, but there was a decent headshot of him alone. She closed the folder and told Marina that they should all get a good night's sleep.

Walter would hopefully have something in the morning. If there was nothing new on Jake Salling, then she'd put his trustworthiness to a vote. Very poor protocol, but about all she had left. They needed a break in this case. Badly.

As she stood up, Donovan eyed the file. He knew what she was planning. But she didn't see any other recourse.

33

It was six a.m. when Eleri woke to the sound of her phone. At first she hit the button to turn off the alarm she'd set, but when the phone spoke to her, she woke up enough to realize that this was a call.

"Walter? Is that you?" She fumbled for the phone as she rolled over, unsealing the cocoon of her covers.

"Yes?" The question came back, and just as Eleri got the phone to her ear, she heard the next question. "Does your phone not have caller ID?"

She almost laughed. "Yes, but I thought it was my alarm going off and I—never mind. What can I do for you?"

More likely it was *What did Walter have for them?*

Walter did not disappoint. "My guy has eyes on Ken Kellen right now. He's been out all night and we think we have a home base for him."

"Oh." Eleri wasn't as awake as she thought. She rolled onto her stomach, trying to be more upright without actually being upright.

"More than 'Oh.' From what I know of him, it's not normal for him to be out all night." Walter barely finished one sentence before starting the next. "Where are you and how soon can you get here?"

"I'm at the Bureau Branch Office and I don't know where you are." Or had Walter said, and she'd missed it? Eleri really wanted to have her next conversation fully awake. She pushed to sitting and as she planted her hand beside her, she brushed the edge of the photo she'd stuck under her pillow. As she pulled it out, the face of Jake Salling stared back at her. Eleri closed her eyes and focused on Walter's words.

Bad idea. She was still tired and with her eyes closed, it seemed like permission for her brain to go to sleep. "You're where?"

Walter had answered but the words had slipped out the hole in the back of Eleri's head. "Currently, I'm sitting outside a gas station, but I'm watching live feed of a camera on a house that Kellen is inside."

Walter gave a few more details and finally Eleri's brain clicked. "Are you in a Jewish neighborhood?"

"Yes, I would say so."

"Is this a new cell?" Eleri was upright, her bare feet hitting the rough rug. This was no five-star hotel, just a corporate apartment at the top of an office building. She wished she'd at least worn socks.

"Seems like, but I'd guess you already know about it." Walter was on top of things.

For a moment Eleri thought that if Walter was the mole, they were fucked. Not only had she gotten inside, she'd gotten them to pay her to deliver intel. But Eleri calmed herself and decided that all she had left was her gut instinct and she was going to have to trust it. Despite all the information they had rolling in from so many sources, they still had jack shit. "You'd be right."

It would be a day for confessions, she decided, as her feet

hit the hardwood floor of the hallway. "How long can you hold out for us?"

The shrug in Walter's voice came through loud and clear. "I can hold out as long as you need me to. You don't have to come at all. But we have Kellen pegged and we are getting some interesting info. I thought you might want to see."

"I do. But I have a few things first." She knocked on Donovan's door and heard a groggy response before turning and heading into the main room. She was in pajamas, but the world didn't wait for her to get dressed. This was why most agents maintained their own apartments. Such was her life; she'd never been "most agents." Eleri flipped through the papers and asked Walter about the address of the cell they'd gotten from the night before. "That's what I have. Is Kellen there?"

"Negative."

Eleri heard Walter shuffling a few things around. A beep here, and soft click there, and then, "But I'm only a few blocks away from that address. And so is Kellen, but in a different direction from me."

"Good to know." Sounded like the cell was staying in the neighborhood. "Can you give me the address where he is?"

In a moment she'd jotted it down on a notepad and Donovan was standing behind her looking over her shoulder. As she turned, she saw his eyebrows go up. She saw that he was more dressed than she. And she saw something else: some kind of fire. He was getting to the stage where he was pissed at these guys and he was ready to bring them in.

That was good for drive, but bad for decision making.

She thanked Walter and got herself ready while Donovan grabbed car keys, put his feet into shoes, and checked addresses they knew. "Who is Walter's second?"

Eleri shrugged into the bathroom mirror, even though he couldn't see her. She yelled her answer out. "I don't know, but whoever he—or she—is, they're good. Did you see the live feed?"

There were a few moments as she brushed her hair up, and slid into yet another hoodie. There were so many ways to blend in in L.A. At least she didn't need a business suit. It felt wrong in this weather.

Eleri emerged with a fun hairstyle that looked casual but would hold up to a run, a fight, or someone trying to grab it and control her. She had on sneakers, as did Donovan, and her jacket was barely thick enough to mostly conceal the gun in the holster at her back. Just another day in weeds in Southern California.

"Feed's not doing much." Donovan spoke calmly over his shoulder. Anyone else wouldn't have heard her come up on the quiet sneakers, but Donovan heard everything.

"Yeah, well, her guy is outside the house sending that back. Ken Kellen is in there." She grabbed her purse and headed for the door, "Let's go."

"Vasquez?" The one word said everything.

"No. Not today."

"The wolf?" He looked a little skeptical at that. But he should. She'd been the one to suggest it the past several times.

"No." Though she let Donovan drive the car, she had plans. "First, go to the hotel that Vasquez is keeping Jake Salling at."

He was headed there, sitting behind cars, waiting at lights, and eventually running through a Jack in the Box for a disturbingly tasty and horribly bad-for-them breakfast. "Couldn't we have called?"

She shook her head, "They're monitoring everything, as they should be. If we call, they'll know exactly what we ask. Exactly what he answers. I don't want evidence."

His eyebrows went up as he took a turn. Once he was through the next light, he spoke again. "I saw you take that stuff from Salling in with you last night. Did you get something? Is that why you want to do this?"

She shook her head again. "I didn't get anything. Or if I did, I don't remember any of it. All I have is a normal gut feeling that I can trust this guy. That he really hasn't had any contact with anyone in his family for going on seven years." Eleri felt her ribs open, her lungs taking in much needed air as she was using up her oxygen on pure anxiety. Though she was outwardly keeping it under check, her body was still burning fuel faster than she could control it. She'd been eating like a mad woman and breathing like a marathoner for the past twenty-four hours, she realized. "What do you think?"

Donovan stayed quiet for a moment. "Honestly, I think the same thing. What do you want to ask him that no one can know about?"

"The cell." There wasn't really time to explain, and it wasn't really bad or good, she just needed some insight that Jake Salling might have. "The Bureau will know we were here, but we're going to question him outside. Away from any recordings. Can you keep an eye out?"

This time he frowned at her, but she was already getting out of the car, and heading into the front lobby of the small hotel. Forcing Donovan to keep up, she climbed the steps, getting her leather wallet ready. Eleri flipped it open, holding the ID card up to the peephole as she knocked on the hotel room door. There was no real security. No agent posted outside the door, no headsets, that kind of thing. In fact, the agent was next door, in an adjoining room. Whoever he or she was, they'd drawn the short straw. But Salling wasn't being held for anything, really. They just wanted to check out his phone, keep him around. Still, they were monitoring all his calls, his interactions. And she wouldn't put it past Vasquez to bug the room.

When Salling opened the door, she smiled, and put the badge down. "Hello, Agent Eames from yesterday—"

He was already shaking her hand. Still a kid, she thought. A kid she had to look up to. But he was finishing her sentence for her, "And Agent Heath. Good to see you again. How can I help?"

That was it. She turned to look at Donovan, who seemed to give her the okay. "Can you take a walk with us? Just a few more questions. Please."

For a moment she prayed silently that he would be helpful. He nodded with a quick, happy bob of his head and reached back to grab a jacket. At the Academy agents were trained to react, just like police officers, be aware that he might not be reaching for a jacket, it might be a gun. But not in here, not unless he'd gone out at night and procured one without the agent next door knowing. Eleri didn't see that happening, as the agent was already sticking his head out the door.

Donovan turned, went back the few steps and talked to him. Showed his badge, and cleared the way for Eleri's questions. She started asking even as she led Salling away from the other agent, away from his room and down the stairs. No one would be listening here.

"Can you tell me a few more things about your father?" She looked up into the young man's face.

He looked saddened by the thoughts he had, but he answered clearly. "What do you need to know?"

"How did he feel about Muslims?"

This time Salling reacted. He frowned, jammed his hands in his pockets as he hit the change in the air out the front door. "I told you, he hates them. He hates everyone not like him. Is he targeting them? Is he planning something?"

This was where she broke protocol.

Massively.

"Yes. That picture last night—the one we asked you to name as many people as you could from—it's a terrorist cell." She should never have said that, but she needed—*needed*—something to work with. She needed to know how the cells were connected, besides visits from Ken Kellen.

Salling stopped dead on the sidewalk. He stared into space for a moment. "A real terrorist cell? Like from nine-eleven?"

She nodded.

"I never thought he'd go that far." The kid almost had tears in his eyes. "I came now because I figured if you put the effort in to bring me back, he must have done something bad. And I can't let him do it. I can't stand back while he hurts people." He sucked in a deep breath, his hands still jammed in his pockets. "Ironically, he's the one who taught me to stand for what I believe in. He made me understand that sitting back and letting the world go to hell is the same as sending it there. Only . . . Only now I see that he's on the wrong side, and if I stand, I have to stand against him." Jake Salling turned on the sidewalk, he saw Donovan coming up behind her, but he looked her in the eyes. "If I'd thought it was this bad, I would have said something sooner."

"I understand." Eleri tried to be as empathetic as possible, but she was judging, questioning herself, wondering if she'd made the biggest mistake in the world and was being taken in by an Oscar caliber actor. She wanted to look to Donovan, get his take, but she couldn't. "You're helping now. That's what we need. So what would it take for your father to work together with Muslims or Jews?"

It broke the spell. Apparently just the thought was too much for Salling; he was already shaking his head. "He wouldn't."

"So say he was, what would it take?" She struggled, "What if they shared a common goal?"

Eleri sensed Donovan going rigid beside her. He had to have suspected this. She had to know she was throwing it all out there, rolling her dice. She wouldn't know if she'd hit jackpot or craps until the whole thing was over. Luckily for her, he stayed silent and let Salling answer. Probably he guessed the damage was already done.

"No. He wouldn't do it."

"Would he convert?" He hadn't. That was one thing Eleri was sure of; the group in Calabasas was clutching their Bibles as tightly as they could. If they were secret Muslims or Hindus, she'd eat her sneakers. Or she'd blow up along with the rest of the city.

"He would never convert. And he hasn't. He couldn't have."

"How do you know?" The kid seemed so sure.

"Because, if he had, he would have contacted me. He would have told me that I'm wrong. Used it as a tactic to bring me back. He tried for several years."

"Was that what we saw on the monthly calls on your cell phone?" Salling looked startled, but as he shook it off, Eleri pressed. "The calls were longer in the beginning."

"Yes, in the beginning, I just left home one day. I believed I only needed to get out from under his thumb. So when he called to tell me what a horrible son I was, I talked to him. I thought I could explain." He looked off to the side, into the trees, toward the subdivision beyond the small forest built to keep the people on the sidewalk from seeing into the houses. They didn't quite do the job, but Eleri left them all to their illusions. "When I quit explaining, he tried to recruit me back. He was right, the longer I was away the more I left the church. Then he got worse, and I quit answering at all. Finally, he said I was dead to him, and I was glad." He paused. "What kind of son does that make me?"

For a moment, Eleri contemplated her mother's Vegas anniversary party and she vowed to not complain again. "It makes you the kind of man who sees the future and the kind who's strong enough to do what's right. It's impressive that you can see the good things he gave you and sort them out. Most people throw the baby out with the bathwater."

"I did at first." He pointed to the holes in his ears, his eyebrows. Then he focused somewhere off into space, before turning back to her. "If he converted, to anything, it would be big. It would be a chance to bring his only son back. He believed my bad behavior—even as a child—was why they didn't have any more sons, so bringing me back was important. Failing with me was a huge failure for him. So, no, he hasn't converted to any other religion. I'd bet everything I have and everything I know on it."

And that was what Eleri was looking for.

She turned to Donovan who seemed to catch the gist. He tipped his head, conceding that she'd gotten something important. She turned their walk back toward the hotel. "Agent Vasquez may have some more questions for you. It's important that you not repeat this conversation with anyone. If anyone asks you these same questions, answer them honestly, but don't tell anyone what we talked about today. If it ever becomes okay to do so, it will be obvious."

He nodded at her, his eyes looking askance at her, then to Donovan. Suddenly, he was wary and she was sorry she'd done that to him, but then she set him free. Told him she'd have Marina get him a burner phone, return his real phone. If the burner phone rang, it meant they had questions. She said the other agent would come back, but she'd take him to his home later in the morning. Then she and Donovan left him back at the hotel with the other agent and headed to their car.

When she closed the passenger door, Eleri spoke. "I think that's as close as we're going to get to confirmation that the cells are definitely not working together. They probably don't even know about each other."

"So none of them have been following Ken Kellen then." Donovan added another conclusion. "Well, it seems Aziza and/or Alya may have. But that would mean Kellen shook them before he did anything important."

"I'm guessing they didn't follow Kellen or they didn't get very far if they did." She thought for a moment as they headed into the Valley to meet up with Walter and her "guy." "Rollins and Kellen were in Fallujah where the two women started. They knew these girls there, as radicals. They supplied the arms that wound up in their hands. So chances are, the women trust Kellen and maybe Rollins."

"I'd agree with you there." He turned the corner, spotting Walter just as she spotted them.

For a while, Eleri harbored fantasies about knocking on the window and startling the former Special Forces operative. Nope. Walter was a Marine. She'd been with MARSOC. She was trained. So Eleri didn't get to sneak up on anyone in her life these days. Her thoughts turned to the text from Avery Darling that she hadn't yet returned. His team had won two games and lost one. She'd love to look up the stats or the highlights or even have a moment to figure out anything about the game beyond 'puck goes in goal,' but she didn't have the spare minute to do it. She stole two seconds to type back the words, "Yay, boo, yay," then turned back to the case.

Eleri closed the car door behind her as Walter did the same, the three of them meeting up casually beside Walter's rented micro-SUV.

As usual, Walter didn't stand on any real ceremony. "Have we got some good shit for you."

She didn't grin. 'Good shit' was just solid intel. But these days, anything was good. Walter's assessment was right.

Eleri just nodded. "Do you want to bring your guy in to brief us? Is it a good time for that?"

Walter nodded. "We're pretty sure Kellen's headed to ground for a bit now. He's been up for twenty-four hours straight. We've taken turns tapping out, but he hasn't. Plus, there are good signs that this is the last stop. I'll have my guy tell you about it."

Eleri nodded again, in unison with Donovan. "Bring him in."

With the faintest turn of her head and lift of her shoulder, Walter brought her mouth closer to her collar. Her lips almost didn't move, but Eleri didn't have to read her lips. She heard the words plain as day.

"Rollins, come on in."

34

Donovan's heart stopped for a second. Walter Reed had just called in to "Rollins."

He took a moment, and when he decided he'd really heard that—partly supported by the stunned look on Eleri's face—he asked. "Is that *Cooper Rollins*?"

"Yes." No waffling about it. No apologies. Just "yes."

"Why?" It was all he could do not to shout it. Had she really just set up Cooper Rollins to tail Ken Kellen? *Had she lost her fucking mind?*

"No," she was calm. "I have not lost my fucking mind."

Shit. That last part must have been out loud. The way Eleri was looking at him, it had been. For a moment, Donovan closed his eyes. He stood at the gas station, trying to catch a reasonable breath and wondering if everything had gone to hell. If he tried, he could conjure the smell of a fresh corpse on his table. He could smell the liver as he removed it. Pick up the tangy edge of metal from his instruments. He could believe his life was made up of simpler mysteries. Or at least ones that didn't leave entire major cities dead over a fuck up like this.

He opened his eyes.

No, he was still standing next to a ridiculous looking SUV type car, and Walter Reed was still looking at him like he was the one who'd lost his mind.

"Can you explain this, Walter?" Eleri asked. Apparently she remembered to use her big girl words. Donovan still hadn't found his yet.

Walter pointed to a restaurant down the street, away from the neighborhood they'd been casing. "How about we head in there and I'll tell you everything."

By the time Donovan slid into a booth next to Eleri and ordered coffee just to rent the table, Walter shuffled in across from them and he was feeling a little better. For a moment he wondered if the booth was hard to get into for her, then he squelched it. One—he didn't care and two—Walter wouldn't want special treatment.

"I hired him because he's the best." She didn't waste time.

Donovan had always admired her; he just hadn't been ready to disagree with her so thoroughly. "But he's also on the watch list."

Walter nodded. "Yes. Guess what I've been doing? Watching him."

"Except when you were asleep." Eleri pointed out. Donovan could tell she was as angry as he was, but she hid it a hell of a lot better than he did. Must be that Southern Belle training.

"No." Walter countered. "I was watching him even then. I put a tracker on him."

Not good enough. "What if he left it somewhere? Do you really think Cooper Rollins couldn't slip a tracker? Did you do it without him noticing? And do you really think you got one past him?"

Donovan petered out, and Walter waited until he was done, paused a beat, then answered. "No. None of us can get one past Rollins. Not really. So, no, of course I didn't try to hide one on him. And yes, of course he could slip a tracker." Her gaze went back and forth between the two of them, daring them to challenge her, to find a weakness. "That's why I handed it to him and watched him swallow it."

She folded her good hand over her metal one and sat at the table staring at them.

Donovan thought for a minute. Aside from field surgery, or a ton of ex-lax—which probably wouldn't have really worked quite yet, and would be beyond detrimental to the job—Rollins wasn't slipping that tracker.

While he thought, Walter pulled out her oversize phone and turned the screen to face him and Eleri. She pointed to a dot on the map. Two blocks from where they were. "He's almost here."

Donovan blinked.

"How did you get him to agree? Why did you even trust him?"

This time she relaxed and started to speak more freely. "I've been following him. Some of it for you—" she looked back and forth between them. "—some of it because I've been following Ken Kellen."

"How does that—"

Her grin interrupted his. "Well, guess who I ran into following Kellen? Rollins, that's who. He's trying to track his old army buddy just like us."

Us.

That's when he realized he was partly angry about her call to use Rollins because he wasn't in the loop. Not because it was bad—though he still wasn't convinced it was good—but more because he wasn't allowed to be part of it. He was also partly mad because it was the second time it had happened this morning. Eleri had simply told him they were going to talk to Salling without telling him what she was going to spill.

He'd had enough. If the city burned, he'd burn with it as surely as they would.

But he didn't yell the way he wanted to. "Go on."

"Rollins is on his own side. He's not in it to blow anything up. In fact, he confronted Kellen yesterday. I was there, and I stepped in because I was tailing him at the time."

Donovan had seen that in her report, but he and Eleri hadn't been able to figure out what it meant. Maybe Walter had.

This time when she looked at her phone, she leaned in, as though telling secrets. "I told him that he was trying to do the right thing, but that if it went down badly, or even if he went down with it, he'd get branded a traitor. He didn't care. Then I told him his wife and kid would live with that, and exactly how they would live with it. I quoted him some stats about kids who grow up with a parent in prison or famous for a crime. It's not pretty."

She was right. Cooper Rollins had been on his own side for a long time.

Just then the man in question pushed through the front door and spotted them. Inside three seconds, he stood at the table, face to face for the first time since they'd brought him in for questioning. This time, when he looked them in the eye, he looked ready to talk. "If you want to come out with me, I'll drive you over and show you where Ken Kellen has been in the past fifteen hours. And I'll tell you everything I know."

Eleri was starting to nod. Donovan was trying to figure out if a car bomb was going to go off when the engine started, but Cooper Rollins wasn't finished.

"In exchange, I want to know that I won't get branded a traitor. That I won't be tried posthumously for treason, not in the public court nor in any other."

Eleri looked stunned. If she hadn't been pinned into the back of the booth, she would likely have jumped up and yelled. "We're paying you for this information. You don't get to barter for it."

"You haven't paid me yet."

"You haven't proved that you aren't a fucking traitor yet!" The accusations were almost harsher for the gentle southern soul that came through on her angry accent. As soon as the words left her lips, she darted her eyes around the restaurant.

Rollins didn't.

Donovan had been watching him and easily concluded that the ex-Green Beret was clearly the superior player here. "I'll ride. Give us reasons to keep your name clean and we'll simply support the truth. How's that?"

Rollins blinked. Once. Twice. He looked like he was going to turn around and leave. He would take with him intel garnered with the help of Walter Reed and the cars the FBI had rented, the equipment the Bureau had provided. Donovan braced to jump up, to chase a man he might outrun but couldn't outfight, probably in either form.

Then, Rollins nodded. "I'm on the right side of this. I don't know if that's your side. But it's the right side."

Then he turned and walked away, expecting them to follow. Without looking to the women, Donovan did. But he heard them behind him. Heard the heavy shuffle of Walter's uneven tread, the light sneakered touch of Eleri's, the sound of her wallet snapping open and the cash trading places with the ticket the server had put on the table. He was already heading out the door into a morning that was colder than he remembered.

If he hadn't heard the car door close, he wouldn't have seen which one Rollins was in. The man started the engine—the car didn't blow up—and headed toward the front of the small restaurant to pick them up. Only once Donovan had slid into the passenger seat did he actually consider that Rollins might tell them something real.

Once they were in, Rollins handed a tablet over to Walter,

and Donovan couldn't help asking about it. He still didn't quite trust the man. "What's that?"

"Tracker I put on Kellen's car. He's almost back to his apartment. If he veers we'll know." Rollins didn't look at him but kept his eye on the road as he pulled out.

"You don't think Kellen would find it?"

"I'm sure he will . . . Eventually. That's why I used one that burns out after two hours. Since he didn't check before he got in the car and the car hasn't stopped, he's on his way home." He took another turn onto the main road and then off, and Donovan realized he was literally along for the ride.

Walter reached up from the back seat and put her hand on his shoulder. Probably trying to tone him down, but Donovan had had enough. He needed answers and he needed to be in on his own investigation. "How do you know that he's the one driving the car? Do you know he didn't switch the tracker to another car? Can he change cars at an intersection without looking like it?"

Rollins didn't flinch. "Well, I watched him get into the car without checking for the tracker. And I watched him drive the car away. The other answer is yes, he could switch out of the car at an intersection with no one really being the wiser, and I'm not dumb enough to mount a camera on his dashboard—because he would find that—so I can't be positive that he didn't do it. In the past he has been awake and alert a lot longer than this. But the car is headed to his apartment and a switch-out at an intersection would require a person waiting there and ready to make the change. So my money says he's on his way home to sleep off the binge."

Donovan didn't want to, but he gave up some grudging respect. The man had training in this far superior to his own. Something that must have come across, because Walter spoke up from the back.

"This is why I wanted him to do it. He's the best."

"Nope. Kellen's the best. . . Actually, Freeman was the best at this, but I dragged him back to base from the last op. Ken Kellen shot him in the head. They needed DNA tests to prove the body was his. So now I'm going to be the best." Though the voice remained calm, the steel under it was obvious.

"We can't have vigilantes, Rollins." Eleri said calmly but firmly from her spot in the back seat. "He may have killed the good guys, but you can't get him, we have to. There's a lot more at stake here than your revenge."

"It's not revenge, ma'am." Rollins pulled to a stop at the side of the road. He spoke to Eleri but looked at Donovan as he did. It took Donovan a moment to figure out that Rollins wasn't giving away the fact that there were two more people in the back seat. Two people pulling up to a curb and chatting—maybe lost—was one thing. A full car, parked and waiting in your neighborhood would get noticed. Especially in this area.

The houses were small and came in varying shades of California. There were whites and chamois colors and the occasional salmon or even Pepto pink. A few of the small homes sported Spanish tile roofs and a few others had trim and art deco curves. Donovan looked around. But Rollins wasn't finished, so he looked at the man as though he were part of the conversation.

"This isn't about revenge. I honestly don't know what Kellen's up to, though recently the evidence has become pretty convincing he's on the wrong side of it. I still don't know about Freeman. Maybe Kellen saved me from him, maybe he just murdered our teammate." Then he changed the subject. "This is the house where he met with what appeared to be a man of Hasidic Jewish origin. Once he was inside, I got some shots."

He took the tablet back from Walter and pulled them up. Donovan checked the tech—a self-contained system like he and Eleri used. No internet. Still hackable—everything was—but harder to get into, at least. A lot harder.

His respect for the man's skills were growing. He wanted to respect the man himself, but he didn't have it yet. Turning his focus back to the information he checked out the pictures. The shots were through several different windows. Like Walter before him, Rollins must have gotten out of the car and aimed the camera through what small window spaces he could find. From the pictures, the shots were taken through wooden slat blinds and maybe a square of glass in a back door. It was hard to identify individual people, but it was clear this was a meeting.

During normal business hours.

Not good.

Donovan slid the tablet back to Eleri, saying, "Hopefully it's the same people he was meeting the other day, or we're screwed."

"You have pictures?" Rollins asked. Then, once again, without turning his head, pointed out that a man was leaving the house with his wife beside him, her hair covered, her dress swishing around her ankles.

"No. Just audio of them finding the bug on Kellen."

Rollins' head snapped to the side. "You got a bug on Kellen that he took to his meeting without knowing it?"

"You're not the only one with skills." It was all Donovan could say. In the back of the car he could hear Eleri suppress a snicker. At least she was smiling. He was loosening up towards Rollins, too. He just wasn't sure if that was a good thing.

Rollins spoke again, and this time he pulled out a book—an old thick Thomas Guide map of Los Angeles. He started thumbing through the pages while he talked. "I've noticed each of the groups has women involved. And several of the women seem to have done something."

Another woman came out of the house then. Her blonde hair was flowing long and curling past her shoulders. She wore jeans and knee-high boots. Her sweater was tight fitting and she was definitely dressed out of character compared to the rest of them. She climbed into a sports car and drove off.

It took Donovan a moment to feel the hand slapping on his shoulder. He tried not to look like he was looking, just in case anyone saw more than two men struggling with a map. He turned a little, then fully as he saw that Eleri's eyes were wide.

"She killed Mrs. Sullivan!" She whispered at him.

He understood.

"You know that woman?" Rollins asked, still pointing at the map and flipping pages.

"She's a suspect in a murder."

"And that's not the car she arrived in." He folded up the map book and subtly pushed the car into drive as the sports car rounded the corner. These blocks were small, a few turns and she would be lost to them if they didn't hug close.

"We're on the move." Rollins announced, doing his job despite the fact that the people who had hired him were in the car and had given no such orders.

Even Walter was all over it. She unbuckled her seatbelt, put her hand on the door and secured her cell phone and tablet. "Drop me at the corner. I'll run for the other car so we can trade off if we need."

"I'm with you." Eleri announced, sliding out of the back seat right on Walter's heels, even before Rollins brought the car to a full stop. She looked Donovan in the eyes as she turned to close the door, staying low and out of sight.

For the first time that day he felt he understood. Divide and conquer. Keep eyes on Walter and Rollins. Find out the rest.

He was on top of that.

Rollins pulled away from the intersection slowly, keeping the car positioned so that the sports coupe would have no line of sight to Walter and Eleri running down the street. "I don't remember her going into the house. But that car pulled up after

I arrived, so I know she didn't drive it there. Changing cars like that . . ."

He didn't have to finish. It was suspicious.

Rollins deftly followed one turn then another, until he started to fall back. Only then did Donovan spot the small SUV in the back, Walter at the wheel. Rollins let them take point, making it harder for the woman in the coupe to see that she was being followed. This was how they'd tracked Ken Kellen.

They were on the freeway, moving pretty well, still letting Eleri and Walter take the lead, when a car backfired next to them. Donovan turned his head to look out the window but didn't panic until his side of the car was within a foot of the truck directly beside them.

The driver honked angrily and Donovan whipped his head around to see Cooper breathing heavily, hands on the wheel, white knuckled, his arms rigid.

"Cooper. Cooper." He tapped harshly on the man, trying to get his attention.

But the other man didn't respond. His eyes were glazed.

Shit.

He was having an episode and Donovan was stuck in the passenger seat. Reaching for the wheel, he saw that it was locked in Cooper Rollins' grasp. When he smacked the man's hand, he finally got a response. It just wasn't what he expected.

Between rapid breaths, Rollins forced out the words "You drive."

Then he was on the other side of Donovan, sandwiched between the passenger door and his passenger.

Reaching over, Donovan grabbed the steering wheel and pushed his foot across into the empty driver's footwell, fighting desperately to control the car heading down a busy L.A. freeway at sixty plus miles per hour.

35

The sound of gunfire set him off. Cooper Rollins felt his brain crack and time loop around on him.

He knew there wasn't gunfire. Or at least he was relatively confident there wasn't. The problem was, this was L.A. and there might actually be bullets. His worst nightmares involved him either hurting people because he thought there was gunfire when there wasn't, or of letting people die, because he told himself it was the PTSD when something real was going on.

Around him, in a fog, cars passed. His passenger tapped him and said something, but it sounded like an old record on slow speed. Like it was coming through molasses.

Cooper couldn't respond.

The front of his brain had taken over.

Though it was his worst memory, he was starting to recognize that it was a memory. Probably that hadn't been gunfire, then. He breathed a sigh of relief and clutched the steering wheel tighter, trying to force his attention back on the road.

But when the man in the passenger seat spoke again,—

what was his name?—and when it again didn't even sound like words, Cooper knew he was going under.

Much like sleep for the too-tired, his body went with it. The memory pulled at him, taking him back. It wanted him stuck in the loop. Back in Fallujah, holding his rifle tight up against his body, fingers firmly on the gun but not the trigger.

A sharp poke. A yell. His hand being grasped too tightly brought him almost into the real world. He was in traffic. *Not safe*—the only assessment his mind was capable of. So he did what he knew to do and vacated the driver's seat, leaving it to someone else.

In the passenger's side, he pressed up against the window, thinking the cold of the glass would bring him back, anchor him here. But it didn't. The roar of silence took over as the twelve men crept quietly through the woods.

His heart had not been calm even when they left. Used to high alert, they trained to stay low and level, react with thought even in crazy situations. On that trip Cooper hadn't been capable.

His brain jumped to another time loop, where he pointed out the shipments of arms to his supervisor the day before. Everyone on the team had seen them, signed for them, watched them disappear. After getting little reaction, Cooper's curiosity sharpened into suspicion and he started an inquiry of his own. So he'd gone into the offices and rifled through the Captain's papers. He saw evidence of the arms shipments coming in from the U.S.

He'd seen the paperwork, and saw that, of the twelve men in the group, each of them had signed for at least two different shipments. Because some were signing for extra—Ken Kellen and Benj Freeman among them—there were well over forty separate shipments of arms.

Son of a bitch.

Freeman was the one standing watch outside while he

snuck in here. Did he know? Was he signaling the captain even as Cooper stood in here thinking Freeman had his back?

Unable to trust his watch now, Cooper slunk out the back of the tent. The Captain would figure it out later, but maybe he wouldn't suspect Cooper. When he came up front to talk to Freeman, he spotted the Captain headed their way.

No signal from Freeman, but their boss wasn't close. There was no way to tell if Benj was selling him out or keeping him safe.

"What did you find?" his partner in crime asked.

"Nothing." Cooper sighed, lied, and wondered if his friend was doing the same. For the first time he wondered if Benj Freeman even was his friend.

The time loop jumped again, to the next morning they'd been sent out. All twelve of them.

Odd.

Cooper thought about the receiving slips. Multiple signatures from each of them. Indicting the whole unit of the fraud. And where were the guns now? Too many to use themselves. More than just what they needed and definitely not the one Cooper now clutched in his hands as they trekked out to check on the family they were sent to scope. This one was his baby. Not a newer model.

He looked around.

Only Ken Kellen held a newer gun. He'd changed his mind on what he preferred to carry recently. Now Cooper saw it with a sinister glint.

The men cleared the hilltop near the family's house. Nothing seemed out of place and Cooper wondered about the intel they were working off of.

This was a rebel family. Father, mother, two daughters—not likely to be insurgents with girl children. But they housed the ones who came through. They fed them, tended wounds, hid the rebel soldiers. In turn, the US fed them, armed them, and maybe more.

The enemy of my enemy is my friend.

Cooper felt his heart thump. The men were quiet. War painted. Stealthy in their big boots. They stopped at the forest's edge and looked back and forth to each other for signals.

Suddenly, Cooper realized he couldn't trust any of them. They all had their hands on the disappearing munitions— including him. Any of them could just as easily believe he was behind it. A jury would surely indict him.

It wasn't unusual to sign for a shipment like that. It was just that the shipments kept coming and the guns and ground-to-air missile launchers were nowhere to be found in Army stock, but the rebels kept turning up with them.

As he looked out over the area, he spotted the girls at the back of the house. In his fugue state, he recognized their eyes. Alya and Aziza were now in America. He *knew* that, but couldn't pull himself from Fallujah, from this loop that played in his head until it played out.

He made a noise in his throat and felt the real world change around him, though he couldn't break out of his own vision. He felt hands on him, heard words around him, not to him. But he was still in the trees at the edge of the clearing. He was still watching the two young women hang laundry, their hair only haphazardly covered because they thought they were alone. They worked easily, ducking between the sheets and clothes flapping in the light wind almost as though they played a game. The heat was a killer, and his gear made him sweat. He only noticed it when he took stock of himself.

Now he took stock of the faces of his men.

Who was really with him?

He looked at each, cataloged previous actions, checked mental histories for suspicious activity, and came up with too much.

Zuckman was counting money he shouldn't have. Ken Kellen was writing in notebooks all the time, notebooks that disappeared and no one could find no matter how they teased him, no matter where they looked. Benj Freeman had a new gun that didn't make sense. And Cooper had no idea who he could trust anymore.

He'd trusted all of them, with his life, up until the day before.

Cooper had looked away from the girls for a moment. When he looked back, he could only see shadows behind the sheets. He frowned, slowly, his brain processing the same thing it had processed at the time—what it processed every time he got stuck in this loop.

Sometimes it was a video playing over top of the real world. Sometimes snippets sounded in his head, as though he was hearing them again. Alya yelling. His men screaming. The jungle of bullets, popping air as they screamed by him.

But now, it entirely took him over as he sunk even deeper. Sight, taste, sound, hammering heart. He couldn't see or react beyond it.

He watched the shadows move and change beyond the sheets. The girls emerged, heads fully covered in the soft beige hijabs they wore around the house. As though they were hidden, or protected, but then it didn't matter when he saw the rifles they held.

Cooper stiffened, his own rifle lowering to take aim on the friends turned enemies. As he looked briefly down the line at the edge of the trees, he saw his fellow men's rifles already aimed. In slow motion, as he lined up for the standoff, he realized he was the last one in place.

Their father rounded the corner of the house, his movements precise and drawn out through the viscous scope of Cooper's flashback. He, too, held a gun.

The shape of it, the exact matte color, the weight of it he could see in the way the man held it—it was American. This man he thought was his friend was aiming a gun provided by Cooper's own country on Cooper and his own men.

He knew that bullets would start singing a split second from now.

He already knew who would die—the father, Benj Freeman . . . the list went on.

But he didn't know who'd drawn first.

ELERI AND WALTER were left following the woman in the coupe. Surprisingly, Eleri was impressed by Walter's skills at tracking the car without giving herself away.

Eleri had classes in this. She'd passed with flying colors, both at the Academy and later by not having the people she was following turn on her. But Walter took it to a whole new level.

Early on, she managed to suss out several cars heading long distance on the freeway, and tucked herself into the pack. The pack changed, but Walter didn't make it obvious. If the woman in the coupe looked back, it wouldn't look like Walter was behind her.

Donovan had tapped out, having to work through an attack with Cooper. Eleri wondered what that looked like, but it was only about ten minutes later that he got on the phone and said they could get back in the game.

Eleri laughed when she heard him ask Cooper Rollins if he was good to go. And then he blurted out, "Hell, *no*, you can't drive."

Even Walter had giggled at that one, and Eleri was impressed once again, this time that Walter could giggle. When the call ended, she asked Walter, "Is Rollins really good to go? He can just have an attack and pop right back up?"

Walter shrugged. "Only he can say if he is. A lot of guys get real depressed after an episode." The other woman looked sideways at her, her one hand never coming off the steering wheel, her eyes somehow still on the road as she checked Eleri out. "You ever have a panic attack?"

"Not really. I've panicked. But it was always at the appropriate time. If there is an appropriate time to panic."

"I'm sure it's not the same for everyone. But it's like that. Heart racing, adrenaline going. Sometimes the guys don't know why they're panicking, and that makes you look around for something wrong. You try to find something bad, so you can justify why you feel that way." She slid casually over a lane, staying far enough behind the yellow coupe. "True PTSD is worse. They relive a traumatic event or events when they get triggered. Cooper's got it bad. Not often, but when it happens, he isn't even here anymore."

"You know some if this from experience?"

"Panic attacks, yes. Not anymore though. I saw a shrink and it helped a lot." She paused and then continued. "A lot of the guys went to Dr. Gardiner. He treated as many for free as he could. Held group classes on techniques to do when you feel it coming on. All on his own time because a lot of the guys downtown don't have anything but the VA and the VA is booked."

"His death was felt by a lot of these guys then?"

Walter nodded. "I'm in this as much to get his killer as anything else."

Eleri bit her tongue. Wanted to say it was Aziza. Wanted to tell Walter that the woman they were following killed Mrs. Loreen Sullivan.

Eleri recognized her, but was unable to say so. Donovan understood, and thank God for that, but she couldn't say anything else. She couldn't say how she had the knowledge. Couldn't say how she recognized her when Donovan didn't. What a fucking mess. Instead Eleri sat in the passenger seat, trailing quietly behind a murderer, checking in with Donovan and Cooper.

"We're out near Westlake Village. How far away are you?"

"Catching up. Weaving traffic like a mad dog. Maybe another seven minutes behind you." He spoke through the phone and she heard some of the conversation and laughed again.

"Yes, you are better at this than me. Except for the part where you suddenly abandoned your post *in the middle of the fucking freeway at sixty miles per hour.*"

Then she sobered up. "Abandoned his post?"

"Yeah, fucker vacated the driver's seat in the middle of traffic. He starts some episode, then weaves, then he's on the right side of me in the passenger seat, and no one is fucking driving the car."

"Holy shit." She did have to admit that was some serious skill to get out of the driver's seat while driving. At least Donovan and Cooper were okay.

Walter tapped her on the shoulder, and she told Donovan what they were seeing. "She's turning off." Eleri relayed the exit number and said she'd text updates before hanging up and paying attention to their quarry.

This woman stabbed Loreen Sullivan with a bomb. Eleri's heart started pounding as the coupe made turn after turn. They were close enough to see the woman start checking the review mirror.

Shit. She was suspecting them of doing exactly what they were doing.

Her phone rang and she hit the button. "Where are you?"

It wasn't Donovan, but Cooper who spoke. He must have grabbed the phone while Donovan drove. "Right behind you. Peel off."

"Turn!" She said it firmly, but made a big deal of pointing to a house up ahead. If the woman was watching, she'd see the two women seeming to find their address.

Walter pulled over, parking at the curb, taking a moment to do a three point turn and face the appropriate way on the street. As Eleri's heart pounded at the thought of losing the woman, she saw the big SUV leisurely pace up the side street. Cooper and Donovan had arrived.

"We have to get out." Walter announced even as she pushed the door open and pulled a purse from the back seat. Eleri wondered what was in it. She didn't think she'd ever seen Walter with a purse before. But the accessory and the softer gait made her new partner look more like any woman visiting a friend.

Eleri got out, too, similar accessory purse in her hand. "Over there?"

She pointed to the house tucked just beyond the cross street. It was close and would get them out of the way, since they couldn't go knock on a door. They had just rounded the corner and Eleri peeked through some tall shrubs when she saw the yellow coupe come around again. "Walter."

She only said the other woman's name, but together they ducked into the bushes as the coupe slowed down, checking on the now empty car.

She *had* made them.

Eleri was already hissing into her phone. "Hold back. She's looping. Don't let her see you."

But Donovan was on it. He'd gone straight through the intersection and Eleri left the phone line open so they could still track the yellow car.

She and Walter watched the woman drive slowly past, look at the car, the house they'd stopped at, and more. Eleri breathed a sigh of relief that it appeared that several people were in the house.

She and Donovan had already mistakenly alerted Ken

Kellen and this cell that someone was onto them. The group already moved their base. They might have changed their plans. Her heart pounded as she hoped they hadn't screwed this up. She hoped the fact that the car was empty, that it looked like they'd gone inside, would help convince the woman in the coupe that it was just coincidence.

The coupe drove past. Her heart started beating again, and Eleri hissed another message to Donovan as it headed another block down and took a turn.

"On it." He spoke back, sounding distant, as though the phone were on speaker. Then a full minute later, "She's stopped at a house. She has a duffle bag in her hand."

"She didn't carry it out to the car with her. It was already inside." Eleri reminded them. That was bad.

Cooper's voice came over. "She's greeted by the occupant. They're talking at the door."

"Get me the address!" Eleri motioned frantically to Walter to use the tablet she'd pulled from her purse.

They were standing on a small sidewalk in an unknown neighborhood, partially hidden by bushes and frantically working on two tablets simultaneously. If anyone was following the woman—a car had gone past—they were toast. Eleri wanted to pray, but she didn't have the time. She had a military database up and waited for Walter to provide a name from her pull of the address.

Eleri input the name and waited.

Just then, Donovan's voice came over the phone, a worried tone underneath the words. "The woman at the house doesn't seem to want the other woman to come in. She's being friendly, though. El, it looks like she's sick. She's coughing."

Eleri tucked the tablet under her arm and shoved Walter. "*RUN!*"

36

Donovan put the pieces together at the same time Eleri did.

"Get out of the car." He pushed on Rollins' arm, a base reaction to the situation. Even as he crouched out the door and stayed low to the road, he pulled the gun from his holster and chambered a round.

Gun or bomb? Too many questions.

The pre-packed duffel bag. The woman at the house was sick. Coughing the same way Eleri said Loreen Sullivan was, right before this same woman stabbed her.

As he watched, the blonde woman applied some sympathy and seemed to talk her way into the home of the now grateful older woman.

Did she have a military connection?

"Do you know her?" Donovan looked at Cooper Rollins.

"No." The other man was now in a stance similar to his own. Donovan had watched him practically roll around the back of the car to join up, his movements far too smooth to be anything other than innate by now. Rollins had also drawn a weapon Donovan wasn't sure he should have possession of. Not after the breakdown he'd seen on the freeway.

"You good with that?" he asked, as though the man would say 'no' and hand it over.

"I'm fine."

Donovan wasn't convinced, but he didn't have other options.

He signaled with his hand to Cooper, not sure if the other man was used to the same system, but it seemed to work and the two of them were partway up the walk when Eleri and Walter came running up the cross street and immediately dropped into position as they spotted the men.

The four of them slowed their movements, all keeping low and approaching the house, weapons out. Donovan thought the women looked a little odd with purses tucked under their arms, and guns out, but it wasn't the time to criticize.

As he watched, Eleri frowned over his shoulder and he saw her pull her badge and hold it up to someone he couldn't see, then put her finger to her lips. She must be signaling someone looking out a window or driving by.

If the police showed up, what would happen?

He only hoped whomever she was motioning to listened. And that they got somewhere safe. He had no solid idea what had been in that duffel bag. He'd put money on one of those knives that exploded, but he wouldn't put a lot of money on it.

Just when he and Rollins made it to the front bushes, Eleri and Walter hit the edge of the house. With a few signals, she opened their phone lines, quickly dialing in the four of them, and whispered, "Walter and I are headed around back. See what you can see."

"Time?"

"I don't know." She answered back.

She'd seen this woman kill Loreen Sullivan. She'd *been* Mrs. Sullivan for a few moments. When Eleri described the scene, it sounded like the woman had talked her way in, gotten close to her target, and stabbed her.

If this story was the same, they didn't have time to wait and case the joint.

Any second they could hear the sound of a human being blowing up from the inside. The sound of failure.

Donovan had seen the results and didn't want any part of being here for that. So he crept closer to the door without waiting for a signal from his partner.

A tap on his shoulder brought him around to see that Cooper was as close as his shadow and was moving around to the front of their little duo. Reaching for the old fashioned knob on the front door, the other man put a finger to his lips and turned it without making a sound, even to Donovan's keen ears.

Impressive.

The finger-to-lips signal irritated Donovan, though he knew it was generic code for quiet entry.

Rollins cracked the door and peeked through before sliding inside. Donovan followed, turning himself sideways to enter without disturbing anything more than they had to. A squeak, a footstep, even just a change in the lighting could alert the occupants they were there.

He pushed the door closed behind him and slowly moved into the living area, stepping where Rollins stepped, as the other man led the way back toward the voices coming from the kitchen. The area had a small table and Donovan was motioning Rollins out of the way. The military man had gotten them in the door, but Donovan knew what was going down here. No one had told Cooper Rollins how this happened the last time.

He heard the younger woman graciously accept an offer of tea, and when he heard the cabinets open, he slowly moved just one eye through the doorway. First he saw the occupant of the house—*Mrs. Deen*, the younger woman had called her— carefully plucking supplies from her cupboard. Then he saw the back of the head of the woman they'd followed here. *Sarah.* Mrs. Deen called her Sarah.

Neither seemed to hear him.

He saw Eleri in the back yard, also watching the scene.

While Mrs. Deen puttered, Sarah leaned over, her long hair swishing to block his view. Unzipping the duffel, she pulled something out and moved it quietly into her lap.

He looked to Eleri, outside the window. Though she'd seen the same motion from the other side, whatever the woman had pulled out wasn't obvious.

He held back. *Don't assume. Don't assume.*

He could look like an idiot if he drew on her. He could kill someone without sufficient evidence. Worse, he could kill her and blow a hole in the entire Fracture Five plot. He couldn't act unless he knew shit was going down.

He held up his hand for Rollins to stay back, and he rolled slowly out of the line of sight. Eleri had eyes on the kitchen. Though it was silent, the phone line was open. She'd let them know if he needed anything.

He waited.

"You sound really sick." Sarah started talking, and he prayed it was nothing; at the same time, he hoped it was gold.

"I have been. I'm usually healthy, you know, but I just can't shake this."

Donovan heard what he assumed was a kettle, heard the rattle and the water glug from the spring water bottle in the corner of the room. Then it went to hell.

"Sounds like a bad infection. Or maybe ricin poisoning."

"Ricin?" The rattling stopped. Footsteps indicated that Mrs. Deen's movements slowed.

Donovan wouldn't be able to look without being seen. And once she saw him, she'd give him away.

"Yes. It's ricin." Sarah was smug. "I put it in your food the other day."

"What?" The breath behind the voice got heavy, and Donovan wanted to move so desperately, but they needed this intel.

Clearly the older woman was a kind, gentle soul who took her tea in china cups, but she was no idiot. Her voice hardened to a brittle sheen. "Why would you do that? I've been nothing but good to you."

Another smug sigh. "But your son hasn't. Did you know he's dealing arms through your house? You had to know. You had to."

The movement at the counter stopped. Donovan didn't know if that meant Mrs. Deen was shocked by the idea or by the fact that Sarah had found her out. He didn't have time to sort the details, so he just kept listening.

"You've been shorting us." Sarah was on the move. She'd stood up, was moving closer to the older woman.

"Sarah, I don't know what you're talking about."

His adrenaline kicked up another notch as he looked out through the window to see that Eleri couldn't really hear what was being said in the kitchen, not through the phone line. But she made a small motion—palms up.

She could not see a weapon. It wasn't time to move yet.

"Tell me where the money is and I'll give you the antidote."

"I don't know what you're talking about." Something hit the counter with a thud, but though Donovan jerked at the noise, Eleri shook her head.

They had to keep waiting, see how it was playing out. They had to walk in with everyone alive and with sufficient evidence for a takedown.

Also, there were two consultants here—not agents, and not under the NightShade directive. The last thing the two of them needed was Rollins or Walter on their asses. So Donovan waited, tense as piano wire, ready to strike, yell, fire if necessary.

"You know where he keeps the money."

"You're going to kill me. There is no antidote to ricin." The voice was steel now. "I'm not telling you shit."

"You will!"

The sound of sudden movement accompanied the words and without conscious thought, Donovan sprang forward. Cooper Rollins was so close behind him, Donovan could not have stopped moving even if he'd tried.

His gun was out, leading the way around the corner. Just as his foot planted on the kitchen tiles, the back door crashed open, Eleri and Walter busting through.

Mrs. Deen and Sarah stood face to face, almost surrounded by the four operatives, each with a drawn gun. Mrs. Deen's back was pressed to the counter and she looked shocked, though Donovan couldn't discern why—there were far too many options. Was she surprised by the turn of events with Sarah? With people in street clothes busting through her doors, guns drawn?

Had she been stabbed already?

Donovan couldn't see. Sarah stood in the way, and she slowly turned around, hands raised, blank look on her face. "It's too late."

She was walking forward, brazen as you please, the walk pegging her as a seasoned criminal. Normal people tried not to get shot, but criminals understood they could walk a good distance if they did so calmly. Sarah took full advantage.

As she moved away, Donovan saw that Mrs. Deen did indeed have a knife in her gut. Her hands wrapped around the handle, holding it carefully in place. She knew not to pull the weapon out. While that was usually sound medical advice, it was all wrong in this case.

Looking to Eleri for confirmation, he saw her nod.

This was that kind of knife.

With Eleri nodding at him even as she turned to follow Sarah, he lunged at Mrs. Deen.

His fingers closed over hers, fresh blood making his grasp slide, nerves making him sweat. He smelled the wound and a tinge of something odd that might be the ricin in her system. There was an overlay of the metal of the knife, mixing with the blood and starting to react. The knife was not entirely plastic. Metal shards were the worst.

He looked Mrs. Deen in the eye, unsure whether she was the good guy or the bad guy in this situation. "Let go. Let me."

She stared at him, wide eyed, in medical shock now, well beyond the surprise of the attack. Donovan didn't have time to comfort her. He was standing so close, he'd at least be injured if the blade blew up. So he yanked it out and held it back.

As soon as he did, he felt the piece removed from his grasp. Holding the knife was just as dangerous as bleeding out. As he moved to try to take care of two deadly happenings at once, Walter yelled at him.

"You can't just pull it out!" She had field medic training, but she didn't understand about this.

He only yelled back. "I'm a fucking doctor." He was getting ready to tell her more, when he heard footsteps. Fast and heavy. It sounded like Sarah was getting away. They could shoot her, but they needed her alive. And they needed Mrs. Deen alive, too, but she was bleeding out through a gut wound and a ricin attack she was never meant to survive.

"Stop!" Cooper Rollins yelled at Sarah, but the footsteps didn't stop, even when he added "FBI" illegally to the end of his command. Donovan scrambled his hands over Mrs. Deen's wound, trying to stuff her shirt into the hole to stem the blood.

Behind him, he heard Eleri yelling to Walter, who must still be holding the knife.

"Throw it!" The desperation in the tone told him. The knife was too close. If Walter was holding it, she'd die.

He heard a soft thud, a grunt, and Eleri yelling at a pitch that nearly broke her voice, "Get down!"

He hunched over Mrs. Deen out of innate reaction rather than anything else and Eleri had barely finished the words when he heard Sarah's voice start to say, "What?"

But she didn't finish her words either. It sounded like she smacked into the door as she spoke, and then the noise hit Donovan's ears just before he saw the red mist.

37

Eleri did not want to open her eyes. One side of her was coated with what remained of Sarah—a woman whose last name she didn't know. And it was her own fault.

She'd seen Walter holding a knife she knew had been activated and would detonate any second. She didn't want Walter near it when that happened. So she'd yelled, "Throw it."

What Eleri hadn't anticipated was that Walter had serious knife throwing skills. She also failed to anticipate that the words "Throw it" would get interpreted to mean "at the woman attempting to run out the front door."

Reaching up, Eleri wiped some of what remained of Sarah from the side of her face onto her jacket sleeve. Not much disgusted her, but this did. It didn't matter; there was suddenly so much to be done. She only wished she'd not been so shocked by seeing the blade fly right into Sarah's exposed right flank as she reached for the doorknob. The woman had seemed shocked that her own weapon had been used against her, or maybe she was just registering pain. But the irony wasn't lost on Eleri.

Now Eleri turned to check on Walter, who still looked stunned.

Her face was worse than Eleri's, as was Cooper's. They heard the yell to get down, but had no idea that Sarah was going to vaporize. They couldn't have possibly reacted fast enough.

There was nothing Eleri could do about that. There hadn't been time to explain.

Walter and Cooper were both using whatever dry fabric they could find to clean their faces. Eleri lamented the lost evidence, but clear faces and open eyes were important. It appeared the danger had passed, but looks could be deceiving. If Sarah had been right, then Mrs. Deen was up to her eyeballs in something.

Eleri looked to find Donovan still tending the older woman. She'd hadn't bled out yet, so Eleri took stock.

Mrs. Deen was down and possibly mortally wounded, but she had a doctor over her. Donovan appeared to have taken very little of the mist and mostly on his back. He was partially tucked around the corner away from the front door, which helped. Still, she checked on him.

"How you doing, Donovan?" It was a simple question, but they were in earshot of a suspect, even if she was bleeding out.

"I'm solid. Grab me a towel?"

She handed him the one remaining clean dish towel. She was turning to check on her consultants when Cooper spoke up.

"What the fuck was that?"

Eleri checked his eyes, and apparently not very subtly.

"I'm still here. Not freaking out." He stared back at her, letting her know he was exactly as he said.

Given that, Eleri didn't give him time to re-ask his question. Cooper Rollins was not a man you wanted to piss off. "That was the way the cells have been killing their targets."

She walked cautiously around what remained of Sarah, trying not to mess up much. At least there was still plenty for DNA collection and the fact was there were four witnesses. She sighed. "That knife was an explosive. They've been stabbing people and blowing them up from the inside."

"That's why Heath yanked it." Cooper was nodding as he took it all in. "Counterintuitive. Most people know not to remove an embedded object." He paused a moment, thinking. "Son of a bitch."

Walter joined in then as the implications dawned. "You didn't want me to get her."

"Nah. Not really." Eleri said. She couldn't lie to Walter, even to soothe her feelings. She didn't think Walter would stand for it anyway. With her, it was all about respect, and Eleri owed it. "I meant 'throw it far away.' I had no clue you had the skills to do that."

"I wouldn't have." Her eyes weren't focused here and Eleri was beginning to wonder if the scene triggered the panic attacks that Walter had talked about in the car. She couldn't tell.

This time, when Walter spoke, she turned and looked at Eleri. "It felt heavy. A bit off balance for a throw. But I misunderstood." Her face fell. "I'm so sorry."

"Don't be." Breathing in, Eleri realized it was up to her. She was commander here on the scene. "I'm calling it in."

There was shit to do, and she did it. She called for an ambulance first and got an ETA which she relayed to Donovan and then passed along an update on Mrs. Deen's condition. She called the Bureau, activating a crime scene team.

Moving Walter and Cooper a few steps back, she had them sit, side by side on the steps that headed upstairs from the far side of the living room. She pulled her tiny camera and took preliminary scene pictures, including shots of the soles of all their shoes.

She was making Walter take evidentiary photos of her own sneaker bottoms—red with the mist she'd nearly slipped in on the hardwood floor—and finally got a chance to speak.

"I would have loved to keep Sarah alive." She'd never bullshit Walter. "But, that knife was going to blow. And you kept her from getting away. What you did was a perfectly reasonable interpretation of my command. The fact is, Sarah came here to kill Mrs. Reed. She also killed Mrs. Loreen Sullivan the same way—ricin poisoning, then attacking her with a knife when she was weak. You ended a murderer before she could get away. That's a fine result in my book."

As Eleri spoke, she watched Cooper turn sheet white.

"Mrs. Loreen Sullivan?"

"You knew her." Eleri knew this. He must not have tracked it when she mentioned "Mrs. Sullivan" earlier. Now that he had her first and last names, he'd put it together.

"She and Mr. Sullivan took in Kellen." He looked from Walter back to Eleri, paying no attention to Donovan and the still-bleeding Mrs. Deen. "Ken took me to them for two different Christmases before I met Alyssa. They made me welcome during a family holiday."

He looked heartbroken, a condition Eleri never thought she'd see on Cooper Rollins' face. Then it got worse.

"I want to say I hope Sarah there died in extreme pain, but that would mean Mrs. Sullivan did, too." Then, as she watched, another piece clicked in. "That's how Dr. Gardiner died. The knife. I'd always thought that scene was very, very odd. . . Son of a bitch. Did she kill Gardiner, too?"

Eleri shook her head, wondering how far into the details he'd want her to go. She couldn't tell him about Aziza.

Turning away from him to thwart his inquiry into things she couldn't answer, Eleri went to the duffel bag. Using a pencil she pulled from a drawer, she pushed the floppy handles out of the way. They wouldn't retain fingerprints, but the rough fabric would possibly hold scrapes of DNA, so she didn't want to touch anything.

Eleri didn't think they'd need it to identify Sarah, but maybe to prove that she'd carried the duffel in. She used the tip of the pencil to hook the zipper and a covered finger to hold the end open as she peeked inside.

"Rollins." She called out when she got a look. "Can you come over here carefully and take a look at these?"

He did so without disturbing anything. Walter had chosen well; Rollins knew his shit. Eleri prayed to any god she could think of that she wasn't putting her faith and a bushel of evidence directly into the wrong hands. "What can you tell me about these?"

They were guns. They were long range, another disturbing development. But they were in pieces, and there was more than one. Eleri recognized scopes and stands, barrels and bolts, but she couldn't tell what specific guns they belonged to without looking up the parts.

Squatting, Cooper kept his hands back out of the way, not even dropping DNA into the bag. He kept his head out of her light and moved around her. She liked him more and more.

She shouldn't.

After a moment's assessment, he spoke. "You have an M16 in there. One. Then you have two Mk 12 SPRs, looks like. There's a modified scope for one. Do you need more?"

"Who uses those?" She asked.

"U.S. Army." It was spoken as though she'd asked what frozen rain in flakes might be called. But it was another link, another step on the same path. The deaths were linked to U.S. Army munitions movements and now at least one cell was linked to that, too. The first set of movements was in Fallujah, the second now here on US soil.

She asked another question. "Is there any legitimate way that she could have gotten her hands on these?"

"Sure. You can buy that gun at any number of gun stores. Though there's supposed to be a waiting period for that." Then he pointed. "But that scope? That's special issue. Armed Forces, Special Units only. They aren't to be brought home with the soldiers either. They're supposed to be accounted for. And the barrels, can you see that they're modified for longer range?"

Eleri shook her head 'no,' but Cooper didn't seem to think less of her for it. "That's also special issue and sometimes hard to get your hands on even in the service. She has two."

"So, not good?" Eleri clarified.

"Definitely illegal," Cooper confirmed, then he put his hands on his knees in a fluid movement that should have led to standing. Instead, his hand flew to her arm, his eyes to Walter's. "We have company."

Eleri started looking around, trying to work her innate reaction and her brain at the same time. "Feebs?"

"No. Definitely not." Cooper strained his head slowly to his left to look out the window better. "He's checking out the coupe."

Eleri did the same and nearly gasped. "I think that's the man that bumped into me downtown."

But he was outside the window. She couldn't pop up, run over. He looked around, then started coming up the walkway.

The yards were small, the walkway measured in discrete feet. "Donovan!" she hissed, even though she turned her head to Walter. "There's someone coming *now*. Keep her quiet."

Mrs. Deen hadn't been noisy per se, but she'd made the occasional soft sigh, moan, or something that seemed like it might be a word.

Eleri held her hand out to Cooper Rollins. "Do you have glasses?"

"I have this." Even as he said the words, the compact spyglass hit her palm. Eleri looked quickly and furtively out the window. He wasn't the man who'd bumped into her, but he looked a lot like him.

Mrs. Deen mumbled something about "my son" and Eleri was grateful to see Donovan's hand slide up and hold the woman's mouth closed. Unless she figured out there was someone to alert, she wouldn't make enough noise to break the barrier of the door. Question was, did he have a key?

She looked at Rollins and mouthed the word "locked?"

He shook his head. They'd probably left the door as they'd found it, meaning Mrs. Deen had not locked herself and Sarah inside. *Well, shit.*

They'd have to wait and see what the son did.

Eleri's muscles tensed as he knocked on the door, waited, and knocked again.

When the doorknob slowly turned, she knew that he knew something was wrong. He'd seen the yellow coupe. If he knew who it belonged to, or even just knew that his mother was home sick today, he'd expect an answer to his knock.

She drew her gun and saw, but didn't hear a sound as Walter and Cooper did the same.

Slowly the door eased open just a crack. In the dead silence of the house—broken only by the sound of traffic on the main street, of others in a busy city going about their daily lives—she heard him gasp.

Eleri couldn't see him, but she saw a shadow of him peeking into the front entry. He must have seen what was left of Sarah whatever-her-last-name-was. He closed the door quicker than he'd opened it. Though she'd thought he'd run, she was shocked to hear him insert a key and slide the deadbolt.

He'd seen the slime and probably one of the few intact parts of Sarah that remained scattered through his mother's living room. Instead of coming and checking on his mother, or even calling out, he'd closed and bolted the door!

Breaking through her surprise, Cooper tapped her on the

arm and motioned a question. "Do you want me to follow him?"

"Yes!" she mouthed back and pointed to the back door. Then she pointed to Walter and motioned for her to go after Cooper, too. Two cars could follow far better than one. That was important since the man already knew something was wrong.

As she watched him out at the sidewalk, the man pulled out another set of keys and opened the door to the yellow coupe that Sarah had driven here. Eleri frowned at the fact that he was now the third person—according to Cooper's original story —who had keys to the car.

The man checked the back seat, the trunk, and looked around a little more before seeming to swear to himself. Then he climbed into the driver's seat and started the engine. By the time he'd pulled forward, both Cooper and Walter were out of sight and she was crouching in a kitchen with a bag of stolen guns, while her partner tried to save the life of an old woman who seemed to have it coming from all sides.

Eleri found herself praying once again.

She hoped the man got away before the Feebs and the techs got here, because she wanted to know where the hell he was going.

38

Cooper entered the FBI Los Angeles branch office as a freshly clean man. There hadn't been time to shower before he and Walter hit the cars and followed the yellow coupe.

He'd just climbed into the driver's seat, partly slimy, and done his best, trading off with the mini-SUV, hanging back, keeping the lines open with Walter. He was disturbed by how much fun it was. Lately, he had just enough money to pay his rent and eat; he'd been following Ken Kellen. Though he'd just watched a young woman blow up from the inside, he felt like a few more rusty bolts were rubbing off the red and breaking free.

He wanted to feel bad for the Sarah woman, but he couldn't. By her own words, she'd poisoned the other woman and showed up with assault rifles and plans to stab and bomb the woman. He'd already put her death aside.

He was still on the fence about Mrs. Deen.

She'd been steely to Sarah. Something in her voice made him think she knew exactly what Sarah was talking about. And if that was the case, if that man they'd followed might be her son, or even a friend of her son, then Cooper didn't have a lot to spare for her, either.

While he'd driven out, he'd prayed he didn't get pulled over. He was wearing human remains, and was considered an active member of a Muslim terrorist cell. That would ruin everything.

They managed to follow the yellow coupe to the end of the line. Hidden themselves, done some quick research and come back in. Walter had called in, and even gotten them permission to bathe. He'd wiped down the car, too, and added a towel that Walter provided from a nice—if nearly empty—apartment she'd gotten very recently. Now he came in through the front door, and the only human remains he had on him were in a plastic grocery bag where he'd wadded up the clothes and shoved them down in.

Agent Vasquez met them and took the bags before ushering him into the same conference room he'd been in last time. He wondered if they did that on purpose, assuming the less he knew about the office, the less of a threat he could be later. But building blueprints existed everywhere. He could probably find something if he needed it. All anyone could do was make crime harder. You could never stop it.

Walter nodded a hello at him but went back to tapping on a tablet she held. She'd gotten new digs and cool new toys these last days. If he didn't just like her as a person so damn much, he'd be very suspicious of her motives. But Walter was a soldier still, fighting the good fight.

He wished he could say that about himself. His own fight had turned very ugly.

She was showing him satellite shots of the compound they'd passed when they followed the coupe, and she was circling an outbuilding. Walter was getting ready to tell him something when Agents Heath and Eames walked into the room.

They'd showered, too.

"Hello." Eames greeted them, her soft smile an odd mix of exotically beautiful and all business. She looked like someone had mixed up their crayons when they colored her, but that someone had a real eye for the tones.

Cooper barely finished nodding when Eames shot her first volley. "You sent us the phone with the pictures on it. Why?"

She wasn't asking about the first part.

"You needed records. You could do facial recognition that I didn't have the capacity to do." He shrugged.

"But you would never get that information back from us. So it was a gift?" She stared at him. She still didn't trust him, and he still didn't really trust any of them. Not to let him do what he needed.

"No, it needed to be done. That's all." He returned the volley. "You put the tracker on my phone."

She shrugged. "You found it inside a day. So I'm sure you didn't take it with you everywhere."

As though the fact that he'd found it made it okay that they'd done it. "I could have been killed if the cell had found it."

"Were you?" She let her face go blank at the ridiculous question and the point she was trying to make.

Cooper didn't answer. Then he opened with his disturbing truth. "I'm fucked now, you know."

She nodded, her face softer. "Yeah, I'm sorry. You could have gotten away doing work with Walter, couldn't you? But after this morning it might be all over."

"Probably." He shrugged. "I guess the question is just how badly they still need a blond-and-blue."

Heath looked at him this time. "You knew that?"

"It's a Muslim group with almost exclusively middle-eastern members." Cooper spoke the words as though that explained everything.

Heath seemed to disagree. "You were in the Middle East a long time. You had a traumatic encounter—at least one that we know of, maybe more. You could have easily converted to any god that made more sense to you. As an American soldier, you're the perfect plant."

Cooper nodded. "I just hope I still am. If there's any chance at all. I can't stay long and I can't stay in touch. Ask me the most important thing and let me go . . . Please."

Heath looked to Eames who was already looking to him. They nodded in sync as though they realized they were thinking the same thing, but the question still surprised him.

"What happened that last day in Fallujah?"

Cooper heard the buzzing in his ears.

Not again. Not another one so soon.

It came, but the sound stayed in the background. As he talked he could see it all again.

Cooper once again felt the arm slide under his chin. An excellent tactical move as there weren't that many places to attack a soldier in gear. He didn't even try an evasive move—it might be expected. Instead he used the butt of his rifle and swung backwards, successfully making contact with something that made the guy let him go. He saw his teammate slide to the ground and he saw the red starting to form at the temple exposed by his turned away face.

Unsure what to do, or who was on what side, Cooper leaned down to check on the fallen man.

When he did, a bullet cracked the air right where he'd been standing.

Though he always thought he heard it—and he must have heard something—it was the spray of bark from the tree it hit that really told him he'd been aimed at.

Cooper checked the spot even as his heart double-teamed and he rolled away. Large caliber. Rifle, not handgun. Coming from the forest.

From his own men.

He scrambled to his feet, staying low, running down the list of everyone on this mission. Who could he turn to? Which direction should he go?

The answers were no one and nowhere. He'd been in the middle of the pack. The insurgent family was in front of him, his own traitorous men on either side and most likely behind. He'd heard more than one set of footsteps running that way. But were they fleeing or positioning themselves to clean up anyone who tried?

"Rollins." The word hissed out of the trees and he turned in search of a friendly voice. What he found was the barrel of a gun. In his haze, at close range, from this angle he couldn't identify the gun. Why that was so important he couldn't say. If he could ID the exact gun, could he ID the man behind it?

The man's face stayed hidden as he aimed at Cooper's head. Not his body, there was armor there. Whether it would do its full job against that caliber at this range was a crapshoot, but a headshot was certain.

Cooper took one last breath. He smelled forest, the burn of fired weapons, food from the nearby house, blood. He saw sunlight through the trees and the open yard with the sheets still swaying in the wind. One had a bright red splatter on it, and he thought he could see the blood still dripping.

He blinked.

In that moment, the man holding the gun on him jerked, his arms coming up with the impact to his torso. His head flung back, eyes wide, glazed. *Jones.* He'd been the last addition to the unit. Self-sure and able to defuse anything. Almost as good at building IEDs as Kellen.

Jones lifted with the impact, the too-large bore bullet hitting him under the arm on the side of his torso where his gear didn't provide coverage. Then he crumpled under the gravity of his own weight.

Cooper looked around frantically, but saw no one.

Who'd taken the shot?

He needed to remember to keep his own arms down at his sides.

Staying low, as if that would help, he made his way to the edge of the forest line. Farther west than he'd been the first time, he hoped to stay out of the way. The man he'd cracked with the butt of his rifle was gone. It couldn't have been three minutes, and yet there was no sign of him. Only a short drag mark where someone had grabbed him and pulled him, and then it looked like he'd gotten up and done the rest himself.

He'd not seen the face, hadn't seen markings that ID'd him. They were there, but it had all happened too fast. The drag marks were important: they meant someone was worth saving. At least two people were in this together.

As he hit the tree line, Cooper saw the man on the ground in the yard, bleeding out. If he was still alive, there was no longer anything that could be done to save him. His daughters returned fire from around the corners of the house. Following their aim, Cooper spotted Benj Freeman, also at the forest line, laying down a blanket of bullets on the girls.

The family was friendlies.

Cooper didn't understand.

The mission was to check on them. They'd been told there was intel that someone was coming for the family, and the teams protected those who protected them. So why were they all shooting at each other?

Cooper gripped his rifle at the ready and patted his handgun, still in the holster at his side, ready to zip out at a moment's notice. When he looked again, he saw Benj Freeman's face explode.

The image burned into Cooper's brain. The back of Freeman's skull remained intact.

He'd been shot from the side. By one of their own men.

Cooper looked down the tree line and saw Ken Kellen lower his rifle.

DONOVAN'S HEAD SWAM. The burner phone was buzzing, but it was a cheap piece of crap, a sister device to another cheap piece of crap. Too much security and it would be obvious. Too little meant the device was of no importance. It needed to seem to be of no importance.

They'd made Rollins memorize this number, he could delete pics, texts, etc. as he sent them. And he could destroy the sister phone and send from other, new numbers as needed.

As Donovan watched from the couch, Eleri picked up the phone and checked it.

"Anything good?" he asked.

"Not yet." She held up the tiny screen. "It's downloading what looks like a bunch of pictures." Then she turned back to her own phone, a faint smile on her lips. She must be finally communicating with the hockey player. That was good. Anything normal to anchor them was good.

Donovan knew that as an important goal from the psych classes he'd taken in med school. He'd found them all ironic given that, unless one of the bodies sat up on the table and declared themselves not actually dead, he was never going to need it. Still, he got top scores in the two classes.

Ultimately, he'd only memorized content. None of it meant anything to him, until now. Until he realized that his 'normal' was the exact opposite of an anchor. All the years of picking up and moving in the middle of the night. The new schools, the superficial friendships and involvements in classes, sports, life. Then he'd gone the other way and anchored everything with his job and his home and nothing else. When the FBI had called, he'd gone nomad again. First to the Academy, then on the road. He'd even gone with Eleri to her beach house the last time they had a break.

He made up his mind to go back to South Carolina the next chance he got.

He also realized that wasn't enough. He needed something normal here. Something in the midst of all this chaos that would help keep him firmly in reality. And he didn't have any clue what that might be.

He'd been shocked by Cooper Rollins' story. The soldier had drawn on his associates. On the very family that had fed him and even hidden him once. But he didn't know if they'd drawn on him first. He'd watched as Ken Kellen turned and shot Benj Freeman right in the face.

Rollins' had paused then as though he could still see it. Given the way he'd fuzzed out on them at the question—and how much it looked like the freeway incident from that morning—Donovan was convinced Cooper Rollins was having another episode. Each time, the man had fought to bring himself back to reality. *Talk about needing an anchor.*

Donovan was developing a grudging respect for the ex-soldier, even if he wasn't sure he completely believed him.

Even if no one else knew what was going on. L.A. was quietly organizing itself. It could go just as badly as shit had gone down on Rollins. He'd turned and fought Kellen hand-to-hand that day, neither of them getting ahead, only inflicting damage. He'd been grabbed from behind; he'd been shot at by his own teammates. He'd seen the black and green and brown on them. And he'd shot back.

It was the only reason he wasn't dead. He'd walked back to base beside three men he no longer trusted. He dragged Benj Freeman's corpse. They'd each dragged a body. And three more men were unaccounted for. One of those had been Ken Kellen.

The man Rollins had KO'd was in the wind now, too. Ken Kellen was the only one of the three missing that Rollins had ever seen again. He'd read in reports that the other two had died that day, but the army had never shipped their bodies home. Location unknown.

Rollins believed there was a hell of a lot more unknown than the army was admitting. Donovan thought Rollins was probably pretty correct on that one.

What Donovan and Eleri had hashed out was that Rollins and Ken had both wound up in the L.A. cell because of their Fallujah connections. Whether or not they'd been on the same side that day, the girls had accepted both men into the group.

They spoke the native tongue—well, Rollins spoke enough of it, he'd pointed out. It was a bigger deal than he'd first thought. The girls had lost their father that day. He'd been left for dead on the ground. Their mother had disappeared later that same night when soldiers came. She'd managed to send the girls out the back first and they'd disappeared, defecting to the U.S. on known visas as rebel friends.

What a crock of shit.

Donovan couldn't wrap his head around much of it. Had Kellen shot Benj Freeman because he knew too much? Had Freeman turned on them? Was Kellen protecting Rollins by killing Freeman and the others? Protecting himself? No one knew.

Donovan turned his attention to the tablet he held. Even as he started working, Eleri came and sat next to him, doing much the same thing on her laptop. "Look."

She pointed to a satellite picture of the compound the coupe had gone to. "It's a militia." She paused for a second. "Damn. I hate this shit."

"You want a good serial killer next?" He almost grinned at the very morbid thought.

"I would not have thought I'd ever say yes, but yes. Please." Then she buckled down. "We can pull sat photos of the yellow coupe. Here." She pointed to another picture she'd down-loaded. "There's Walter and there's . . ." She scrolled. "Cooper."

"If we could find photos this easily, so can they. We have to assume they know the coupe was followed."

She nodded glumly at him. "If they're any decent at this, and it appears they certainly are, they have cameras on the entry and at various points. Cooper turned around as soon as Walter passed the gate, so they at least saw her, but I'm guessing they got him too. If they ran the plates they figured out the cars are rentals and can't be tracked back to the owners."

Donovan filled in. "Two rentals on a nearly deserted road, tailing their guy? That's bad."

He looked at her and waited until she glanced up from the screen and caught his eye. "We opened a shitcan of worms today, didn't we?"

"No. Sarah did that."

"No, she didn't. If she'd killed Mrs. Deen, that *might* have started something between the Jewish cell and the militia where they must have been getting their guns. But us being there, Sarah winding up dead, and Mrs. Deen in Federal custody, that's not good. *We* did that."

She shrugged. "We have a witness. She's alive."

"She's a crap-ass witness."

"True." Eleri agreed. The old woman was holding out on them.

Any concern Donovan had about her being poisoned and innocent had flown out the window. She'd come around in the ambulance and bitched about her constitutional rights. She demanded her guns, demanded that she be released—she couldn't have health care forced on her!—and tried to beat up one of the EMTs. Donovan had pushed on her sternum, a great martial arts move that pinned her down and left her floundering like a bug. And he'd called her a bitch to her face.

Probably inappropriate, that, but he still didn't care.

There were agents on her at the hospital—it turned out

they *could* force health care on her. She'd given them nothing so far, even as they tried to save her from the Ricin.

"Sounds like the little crappy phone is done."

Eleri showed him a text first.

— KK VOUCHED FOR ME. I have this now. Don't come.—

THREE PICTURES POPPED UP NEXT.

A zippered brown backpack was in one.

The same backpack was opened in the second picture. Wires spouted from C4 stuffed in the neck of a bottle with clear liquid. Motherboards and timers protruded. A simple switch showed in one place, a cover protecting it from accidents.

Donovan thought something about it looked familiar, then he caught it. "My money says that's a Colonel Ratz design. Or at least part of it."

Eleri's eyes widened, then she nodded in agreement.

In the third picture, there was a handheld piece.

Donovan spoke the words out loud though he was sure his partner already understood. "That's a remote detonator."

39

I t was still dark when the pounding sound woke Eleri from her spot on the couch. She'd curled around the tablet like it was a teddy bear.

The sound came again, only this time she recognized it as knocking. Donovan's frown turned into acceptance as he, too, uncurled from the other end of the couch. He figured it out before she did. "Vasquez."

Well, at least she was already dressed.

She checked the clock. Five-thirty a.m. Interesting.

Something must be good for Marina Vasquez to be waking them now. Eleri opened the door to see that Marina didn't look much better than either of them.

"Sorry." She said it as she came through the door, though she seemed too busy to actually be sorry. Her usual bag was over her shoulder, her tablet in one hand, a cold can of that weird soda she liked in her other. Eleri wondered how long she'd been pounding the caffeine.

"About what? The time? The case? The universe?" A smile tugged at Eleri's lips. At least she had good people to work with these days.

At the Behavioral Analysis Unit, the work had been the only real good part. Her fellow agents distrusted her for her instincts. Her boss had even written her up once, causing a bone-deep mortification.

As Donovan had joked before, serial killers were small potatoes compared to a city like L.A. getting attacked by multiple individual but simultaneous terrorist cells. "What do you have?"

"An eight a.m. meeting for all of us. With other FBI agents. I'll explain. Give me a few minutes." Marina sat at the table in her usual spot. The fact that she had a usual spot was telling, since they'd only been here a few days.

The small lump under her shirt made Eleri think. "You're still wearing the grisgris."

"You're wearing yours." Marina pointed out.

"She's my grandmother. Great-grandmother, but whatever." She smiled.

"Sure, but she matched the outfit I was wearing the day it arrived. And the package was waiting in a room Donovan had just picked. I don't turn down protection of any kind, let alone *that* kind."

Eleri laughed. "You also researched the hell out of it, didn't you?"

"I did." Vasquez clutched the grisgris through her shirt with one hand while with the other she finished arranging her things. Then she once again turned her tablet to face Eleri. "This is what I have on the militia."

She pushed a piece of paper across the table at the two of them. As Donovan took his seat, Eleri realized she heard the coffee maker burbling and she felt something decent seep into her bones at the sound. She scanned the list. "It's what? Forty-five people?"

"Sixty plus. Though I'm not sure they're all currently active. The problem is that they very well might be networked." At

Donovan's frown, Marina continued. "There are well over fifteen hundred active militias in the U.S. today. And that's just known, anti-government militias."

"There are other types?" He asked.

"Sure, religious—"

"Our Texas case bordered on that. They were a cult that also armed themselves heavily. But they were probably a cult first." Eleri explained.

"Yeah, those aren't counted in these numbers. Neither are those who are pro-government, but consider themselves their own small branch of the military. They train in their own time, in their own way, and aren't planning to overthrow the government, but to protect it when our regular military fails or needs help. Then there's the gun-nuts who form groups. They love guns and they get organized and train. So not really military-like even though they like to play war games and wear camo." Marina sighed. "This group is definitely anti-government. No religious affiliation."

"The one thing we managed to weasel out of Mrs. Deen is that those guns are from her sons' group." Eleri added, not sure if Marina already knew that.

"And Cooper Rollins was right. Those guns were U.S. Army issue. Special order, serial numbers track back to the Army holdings. They should never have been in the hands of civilians."

Something about the look in the other agent's eyes made Eleri tip her head.

Marina held her hand up. "You do not want to know the earful I got from the Army. Where were they? How had I gotten them? No, they were not FBI evidence but U.S. military property." She sighed. "He threatened to put me in jail."

"We won't let that happen." Eleri reached out.

"There are actually quite a few agents named Vasquez. So he can probably find me, but it should at least take him a while." She sighed. "I hung up on him, but I can't get prosecuted for rudeness."

Eleri tried to steer away from that. Vasquez couldn't get prosecuted for her work, but Eleri had seen harassment from a person or group in one branch toward another. It wasn't pretty. It would get less pretty if Eleri and Donovan identified exactly how the Army guns were leaking out of U.S. holdings. It happened all the time, to be frank, but Eleri was trying to prove that this was an organized operation.

Marina's voice brought her thoughts back to the table. "Here's what I have."

She started scrolling through dual pages. One side had a head shot, most of the time. The other side listed bio info about the person. Eleri took over, Vasquez had put this all together, so she'd already seen it.

Starting back at the beginning, she looked over each one.

"This." Marina pointed to the first one—Madden Deen. "This is the son that came to the house and left, the one Cooper and Walter followed. Word is he's the front man. Known in the community. He's got a law degree but only uses it on constitutional cases. Keeps up relations with a few local businesses."

Eleri showed it to Donovan. "Would you recognize him? Did you get to see him?"

Donovan pulled the tablet closer. "Not at all. I was trying to hold that old woman together."

Eleri felt her eyebrows go up.

"Hey." He protested at her look. "So my bedside manner sucks? I'm an FBI agent with special skills and I think she was a rank bitch. You should have seen her in the ambulance. Tried to stab the EMT with a needle."

Eleri nodded in concession and went to the next picture, then the next. "Hey. This is another Deen son, right?"

She turned the page on Maxim Deen around to face Marina, who nodded back at her. "He's the oldest. Rarely leaves the compound. Runs the drills. Up to his neck in this shit. In fact, the shit is so bad, that the FBI already has agents on them and is looking to run a raid. They'd already figured out the group isn't just practicing but running guns they're getting through U.S. military lines. I may have almost messed that up a little bit."

When Eleri looked up, Marina explained. "Let's just say it's a good thing that Walter Reed and Cooper were tailing them and not any of us. Those two—if they are identified—are ex-military. They could maybe, *maybe* claim they wanted in on the action. But if agents had been seen tailing a Deen boy to the compound it would have blown a year's worth of plans."

"Ouch. So we need to get together with these agents." Eleri added.

"Exactly. That's our eight a.m."

Eleri frowned and looked at her phone, the meeting was now in one hour.

Eleri motioned to Donovan about the time. Marina didn't notice as she was at the refrigerator reaching for more to drink. The junior agent might need a blood transfusion when this was all over. Not that Eleri was doing much better.

She held up the phone to show Marina. "So we're on for this ASAP?"

The junior agent nodded. "I set it up at three a.m. Honestly, I let you sleep as long as I thought I could."

She had. But this was not the eight a.m. meeting Eleri had been expecting. Marina was left waiting while they cycled through the showers. Eleri had to dry her hair. She wasn't going out walking the streets of L.A. trying to dress so she could blend in at a meeting or hop the fence at the Square. She was heading into a full FBI investigation—non-NightShade.

She asked Donovan to get in touch with Westerfield and get some guidance on how to proceed with an interlocking investigation.

When she was finally ready, there were only about ten minutes to spare. Eleri entered the main room as Donovan was slipping into his lightweight suit jacket. She hadn't realized before that Marina had arrived ready for the meeting.

Eleri looked to Donovan. Had he talked to Westerfield? His small shrug said no. They were going into this with no guidance, and once again Eleri fought the nagging sensation that Westerfield was poised to leave them under the bus should anything go wrong.

"Are you set to present this?" Eleri asked Marina, "You did all the research. We haven't even read it all. Grab your shit, people. Let's go see what's up at the compound."

They were in the conference room, having just poured round two of coffee for the morning, when two other agents walked in. Eleri was disappointed. She'd harbored a secret hope that she would know one of them, but she didn't.

They nodded and sat down, the older gentleman looking like a kindly grandfather with a stern Bureau gaze. For a moment she thought he might be wondering when they started letting women into the bureau, he looked that old and that set. But luckily when he opened his mouth he seemed to have none of that good-old-boy vibe.

"Agents." He nodded, barely bothering with introductions. "Vasquez tells us you have a case that intersects with our investigation of the anti-government militia in Fontana."

It was a statement, not a question. Eleri had no idea what Marina had told them other than, yes, it did seem to intersect. She sat down, mug in hand, and leaned forward. "I sure hope so. Ours is all over the map. But it looks like big time terrorism and it seems your guys are involved."

They started by matching the address—or coordinates—of the physical location that Walter and Cooper had followed the yellow coupe to.

"You had agents follow them to the front gates?" The

younger one leaned forward this time, his tone clearly conveying what he really wanted to say. *How could you be so stupid?* It was the older agent who put a hand on his arm and held him back mentally if not physically.

"They didn't know. They followed a lead that brought them to our front door." He shook his head. "I've always thought we should have a fucking newsletter or something that said, 'hey, here are the other cases in your area.' So shit like this wouldn't happen."

"You followed someone off the main roads!" The younger one yelled, the hand-on-arm move having not really worked. "Where the hell did you think that car was going? A yellow sports coupe with black racing stripes and guns in the back seat. What else could it have done?" He went on about how they were so stupid, making sure to aim his vitriol equally at all three of them.

Marina flinched. Eleri moved her leg to touch Donovan's in a signal, then sat still, waiting with a purely flat expression. When he ran out of steam, she made sure she sounded bored as hell. "Are you finished?"

At least the older agent wasn't mad. He just seemed a bit embarrassed by his partner. There was no right to be angry, but many agents didn't recognize that when their hard work was compromised by other agents just doing their jobs. Eleri had been on both sides of it, but she'd never yelled at anyone for what they hadn't known. So she was ready to pick up and walk out if the agent went off again. When he didn't, she asked another question. "Are you ready to hear what really happened or would you like to keep bitching about the way you made it up in your head? Because I have shit to do."

At least he looked contrite as he sat down. He was still angry, but he was finished.

So Eleri turned her attention back to the older—more sane —agent. "The coupe didn't have guns in it. The guns were in our possession at the time after stopping the attempted murder of Mrs. Deen." Eleri pulled up the picture and turned it around. "I believe she's the mother of the group's leader?"

The older one nodded, and Eleri tried to aim her discussion toward what was important to them until she had things more sorted out. "The guns came to Mrs. Deen's house with a delivery woman named Sarah. No last name yet. Now deceased. Madden Deen, another son of hers, pulled up in a different car —which we have impounded—checked the front door, saw the body of the deceased and left in the yellow coupe." Then she turned her attention to the younger agent, "So you can sure as hell bet we followed that car. I'm just sorry your people weren't already on it. By the way, it was two Army consultants who followed them, so not agents at all. And the second turned around about five miles back, once they realized where he was heading." She stared a moment, daring him to call Walter and Cooper stupid again. Then she explained the connection to the Jewish cell, asked if they knew about Sarah? Alya, Aziza?

"Those are women. Muslim women?" The older agent asked. "So what makes you think they're involved?"

"Honestly, sir, it's brilliant. They violate the dictates of a strong religious order, but they do it for 'God's work' or 'Allah's' or 'Saint Issa' and no one suspects them. Think about it. Almost our entire terror watch list is men. No one is watching these women. Except us." She pointed at the three on her side of the table. Then she turned the conversation back to the compound, since they didn't seem to know much about the cells' agendas or why Sarah would try to kill Mrs. Deen. In fact, if the ricin poisoning worked, she still might succeed. But the other two agents did know about other gun deals.

"That's the Indian group." Donovan pointed to a trade location on the map they gave.

Eleri shook her head. "The address was phantom."

"It's a letter and number off on each part. It's not phantom, just coded. Look." Donovan pulled it up, suddenly in the mix after having been silent for most of the time.

"You know the group they were selling to? We have nothing on them." The younger agent frowned but was civil, now that the trio had proved to have something he wanted. *What a dick.*

"We don't have much. Only that they exist. They committed a murder associated with a string of murders and we think they're in line to be part of a coordinated terrorist attack."

He explained a little more about the groups and Eleri let him. Being a brick wall to an asshole was draining, but she kept up the front.

"Can we have a few minutes?" the older agent asked.

Though he was polite, Eleri had had enough. "Certainly."

So she kept her butt planted in the seat and took a careful sip of her coffee while looking toward the door. They could leave. The message was clear.

With a nod of acceptance for the assholery his associate had displayed, the older agent pulled a few papers to head to the hallway.

Eleri waited until the door closed.

Marina breathed out a sigh of relief, and words followed right on its heels. "You were so badass. I want to be you when I grow up."

Eleri laughed out loud, some of the tension leaving her.

"At least you didn't do that thing with your eyes." Donovan said before he realized. Then he covered quickly, leaning toward Marina. "She gets this glare that no one else can do."

He gave her a slight tip of the head indicating that he hadn't lied. She still hadn't seen what he had, so she dismissed it. "Let's get something done. I can hear the clock ticking on this one. I'm just hoping the younger one can get the big stick out of his ass and be useful."

Marina smiled again, but picked up with info over her cup of coffee from where they'd left off in the apartment earlier.

"There are four Deen boys total. Actually there are ten Deen kids, but some are cousins. Gotta love that. Four are Mrs. Deen's kids, probably part of why she's not talking. The third oldest is Madden—who came to the house. Second is Magnus. He's ex-Army, the only one who served. The general consensus on him is that he served solely to get information for the militia. Guess where he was stationed?"

"Fallujah." Eleri and Donovan said together, almost like it was a game show. Then Eleri added. "We have to get these photos to Cooper and even Walter. See if they know this guy. It's a long shot, but..."

She made mental notes of task after task that had to be completed. If anything fell through the cracks, the world just might burn. She turned back to Marina. "Who's the fourth son?"

"Marvel."

"Marvel?" Donovan asked, right as Eleri was asking "Are you serious?"

Marina sat down again even as she shrugged. "Ran out of M names? Maybe she was high?"

Flipping through the screens, Eleri almost passed him in the short bios, but she recognized the face. "He's the one who bumped me downtown."

Eleri looked at the two of them. Did they know what that meant?

"What?" Donovan looked at her.

"Marvel Deen. He made me." She almost whispered it. "*They* made me. Before I even knew they existed. Our groups have been working in explosives, knives, that kind of thing up until now. They're only just now getting guns into the picture. But the militia that's supplying them, or whatever, realized we were on it and they put a tracker on me!"

Her heart was racing. That was bad.

He'd come by after Walter had helped her out of that little

altercation with the lobomau. If he was paying attention, he'd seen Walter, too. If they'd spotted Walter at the compound . . . If they had security that got facial pictures of the drivers going by —and they *had* to have that—then he could pull out Walter as being associated in some way with the FBI. With Eleri.

Her brain turned over. "So even if these agents don't know about the cells, the militia sure does. Enough to loop back around to me. Other than being a Bureau agent, I'm not associated with the militia case at all. Hell, I'm not even on the Los Angeles roster. Fuck." Her brain turned over yet again. "Donovan?"

"I'm on it." He already had his phone to his ear. "Walter?"

It was all she heard over the pounding of blood in her veins.

When she focused, she heard him asking Walter to come down and ID names and faces. She was shaking her head 'no' and he was nodding 'yes' as the other two agents returned.

Donovan's voice was clear to all of them. "Wherever you are, get out fast and get out clean. It's not safe. Let us know when you're in route."

"You're pulling your operative?"

Eleri pushed the tablet forward. "Your guy, Marvel Deen, tagged me with a tracker downtown two days ago when I was trailing one of our main cell operatives. Whatever you don't know about the cells, I'm pretty certain your militia guys do."

The agents didn't flinch at the barb. But the older one ran his hand through his hair. "They've been ramping up these past few weeks. More than the past months. About nine months ago they went from a watch list to active investigation because of their change in quantity—"

Eleri interrupted. "That's when our cells started getting active."

"Shit."

The younger agent picked up the slack. "They ramped up again about a month ago—doubling their supply and sales.

More of them moved out to the compound. There are more drills, and they've been running ground-to-air missiles for three months now."

He paused, but then continued.

"We have reason to believe they're planning an attack in two days at the most. Maybe today."

Eleri's blood ran cold.

40

C ooper Rollins was in 'go along to get along' mode. It wasn't a place he was comfortable, but comfortable had left his sphere the day he'd turned his rifle on his teammates.

This was particularly bad, though.

He had the backpack over his shoulder and was walking down the street as though he didn't have the means to blow them all to high hell. If he hadn't carried explosives before, if he didn't know how to double-check the damn thing himself, if, if, if .o..

He remained calm. He didn't sweat or overact like an idiot. He held the weight of the backpack over one shoulder, ready to throw it as far as he could should that be necessary.

The downtown streets of Los Angeles teemed at this hour. Though it was nearing winter, the city was still relatively warm. A guy with a backpack was no big deal. That he clutched the strap of that pack with a death grip also wasn't unusual. It was a big city; he was just preventing theft.

Where his skills came into play, what really made him want to lose his shit, was the trigger. He'd sent the pictures. He'd checked the connections. The remote he had was in the pack, which led him to believe he was to plant the bomb in one place and retreat to another to detonate it.

That should have made him feel better, but it didn't. The problem was, he didn't have the only remote detonator.

Alya had distributed the packs. Told him not to open it until he got home.

Five backpacks sat on the floor of the apartment where they met. The colors varied, but none was bright. The designs varied a little, just enough so no one would notice five identical packs.

"You choose. You are first, Cooper." Alya had said as she stood behind the line.

At that time, he hadn't known what was in the packs, and he asked.

She ignored the question, waving her hand at the book-bags. "You choose the pack you like. Pick a color that suits you, something you feel you can carry around town and look right."

So he'd picked the black leather looking one. He'd hefted the weight, tested the straps and felt that something sloshed just a little inside. Cooper set it back down and went for the brown.

It was a test.

Were they all the same? Did they all contain the same inner workings? He stuck with the brown suede, not wanting to look like he was doing what he was doing. But he watched as each pack was in turn picked up and hefted. He saw where the weight shifted, listened for the sounds of liquid. He guessed that the liquid containers were relatively full. Everything appeared padded, too, so that the heavier parts didn't slip to one side, make telltale bulges in the sacks.

When only two packs remained, Aziza and Alya chose their colors together. Aziza leaving with the dull red and Alya with the blue with black stripes. Both girls slung both straps over their shoulders like college kids might. They could have been carrying books and laptops from the looks of it.

At his own apartment—he could hardly call it home— Cooper was not surprised when he opened the bag and saw the bomb and detonator. He'd sent the pictures, turned the phone off, and stuffed it into a dug-out section under his cheap mattress. Then Ken Kellen called and told him to get a good night's sleep, and Cooper tried not to laugh in response.

He imagined a life where he lived with his wife and little boy. He logged into his bank from his phone and permanently blocked the transfer of money that usually came from the family account. If he lived, he was going home. He'd find a way to be okay again. If he didn't live, then Alyssa would need it all.

Then he slept. He knew how to fall asleep even under hail of bullets.

These were tasks he once considered manly. Now he knew them for what they were: simply crazy.

He'd been activated this morning. No one had said anything. But Alya had showed up and knocked on his door. She'd waited while he dressed, something he didn't do too quickly. She knew he was a soldier. She'd watched him fire on his men. She'd fired on them, too. She'd fired on him.

But there she was, sitting on the cheap chair as though she were his friend.

He didn't know.

They'd walked out of the building together, and he knew she was keeping an eye on him. Then, she casually said an address, subtly handed him a tiny earpiece, and peeled off to go her own way.

She didn't tell him first that she was giving him important information. She didn't repeat it. Despite the play of her sitting and waiting on him, she knew he was a soldier.

Turning the corner, he found the building and made his way up to the apartment number he'd been given. It wasn't what he'd expected, and he had no idea if he was meeting someone, supposed to detonate someone, or himself?

Cooper stayed on high alert.

The apartment wasn't one he'd been in before. It was nicer than he'd expected. He was surprised when Ken Kellen answered the door.

For a moment Cooper took stock. He sniffed the air, listened to the sounds around him, and assessed the possibility. He was about to ask, when Kellen spoke.

"We're alone." His face was grim, determined. "We're not bugged. Say what you want."

"What the fuck are you doing?"

"I have to do this." He sipped at a mug of coffee he must have set on the table before answering the door. He'd known Cooper was coming even if Cooper hadn't. He knew what was in the backpack, but he'd made coffee like Sunday morning.

"Why?" Such a small question for such a massive need.

Kellen shook his head. Shrugged. Sighed. "You know. You know about the arms in Fallujah. I saw you going through the Captain's papers. Freeman told me you'd figured it out."

Neither nodding nor denying, Cooper waited.

"It started small. Reasonable. We armed the right people. The enemy of my enemy is my friend." He set the coffee down a little too harshly and Cooper saw it slosh over onto the table, but he didn't take his attention off of Kellen, off the pack he still clutched. He felt the weight of the gun holstered at his side and hoped he didn't have to use it. He was afraid he was going to.

Kellen spoke again, and for the first time he looked worried. "We had to sell the guns. We couldn't give them out. You were part of it."

"Of course, there's a normal exchange there." The U.S. armed local groups that were friendly to U.S. efforts all the time. Normal enlisted never got their hands on that, but sometimes the special teams did. They'd delivered some of the crates of weapons, just like they delivered food and medical supplies. As he was considering a possibility, Ken Kellen spoke again.

"It wasn't all food. You transported some of it."

"I checked the crates. Every one." His anger rose, but he had so much practice holding it in check.

"Captain had two of us on it originally. Me and Freeman. We traded your crates, or repacked them."

"The weight was the same. The—"

Cooper stopped when he saw the look on Kellen's face.

"We're all good. You would have done the same thing. Repacked with care, watched the weight and the balance. The thing was, you didn't suspect us. So why would you check again? We were doing what was necessary to put down the forces we fought."

"Why the extra? We were already giving them guns!" The weight of the bomb grew heavy on his back and he wondered why Kellen was telling him this. His only security was that if Kellen held the other remote, he'd blow himself to hell, too.

"It wasn't enough. They needed more. They needed better weapons than we could hand them on the books."

"No, they—"

"Yes. They did. You *know* how strapped we were. You *know* that we knew where the strongholds were. We *knew* where the enemy was, but we were bound by convention, by code, by the creed of the Army. These guys weren't. They took out so many for us. And they paid for the guns. It was good for everyone."

"Then it wasn't." Cooper guessed.

"*You* figured it out."

"Freeman tipped you off." Cooper took two steps back, wanting to be out of arm swing should Kellen decide to stop talking. He quit gripping the backpack and reached slowly for the butt of his gun. "Why did you shoot him?"

"I had to." Kellen looked around. "You have to go. You have a point to get to. Take the pack, set it up, and get away."

"As though I'm going to live through this?" Cooper didn't believe a minute of it.

"Yes. I'm trying."

"So I can be tried and hanged as a traitor? I'm screwed twelve ways just carrying this shit down the street, Kellen. What the fuck is really going on?" He held his tone in check, didn't let his anger make him loud. But it didn't mean he wasn't angry and afraid that he wouldn't live to see the sunset.

"You won't be. You'll come out a hero."

"You're a crap ass liar." It was all he could say.

"You have to do this."

Cooper didn't pull his punch. He nailed Kellen square on the jaw, the other man pulling back only enough to make the hit glance off rather than leave him cold.

He fought back, arms up, and three hits later, Cooper realized that Kellen was defending, not fighting.

"What the fuck, man?" This time he was louder than he intended to be.

"Trust me."

"No fucking way." Inside half a breath, he had Kellen on the floor. His head made a dull thud against carpet that wasn't padded well enough to stop the hit.

Still, the other man tried to speak.

Cooper tried to listen.

"They got us in. They made it reasonable: we distributed guns at the orders of our superiors. But then we were in it up to our necks and had to do what they said." His eyes finally contacted Cooper's, and for the first time he saw the bleakness in them.

But what did it mean?

"So?" he asked, his hands on Kellen's shoulders, an inch from his neck, a moment from choking the life out of him. "If you and Freeman were in it together, why did you kill him?"

"He turned on me!" Kellen offered a plea. "I have it worked

out. Go, plant it. I've taken care of it all. You have to trust me. They set me up!"

In that moment, Cooper understood. Kellen was running off righteous need for revenge. But against whom?

"You killed Mrs. Sullivan! She fed us, she kept us for Christmas."

Kellen's eyes squeezed shut. Cooper had been certain that his friend thought of the Sullivans as the parents his had never lived up to being. The air fled Kellen's lungs. "I had to. You don't know."

"No. And I don't understand."

"When this is done, come back here."

"No." Cooper refused. He sat astride the other man, holding him down. Kellen was in no position to make those demands.

Then he was.

In the heartbeat where Cooper hadn't paid attention, Kellen had switched their places. It was Cooper's head that thudded against the carpet, Cooper's hands that were held down.

His pale complexion glowing with rage and some inner need, Kellen leaned in close to Cooper and whispered six words.

ELERI JUMPED as her pocket buzzed.

She was still at the Bureau but back in her jeans and hoodie, gun tucked into a holster that was—as usual—only mostly concealed. Donovan looked much the same. Casual guy, out in L.A. Because L.A. didn't see the shitstorm that was coming.

Walter looked much the same, her shirt untucked, hoping most people wouldn't even see the metal she sported. The more they blended in, the better.

The buzz came again. *Wade?* She'd texted him that he'd

been right. *Avery?* She'd sent him something sweet, short, and probably a little too cryptic. But her phone was blank.

Not even news from the agents on the militia raid. They were going to signal if they had to go in, but in the meantime, they were waiting on word from Eleri, who was hoping they'd have something from the variety of boots on the ground. They'd sent out thirty agents, each with a different target.

Not all the targets had been found. But the ones that had were all on the move.

Not good. Statistically that shouldn't happen. Some should be asleep. Many of the people had jobs, but they weren't at work. To a man, they were off sick today.

Her stomach turned.

The women were not at home. They should be.

Eleri's breathing was slowly ratcheting up.

"Look." Donovan showed her his tablet. They were both getting photos from a variety of agents out on the streets following their respective targets. "We have four backpacks that look like siblings to Rollins'."

"The girls carry backpacks all the time."

"Not these." Marina was looking over her shoulder. "Look." She did a search, pulled up old pics of Alya, who was often seen with an army green backpack. "I've never seen her with that one before. Aziza usually carries a gray one." She was flipping pictures too quickly for Eleri to follow, but the intel was good.

"Bags." Donovan pointed to different pictures. "These guys don't have backpacks, but they all have bags. Bags big enough to hold that same bomb. Look."

One woman had her hair down like Sarah. Marina identified her as being from the Jewish group. Another woman had two bags, one of which she set down and walked away.

The voice of the agent trailing her popped on the speaker. "Follow the girl or the bag?"

Fuck fuck fuck.

Eleri's head raced. "The bag. Stay with the bag."

She hoped it was the right thing to do. She wished she knew where to go, but was only grateful that the Bureau office was relatively central. So she stayed put. Agents were all over town.

Pings came in from everywhere. Four agents were on buses. One out of communication while hitting parts of the subway. Just as they lost him, another reported getting on the subway on the opposite side of the system.

"Are they converging?" Eleri asked the room at large. She was now commanding a hastily assembled team of analysts and agents.

"Maybe." One voice was steady. A slightly older woman; a statistician, Eleri remembered. "I was just getting ready to say that."

"Where?"

The woman shook her head. "Not Calabasas. Not Downtown. Not Santa Monica area. Those are all headed the other way. Maybe Hollywood? Westwood?"

Eleri looked to a map of the city she'd gotten to know a little better while she was here. It was so sprawled out it was more like fifteen different cities, thirty maybe. Even the focus she'd just been given was far too big to pinpoint.

"Let's start moving that way." She took a breath and began gathering what she could. "Vasquez, Heath obviously. Fisher." She used Walter's real name to the room at large, then picked two other agents who looked street ready and left the others behind as they bolted for two SUVs.

She let the other agents follow with Walter in a second car, wondering if they looked too official in their black Lincoln. At least Eleri and Donovan had a colored, sportier SUV. If she lived, she'd thank Marina for that forethought.

Donovan reported from the passenger seat. "The Christian group is all carrying packs, too. They have bags or backpacks with a cross and some saying on them. Each group has a theme. Each group has a handful of people on the ground carrying what is very likely explosives."

Her phone buzzed, and this time it wasn't blank. She handed it to Donovan who put it on speaker.

It was the older woman, the statistician. "They aren't really converging. I'm sorry. It looked like they were."

As they wound their way up the street, not sure where to go now, she thought about the blank screen on her phone the last time it buzzed, and she smacked the pocket on her cargo pants. The burner.

Pulling it, she handed it to Donovan while deftly handling the car in the crushing traffic. She didn't know where to go, but now Donovan did.

"It's Cooper. Listen to this: On the move. Still have the tracker. Don't show yourselves. Follow me."

41

D onovan sat in the passenger seat, taking updates from Walter as she followed the tracker Cooper Rollins admitted he still had in him.

Rollins was headed in the direction the statistician had originally predicted as a possible convergence point. Eleri followed the best path of traffic taking them into North Holly-wood even as Cooper Rollins moved northward just to the east of them.

Donovan had resorted to sticking an earpiece in. He'd learned their uses at the Academy, and even used one for a raid during their last case, but he still found the things awkward. He hadn't yet come to terms with his inner James Bond and wasn't sure he was ever going to.

He almost startled when the voice came through his ear. First one voice, "Patching you through." Then a second voice, "The bag has been picked up. A woman in jeans and a patterned shirt. She looks to be . . . Indian in origin."

The agent would have said "Native American" if he'd meant that. "Indian" meant from India.

"Follow her!" Donovan shouted back before turning to Eleri.

"Someone picked up the bag. Looks like a woman from the Saint Issa cell."

Eleri had an earpiece, too, but hers was attached to Walter in the other car. The agents in that car were linked to the home base at the Bureau and everyone was barking at everyone else. It was chaos, but the only way to keep all the info from pouring in to everyone all the time. Eleri processed what he gave her then added her own two cents. "Holy shit. Make sure he knows he's the only eyes we have on that cell."

Donovan relayed the message and listened as more info poured in.

"No ID yet, but she walked by and picked up the bag in a practiced motion. This is not coincidence, she's either a criminal stealing a bag she found or this was a handoff."

Donovan thought for a moment, trying to figure out what he wanted to know. "Did she make any contact with the other woman? Is there any evidence of communication between them?"

"No. The first woman is gone. Long gone. She set the bag out as smoothly as this woman picked it up."

Damn. He wondered if they knew each other. Or if the first and second women had simply been told the other was a sympathizer. As far as he could tell, they weren't even in it for the same cause. And they still had no clue who was running the fractures above Ken Kellen.

Kellen had once been, or seemed to be, a dedicated soldier. Had he gone to the other side willingly? Was it money? A misguided sense of justice? There were so many sides to the wars these days. It was no longer Hitler and crimes against humanity. You couldn't just storm North Hollywood; it wasn't Normandy.

More information came in from Walter about Rollins, but it didn't make any sense. "Where the fuck is he going?"

"Here." Walter rattled off a link complex enough to take three tries to enter it correctly. He didn't want it recorded on email, not that it would be good much longer, but they were already at a huge risk out here on the road. No system was secure enough.

After he finally got it entered right, a map popped up and he was seeing what Walter was. And it was just as crappy as what Walter thought.

He sighed, and when Eleri gave him a look, he shook his head. "Rollins was headed north at driving speed, but hit an intersection and turned almost due east. Looks like he's on foot now."

"It's as though he's trying to keep people from following him." She mused.

"But he told *us* to follow him." Donovan countered. "We have a tracker on him, unless he lied."

"I don't even want to contemplate how he might have gotten that tracker on someone else."

Donovan made a face. "So it's him."

"Should we follow him more closely?"

Despite fighting traffic, they'd made good progress. While Cooper had turned and was no longer on a course that would cross theirs, they weren't far away. Donovan pointed this out to Eleri, and almost in tandem, the two cars turned east to see where Cooper was headed.

Ten minutes later, Eleri spotted him walking up the street, backpack slung over his shoulder.

"People don't tend to walk much in L.A.," she commented. There were some people about. Some loitering on street corners. Others walked briskly with someplace to go, but it wasn't like New York or even downtown Chicago with foot traffic being the norm. "If Rollins is trying to shake a tail, that means he thinks he has one other than us."

Donovan wanted to call the man, but that was an impossibility. If they called him, it might alert whomever he was working with. If someone was tailing him and saw him on a phone, that could be problematic, too.

Donovan turned to Eleri. "They haven't made me. Can I get a device, a microphone, to Cooper? Bump into him on the street?"

Marina Vasquez spoke first from her spot in the back seat. She'd been tapping away in the back until now. "You can't be sure they didn't make you. Marvel Deen got a tracker on Eleri. So who's to say they don't know about you, too? About me?"

"That's a valid point." Eleri conceded. She looked at him and shrugged.

"What if I looked *enough different*?" He tried to put just a little emphasis on the last two words for Eleri to understand. If he could find a spot to change, he could walk right up to Cooper Rollins as the wolf. If the wolf handed him a tracker, then Rollins would understand that the dog he'd seen downtown was a trained asset. But maybe that was worth it. It seemed they were coming up on an endgame.

"How in hell would you get . . . enough *different* looking to make that play?" Eleri looked sideways at him.

For a moment he thought she hadn't understood him. That she thought, as he hoped Vasquez did, that he was talking about some sort of disguise. But she'd understood.

"I could drop you off, but you'd have to find somewhere to head into, and change enough to make a difference, and that place would have to be so private . . . Just in case someone else is following him. Then you'd have to change back and get back here."

Shit. For a moment he'd thought he could duck somewhere, but as he played it out further in his head, he couldn't think of that place. They were in North Hollywood. Though there were a few abandoned buildings downtown, there wasn't much up here that would allow him to walk in as a man and walk out as a dog. Or leave his clothes behind untouched for when he came back.

The idea of returning and finding his clothes had been taken would leave him either naked or running around as the wolf. "You're right. There's not enough time nor is there a good place. Shit. I want to talk to him."

Eleri kept her eyes on the road, making random turns and staying out of sight, but close. "We can only do this a little while. Someone's going to realize there are two cars out here driving like drunks."

Marina stayed on Donovan's topic, and at least made him feel a little better about his probably really stupid idea. "Even if you got an open line to him, there's a good possibility he still can't talk. If someone else has a line on him, he won't be able to say anything to us at all for fear of alerting the other line."

Donovan sighed as Eleri took a turn away from Rollins and looped around a block. She was right, they were starting to look very, very suspicious.

The other car did a slow track past Rollins then headed up the street. He kept a good clip for being on foot but the cars couldn't follow without being obvious. Eleri had just taken a cross street as the other car passed, and Donovan caught a glimpse down the street. He didn't see anything.

But Walter did.

Eleri grinned even as Donovan heard the low chirp of Walter's voice in Eleri's ear, and he waited for Eleri to relay the information. "He's in a holding pattern."

"What does that mean? Can he tell her where he's going?"

Eleri asked then replied a moment later. "It's military signals, not sign language. It's pretty generic stuff. The teams apparently have better language, but Walter was MARSOC, not even Army." She shrugged. "I think we're lucky we got this."

Then she grinned. "He worked out a code with Walter, we can head off but stay close and follow him when he's on track again."

It took four minutes to find a parking lot with two spots adjacent to each other. Actually pretty lucky for a weekday in Los Angeles. It was easier to pay the fee than to flash badges and alert anyone that anything was up. Soon they were all out of the cars, standing around and talking.

He and Eleri looked almost like random kids. Walter bordered on military goth, with an out of place cheerful ponytail. The agents looked like . . . well, FBI agents in street clothes, but there was nothing Donovan could do about that. They'd come in to be part of the home base. They hadn't planned on being on the road. To be fair, if they needed to draw down on anyone, these two would wield a whole lot more authority than either him or Eleri in their jeans and hoodies.

Marina Vasquez was the one who first gave up anything useful. "If he's in a holding pattern then he has both a direction and a time."

"What?" Walter asked her.

"If it doesn't matter when he shows up, he'd keep going." Vasquez explained. "The fact that he's biding time means there's an important or planned time of arrival and being early and hanging out is not an option."

Eleri looked back and forth between the rest of them. "Coordinated arrival . . ."

"So if they're all going different places, then they each arrive at those places at the same time?" Donovan asked.

"Makes sense." Eleri and Vasquez both said it at the same time, though Vasquez seemed contrite about speaking over her senior agent. Eleri didn't even seem to notice. Donovan was trying to pay more attention to these things, but maybe now wasn't the time.

"Can we figure out where they're going?" He asked.

None of them looked at the other. Six brains, all intelligent, all working overtime, were trying to crack what was going on. And they'd all been trained to throw out what they had, no matter how crappy.

Walter went first. "How many backpacks are out there?"

"Five." Vasquez knew that one. "But that's just backpacks. Assuming you mean all the bags? That's twenty. Maybe twenty-five."

Eleri frowned. "It's fifteen. Five backpacks, five from the Calabasas group, five from the Valley group."

But Donovan saw where the junior agent was thinking. "But we know there's an Indian cell, too. At five from each group that's twenty. The militia or another group would put us at twenty-five."

Even as they tried to calculate the number, Donovan got another transmission.

"My guy—Officer Davies—had no bag when he left, he just picked up a black leather bag sitting under a bench."

"Who dropped it?" Donovan nearly yelled into the mouth-piece. He hadn't even told Eleri what they had.

"No idea. I'm still following him."

"How did it go down?" Donovan was desperate. Not only were a handful of terrorists out and about with bags—at least one of which contained a bomb and a remote detonator, and most likely all of them did—now there were multiple hand offs.

"He drove into Hollywood. Parked. Hit a shop, then walked up LaBrea and over on Franklin. There's a little park there. He sat on a bench and a moment later he'd pulled the bag from where it was stashed under the bench."

Holy shit. Coordinated tradeoffs between groups that might not even know the other existed.

Donovan told Eleri. "Do we know of a group with . . . hold on." He spoke into the receiver. "Can you describe the bag?" Then he turned back to Eleri and Vasquez. "Black leather messenger bags?"

"Does it have any Christian insignia on it?" Vasquez asked without looking up from the pictures she scrolled through.

It took just a second for the relay, but Donovan told them what he got, "No."

"Good." Vasquez didn't look up until they all stared at her.

"Well, currently we have five bags per group. This trade off tells us that there's at least one other group out there running bags. Like I said, probably twenty. If there's another cell involved or if the militia is involved, then there's another set of bags."

"Shit. She's right." Eleri plucked her phone out and called the agents from earlier. "Are your militia members all still inside?"

By the look on her face, the agent confirmed it. They had satellite eyes on the compound and noted that none of them had left. But if the Bureau started plucking these guys off the street, there was every possibility of a tipoff of some kind and the raid on the compound would be compromised. There was a second, worse, possibility, that if they pulled any one of these people, they would activate a backup plan.

And they had no clue what the backup plan might be.

"Are we still on hold?"

"Yes," she answered, hanging up even as she turned back to the assembled group. "They're all in the compound. So unless someone snuck out some super-top-secret passage that these guys don't believe exists, they're waiting. There is activity at the compound, but it's all internal."

"Do you think they could be on the line with all the people with bags? Are they coordinating the movements?" Vasquez asked.

Eleri and Donovan both shook their heads at the same time, but he spoke. "That would require the whole compound being part of the fracture. They would have to know as much as Ken Kellen and there's no evidence of that at all."

Vasquez was nodding along with him even as he said it. "In fact, there's evidence to the contrary. Okay, so we have all these people and all these bombs out on the move. They aren't converging, even though they looked like they might be. So twenty-five separate targets?"

"That would be impressive." Eleri considered it, folding her arms against the slight wind that had come up. Then she stopped for a moment and Donovan saw her thinking. "What's the capacity of that bomb?"

"I don't think it's that big." Donovan said. He didn't know bombs. Cooper Rollins might, but he wasn't here. "Show them."

Though the words themselves were unclear, Eleri understood, and she pulled out the burner phone and showed the others the pictures of the bomb in the backpack.

It was Walter who managed some initial assessments. "It will take out the immediate area. But it's not Oklahoma big. Not by a long shot. It's . . . suicide bomber big. Does that help?"

They all nodded.

They all knew there was at least one bomb in the pack Cooper Rollins was carrying. And they knew he'd been allowed to pick his pack, insinuating that there were bombs in all of them. "What if the others are dummies? Maybe Rollins just drew the short straw?"

"Could we get close enough to tell?" Eleri looked at him and Donovan stared back. If they hadn't made him, he could. He could smell it if he got close enough. But how in hell would they be able to tell the others that?

Eleri didn't even pause with that, she was already on the line to home base. "Is there anyone else carrying a pack near us?"

She looked up excitedly. "There are two, maybe three depending on how we want to go." Then she turned to the others. "You stay on Rollins; Marina, come with us. Donovan has a really good sense of smell, if he can get close enough maybe he can tell."

"You have a really good sense of smell?" She looked at him quizzically.

He didn't get a chance to answer, Eleri did it for him. "He gave up a life of sniffing armpits or perfumes for one of the big corporations to fulfill his dream of smelling dead bodies all the time."

She always had a ready comeback for whatever was weird. Except when it was her. Her dreams were "normal." Her visions were sometimes devastating, and her eyes? She still wasn't even acknowledging that, but Donovan? She could sell his special 'talents' to anyone almost like a used car salesman.

They made Marina drive. At the first place she let him out three blocks in front of the woman the agent was tailing. Donovan put on headphones and pulled his hood over them. He shoved his hands in his pockets and walked down the street moving a bit to music he wasn't even playing. He took deep breaths as he went, cataloging the background smells, and as he passed the woman he tipped his head slightly and inhaled.

A block later, he heard Eleri in his ear, the FBI earpiece tiny and still in place. "Agent confirms she didn't suspect you. Not anything that showed anyway."

"The bag's positive. Pick me up at . . ." He looked up at the street signs. "Radford and Vanowen."

In less than a minute the car pulled up and he hopped casually into the passenger seat. Marina Vasquez already had them on the way to the next one. This one was male, Eleri hopped out with Donovan, insisting they hold hands like a couple for cover. He argued. She reached for his hand. Since he had to lean in close to the bag, it might look weird if they were holding hands. He pulled his hand back. Well, now they looked exactly like a couple.

Though they moved slowly, the man with the bag was coming right up, but unlike the girl before, he held the bag down at his side. It might reek of explosives but Donovan wasn't taking a chance. Pulling away from Eleri's hand again, he said, "There's something in my shoe."

"Are you fucking kidding me?" She pulled off 'exasperated' very well. He was already leaning over, his head down by his feet and he had the shoe off as the bag went by. He put the shoe back on and declared his foot better and even held Eleri's hand. When they climbed back in the car they got confirmation of success from the agent tailing the man. He didn't seem to have noticed them.

Donovan nodded at them. "He's positive."

"You can smell it?" Vasquez asked.

He nodded, and shrugged. "Some explosives are really stinky."

"Hmm, I handled some C4 before and I don't remember it having a smell at all."

"C4 really doesn't." He lied through his teeth. He could smell C4 on someone's hands. "But a lot of the liquids involved have low vapor pressures and they leak fumes and smells."

These were pretty tightly sealed, but he didn't tell her that. "Do we want to do a third?"

Eleri shook her head. "We are one hundred percent positive from our spot checks. We know Cooper has one. We know this woman from the Calabasas cell has one, and we know that man from the Valley Glen cell has one. Unless these three each drew the short straw . . ." She shrugged, pointing out the unlikelihood of that.

"But what if they did?" Donovan perked up, his brain in overdrive. "These three are all heading one way. What if the ones with bombs *are* converging?"

Eleri went a different direction. "It's been almost an hour. Rollins is still in a holding pattern?"

Walter's voice came in reply. "I haven't gotten the signal yet."

"Do you trust him not to slip the knot?" Eleri's voice held the exasperation that Donovan suddenly felt. Had they trusted Rollins and he'd screwed them?

"I have to." Walter answered. "Yes, I do." Then she laughed. "We just got the signal."

Donovan jumped in. "He's headed south isn't he?"

"No, north."

Donovan frowned. They were down at Hollywood and Western. Cooper was up in North Hollywood still. The other woman was in Burbank heading south. They sat in the car, confused.

Just then they heard a comment. "My guy just got on a bus. I'm on with him."

"I've been walking north, but just turned west."

"Rollins just hopped a bus."

The information started sounding off like popcorn. Everyone was on the move, changing direction, hopping busses. It was time.

Then, the info Donovan had been waiting for. "Rollins' bus says it's headed toward Griffith Park."

He turned to Eleri. "Griffith Park is one of the points!"

She was frowning at him, but he was already on the line to home base. "What if there isn't one convergence and there aren't twenty-five targets? What if there are five? Five bags, one member from each cell to each place?"

Eleri got it then. He could see it in her eyes. "Shit. Griffith Park is one of the targets! Hit it, Marina."

42

E leri felt the car lurch forward, felt herself being thrown around more in the back seat. Her brain was too busy to think about bracing for turns. She picked up her tablet clocking Cooper Rollins' movements. Then she called in to the Bureau.

"We're thinking we have multiple points of coordination. Five of them. One is Griffith Park."

Then she held her breath. The statistician didn't speak for a few minutes, then, "I've been considering multiple points as well. That these people will meet up. But you said they don't seem to know each other, so why would they meet up and work together?"

Good point. "I don't know that they will. I don't think they'll recognize each other. However, the burden of each bomb doesn't look like it's big enough to take out a city block, but if you put them together . . ." She hated saying it. Hated thinking about what would happen if they didn't stop it. Stopping it required a very precise strike. One that didn't trigger any backup issues they couldn't *also* stop.

The statistician's voice came back again, and Eleri could

almost see the woman. She seemed so calm, just working her numbers and occasionally speaking something important. "So, five points because one person from each cell will meet up? Is there something different about each of the bombs?"

Eleri asked Donovan but he shrugged. So nothing smelled different about them. "I think it's just an increase in blast load. They probably don't know they're meeting up. Also, the one we saw has a remote detonator, so the cell members can probably survive the blast."

"Give me a sec." But she only took a second to produce the first one. "Santa Monica." Then she paused. "Downtown . . . But not sure exactly where in either place."

She was on speaker at the home base. "Send teams."

She wanted to send in SWAT, but "Santa Monica" and "Downtown" were too big to get anyone into position, and they couldn't just drive around without being seen.

Eleri started pulling up maps, as she zoomed in, the woman's voice came again. "UCLA. Remember these are my guesses. UCLA is at least a smaller target. If I had to guess Santa Monica, I'd go for the pier. Downtown there are a hundred tall buildings."

Eleri wanted to say "one more" but she bit her tongue. What if she was wrong? There could easily be more than five, so she didn't say it.

The statistician did.

"Pasadena!" She was excited. "If I use five as the expected number, it works. I think this is it. Do you want to dispatch more teams?"

"Yes." Eleri tried to stay calm. Tried not to yell, "Yes! Dammit, *Yes!*"

"Donovan," she spoke his name clearly, so those listening over the speaker at the Bureau wouldn't get confused. "Call the other car, have them turn and head downtown. Tell them Walter knows it like the back of her hand and they should listen to her. Also tell them she's been tailing Ken Kellen for days and she'll have some insight."

She only half heard him as he repeated all of that. She didn't even see the other car peel off and turn. Eleri stayed in the back seat. The SUV stopped and started, but she wasn't looking out the window, she was staring at the map, zooming in and out. Then she asked the statistician, "The Rose Bowl?"

"That's what I was thinking. I'm currently checking that."

Eleri had no clue what math the woman was doing exactly, but she was checking the convergence of the routes against the likelihood of a place being a target.

"The numbers look good," she said. And by 'good' she meant 'likely to be hit' which was 'bad.'

Five targets. She had three agents who understood what was going on. She had two consultants who knew the game, but one was carrying a bomb and out of communication—not to mention possibly almost rogue. The other was just a consultant and couldn't lead a strike.

Eleri leaned back against the seat, taking long deep breaths.

This was what the FBI was good at.

Though they weren't all NightShade and had no Night-Shade directive, they were great at coordinating and taking down. It's why no one knew about the Red Line Ricin Attack or the Candlestick Park Bomber. There were others, too, but these had been cases that Eleri was personally involved in. She'd been profiling at the time of the Red Line Ricin Attack and had been low man on one of the teams.

So she had to trust that these guys would step up for her and take the cells down before they could inflict any damage. Just like she had stepped up when they called her in the past.

"Oh shit." Marina spoke from the front. She must have been looking at Donovan's set up even as she drove. It was Donovan who filled Eleri in.

"Rollins is headed up the front walk of the observatory."

"Of course he is. It's heavily populated."

Then she heard a spark from home base. "I just lost my guy. He walked up to the woods and hopped a moto-cross bike. I can't keep up. I'm sorry."

Eleri was just getting ready to ask, when he volunteered what she needed. "We are on Western Canyon road and he headed into the woods toward the observatory."

"Sounds like confirmation to me." The statistician came in.

"Can we get SWAT close, but hidden? We can't run a take-down if they're hitting different sides of the building. Fuck." She whispered the last word, as though by not barking it she took away some of its power. She whispered her next line too. "We need to get out of the car."

When she realized no one heard her, she said it again. "Marina, take us to the front, drop us off and park. Come find us. We need to get out of the car."

She spoke then to the home base office. "Tell them all we need boots on the ground, but plainclothes."

That meant not SWAT. It meant the officers. She kept talking even as she climbed out of the car. "Tails should keep following. Weapons at ready. Patch me through."

She looked up suddenly, trying to appear normal as she entered the observatory. Where was security? Eleri glanced around.

There were several guards, but if there was a detector, Rollins had passed it cleanly. She wouldn't. She was packing. She would light the place up and that was bad.

"Donovan, go grab that guard and get us in with no fanfare." She didn't even look at him, just faked a smile and caught Rollins heading around a corner.

Shit.

She had to catch up to him, but there hadn't been enough time to scope the place out, to make plans. That must have been the plan all along.

Double shit.

Stepping to a corner, she tucked her head down and her shoulder up, she even tried to look like she was on her cell phone. "Rollins is inside the observatory. Which means we are close to time. What are the other targets?"

They should know them by now. The cell members should be dead on and starting to converge. Unless it was staggered timing, but that would be bad news for the last group.

"Just getting ready to relay that. One—Rose Bowl. Two—Pier. Three—UCLA Medical Center. Four—you, Griffith Park Observatory. Five—downtown Tower Theater. All have plain-clothes agents getting into place. Most have three if not four cell members reported entering. SWAT standing by at all except Pier and Tower Theater. ETAs are five and eight minutes."

Eleri fought to keep her breathing under control. Five minutes would be fine.

She kept the tablet tucked away, she didn't need it to track Cooper. Yet.

Her eyes frantically scanned the room until Donovan appeared at her side and the guard let them through, sending them into the main part of the Observatory cleanly. No beeps, no bells. She let out a small sigh. Step one of a thousand.

Just then, Marina Vasquez appeared at their sides and had the guard let her through with them.

Eleri smiled at her like she would a friend, then offered her a hug as though she hadn't seen the woman in a while. While she was close, she whispered. "Head to the right. See if you can pass a cell member or an agent. See what you can get. Keep us posted."

Marina offered a squeeze back and a reassuring, "Got it. See you on the other side."

Eleri hoped like hell she meant on the other side of the

building and not anything more ominous. But there wasn't time to clarify.

"This way." She motioned to Donovan as though she really wanted to view the exhibit and steered him through the center portion of the building and off to the left.

Her heart matched her feet as she fought to keep up with the pace Cooper Rollins set, even though she could tell he was hanging back to help them. She was practically skipping to keep up, and it was difficult to look as though she was simply wandering the exhibits.

Donovan put a hand on her arm. "We're good. He's leading us."

"Sure, but what if he doesn't lead us to the other three? What if the strike points are different?" How would they find all five? If even one bomb got through, people would die.

A voice came over her earpiece. Hers was concealed, Donovan's not so much. His slight jerk indicated that he got the same message.

"Three people already entered the Rose Bowl. They are heading down into the tunnels. Fourth member appears to be arriving. We are putting an agent on him."

"Updates." She spat out the word. She wanted a snapshot of where everyone was. She got it—so much rapid-fire information that she let Donovan tug her along behind him as he followed Cooper and she assimilated and organized everything she thought she understood.

Cooper Rollins disappeared through yet another doorway as she put it all together. They were getting in place but if the cell members were meeting up, they weren't there yet.

She was counting on them meeting up. Unsure if they were suicide bombers or hoping to get away in the chaos of the crowd afterward, she couldn't tell what the set-up would be, but she was praying they were smart.

And Ken Kellen was smart.

He knew how to build the IEDs. He was operating with additional information from Colonel Ratz on how to make the bombs better. He'd made them lightweight, with a relatively light load. But if he put them together, he'd get a lot more out of it. That was the smart move.

So Eleri had to count on those backpacks and bags getting as close to each other as possible.

And if she was wrong?

If she were close enough when she was wrong, she'd pay for that mistake with her life.

No one was setting down their bags yet. No one had yet met another member and shaken any hands. Not one agent had passed another tailing agent. Yet. So there might still be time.

Or it could all come together in the next five seconds.

Eleri held her breath and took the next turn to see Cooper Rollins take a door to the outside. Once again, he turned to the left, taking the terrace around the building. He could go right back to the parking lot from here, and Eleri frowned.

Almost no one was over here, and why would they be? It was out of the way. There were no exhibits here, not a great view, unless you liked the canyon and the drop-off area.

Rollins paused, admiring the tops of the trees he could see from where they stood. They were tucked too far around to see much of anyone else. Eleri whispered into her mic. "Vasquez?"

"Far right terrace. No activity."

Eleri whispered another check in for the observatory and found two others, the one on his dirt bike only somewhere ahead of the agent who was on foot still tracking and only able to give a general direction. Another agent was following the cell member up from a bus drop-off toward the front of the building.

Each time they got closer together, Eleri felt her heart rate increase.

Just then, Cooper took a small turn, and looked at the other people milling just beyond the corner of the building. Then with no fanfare he looked at her and Donovan and tapped his ear.

He was getting something.

Then he jumped a little and disappeared.

She'd blinked and he was gone. "Donovan!"

Her harsh whisper broke the air of the beautiful day but didn't solve anything. Donovan didn't even look at her. "Hands."

Sure enough, as she looked at the railing, she saw fingertips let go. Then he really was gone.

Cooper Rollins had jumped the fence.

43

E leri found herself at the terrace railing, her feet having flown to the spot where Cooper Rollins disappeared. It wasn't too far a drop to the canyon floor, but the ground rolled away in a steep slope.

Hands already planted on the rail, Eleri didn't think twice. She hopped the railing just like Cooper.

Okay, not just like Cooper. Her jump was far less graceful and for a moment, as she hung on the other side seeing the drop now at a more accurate measure, she was afraid.

But she was far more afraid of those bombs going off. Despite all the tails and all the agents out today, Cooper Rollins was their best lead. And he was disappearing into the woods in front of her.

So Eleri let go.

Her feet hit the ground with a sharp sting to the soles despite her cushy sneakers. The impact slammed all the way up her legs even into her spine, but she didn't have time to get her feet under her. Gravity and the slope of the ground pulled her forward, and she was falling and stepping while at the same time trying to stay upright.

She'd made it two feet when she was slammed into with a grunt.

Automatically, her hands came up and she managed to grab an elbow and get a hand flat on a back.

"Donovan!"

He'd tipped into her, the grunt from the hard landing to his already sore ankle.

"Are you okay?" It was low, frantic, the sound of the worry deep in her soul.

"Fine." He pushed it out through the lie of his clenched teeth. The sharp intake of his breath snapped as he, too, was forced into a downward run lest he take her tumbling with him.

There wasn't time to worry about old injuries. New ones would be far more devastating, and even as she couldn't see her feet or pay attention to the uneven ground she was running over, Eleri looked up to see Cooper, Donovan, and the backpack disappearing into the trees.

What the fuck was he doing?

There was no one out here.

Then she heard the buzzing in her ears for what it was. Updates.

The cell member still up at the observatory was headed around the left—meaning he was coming to her side. He'd skipped the entrance all together and simply hopped a low fence and walked into the canyon. She was pretty sure it was national or state park territory. What that meant legally she had no clue. There had barely been time to figure out where these guys were going, let alone what the rules and regs were in the locales.

Her feet pounded along beside Donovan, far behind Cooper Rollins as another update came in. The two at the pier had turned from the end and headed around the back of the community center. The agents voice sounded puzzled. "It's closed."

"Us, too."

"What?" Eleri asked, stopping for a moment. She could chase Cooper, she could listen, she could think, but she couldn't seem to do all damn three. So she stopped and waved Donovan on, thinking she'd catch up to him.

"Downtown, Tower Theater. They left. My guy is headed now into the building for The Lofts. They're closed for remodel. He had a key."

"Closed?" She felt her face contort with the stupidity of the information.

That wasn't the smart way to bomb someone. One of the cell members had been under the pier with a bomb. The smart thing was to take strategic pylons out. Not head to the top or into a closed building.

Downtown, in an empty building. What did that prove?

"Rose Bowl." She stated it, but they understood.

Three agents there. "Full of fucking people. Kids. Some kids' concert thing."

Her heart stopped.

The signal scrambled then. A moment of static and it was just gone.

Eleri looked up, scanning as far as she could through the relatively dense trees and scrub. Where was Donovan? Why had she thought that she—five-foot-two to his six-plus—could catch up to him? He'd run track, and she couldn't have been any more stupid.

Scanning the forest for any movement, she got more and more disheartened. She should be running, moving, but she didn't even know which direction to start. Eleri tried a deep breath, knowing that panic was not the way to go, but she'd lost her comm and her partner and her back-up was on the other side of the fence.

She tapped frantically at the earpiece, but nothing

happened. She took it out, put it back in. It simply was not working.

For a moment she closed her eyes and slowed down so her breath soughing in and out of her lungs wasn't the only sound she heard. When she did, she caught the faint burr of a motor-bike and her mouth curved a smile as her feet took off in that direction.

Her first thought as she picked up speed was to call it in, but her comm was dead.

She was just thinking that was bad, very bad, when she heard another sound off to her right.

"El!"

Short and sweet, maybe only she knew it was for her. She stumbled as she turned and only then did she catch sight of the dull red t-shirt Donovan wore. He was shrugging out of it, stuffing it up in a tree.

"I think Ken Kellen's here."

"What?" Her shock almost made her shout it.

"I think I smelled him. Is your comm out?"

"Shit. Yes." She shook her head trying to sort out what might have taken out both their comms, why Ken Kellen was here, and what the hell she was going to do now that she had no communication at all even though she'd found her partner . . . who was slowly stripping his clothes.

"Donovan." She only said his name.

"He's that way, following Rollins as best I can tell." Donovan pointed her in that direction and gave her a shove, still not wanting her to see him change.

She granted him that and would have looked over her shoulder to tell him to be careful, but the ground was still falling away beneath her feet as she sunk deeper into the canyons and deeper into the plans of a madman. She didn't want to disrespect Donovan, so she wished him good luck the only way she could right now.

Eleri clutched the grisgris still at her neck and said a prayer she knew from Grandmere, from a summer childhood a lifetime ago.

"Bon Dieu, keep him safe. Bind him from trouble. Aida-Weddo, protect him from this forest he walks."

So Eleri ran toward the sound of the bike, until it stopped and the forest around her went dead silent.

DONOVAN KEPT HIS HEAD LOW. He hadn't been able to smell clearly when he was upright, but down on all fours, his nose to red clay, his nasal passages more open in this form, he got the scent for certain.

Ken Kellen *was* here. Now.

The thought made no sense to him. None of it did. Why were the ones at the pier going into the Community Center?

Were they staying safe when the others were out of the way? Maybe they didn't all have bombs. Maybe they were just decoys to use the Bureau's time and resources. To take critical agents out of the loop at just the right moment.

He couldn't hold his breath, not at this speed, but if he could have, he would. The world might blow up in front of him at any moment. He kept his head low and his speed high. A few times he lost scent, veered off track, and wasted precious time getting back on it. When he did find what he needed it wasn't because of his skill. It was because of the noise.

The slap of skin on leather was the first thing he heard, followed by a grunt, a hit, a stumble. Then he ran fast enough, changing his course to find the two men locked in a struggle.

Cooper Rollins expertly removed himself from a chokehold and whirled around to face Ken Kellen. Both men stood forward on the balls of their feet, ready for anything. Hands out, they circled each other, both knowing that movement was a better starting point than standstill if you wanted a good hit.

"What the fuck, Kellen?"

"Give me the bag." Though the men mirrored each other, Kellen held out his hand, the lift of his arm making Donovan nearly flinch at the stinging scent of fear that came on the air. Why would Ken Kellen be afraid?

"You know what's in it."

"I told you to trust me, and you've been communicating with *them*. They'll fuck it all up." He made a move, feinted left, and Rollins expertly dodged it.

"And I don't trust you."

"You don't have to." Kellen spoke, his eyes angry now. "I shorted the systems. They can't find you."

So that's what had happened to the comms. It also meant Marina and Walter could no longer track Cooper. They'd have only a last known transmission point to help locate the three of them. As he watched in abject horror knowing the bomb could go at any time, the two men circled each other. Sounds of other people came through the woods to him. Eleri crashing through the trees and dry brush on the other side of the men, a dirt bike coming closer, a lone hiker coming up behind them, someone in the distance closing ground.

Kellen made an offer, his hand still out. "All my journals. The whole thing. You always wanted them. They're in the closet in my apartment. Usual way. Is that enough?"

Cooper didn't answer.

The dirt bike came to a stop and Ken Kellen heard it. The sound only made him get more desperate. His look, his voice, even his smell, told the same story: he was about to crack. His tone was a harsh whisper to the wolf no one had noticed. Yet.

"I have a remote for all twenty bombs. If you don't give me the pack, you'll die. I will set them off. I have to." He spat the words low, held his hand out, waiting, despite the fact that Cooper wasn't responding.

Only then did his eyes flick to a spot behind Cooper, and though Cooper didn't fall for it, Kellen took advantage. In a piece of a moment, he was on Rollins with a punch to the face.

Rollins defended, but Kellen used it to get the backpack.

Donovan hung back, ready to jump into the fight, but not sure what he could do in the midst of two trained warriors such as these.

The backpack was bulky, and it was Rollins' downfall. Kellen grabbed it, using the momentum of the weight inside to pull Rollins to one side and trap his arm. He took advantage of the opening with a quick blow to the side of the head that dropped Rollins like a rock.

Kellen peeled the backpack from his fallen teammate and took off like a rocket in the direction of the bike.

Donovan heard the hiker coming up quickly behind him and Eleri on the far side. He made a decision, giving Rollins one quick tug on his arm. When the man didn't respond, Donovan took a firmer bite and dragged him as far back as he could. There was every likelihood something was going to blow up.

Once he had Cooper hopefully safely out of the way, Donovan took off after Ken Kellen. But he quickly came to a stop when he saw Kellen slow his pace and come face to face with the man who'd likely gotten here from the dirt bike, given the looks of him and his direction of approach.

Donovan recognized him from the Calabasas cell.

"Sir. I didn't expect to see you here."

Kellen offered a comforting smile. "I told you, I'm in this with you."

"Are we ready?"

"Sir?" A new voice, female. Donovan looked up as a hiker

came out of the woods, her bag slung cross body. She seemed as confused as the Calabasas man.

Kellen nodded to her. "Avital."

"What's going on?" she asked him, clutching at the bag, snaking her hand inside, presumably to go for the remote. She started to lift the strap over her head, her movements nervous.

Donovan felt his heart kick up.

Kellen put his hand out flat, palm toward her. "Wait, Avital. All is according to plan. We need one more."

His words held the tremor of fear and Donovan wondered if the others could hear it.

The hiker came up to his left, but he saw the people, now standing in a small circle and didn't seem to notice the very large wolf he'd walked within ten feet of. A rustle came behind Donovan, but he kept his eyes forward.

"Ken?"

The hiker became angry, not ready to be calmed or surprised like the others. "What the hell is this?"

Turning, Donovan saw a man of Indian origin. One of each. With Kellen replacing Rollins as the representative of the Downtown cell. The click of a bullet being chambered turned all their attention back to the center of the circle, where the Calabasas man had drawn his gun.

The Jewish girl was reaching for hers, and the rustles beside him turned into human movement.

Cooper Rollins was less than eight feet away. He must have come to and snuck up. Donovan kept his eyes on Ken Kellen.

He addressed the small circle. "This is the mission. It always was."

He reached into his pocket and Cooper Rollins turned on a dime beside Donovan.

It was the only clue Donovan got, but he, too, turned and took off after Rollins. He hadn't turned as fast as he should have. He'd kept watching. The only advantage he had was that no matter how fast a man was, the dog was faster. Donovan laid himself low and stretched for each leap, but it still wasn't enough.

He didn't hear the sound.

He only felt the shockwave lift him into the air and send him flying somehow faster than he'd been running. It was the last thing he remembered.

44

Eleri woke to ringing in her ears and the slow creak of unused muscles. She rolled her shoulder, and tried to pop her neck before she felt the rub of her face against the dust of red clay.

She tried to sit up, but her back burned, and just the thought of it snapped her back into reality.

She'd heard Kellen say something and she'd run, even though she couldn't see them, something about his tone told her to get the hell out. But she hadn't been fast enough. She'd been thrown to the ground, or the ground had been slammed at her, she wasn't sure which, but she knew it was because of the blast. She was confident that Ken Kellen, still holding Cooper Rollins' back pack, had set it off.

Her right knee ached and she was pretty sure she'd cracked her kneecap on a rock jutting out of the ground for seemingly that exact purpose. Below that, her shin was bleeding from a cut she couldn't quite see through the dirt and blood and the tatters of her jeans.

When she rolled her shoulders, she felt the pull of the skin on her back again, and a deep cold seeped into her heart at the thought that she was maybe severely injured. When she reached up, the back of her jacket felt wet. If it had been burned onto her, attempting to remove it was the last thing she should do. But the feeling of fear crawling under her skin, the desperate need to be rid of the jacket overruled any medical sense she had, and Eleri peeled it. Part of her was relieved and the other part prayed she hadn't removed a layer of skin with it.

Pulling it around, she saw that the back was coated with debris. It was bloody in a few spots, so she had some nicks and cuts there. Eleri looked around, realizing there was a good chance that large splinters had flown into her back, thus giving her the cuts and maybe even the feeling of the burn. But the fabric didn't appear scorched and her breath wheezed out of her in exhausted relief.

She patted at her gun, still blinking away the dust in the air, still trying to hear anything beyond the ringing sound. She was just getting to her feet as she felt the first sharp stabbing in her knee. Eleri almost tumbled back down, but she fought the feeling and took another step.

"Eames. Eames, are you on?" The ringing in her ears was the comm.

Ken Kellen had jammed it, and he was gone now. She hadn't seen it actually, but he couldn't have survived that. Could he?

Donovan!

Her heart kicked up and she ran to where she'd seen him last, wondering why he hadn't been her first thought.

"Eames, if you don't respond I'm handing command to Decker."

Who the fuck was Decker?

"I'm here." Honestly, she had a damn fuzzy definition of 'here' right now and she probably shouldn't be in charge if she didn't remember who the hell Decker even was. But she wasn't handing it over. So shoot her. It wouldn't be the worst that happened today.

"We're ready to raid the militia. Is it a go?"

"I've been out. How many blasts?" She was still running, still trying to account for the people she needed. In her peripheral vision she saw an arm in the dirt. At least that's what she thought it was. Ahead of her, there looked to be a man lying face down. That was more important and she didn't check on the other.

"Five blasts. Shockingly simultaneous."

"Raid the militia. It's a go." She gave a firm command. It didn't matter that children in the Rose Bowl were likely dead on a sunny if slightly chilly afternoon. She didn't know how much of the UCLA med center was still standing. She could get that later. She couldn't bring those people back.

But she could stop the next wave. The militia had been prepping this morning. None had left. Agents that could have been on the Fracture Five case were assigned to storm the compound. Let them get to it. At least they'd had months to plan their attack. She'd had minutes.

At the home base, messages were barked, orders relayed from her to the men and women waiting just over an hour away in Fontana. Within seconds they'd be on the move, coming out of the woods surrounding the compound. They'd come from far back, staying out of sight of the hidden cameras they knew were there. If they were lucky, they would be done in a matter of minutes.

Eleri was not certain the day would be lucky.

Despite the stabbing sensation in her knee, she made her way to the prone man, even as she still looked around for Donovan. The man was not Donovan. But friend or foe, she didn't know, and Eleri pulled her gun, bracing it in two hands she was surprised to find were shaking.

She stood to one side of him and nudged him with her toe.

Nothing happened. He didn't wake, he didn't seem to respond, but he did move like he was alive. Despite being out, despite the number of ways a brain could lie and believe someone was alive when they weren't, there was almost always a distinct shift in the way the body moved when still inhabited. This one was.

She nudged it again and it moaned.

Still aiming her gun at the back of his head, Eleri scanned the area.

Where was Donovan? Because he was out here as the wolf. Unless he'd gotten away already. She had no idea how long she'd been down, but what if he'd been hurt? Who would help him and how could they?

"Who are you?" She barked it when she really should have been quieter. She had no clue who was still out here.

"Eames." He frowned up at her.

No, she thought, *I'm Eames*.

But it was just recognition. Cooper Rollins was rolling to get up. He'd said her name, and he was moving with a fluid ease that she was extremely envious of right now. Just standing felt like having a two-foot straight pin shoved up the middle of her shin. But she didn't flinch. "Are you okay?"

"I'd feel better if you weren't aiming that gun at me." He reached up to wipe dirt from his face, his movements slow enough to show her he wasn't going to do anything that might make her want to pull the trigger and deliberate enough to tell her he didn't give two shits about her trigger.

"Are you okay?" She asked again as he got to his knees. Eleri considered taking a safe step back, but this was Cooper Rollins, their informant. He wouldn't—

He did.

Faster than she could blink, he was on his feet, his hands grasping hers, one in front of the other, right around the gun. He rocked the slide back, stopping a bullet from leaving the chamber, just like the skilled professional he was. It was a risk, but he knew how to take it.

He twisted her hands around, forcing her to let go of the gun, and Eleri cried out with the pain of having her freshly bruised wrists forced to drop her only real security. He'd grabbed her the right way, with her smaller hands encased in his, she couldn't get out of it, so she gave up the gun.

For a split second, she imagined Donovan, leaping into the fray, twelve-hundred psi jaws clamping around Cooper Rollins' arm and pushing him sideways. But the assistance didn't come and Eleri stood before Rollins as his victim.

She was afraid.

He was a big man, definitely bigger than her, and far better trained than she. He'd been aiding and abetting terrorists the whole time he'd been helping the FBI. Two minutes ago, she hadn't known what side he was on, and right now she still didn't, but she knew one extra thing: it wasn't her side.

Donovan was still out there, possibly hurt. She hadn't heard a single sound that might be him, what she did hear was the sound of agents and SWAT teams. The dry bushes and near-dead trees rustling with every movement, making whispers of the coming plague of agents. Well, enough to get her out of this.

Rollins' heard it too, looked over her shoulder and grabbed her hands to drag her along and finally triggered her 'pissed off' button.

As he pulled at her still clasped together hands, she pushed. When he adjusted, she pulled and then pushed with one hand and pulled with the other. He'd hold one, but she'd gain one. Only he didn't.

Cooper Rollins took one look at her and reared back.

"Get the fuck off of me!" she yelled and took immediate advantage. She roared out her anger at him, her hands coming up to attack even as he raised his to defend his face. She faked a punch to his midsection and kicked him in the balls with everything she had.

His hands dropped like stones as he started to crumple. Eleri caught one and spun him around, tugging his arm up behind him until she felt his shoulders give, then she planted a foot in the middle of his back and pushed him back to where he started—face down in the dust.

She pulled her cuffs and ratcheted those suckers down, hoping she caused him pain. Then she leaned over and whispered harshly at him. "Do not fuck with me, asshole."

He didn't respond, didn't look at her, just watched the people in full black gear approaching with rifles raised, as he sucked in air through flared nostrils. If she didn't know his background better, she'd say she actually scared him.

"Ma'am!" One of the Bureau agents called out to her. "Drop the gun and surrender."

"You have to be shitting me." She muttered under her breath, but she knew how this worked. Loud enough for them to hear, she said, "I'm Agent Eames with the Bureau."

"You don't match the picture we have, ma'am." He hollered out, so she raised her gun, holding it by one finger through the trigger. And thought, *that's because my Bureau ID doesn't show me after I've been coated in bomb resin, tree blast, and red clay. But hey, you do what you gotta do.*

She wanted to move her foot, plant it on Cooper Rollins' back and keep him down. So help her God, if he moved one muscle she would shoot him dead. "Reaching for my badge."

Her heart pounded triple time from all the rifles aimed at her, though her movements were like cold molasses. Eventually, she got the wallet out and flipped it open in a slower version of her practiced wrist flick.

By then, two of the team members had scoot-stepped their way up to where they could see it, and her, better. "Yes, ma'am. Sorry. Orders?"

Just like that she was on top again. No time to be pissy about nearly being taken down as one of the terrorists she'd spearheaded catching. "This is Cooper Rollins—informant and maybe terrorist. Take him in."

Two agents were reaching to pull him up and haul him in and she was getting ready to speak again, but she was puzzled by the way he scrambled to go with them. Eleri shook her head.

"This is the blast site." She pointed behind her, trying to be careful about saying what she knew. Donovan had smelled Ken Kellen, and she'd heard what she thought was him, but . . . "I heard people, several of them, just prior to the blast, then I was knocked out. How long was I out?"

She changed tacks without warning, but they turned with her. "Blast was about four minutes ago, Agent. We held back just a minute waiting to see if there would be another one. We got satellite confirmation of no movement and then we came in formation."

She nodded at him. That was as it should be. Eleri set them to checking the clearing, to calling forensics to be sure there were enough parts or DNA to confirm four people had died in the blast. She needed more information on the other blasts. But more than that, she needed Donovan.

Eleri turned to the man, "My partner is still missing, but I think I know where he is. I'm off to get him."

"We'll help."

"No." She barked it. "You're needed here. We have no idea if there are more terrorists around." Eleri spoke even as she pulled the jacket from her waist and put it back on. It was disgusting, but her t-shirt had been chosen for blending in. She needed to be a beacon now. She pointed to it, looking from one agent to another. "Don't shoot. I'll wear this. Tell everyone. I'm out searching, I'll call in backup anywhere I need it."

Then she took off in the other direction. She jumped over fallen trees, and the occasional body part, scanning and calling out as she went. She yelled louder than the scream of pain in her leg. "Donovan!"

Nothing came back. Not a whimper or a bark or a shout.

She was searching the same area a second time when she almost tripped over him. Not too far from where Cooper Rollins had lain when she first found him, Donovan was farther from the blast center, but a tree had fallen across him.

She couldn't call his name. He was the wolf.

There were too many others here. Too much of a chance of being found out. So she stayed quiet, trying not to alert the agents working the woods, searching, just beyond where she was. Intel was coming in her ear about the other blast sites, but she wasn't listening. She was on her knees in the dirt and debris, feeling for a pulse.

45

onovan had woken to pain. And he'd woken to Eleri, pushing on him as though he were in bed and needed to wake up. He'd tried to tell her to go away, to shut up. He'd tried to say her name, but his mouth wouldn't work.

Then he remembered.

He was in the canyon below the Griffith Park Observatory, and he'd been out cold. He'd only slept as the wolf a handful of times before. This was not planned.

"Go," she'd whispered. "Go."

He heard the crunching of leaves as agents approached her. "Everything good, Agent Eames?"

"Just a dog out here. Maybe belongs to someone." She gestured off beyond the edge of the woods where there were in fact houses, but they were far away. "Looks like he got caught in the blast, but he's okay."

That was a fat lie.

Donovan stood up on all fours, looked at Eleri, and walked away. He fought against the sharp pain in his ankle, the deep, dull pain he pulled in with every breath.

He heard the agent as he turned. "Looks like a wolf to me."

"You think?" Eleri's disagreeing tone followed, always covering for him.

He made it out of sight before he gingerly lifted the back leg he shouldn't have been walking on and limped the rest of the probably two-mile loop back to his clothes. He'd had to walk on it while they were watching. He couldn't afford sympathy. Even more, he couldn't afford to be shot as an injured and possibly aggressive animal.

When he got to the place where he'd left his clothes, they were missing. But after a moment of panic he'd spotted the very clear trail in the debris to where Eleri had tucked them under a bush. Somewhere safer, somewhere not crawling with agents.

So he'd grabbed the clothes and limped away, tucking himself beneath a tree, behind some bushes, up against the wall that led up to the terrace a full story above him. Only if someone looked directly down at him might they see anything. But he simply couldn't go any further.

He rolled his shoulders into place, popping his elbows out and finally his fingers. His ribs were cracked. He could feel it, but he pushed through the pain, there weren't other options. He managed to put his left leg back, but it hurt too much to do both at once.

Donovan stopped now, almost entirely human, naked and panting heavily from the strain, hiding behind what he hoped was adequate cover of brush. It was the right leg that gave him trouble. If he'd thought the left hurt, he hadn't accounted for a broken ankle. He tried to push back but couldn't. He was stuck this way. He couldn't change it.

"Fuck, fuck, fuck," he whispered to himself as he broke out in a sweat trying again.

The muscles wouldn't pull the leg back. His ankle wouldn't bend and the tendons wouldn't slip into human position. He flexed his toes, sending spikes of pain that almost made him scream.

He couldn't make noise. They were looking for Donovan Heath. This would not do. So he did the only thing he could think of, because no one else could do it for him. He shoved a nearby stick in his mouth and bit down. The bitter taste of the resin didn't register as he grabbed the ankle with both hands and twisted it back into place.

He didn't scream.

He spat the stick as he vomited and fought to keep from passing out as nausea set up a standing wave in his system. It was only after he vomited a second time that he was able to sit back and start to breathe.

"Donovan?" The voice was soft. She'd come. She'd done what she could, and she'd come.

"Not yet." He panted it out, still exuding the cold sweat of the tortured.

"Okay."

She waited what seemed like forever, standing guard five steps away. Her blue-green hoodie marked her for all to see. She told them her partner was coming up. She was covering for him. Again.

Donovan pulled on his shirt, and found his pants to be harder to deal with.

He managed his socks and his left shoe while Eleri took in details of the day. She was relieved to find him and he was relieved to have her standing guard, but he wasn't out of the woods yet. "El?"

She crouched down, finally coming face to face with him, her relief a small shock wave that hit him as she looked him over. "Yes?"

"I can't get my shoe on." He had the left one on. It had hurt, but the right threatened to make him pass out. "Can you?"

She tried. Three times she tried. But she couldn't grab his

ankle to guide it in or push the shoe onto his foot without nearly making him pass out. Finally, she shrugged and tossed it into the brush. "You lost it in the blast."

"I'm ready."

She shook her head. "No you're not. Once again, your clothes are too clean. Can you roll?"

No. No, he could not fucking roll. But he did it anyway, feeling the cracked ribs all over again. Tree bits, red clay dirt, and pieces of weeds stuck to his clothing and having her brush him off was almost as painful as trying to grind it in.

"Now," she declared, and shoved her shoulder into his ribcage as gently as she could. It took him a minute to figure out she was trying to help him up. He accepted. All movement hurt, but it got him where he needed.

Once they'd made it about three feet, she set up a hue and cry that she'd found him. That he was injured, that he needed medical.

They had a brace on him in no time, which hurt almost as bad as not having a brace. They felt for broken bones and he winced at each touch, threatening to vomit on the med tech checking him.

She'd set up forensics at the scene, left the agents to their checking and hopped in the back of the ambulance with him. The EMT couldn't leave them alone, so it was a while before he got to check in. He'd been admitted to the ER and x-rayed before the hospital made it clear he still couldn't put his earpiece in.

Eleri had relayed what she could.

The Rose Bowl bombs had all gone off, but the Rose Bowl was fortified for something like that. "They were planned strategically where they would do the least damage. From the location of one of them, it looks like the bomber figured that out. He moved to a more structurally important location and tried to inflict some real damage. He did some. But only one bomb, it didn't kill anyone."

"So no one at the Rose Bowl?" Donovan was in awe.

"There are injuries, but no deaths." She smiled, her relief again palpable and Donovan wondered if she would run out of it. Just deflate and disappear. "At the Santa Monica Pier, Kellen put them into the Community Center—which is closed today. No one was there that we can tell. It's almost completely destroyed, but no one was hurt—except the bombers. And at UCLA he turned them to an old theater across the street. It's getting refurbed, same with the lofts downtown, they were next to the Tower Theater. They destroyed the building and themselves, but not anyone else."

He heard footsteps in the hall. His doctor—the man had a slightly uneven gait. Donovan asked quickly. "The bombers?"

She looked down, shook her head. "All gone. I think Kellen set them up with remotes and then set his own remote. They all went, they must have known—"

The door opened and Eleri looked up but finished her sentence as it was meaningless without the rest of the information. "That they would get alternate last minute instructions." She leaned close to whisper the last part before moving back out of the way. "He planned the whole thing to look like a real attack but then turned them toward each other and detonated all of them, still holding their bags, as soon as they were in place."

Donovan almost smiled, but the doctor looked grim. "Dr. Heath."

He nodded. It had been a while since he'd been addressed that way. He was almost used to "Agent Heath" now.

"This isn't good. But you probably already knew that." The man was older, white haired, with horn-rimmed glasses. He seemed amiable, but not like the kind of doctor that would do anything aggressive to treat things. Then again, Donovan clearly needed something done. He'd had only a dose of Advil relatively early in the process.

The doctor posted the x-rays on the light box and flipped it on, seeming surprised when Eleri took a closer look. But he turned his attention back to Donovan. "It's broken. You can see here."

He gestured with the pen at an obvious crack in one of the bones that fit together to make the ankle, then another. "And here. It's a toss-up between casting it and surgery."

Donovan nodded, waiting for what he knew was coming.

"Son, you're a physician. You have to be aware that you have some unusual anatomy."

Despite the fact that Donovan nodded, the doctor continued to talk, pointing out one anomaly after another. Nothing was horribly out of place, nothing too abnormal, but Donovan knew, one oddity in a bone was just that, an oddity. What he was was something far more.

"I'd love to write this up in a medical journal. Take more x-rays—"

"No." He stated it firmly and wondered if it would hold.

"You have to know what these things mean to medicine, son. You have a duty—"

"No." He stared at the man. "I am a physician. I know exactly what happens when these things get written up. I'm also an FBI agent who is incapable of doing my work if I have physicians wanting my x-rays and writing me up all the time. So, yes, I know exactly what's at stake." *More than you do.* But he didn't say the last part.

"It wouldn't be invasive. People on the street wouldn't stop you."

"I know exactly what it is. And the answer is 'no'." He looked at the older man, who still seemed to want to push. His expression at Donovan's conviction still seemed doubtful.

Eleri held back, not saying anything, but watching carefully.

Donovan did what he had to. "If any of this turns up anywhere, even at your dinner table, you'll hear from the FBI. Do you understand?"

The man looked a bit dubious until Eleri stood next to the bed, feet planted and pulled her wallet. She flipped it quietly open as if asking the doctor to check her credentials. "Doctor-patient confidentiality requires that you respect my partner's wishes regarding any dispersal of his medical information. He's been aware of the malformation for years, he worked hard to pass all the Bureau physical tests—"

Donovan almost laughed. She was playing the handicapped card.

"—and you have no right to interfere with any of this. Now, will you treat him as he requests—which is any patient's right —or will we need to enlist the help of another physician?"

"I'm good."

He finally backed down, assuring them he'd be back to set the ankle shortly.

Even though Donovan was sure the doctor had gone, he'd still whispered the next line. "Good thing he didn't get x-rays of the rest of me."

She smiled, then jerked. "Oooh. Wait." She spoke into the air, then to him. "Put your earpiece in."

She motioned as though he could will it into his hand from where he lay in the bed, only partially clean after getting blasted and rolling in the dirt. He'd accepted the stupid gown, knowing that not wearing his clothes would make the staff less likely to see the massive discrepancies between the clothing and his injuries. So far, no one had asked and his clothes were wadded in a clear plastic bag, waiting to be burned. The earpiece was down in there and he motioned to Eleri to dig it out.

Once he finally had it in place, she said, "Go" and information started pouring in.

Walter was on the line. "So Rollins said he had intel to trade. And I still think you didn't need to bring him in. I think he's on our side."

"He *attacked* me." Eleri protested. "And I only cuffed him, I didn't arrest him or even Mirandize him!"

"He says he was just trying not to get hanged for treason—hey! Don't shoot the messenger." Walter added the last preemptively. "I think he's okay. He's trying to prove it. Eleri already knows this; she gave the go-ahead for the search of his apartment. And we looked exactly where Cooper said. Well, we got a lot of something."

"What?"

"Fifteen notebooks—almost diaries—kept by Ken Kellen."

"What!" Donovan nearly shouted, startling the tech who wheeled in the cart with all the supplies for a plaster cast. Donovan looked at the young girl and shook his head no. No plaster cast. "Air boot" he mouthed.

"The doctor ordered a plaster cast."

"Yeah, but I want an air boot." He told her.

"What is he talking about?" Walter asked into his ear and he let Eleri field it while he explained that he wasn't taking a full plaster cast.

He caught the next part as the girl wheeled the cart out of the room. She probably wasn't a girl. She was a tech, she just looked young and he was only half focused on each side of the issue, his care and the intel coming in simultaneously. He focused back on Walter.

"We're going through them now, but the latest entries document him planning exactly what he executed. Telling his superiors that he was hitting major targets, then, on his own, diverting the locations and blowing up only the cell members."

Donovan sat up. "Is Ken Kellen really dead?"

"Forensics seems to say so." Eleri answered both to him and to Walter as the doctor walked back in.

"Air boot," he said to the man.

Maybe if he repeated it enough, he could get out of here. He was starting to believed he *needed* to get out of here. Once the man finally wrote up that the air boot was not his recommendation and had Donovan sign himself out on an AMA—against medical advice—form, he spoke briefly, "I still have to set the ankle."

The medical grade brace was coming, along with crutches. Not ideal. But neither was the situation.

"Can we recover some of the tech from Kellen. From his body? From his place? Can Rollins find it?"

"Probably." Eleri looked confused, like she would say more, but he didn't let her.

"Kellen was the link to the top of the chain." Donovan pushed the words out fast, as though maybe saying them quicker meant he wasn't as crazy. "Maybe we can track who he talked to and shut down more than just this. Ken Kellen *was* Fracture Five."

46

Eleri wanted to rush into the offices at home base, but she couldn't. She had to drop Donovan at the elevator and it took a minute for him to operate the crutches and get out of the car without putting weight on the bad ankle.

Despite his demand for an air boot rather than a cast, he wasn't going to mess with it. Eleri had no idea how his ankles worked other than his one-off explanation a long time ago that it was "kindof like being double-jointed, everywhere." But she figured he knew how they worked.

Donovan had taken a huge risk for the case. She would never get in the way of him being healthy, but she desperately wanted to drop the car and race upstairs. Instead, she parked, walked back to the elevators to find that Donovan was holding the door propped with a crutch and waiting on her.

Marina had been leading a rapid fire "read and report" from Ken Kellen's journals. So Eleri wasn't surprised to find the room ready to update them. What she was surprised by was the cheering and clapping.

For a moment she was flattered. But she'd been on a team, and they weren't done yet. She said as much.

"Have we confirmed cell members at each explosion site? So we have a record of the dead?" Eleri turned to Marina for that. They could cheer later.

"Yes, for four of the sites. We have three unidentified total there. And we have only Ken Kellen at the observatory. The other three are unknowns."

After checking the lists and finding names she recognized —Aziza, Alya, Officer Davies, and more—among the dead, Eleri heard Donovan speak up about the unknowns at the observatory. "I have those."

"What?" Some people turned and looked at him. "There was one agent on one woman, and he lost her going around the side. The other agent lost his guy on a dirt bike."

"And how would you get the fourth member?" Another agent asked.

"I was there. I was just outside the circle right before it exploded. I can get you faces, thus names." He hobbled over to the table and sat down, pulling the head shots—some were mug shots—toward him and he pushed three back. One Indian man, one Calabasas man, one Jewish girl. He pointed to the last. "Her name is Avital. I don't know her last name."

"Ben-Adam," another agent commented. "I knew you'd been near the blast, but not that close. How did you get away?"

"I ran. I ran track all through high school. I guess some things don't leave you." He put that out there as though it explained clocking forty plus miles per hour sometimes. There were advantages and disadvantages, Eleri guessed. She scanned the faces, finding Cooper Rollins sitting in the corner, still hand-cuffed. He looked at her and leaned back, as though he were pulling away. *Odd.*

She ignored him. "Okay, that's the ones in the blasts. We have no other deaths accounted yet? No missing reported?"

There was a round of no's, and Eleri was supremely glad. "How are we doing rounding up other known cell members?"

She listened to that for a while, a detailed rundown of who was in custody, who was still being tailed, and who was in the wind. What intel did they have on the missing? At least for the Calabasas group, not-so-favorite son Jake Salling was happy to help with anything he knew. He'd revealed a hidey hole in one house that gave up three members and a slew of guns. No one had been hurt.

"Where does the militia raid stand?" Eleri asked next to the room at large.

As she took stock, she realized it had only been that morning that she and Donovan had met with the two agents who were angry at Walter and Cooper for following the yellow coupe and ultimately cracking the case.

"It's ongoing. There's gunfire. We have wounded. They have dead. But they're hunkered down. It's not going anywhere for a while." The report there was somber. "Injured" often turned into "deceased" as the night went on. She took a deep breath and tried to take it all in.

"So where are we with Ken Kellen's papers?"

That was where shit got interesting.

The words came at her rapid fire. "He started moving the guns in Fallujah as a matter of course. Thought it was all up-and-up. Later found out that it wasn't. Then was coerced into continuing because he was already up to his neck in it. He still seemed to think they were selling to the right people, though."

"There's a whole piece on the last mission. Basically, they were sent out to kill the guys who didn't know. Rollins among them." The agent, holding a composition book, gestured to the man in cuffs as though she was talking about his shirt color and not that his teammates had been ordered to murder him. "The handful that were moving guns were in deep enough that turning seemed legit to some. Not to others. Not to Kellen— according to these writings—so he took out Freeman and another."

In the background Eleri saw Cooper almost getting sick. He should be.

Another agent spoke up. "Kellen was tracking all of it. He has papers with the signatures and ID from Vivian Dawson. He has shipments of IED's designed by . . . Um. . . ." He flipped pages and it was Donovan who filled in.

"Let me guess, Colonel William Ratz?"

"Yes!"

"Shit," Eleri muttered, even as she heard the sound coming in stereo from Donovan. "And Sullivan? Loreen Sullivan?"

This time, it was Rollins that spoke up. "She was like a spare mother to Ken. The Sullivans took us in for Christmas a few years. Kellen's family was shit, but the Sullivans were good to him." His voice pled with them to keep the Sullivans clean. To make the death meaningless in that scheme of things, at least.

The reporting agent didn't pick up on that. "Says here that the two of them recommended Rollins to the group, along with Ratz, thinking he would go along. They were in it deep. The Sullivans were covering tracks."

Eleri had never seen Rollins so close to breaking, but he was close. "Dr. Gardiner?" His voice was flat, not matching the near tears as his eyes fought to stay clear.

"Ken Kellen didn't order Dr. Gardiner's murder."

"Then why?" Rollins tried to gesture at the futility of it, forgetting his hands were cuffed, and he just made them clink.

Sighing and deciding it didn't make much difference anyway, Eleri marched over and pulled her handcuff key, then watched as Rollins flinched.

"Jesus, Rollins, I cuffed you because you deserved it." She muttered even as she unlocked the handcuffs. She'd put him in, she could take him out.

He leaned back as though staying away, then he leaned in and whispered, "I saw what you are."

"What?" She frowned at him. *What the hell was he talking about?* She had no clue, so she said it out loud.

He looked at her like she was crazy, then he stared her down and said, "I saw your eyes go black. Full black. Like a demon. You were crazy strong, and you were something else. I know." He whispered the last two words like a threat, even as her stomach turned.

What the hell were people seeing? What was happening when she got mad?

Her hand flew to her chest—the grisgris. Had Grandmere done something to it? She could easily have enchanted Eleri's and not the others, or not the same way. She was going to throw the thing in the trash first chance she could discretely do it.

"You'd just taken a concussive blast to the back of the head and been out cold for several minutes. Plus, I nailed you in the balls. Hard. I don't think you saw what you think you saw." She pocketed the cuffs and walked away, trying to hide the disturbing voices nagging the back of her brain.

At least he could move his hands. Maybe it wasn't so bad that the big, bad soldier was scared of her.

As she turned back to the table, she saw an agent holding up some loose pages Kellen must have been keeping at one point. "So, once Kellen saw Cooper in L.A. he tried to get Cooper into the cell. But he couldn't risk telling you. The two women in the cell murdered Gardiner on their own. They wouldn't take you if you had a confidential place to tell what they were doing. The doctor would have been obligated to report any kind of terrorist activity you discussed."

"Great." Cooper slapped his thighs in disgust. "So you all don't just think I'm a terrorist, you think I'm a dumb one, too."

"Nah." The agent grinned. "Ken Kellen pretty much lays out what happened today. He was going to send you out with the bomb—prove that you were a worthy member, that you'd just shot at the girls in Fallujah because you didn't know which side people were on. Then he was going to swap with you, give you the way to find all these notes and push you out. Leaving you alive to tell the tale. He did not plan on the FBI, you wearing a tracker, Walter following him—I don't think he even knew that. Did anyone have that? I just have general paranoia developing round about the time she started."

"That's fantastic." Walter replied, low key, and Eleri couldn't agree more. There wasn't a much better recommendation one could earn in surveillance.

Eleri turned again. She would read all fifteen notebooks, all seven years Kellen had been in on this. Eventually. But for now there was one more step. "If Kellen was the fifth fracture, does he know who he took orders from?"

"Not much." It came from several different agents at the same time.

"Shit." She spat it out even as she paced at the windows. "What do we have?"

"The person was originally involved in the gun sales. I.e. a rebel getting the guns on the other side. That's how Kellen started talking to him. He was recruited in a purely military sense before realizing he'd become the other side without even knowing it. Those are his words."

"Any names? Any?" she asked the room at large.

"Hadad."

"That's it? It's so common. That's like having 'Ben' here in America." She was so frustrated.

"Yes, but it's better than nothing."

Donovan piped up with forced cheer that he managed despite being in obvious pain. He'd refused anything but Advil, wanting to be an alert part of the team. "Where's the tech? It doesn't matter what his name is if we can call him."

"Holy shit." Donovan was right. If they had Ken Kellen's equipment, they might be able to trace it back. "Where's the tech?"

"We have what he was wearing when he died. There's an earpiece and a comm. They don't work anymore, but we cracked them. They seem to be a closed loop with the other cell members. So that's a bust."

"Tech from the warrant executed at his place is on its way."

"How far?" she asked just as she considered eating something. It was full dark outside—or as full dark as L.A. seemed to get. She'd had no food all day and was running on fumes and stale adrenaline.

A knock came at the door and she saw it was opened and a bag delivered. She prayed it was food. She prayed it was Ken Kellen's cell phone and computer and more.

It wasn't food.

And she didn't get any of the pieces of equipment. Hacking wasn't her specialty.

A bowl of fruit sat on a side table along with water and she downed a paper cup-full then a second before thinking to take one to Donovan. She nudged him to drink it, unsure how much he was paying attention given the pain his ankle had to be causing. But the fact was he'd contributed twice and he'd been useful, despite not being truly fully in the conversation.

Eleri went back and grabbed two bananas, handing one to her partner before filling her water again and sitting for just a moment of nothing. The food hit the spot. She pulled up her own cell phone and started looking up info as she ate the last bite. It wasn't two minutes later that she heard, "I think I've got something."

"What do you have?"

"Number. A cell phone number."

Eleri was about to ask why this number amongst the handful at least that must have been found, but the agent was already on it. "It's been dialed regularly from this phone—and there are only three numbers on this phone. So it's minimal use. Two of the three numbers go to cell phones in Iraq. And I can trace the origin of purchase on one to Iraq as well. Do you need more?"

What more could she ask. "Does it belong to someone named Hadad?"

He shrugged. "It's a burner, so who knows? But I think this number is the one because it was bought less than twenty-four hours before the mission where Ken Kellen shot his fellow teammates and went rogue."

"Holy fucking bingo." Eleri blurted her excitement. Then she turned to the room at large. "So how do we use the phone to trace him?"

It was Cooper Rollins who answered. "That's exactly the kind of thing you'd use my team for. We'd get the trace, infiltrate, and take out."

She turned to him. "That's the problem. You guys are exactly who we need, and your team is all either dead or in the wind. You're half made up of traitors. I can't call *any* Army team, I can't even *alert* the Army to what we have, because right now I don't know who to trust."

47

Cooper Rollins stood up. "You don't have to trust me."

He could see from their faces that they didn't. Some of them were okay with him. He looked at the papers in front of each of the agents. The ones who'd read Kellen's manifesto—for lack of a better term—knew Cooper wasn't a terrorist.

He hoped they couldn't see how ashamed he was.

He'd joined the army full of hope and forward momentum, and look where he'd wound up. With severe PTSD that kept him from being with his family and now barely out of cuffs for being suspected of treason.

When he'd started, Colonel Ratz had been a mentor, and it turned out he'd been sending IEDs into enemy hands. Cooper wanted to hate the old man. At the same time, he wondered if Ratz had been taken in the same way they all had. Someone was at the top pulling strings, and each person below that was pulling strings. Just like Kellen had done here. He'd blown them all up, turned them on each other.

Had he learned that from their superiors' orders that last mission in Fallujah?

Cooper probably wouldn't ever know. Ken Kellen had inserted himself into a terrorist plot. Probably, it was more that he'd been like Cooper at the beginning. He'd had no plans to run guns. He'd been making legal army deliveries, he'd thought. His hands were dirty before he even knew he was playing.

Kellen may have been in the fracture just by virtue of keeping himself alive despite the team imploding. Cooper had some guesses about how that had worked. Ken Kellen had probably had a place to go in Fallujah, had a friendly rebel family that took him in. He may have joined some form of the resistance. He was a good soldier, took orders, and spoke all the languages.

Cooper wasn't as good at that, but he volunteered. "I speak their tongue. Not like a native. Not like Kellen. But if you get me on, I can talk and maybe get some intel before they realize it's not him."

"Would they recognize your voice?" Agent Eames asked him. She gave him the squirrels since he saw her eyes go wild. That was not from a blast to the head, but no one else was giving it credence. He was trying to talk himself down from what must have been another episode. She still gave him the squirrels.

He tried to act like he wasn't bothered. "In the past, when the connection is bad, people can confuse me with Kellen. Don't know if that's enough. But unless someone has a closer voice, and a grasp of the tongue, I'm what you have."

Eames nodded at him. As did her partner. He'd been in obvious pain since his return from the ER, but Cooper respected his need to stay in the game and stay sober.

Agent Heath looked at him. "It's nice that you can speak the native language and might be able to talk to them. But you can't get a team in there! So what good is it? Plus, I'm not sure I trust you."

The room went dead silent at that, and Cooper's heart stilled. It was possibly the worst thing a dedicated special teams member could hear. Everything he'd done had been based on trust. Until he'd had to trust no one. Until he'd followed Kellen and decided that he might get pulled under, but he'd get to the bottom of things.

Well, he was sure at the bottom of things now.

Then a voice spoke up. "Sir," a younger agent addressed Heath. "I've been reading this. He's not implicated. In fact, Kellen pulled him in to give him these papers. To exonerate Rollins and give Kellen back some of the . . . dignity, I guess, that he'd lost in the job."

It was Heath at the bit now, and Cooper felt every pull. At least he wasn't a freak like his partner. Then again, he shouldn't think that. He did have a tendency to hallucinate. Heath held out. "How do we know Rollins didn't write this shit and bury it?"

Another moment of silence. Another voice popping up. "I don't think Rollins is a problem either. There's even some stuff in the early pages about how obnoxiously goody-two-shoes Rollins was. It was why he wasn't brought in on the deal in the first place. This is all hand written. A good handwriting sample should do it."

Great, now he was obnoxiously good. But if a handwriting sample would get them what they needed, that was easy enough.

Without being asked, he picked up a cheap pen, one of many scattered on the table, and began writing on a paper tablet he grabbed. He sat at one of the few empty chairs and wrote out "the quick brown fox jumped over the lazy dogs." Next he wrote the Lord's prayer, then started on the creed he recited when a soldier fell. Maybe he was writing his own.

Agent Eames was looking over his shoulder, her big freaky eyes on everything. He didn't get much further.

"I was with the Behavioral Analysis Unit. I'm a good enough graphologist to say he didn't write Kellen's notes." Then she turned to him. "Even if we could connect you, how would we trust the team to follow through? I mean, if they don't, if we get through to our guy, and then they bury him deeper, we've got a worse problem."

She turned to the room at large. "We have an advantage. Fallujah is eleven hours ahead of us. We just took down their guy and their people a few hours ago. It's very early morning there. So there's a possibility that they don't know about Ken Kellen. But that window is getting very small to put Rollins in as Kellen and check this shit out. How do we make it work?"

Cooper stood back up. "You don't use an Army team. I don't know who to trust there, but I do know who to trust here."

He looked at Walter Reed, standing opposite him where she'd planted herself at the table a while ago. "Walter—Fisher —is MARSOC. She's a Marine. Use a Marine Special Forces team. I bet Walter knows exactly who she can call."

Cooper stared at her, praying he was right.

IT TOOK TWO HOURS, and Eleri held her breath for every single minute of it. She was running on fumes, stale adrenaline, and one banana now.

With every moment that passed, the cell waiting to hear something in Fallujah might realize their link was dead. The faster she and her team did this, the more likely it was that the man on the other end of the phone would think it was Ken Kellen on the line.

They'd put Walter through to a forward operating base, and she'd woken an officer she once worked under. He'd been excited to hear from her and glad she was doing well. For a moment Eleri had enjoyed hearing the pride that rode along with the urgency as Walter explained the situation.

He started naming a team, told Walter he wished she was on it, and Eleri watched her grin. This was not the same woman who was sleeping in the square a few weeks ago. She probably would never be that woman again.

Eleri counted the positives before she opened her mouth to identify herself, Donovan, and even Vasquez and Rollins. They were the core team here.

Walter's contact would be boots on the ground half the world away.

The home base team had caught short naps, read Kellen's disturbing quantity of papers, ate snacks, and waited. Occasionally they jumped up, tense, only to ease back down for another round of waiting.

They did this when the team first reported they were boarding the chopper. But the ride was longer than Eleri expected, and she'd almost fallen asleep, then jerked awake suddenly with word that the team had hit ground. But they weren't there yet.

Each milestone was helpful. Each report that they weren't there yet was another stretch of time in which it could all go wrong. So when they reported that they were, in fact, in place, Eleri found herself on a yo-yo string.

She forced out the words. "We'll get our guy in contact. I'll give you go/no-go as soon as possible."

There was every likelihood that they hadn't found the right person, or the phone might have changed hands or it might be pizza delivery. Or it could just be that he wouldn't say anything that Cooper could distinguish as sufficient evidence to storm the place.

She hand signaled to Rollins to make the call, and the room came to a dead hush. Rollins was on a headset that would filter out noise, and they were all listening in.

Though she understood it wasn't her native tongue, for some reason Eleri was frustrated by her inability to make out even a little. She knew a reasonable amount of French, was passable in Spanish and Italian and even American Sign Language, and she understood exactly jack shit of what was going on.

Rollins could be checking his damn dry cleaning for all she knew. He could be angrily telling the man to run and hide. Just as she was thinking that she *had to* trust him, Eleri felt a hand on her arm.

Walter mouthed, "They think he's Kellen."

Eleri pointed and mouthed back, "You understand?"

"Enough." If she'd read Walter's lips right.

Just as some of the tension eased, she saw Cooper Rollins frantically start to motion to her.

This was the guy. This was Kellen's contact.

She switched her comm to the Team Leader, then she checked it and checked it again. Now Cooper had to keep the other end on the line until the raid went down. *Don't let them suspect.* Eleri fucking up her channel switch would do it. She triple checked.

Then, with her heart in her throat, she whispered, "Go."

It wasn't three minutes later they heard gunfire. Followed by shouting in two, maybe three languages, then more gunfire.

She held her breath.

She'd said 'go.'

Donovan looked up at her, his crutches resting in his lap, his eyes full of sympathy. But she was the senior agent; it was her shoulders this world rested on. It was her junior partner she'd sent in for a recon she couldn't necessarily get him out of. They'd been lucky.

There were dead men at the raid in Fontana. She still hadn't heard all the details there. At least it wasn't her raid.

Now there was gunfire, so far away. At her command.

It slowed. It stopped.

She waited.

She heard the voice Walter had been talking to and watched as her friend dropped the tension from her own shoulders upon hearing her old commander again.

"They had eight present. All tango uniform."

Eleri frowned to Walter who mouthed, "tits up."

Oh. All dead.

"Your guys?" Eleri dared to ask.

"All alive. Some wounded, none serious." She was going to thank him but she didn't get the chance. "This is the best score yet. This place is crawling with American issue munitions. There are IEDs in a variety of states; they may have been assembling them. We're going to hold this place until a proper clean up and evidence can be gathered. Great tip, Fisher."

It took Eleri a moment to translate that last line into praise for Walter.

She gathered a few more pieces of intel and disconnected to let the soldiers guard their stake.

She turned to Cooper Rollins, who was white as a sheet, but she didn't mention it. "Good work, Rollins. You nailed it."

"Thank you, ma'am." He sat down hard and she motioned for Donovan to check if he was having another episode. At least he'd held it together when he was needed. But then Rollins popped his head back up and breathed deeply. So Eleri turned to Walter who got a firm handshake and a sincere thanks.

Marina Vasquez got a hug and a "We could not have done this without you. Give me until tomorrow, or maybe next week, but I'll put whatever recommendation you want into your file."

That earned her a smile.

There weren't any cheers this time. There were men dead. Men fighting a war that Eleri didn't understand and wished she'd never fallen into. She thanked the other agents, and they all started to walk shakily away. She was glad she wasn't the only one.

Before they left the room she did make an announcement.

"We only recently learned about these cells here in L.A., and we also learned that they were what's called a 'fracture.' A disconnected cell with no reasonable way to trace up the line. These cells were so far removed from the core, as you know, their passcode was 'Fracture Five.' But thanks to all of you here, Fracture Five is gone. And so is at least part of Fracture Four—the level above them. Levels one, two, and three are beyond us, but we'll hand this up to the Pentagon and maybe they can get the right people on it. You did very good work, these last few weeks . . ." She turned to Walter and Marina and Cooper, "Days," she pointed out several agents, "Or even just since you were thrown in this morning. Thank you.

"We'll debrief at eleven am tomorrow. Get some sleep."

Though they'd all been gathering up, that was the official signal and the door opened, mixing air outside the tense room for the first time in hours.

In a matter of minutes, even Marina had begged off to sleep and only Eleri and Donovan were left.

"Oh shit!" She sat up. "Westerfield. It all went down so fast that I didn't—"

Donovan's hand on her arm shut her up. "I patched him in about two or more hours ago. He signed off when the raid went down."

"Oh God, thank you!" She wanted to throw herself at him, but was pretty sure he wouldn't appreciate it with the cracked ribs and all. The ones he'd had them bind at the hospital, but not x-ray. That doctor sure suspected something.

"Donovan," she started on a tired sigh, "I owe you a huge apology. I should never have sent you in today without a better extraction plan. That was pure insanity and almost got you killed. I'm so—"

"*I* sent me in. And yes, we need a better extraction plan in the future. We need to have a standard plan and a backup and maybe a plan C. I don't want to repeat today ever again." She felt that to her bones, but he stopped her before she could say anything. "I did the right thing today, and we did get out. I'll heal, and I was the only one able to ID the members at the observatory. It's helping them pick up the rest."

She nodded. "There are some members of that Indian cell that we still have no clue about. I wish we'd had more on them."

"We took down a fucking terrorist cell plot, El. I'm sorry you didn't manage to perfectly capture every member of *four separate cells*. We did good. Deal with it." He smiled. "We'll write it up, hand it off to the Pentagon who will investigate the Army, and we'll take vacations."

She nodded. "You can go back to FoxHaven if you want. I'll give you the key."

"Nah. I'm going home. I need to go *home*. I thought I was going to do a lot of running while I was off, but . . ." He shrugged.

"Once vacation time is over, we'll be on paperwork duty for a while. While you heal." She nodded. "You have what? Five to eight weeks on those things?"

"Oh no. Not on the crutches, but before I'm field-ready, yes."

So she'd do desk work. Be an analyst for other cases as she could. Did NightShade Agents fill those spots like other agents did?

Donovan's voice interrupted her. "Are you not going back to FoxHaven?"

She shook her head. "I have people to visit."

"The hockey player?" He grinned at her, and that was good to see.

"Yes." She admitted. "Now take a Percocet and let's get some damn sleep."

48

Eleri met up with Avery Darling in Minnesota, where winter was really winter, and hockey was king.

"It's good to see you." He grinned and she grinned back. He kissed her and she melted.

"Have you been watching the games?" he'd asked as he tugged her and her suitcase into his waiting car at the airport. He really didn't have time for this. But his team had a day off, so he'd come out here to meet her, and then would play tomorrow night.

"No." She shook her head. "Not at all."

He shrugged. "Too busy?"

She nodded, wondering if this was where it all fell apart. If he couldn't handle her occasional sabbatical from life to solve a crime.

"What were you doing?"

"I can't specifically say." She shrugged, waiting for a shoe to drop.

"Was it big?" He was still grinning, and that smile got her right at the core.

So she said, "Yes."

"How big?" He'd started the car and was pulling out of the pickup area and almost onto the freeway.

"Well, if it had gone through. If the team hadn't stopped it, maybe several thousand people might have died." She tried to calculate the possible loss at the theater, the pier, the observatory, the rose bowl and the medical center.

There were no real numbers. Only Avery's very appreciative, "Oh shit. And what position were you on this team?"

She wanted to smile. He was a hockey player; he would think in terms like that. "It was my team. Mine and my partner's. Donovan, you met him."

"And you're the senior agent between you. So your team."

"Kind of." She shrugged.

"Well then, you deserve a vacation. Would you like to see your first hockey game tomorrow night?"

He took her to dinner and explained what a goalie did. He taught her about icing and how one got in the penalty box.

Three days later, she showed up on Haley Jean's doorstep.

She was hugged and fed home-grown vegetables just like she'd imagined. They toured the warm greenhouses under their light dusting of snow. Undergrads came out and cleared the roofs some days, letting the sun in.

Eleri commented that she was surprised Haley Jean hadn't just built one to spec that was too steep to keep the snow. Apparently she had, this one was a historical model that she was trying to recreate traditional methods with. "It's a forcing house."

Eleri nodded as though she knew what that meant.

One day, Haley Jean had lined up meats and cheeses and bakery breads and made sandwiches until her wide kitchen counters were covered. She popped open plastic bags with handles, and created a small assembly line with Eleri as her lackey.

They made lunch kits to last someone several days, with

Haley Jean adding all kinds of extras. They folded the seats of her friend's big SUV into the floor and piled in more bags than Eleri thought they could possibly give away. When Haley Jean pulled into the lot at the local park, there was a line of people waiting in the cold for the bags. They gave out every one.

When Haley Jean went out of town the next week, Eleri considered going to Patton Hall. She'd had her things put into storage before she went into the mental hospital. She hadn't had a breakdown per se so much as she had issues. So she'd had time to get her affairs in order before she checked in, but she didn't have a home at all now.

"Stay here. Keep the house warm, keep an eye on my grad students." Haley Jean had told her. "Run the park for me next week. You saw how I do it. They'll be waiting."

"I *saw* you do it, but I don't know *how* you do it." Eleri commented as she tucked feet covered in thick cotton socks under some blanket that was softer than baby ducks and probably something Haley Jean had knitted herself. "It was overwhelming."

"And what you do isn't?" Haley Jean had offered a sad half-grin. "We all save the world in our own way."

So Eleri had done the park run, adding a pile of warm coats to the back seat of the SUV. She handed out everything. Then headed back to Haley Jean's big comfortable house. It wasn't really empty with the cat and the feeling of being occupied even though her friend was gone.

She filed all her remaining paperwork on the case. Answered questions and sent documents to the Pentagon. Handled Westerfield and his concerns about Donovan healing.

She talked to her partner who asked if her eyes had changed color again. "No."

"Didn't get mad?" he'd teased her.

"I think it was the grisgris. I think mine was special, and Grandmere is known locally for her . . . special skills, shall we say?" She'd shrugged though he couldn't see her. "I never really took it too seriously, but after those eye comments. . ."

"Eleri."

"What?"

"The first time happened *before* you got the grisgris." His voice was soft.

So was hers. "Well, shit."

DONOVAN HAD SETTLED IN, glad to be home. The weather had gotten colder, but not that bad. Not in South Carolina. Though he couldn't run, he did get out in the woods with his crutches. It was slow and clunky and beyond ideal, but the air and the trees did him good.

After two weeks he and Eleri were officially back at work on desk duty from home, and he'd ditched the crutches. Not even wanting to follow up with anyone about his strange bones and the fact that he wouldn't let the doctor x-ray his ribs. It wasn't his ribs so much as his scapulae. Even Eleri had noticed once. Better to stay silent.

Another three weeks and he got himself a smaller brace.

A week later he went on a long walk in the woods and waited for the ankle to protest. Another week after that, he ran on the long winding roads leading to his very isolated house. He wanted to run in the woods, but sneakers on flat ground were safer.

He was still scared.

So he waited another week before he tried changing.

The wolf almost collapsed in relief that it had worked. It was never easy. The metabolic load of the change alone was rough. But had the ankle not healed right . . .

Donovan didn't want to think about it. Instead he trotted

into his forest, under the light of the full moon and thought about home.

He'd made anchors and weighed himself down with them. He made routines. Worked cases for Westerfield, set timers, read, and settled in. Maybe, maybe next time he was home, he'd try his hand at dating. That was normal. Wasn't it?

Eleri was dating. Wade was dating. Maybe he could, too. The lobomau were not his ideal mate, but it had occurred to him there were more like him out there. And maybe someone didn't have to be exactly like him to understand.

He went into the Medical Examiner's Office to see how it was working with the new M.E. and was shocked at how out of place he felt. A few people said hello, but no one seemed glad to see him. They weren't upset, but he was merely interesting, not missed.

In between analysis assignments with the Bureau, and filing reports through Eleri, he emailed Walter—and asked how her PI business was running. It was picking up, she said. Apparently Marina Vasquez had thrown a few recommendations her way. Donovan wished he'd had some to give.

So he emailed Marina Vazquez—and asked what she was working on.

Then he emailed Cooper Rollins. He wrote back right away. He was in a treatment center, but doing much better. The feeling of the loss of control had mostly gone away.

Donovan pulled his old Psych 101 out and mulled that over, thinking it had made sense. Rollins struck him as a man of structure. He'd handled the perils of war just fine until his structure not only disappeared but turned on him. The case had given him some structure back. Some understanding of the pieces he'd been left wondering about ever since that bad mission in Fallujah. The soldier spoke of dating his wife, and Donovan had laughed but thought that was probably a very good thing.

He'd had a brief moment, sitting at his computer, and he'd decided the sun was just right and so was the temperature and he did what he'd bought the house to do. Donovan stripped in the den, opened the back door, then the back gate and when he passed through, he was the wolf.

For the first time, he ran.

He pushed for every step, making long gliding strides. His ankle held up. The scent of pine came down and invaded his nose in fifty different ways while the loam crept up and made bottom notes of deep earth.

He stayed out until dark. Passed through the gate as the wolf, then opened his back door as the man. Donovan showered, dressed again, and checked his email.

Then he picked up his phone.

"Eleri. Did you see?"

"Yeah, just now." She sighed but he could hear the grin in her voice. "It's a skeleton with a full set of anomalies. Do you think it's a lobomau?"

"Doubt it." He said, rolling his ankle around to test it, but he didn't feel any lingering effects. "If it was, wouldn't Westerfield have said so?"

"Maybe he doesn't know." She turned the conversation. "Are you ready? Are you healed?"

"I'm good to go. Went for a serious run today. I'm all in. I think the question is: are you ready? You wanted something different. I think a skeleton in Michigan is definitely different."

"From the way the email is worded, I think Westerfield thinks there will be more than one." She paused. "Meet me at the airport in Grand Rapids tomorrow?"

"I'll be there."

ABOUT THE AUTHOR

A.J.'s world is strange place where patterns jump out and catch the eye, little is missed, and most of it can be recalled with a deep breath. In this world, the smell of Florida takes three weeks to fully leave the senses and the air in Dallas is so thick that the planes "sink" to the runways rather than actually landing.

For A.J., reality is always a little bit off from the norm and something usually lurks right under the surface. As a story-teller, A.J. loves irony, the unexpected, and a puzzle where all the pieces fit and make sense. Originally a scientist and a teacher, the writer says research is always a key player in the stories. AJ's motto is "It could happen. It wouldn't. But it could."

A.J. has lived in Florida and Los Angeles among a handful of other places. Recent whims have brought the dark writer to Tennessee, where home is a deceptively normal-looking neigh-borhood just outside Nashville.

For more information:
www.ReadAJS.com
AJ@ReadAJS.com

Made in United States
North Haven, CT
06 July 2023

38631080R00289